STEPPING STONES TO THE STARS. . . .

For forty-seven years humankind has been reaching for the stars, with satellites, rockets, space shuttles, and, of course, orbital space stations. It seems obvious that to make our way to the other planets in our own solar system, and ultimately to distant stars, we will need to establish permanent manned space habitats. But what form will such space stations take, and what fates will await travelers to these stations as well as those who live and work in them?

The fourteen tales included in this volume offer an extraordinary range of possibilities, including:

"Mikeys"—Don and Sas were the advance team, their mission to land on Deimos, and construct a space station so the next team could actually touch down on Mars and do the real exploring. No one could have foreseen just how important the Deimos station would become. . . .

"The Franchise"—They had come to Hamilton Station to help rebuild, but it was soon obvious that Hamilton was determined to keep enemies and friends alike from getting in. . . .

"Follow the Sky"—As a young child, she dreamed of flying to the Wheel, and from there to other worlds. But it was only by losing everything that she might make her dream come true. . . .

More Imagination-Expanding Anthologies Brought to You by DAW:

MICROCOSMS *Edited by Gregory Benford.* Thirteen original tales of worlds within worlds by Stephen Baxter, Pamela Sargent, Robert J. Sawyer, Robert Sheckley, George Zebrowski, and other masters of miniaturization. From the tale of four physicists who created their own universe . . . to a microcosm inhabited by sentient atomic particles . . . to a future where all the people of Earth—with the exception of a tribe in Africa—have become one communal mind . . . open the portals into unforgettable universes that exist on the innermost frontiers of the imagination.

STARS: Original Stories Based on the Songs of Janis Ian *Edited by Janis Ian and Mike Resnick.* Twenty-nine stories by a stellar constellation of authors, including Tad Williams, Joe Haldeman, John Varley, Mercedes Lackey, Gregory Benford, Robert J. Sawyer, Spider Robinson, Harry Turtledove, Orson Scott Card, and more. This is a unique volume of stories inspired by the songs of Janis Ian, and the contributors are the top writers in the field today.

SPACE, INC. *Edited by Julie E. Czerneda.* From such visionary authors as Josepha Sherman, S. M. Stirling, Robert J. Sawyer, and Tanya Huff, here are fourteen tales of the challenges, perils, and responsibilities that workers of the future may have to face—from a librarian who could determine the fate of an alien race . . . to a pair of space mechanics assigned a repair job for a species that despises humankind . . . to a ballet instructor who must find a way to tailor human dance forms for multilimbed sentient beings. . . .

SPACE STATIONS

Edited by
Martin H. Greenberg
and John Helfers

DAW BOOKS, INC.

DONALD A. WOLLHEIM, FOUNDER

375 Hudson Street, New York, NY 10014

ELIZABETH R. WOLLHEIM
SHEILA E. GILBERT
PUBLISHERS

http://www.dawbooks.com

Cover art by permission of Corbis and Getty Images.

DAW Book Collectors No. 1288.

DAW Books are distributed by Penguin Group (USA) Inc.

First Printing, March 2004
1 2 3 4 5 6 7 8 9

DAW TRADEMARK REGISTERED
U.S. PAT. OFF. AND FOREIGN COUNTRIES
—MARCA REGISTRADA.
HECHO EN U.S.A.

PRINTED IN THE U.S.A.

ACKNOWLEDGMENTS

Introduction © 2004 by John Helfers.
The Battle of Space Fort Jefferson © 2004 by Timothy Zahn.
Redundancy by Alan Dean Foster; © 2004 by Thranx, Inc.
Dancers of the Gate © 2004 by James Cobb.
Mikeys © 2004 by Robert J. Sawyer.
The Franchise © 2004 by Julie E. Czerneda.
Follow the Sky © 2004 by Pamela Sargent.
Auriga's Streetcar © 2004 by Jean Rabe.
Falling Star © 2004 by Brendan DuBois.
Countdown © 2004 by Russell Davis.
Serpent on the Station © 2004 by Michael A. Stackpole.
First Contact Café by Irene Radford; © 2004 by Phyllis Irene Radford.
Orbital Base Fear © 2004 by Eric Kotani.
Black Hole Station © 2004 by Jack Williamson.
Station Spaces by Gregory Benford; © 2004 by Abbenford Associates.

CONTENTS

INTRODUCTION

by John Helfers

IT'S amazing what the human race can accomplish when we put our collective minds to something. Whether it's exploration, fighting disease, inventing new technology, or changing society, mankind can be an awesome power when it chooses to be.

Consider space exploration, for example. While scientists have been studying the stars for centuries, getting a man to walk among them has been quite a different matter. As the study of our universe goes, it is one of the most recent fields of scientific endeavor, primarily because of the advances in technology that have made it feasible. Since the launch of the first satellite by the Soviet Union on October 4, 1957, the United States and the rest of the world have been looking to the skies, and the universe beyond, as the ultimate last frontier.

And what an incredible forty-seven years it's been. Since the first space race between Russia and the United States, the world has seen men land on the Moon, the first unmanned exploration of the surface of Mars, China join the other space faring nations, and a renewed interest in the vast galaxy beyond our own planet.

Along with this activity comes new ways to study and explore space. From the Hubble space telescope to the Voyager and Galileo deep space probes, we have pushed farther and farther past the boundaries of what we once knew.

One of the best ways to do this is right in our own backyard, so to speak. No matter how sophisticated the technology, satellites and machines cannot replace man when it comes to exploration, at least, not completely. Space stations, platforms where men and women can study the galaxy around the clock, have become the best way to gain practical results from space, whether it is manufacturing new medicines and materials in the weightless conditions, or exploring the heavens and planning to use the space station as a jumping off point for trips beyond.

There have been several permanently manned space stations during the history of space exploration. The Russians beat America into space again with the launch of the first orbiting station, Salyut, in 1971. A Russian crew was the first to live in space for approximately twenty four days, but tragically died upon returning to Earth. The U.S.'s first space outpost, Skylab, was launched in 1973. It was not intended to be a permanent station, but was used to study long-term effects of space and weightlessness on humans and animals. The longest-running manned space station, the Russian Mir station, managed to stay aloft for fifteen years despite being used for years after its proposed duration and suffering several accidents that at times severely hampered its capabilities. In 2001 Mir was guided back into Earth's atmosphere, where it was destroyed.

The most exciting development in the field of manned space exploration today is the International Space Station, a joint project that began construction in 1998. Funded and supplied by sixteen countries around the world, its purpose is to create a permanent station to take the world's space program into the next century and millennium. When the station is completed in 2006, we will have the best platform to begin the next stage of exploration, leading back to the Moon, perhaps to Mars, and beyond.

The ISS has fired the imaginations of people around the world, and science fiction authors are no different. Fourteen of today's best writers have given us their ideas of what the next generation of space stations will look like. From Timothy Zahn comes a story of a station that everyone thought was past its prime, until the time came for it to take part in a most unusual battle. Alan Dean Foster explores a space station that takes care of even its smallest inhabitant in a very special way. Brendan DuBois takes us to a future Earth where the dream of space stations took a detour that grounded humanity forever. And Gregory Benford reveals a completely different view of a space station in our final story.

Fourteen visions of the future created by the finest authors of speculative fiction. So turn the page and prepare for adventures beyond your wildest imagination on these space stations of tomorrow.

THE BATTLE OF SPACE FORT JEFFERSON

by Timothy Zahn

Timothy Zahn was born in 1951 in Chicago and spent his first forty years in the Midwest. Somewhere along the way toward a Ph.D. in physics, he got sidetracked into writing science fiction and has been at it ever since. He is the author of over seventy short stories and twenty novels, of which his most well-known are his five Star Wars *books: The* Thrawn *trilogy and* Hand of Thrawn *duology. His most recent book is the* Star Wars *novel* Survivor's Quest, *published in 2004. Though most of his time is now spent writing novels, he still enjoys tackling the occasional short story. This is one of them. The Zahn family lives on the Oregon coast.*

EIGHTEENTH April, 2230," Ranger Bob Epstein said into his log microphone. "Morning report. Three more days to President Ukukho's visit."

He gazed with satisfaction at the sentence on the screen as he picked up his slightly stale bagel covered thinly with cream cheese. A little lox would have been nice, but lox was hard to come by on United Colonies Space Fort Jefferson.

Actually, pretty much everything was hard to come by on Space Fort Jefferson. Tourist-free tourist attractions, as he'd often been told over the past seven years, rated very low on the Park Service's priority list.

He scowled as he set the bagel back onto its plate. It wasn't a fair assessment, as he'd argued back for most of those same seven years. Granted, for much of its four-point-three-year orbit Space Fort Jefferson was largely deserted, with only its five-ranger crew here to keep the decks and empty weapons emplacements company.

But for the four months when its elliptical path carried it near the asteroid belt's Anchorline Archipelago, there was quite a bit of activity on the old fort. Granted, it wasn't Disney Ceres, but it was still busy enough to keep the rangers hopping. And even during the long down-time, there was always a trickle of visitors willing to endure the long and boring trip to set foot on a piece of genuine, if obscure, history.

But that was going to change now. Earth President Ukukho himself was on his way; and for the first time in a hundred years, someone in actual governmental authority was going to visit the station.

And since the public lapped up everything Ukukho said or did, that meant that billions of people who'd never even heard of Space Fort Jefferson were going to be brought face-to-face with it.

And what billions of people saw, millions of people went touristing to. Or so went the theory. Bob took another bite from his bagel, visualizing the list of improvements and renovations he would be submitting to the Park Service as soon as the crowds started arriving. At the top of the list would be to finally finish the renovation of Decks Three to Six that had been started two years ago and never completed. The mess made the fort's original gunnery control area nearly impossible for even the rangers to get to, and visitors always liked seeing control rooms.

There was a gunshot-crackle from the intercom. "Bob?" Kelsey's voice came distantly.

Bob reached over and flicked the switch. "Yes?"

"Bob?"

Muttering under his breath, Bob flipped the switch off, gave the side of the box a sharp rap with his knuckles, and flipped the switch back on. On second thought, maybe it would be the intercom that would head the replacement list. "Yes?"

"Got a ship coming in to dock," Kelsey reported.

"The GenTronic Twelve?" Bob asked, frowning. The

yacht had been on their scopes for the past thirty-two hours, bringing in the latest batch of off-season tourists. But last he'd checked, it shouldn't be here nearly this soon.

"No, they're still three and a half hours out," Kelsey confirmed. "This is a Fafnir Four."

Bob felt his eyebrows lifting. "A Fafnir *Four*?"

"Yep," Kelsey said. "Government issue, fully stealthed—Hix didn't even spot it until it hailed."

"Yes, but a *Four*?" Bob repeated. With the President on his way, the Secret Service would naturally be stopping by to check things out, and Fafnirs were the ship of choice for most government agencies.

Problem was, a Fafnir Four only held two people, not nearly enough for a Presidential advance team. The advance team for the advance team, maybe?

"It's a Four, all right," Kelsey insisted. "I'm in Dock Obs, looking straight at it."

Reaching to his recorder, Bob flipped the switch from "standby" to "off." He'd finish the log entry later. "I'll be right up."

The two visitors were already in the entryway reception room by the time he arrived. The older man, about Bob's own youngish forty-five, was studying one of the information plaques lining the wall. The other, twenty years younger, was standing at a sort of stiff at-ease, his eyes shifting between the door and a nervous-looking Hix. Apparently, he didn't have the time or the interest for anything as job-unrelated as mere history.

"Good day, gentlemen," Bob greeted them cheerfully as he stepped into the room. "I'm Ranger Bob Epstein—Ranger Bob to our visitors. What can I do for you?"

"We're not visitors, Ranger Epstein," the younger man said, his voice as stiff and government-issue as his posture. "We're here on official business—"

"At ease, Drexler," the older man said dryly, straightening up from the plaque he'd been looking at and giving Bob a slight smile. "I'm Secret Service Agent Cummings,

Ranger Epstein; this is Agent Drexler. We're here to check things out for the President's flyby."

Something seemed to catch in Bob's throat. "His *flyby*?" he asked carefully. "We thought—"

"That he would be visiting the station," Drexler said briskly. "I'm afraid that's been changed. The organizers realized that a stop would take up too much time and fuel, so *Space Force One* will merely be flying past."

"I see," Bob said, trying hard to hide his disappointment. Hix wasn't nearly so good at it; his face was a map of crushed hopes and expectations. "May I ask when this decision was made?"

"That's none of your concern—"

"A week ago," Cummings spoke up. "I know this must be something of a disappointment for you."

Bob took a deep breath. A week. Seven days. They could have told him. "We'll get over it," he said, trying to keep his voice steady.

"I'm sorry we couldn't give you any kind of heads-up," Cummings went on. "But the President's itinerary isn't the sort of thing you broadcast across the Solar System."

"I understand," Bob said, glancing over at Hix. The big man still looked like he wanted to cry, but he was starting to pull himself together again. "It's not like Space Fort Jefferson is an indispensable part of a historic Presidential tour."

"Or of history itself, for that matter," Drexler added.

Bob felt his face settle into familiar lines. "That's hardly fair, Agent Drexler," he said. "Space Fort Jefferson has had a long and hardly insignificant history."

"Really?" Drexler said, regarding Bob coolly. "Which part do you consider to have been significant? The thirty glorious years it spent as a prison for the Archipelago? The fifteen it did duty as a jabriosis quarantine center? Or the twenty-two it's now spent as a tourist attraction?"

Bob took a deep breath, his mental argument center loading Defense Pattern Alpha—

"All right, Drexler, you've made your point," Cummings put in quietly. "It's not Ranger Epstein's fault that Space

Fort Jefferson never got to serve in its primary capacity. Not really Space Fort Jefferson's fault either."

Drexler snorted in a sedate, government-issue sort of way. "Maybe if the designers had had the foresight to build particle shielding into the hull, they'd have gotten some actual use out of it."

Bob sighed. He got so tired of going over this same territory with people who'd never bothered to check their history. "Particle weapons hadn't even been developed when they started building the station," he said.

"He's right," Cummings agreed, tapping the plaque he'd been studying. "Construction began in 2082. The first successful test of a particle weapon wasn't until 2089."

"The shielding they put in was more than enough to handle anything known at the time," Bob added. "If Xhong hadn't made his technical breakthrough when he did, Space Fort Jefferson would have been a perfect defender of the Ceres-to-Earth shipping route."

"Perhaps," Drexler said. "But part of a designer's job is to anticipate future trends and incorporate them into his plans."

"But we didn't come here to discuss history," Cummings interrupted diplomatically. "We need to give the station a quick once-over for any possible danger to *Space Force One* and its escort. Just routine, of course."

"After all, we wouldn't want a section of hull to fall off and float into their path," Drexler said under his breath.

Cummings sent him a strained look. "For what it's worth, I understand the commentators will be giving some of the station's history during the approach," he said. "I know it's not a Presidential visit, but at least it's something for your trouble."

"Yes, sir," Bob said, nodding. "I'm sure we all appreciate it."

Cummings nodded in return. "Now, if you'll take us to the main control complex . . . ?"

"Of course," Bob said, swallowing his annoyance and gesturing through the door. "This way, please."

* * *

A full self-guided tour of the station, including a reading of all the information plaques, was timed to take about five hours. Adding in a lunch break—carry-on bubblepack or back aboard your own ship; the visitors' cafeteria hadn't been open for ten years—the whole thing was a pleasant day's touristing.

Cummings and Drexler didn't bother with the plaques, and they weren't interested in lunch. But unlike standard tourists, they also insisted on seeing the rangers' living quarters, workshops, and storerooms.

It was nearly four hours before Cummings pronounced himself satisfied that Space Fort Jefferson was safe enough for President Ukukho to come within five miles of. What Drexler thought he kept to himself.

"We'll need to stay aboard until after *Space Force One* has passed out of magscope range," Cummings told Bob as they headed back toward the entryway. "We'd like to set up as near the main control area as possible."

"Certainly," Bob said. Ahead, he could hear a murmuring of unfamiliar voices from the reception room. Apparently, the GenTronic Twelve had arrived, and Bob tossed up a quick prayer that there wouldn't be any bored teenagers or inquisitive toddlers in the group. "The station was originally designed for a crew of fifteen hundred, you know. There's a duty dayroom just off the control complex you can use."

They came around the corner into the reception room, and Bob breathed a quiet sigh of relief. No toddlers; no teenagers; just nine youngish, pleasant-looking men in upscale bulkyjackets spread out around the room reading the plaques. Probably rich enough to be sued if they broke anything, which meant they would be careful not to. Hix was hovering nearby, looking like a combination proud mother and nervous curator, all traces of his earlier depression gone from his face. Hix loved showing off his station to visitors even more than Bob did.

"Ah—here's Ranger Bob now," Hix said as Bob and the agents stepped into the room. "I was just telling Herr Forste here what a good job you've done keeping Space Fort Jefferson running."

"Nice to meet you, Ranger Bob," Forste said, smiling. His English had a pleasant North European accent to it. "And who are your friends?"

Bob looked at Cummings, wondering what exactly he was supposed to say here. Cummings moved smoothly into the gap. "My name's Alan," he said. "This is my friend Thomas. You and your friends come from Ceres?"

"Not exactly," Forste said. "We're from Free Norway."

Free Norway? Frowning, Bob turned back to him—

And caught his breath. From beneath their bulkyjackets, all nine men had suddenly produced small but nasty-looking handguns. "You will all please put up your hands," Forste said.

He smiled genially. "Especially you, Secret Service Agents Cummings and Drexler."

They picked up Kelsey as he filled out duty logs in Dock Obs, Renfred as he polished plaques in the Number One Fire Control Center, and Bronsoni as he sneaked an unauthorized nap in the Number Thirteen-D torpedo launch tube.

"Which leaves only Gifford Wimbley," Forste said with satisfaction as he and four of the other gunmen herded the prisoners into the Number Three Defense Monitor Complex. "Where is he?"

"He's on a supply run to Ceres," Bob said. "He won't be back for another two weeks."

Forste's eyes narrowed. "Really," he said, lifting his left thumbnail to his lips and tapping the tip. "How very convenient. Sjette? You up in Command yet?"

"Yes, I'm here," a voice came back, just loud enough for Bob to hear.

"Check the duty log," Forste ordered, his eyes on Bob. "Is Gifford Wimbley off the station?"

Bob cleared his throat. "Uh . . . Giff usually doesn't bother to check himself out," he said. "Since there are just the six of us, and we always know where everyone is—"

"No sign of anyone checked out," Sjette's voice came back. "According to this, everyone should be here."

Forste's eyes bored into Bob's face like rust remover on a gun turret that's been neglected too long. "Where is he?"

"I told you, he's on Ceres," Bob insisted, feeling sweat starting to break out on his forehead.

"He's hiding," one of the other gunmen said, sniffing the air distastefully. Defense Three was far off the standard tourist route, and it hadn't been properly cleaned in ages. Even for Bob, who was used to such things, the scent of old metal and new mildew was a powerful combination.

"Of course he is," Forste said, lifting his gun another couple of inches. Bob held his breath; and then, to his relief, Forste merely smiled and took a step back. "But that's all right," he said. "We have three days; and Space Fort Jefferson isn't all *that* big. We'll find him ourselves."

"Three days until what?" Drexler demanded.

Forste regarded him coolly. "Three days until President Ukukho comes within firing range of this station, of course," he said. "Three days until the people of Earth and the Colonies are brought face-to-face with the determined men of Free Norway."

"Free Norway?" Bronsoni asked, a puzzled look on his face. "I didn't even know it had been locked up."

"Don't be an imbecile," Forste snapped, his eyes suddenly glowing with revolutionary fervor. "All of us are locked up in our own ways. Norway in particular has been imprisoned by a corrupt press, a bloated welfare bureaucracy, and the insidious, multitentacled cod industry. It must stop."

"How will killing President Ukukho help you?" Kelsey asked.

"It will bring system-wide attention to our plight," Forste said, his eyes blazing even brighter.

"Yes, but—"

"How exactly do you intend to accomplish this?" Cummings asked calmly.

Forste focused on him. "Of course," he said, the fire in

his eyes fading back to something approaching normal. "You want to learn our plans in hopes of defeating them."

He shrugged. "But since you have no way to communicate with anyone outside this station, I see no reason not to tell you. It will be a rapid-fire, three-pronged attack as they reach their closest approach. First, a carefully targeted spread of laser blasts will blind their antimissile defense sensors. Next, two Disabler torpedoes will be launched to paralyze the escorting ships. And finally, a single Hellflare missile into *Space Force One* itself . . ."

He left the sentence unfinished. "And the whole Solar System will suddenly understand your problems and tribulations and flock to Free Norway's side?" Cummings suggested.

"Of course," Forste said, as if that was obvious. "All the oppressed peoples of the System will rise up as one."

"And destroy the evil cod industry."

Forste's eyes narrowed again. "I don't like your attitude, Agent Cummings," he said.

And flipping his gun casually toward Cummings, he fired.

Bob gasped as the boom of the shot hammered into his ears. Drexler shouted something and started into a leap that would probably have cost him his life if Hix hadn't grabbed his arm and kept him back from the terrorists.

As for Cummings himself, his expression never even twitched. He glanced down at the red stain spreading rapidly across his chest, looked back at Forste, and collapsed to the deck.

"Get him to the medpack!" Bob snapped, taking a step toward the fallen man.

"As you were, Ranger Epstein," Forste snapped back.

"I'm a Park Service Ranger," Bob countered, ignoring the order and kneeling beside Cummings. "I have an oath to keep, and that oath includes rendering aid to anyone on my station who needs it."

He looked up at Forste, trying to ignore the gun now pointed directly at his left eye. "And even the oppressed peoples of the System," he added, "don't appreciate someone who guns a man down in cold blood and then refuses him medical assistance."

For a long moment Forste seemed to think that one over. Then, as casually as he'd shot Cummings, he raised the muzzle of his gun away from Bob's face. "I suppose they don't," he conceded. "Very well. Take him away."

The medpack was probably two generations behind standard Park Service medical equipment, which meant it was at least five generations behind state-of-the-art for the rest of the Solar System. But it was good enough to diagnose the problem, remove the bullet from Cummings's right lung, and plug him into the coma-nutrient rapid-healing system.

"It says he'll recover to within ninety-seven percent of normal capability," Bob told Forste, peering at the medpack's display. "Looks like he'll be in a healing coma for . . . sixty-two hours."

"Sixty-two *hours*?" Forste said incredulously. "That's ridiculous."

"That's what it says," Bob insisted, pointing at the countdown display.

"Any medpack I've ever heard of could patch him up in a tenth that time," one of the other terrorists insisted suspiciously.

"This is an old and discontinued model," Bob told him. "It has a lot of problems."

"Doesn't matter," Forste said. "Two and a half days. That will still have him up and around in time to watch the show."

He took a step closer to Bob. "Now. I've done you a favor by letting him live. Your turn. Where is Ranger Wimbley?"

Bob sighed. "I already told you. He's on a supply run to Ceres."

Forste lifted his gun in front of Bob's eyes. "You know, I have enough rounds in here to give each of your rangers three of them," he pointed out darkly. "And I'd still have enough left for you."

"I'm sure you would," Bob said, starting to sweat again. "But it wouldn't change the reality of the situation. Giff isn't here."

"Want me to take him to one of the storerooms?" one of the other terrorists suggested.

Forste shook his head. "A waste of time. Where did you say all that construction was?"

"Decks Three through Six, West Quadrant," the other said. "I only glanced in there, but it's a real maze."

"That's where he'll be, then," Forste decided. "You and Niende go find him."

"Right." The other flipped an abbreviated salute and left the room, taking one of the others with him.

"And as for you," Forste added, gesturing to Bob with the gun, "it's time for you to join the others."

The other rangers were gathered in a tight conversational knot in the back of the monitor complex as Bob was escorted back in. The knot broke as the pressure door slammed shut behind him, surging forward like bees whose hive has just been hit by a thrown rock.

Even so, Drexler got there first. "How is he?" he demanded.

"He'll be all right," Bob assured him. "He's out of danger and in a quick-heal coma."

Drexler looked back toward the pressure door, his eyes simmering like overheated circuit coils. "Damn them," he ground out. "Damn them all."

"Careful," Kelsey warned. "They could have painted a bug or two on the wall before they put us in here."

"There aren't any bugs," Drexler said. "I've already checked."

"So what about this plan of theirs?" Renfred asked, playing nervously with his mustache. "It can't possibly work, can it?"

Drexler's lips compressed. "Well, that's the real hell of it. It just might."

"You're kidding," Bronsoni said, his mouth dropping open.

"Do I *look* like I'm kidding?" Drexler growled. "This place was designed to take the biggest sub-nukes they had available back then, which means you've got a hell of a lot of metal and collapsed ceramic in your hull. That means a lot of sensor shielding; and *that* means the escort ships may very well not spot the telltale missile and laser EM signatures until it's too late."

"But what about you?" Kelsey asked. "Aren't you supposed to check in or something?"

"Of course we are," Drexler bit out. "But Forste has to know that. I'm guessing they've either cracked our code and can fake a message, or else they've got an agent on one of the escort ships who can do it for them."

"And they *did* know who you were," Hix murmured. "That means they know a lot about the President's plans."

"That point had not escaped me," Drexler said icily. "Regardless, we can't assume that this scheme will be cracked at the far end. That means it's up to us."

He looked at Bob, visibly bracing himself. "So we need a plan; and Part One of that plan is getting us out of here. Is Ranger Wimbley clever enough to figure that out?"

Bob shook his head. "I'm sorry. But like I've told everyone else, Giff is on Ceres."

"That's ridiculous," Drexler insisted. "You flinched when Forste asked you about him. Why would you do that if he was on a simple supply run?"

Bob glanced at Kelsey, and the pained look on Kelsey's face. "Because it's an illegal supply run," he said reluctantly.

Drexler frowned. "An *illegal* supply run? What's he getting, elephant tusks?"

Bob sighed. "He's picking up a shipful of electrical equipment, plumbing supplies, and enough construction webbing to at least start putting the West Quadrant back together again."

Drexler frowned even harder. "What's illegal about that?"

"The fact that we're buying the stuff ourselves instead of going through Park Service Procurement," Kelsey told him.

"Bypassing bureaucratic banana slugs is a Class E felony these days. Or didn't you know that?"

"No, I didn't," Drexler said between clenched teeth. "So that's it. The entire opposition is conveniently locked together in this room. Terrific."

"Don't give up hope yet," Bob said. "We still have one ally that Forste may not have figured on."

"Who?" Drexler asked. "Our comatose Agent Cummings?"

"No," Bob said, smiling the smile of a man stuck too long on the same dead-end post. "Space Fort Jefferson."

Tredje got the door halfway open before it jammed. Cursing, he eased his way sideways through it, hoping his barrel chest wouldn't get stuck.

"We could try one of the other doors," Niende offered from behind him.

"Shut up," Tredje advised, exhaling and pushing. A second later, he was through.

He stepped to one side as Niende joined him. The whole area, as far ahead as he could see, was one huge collection of scaffolding, barriers, supply piles, and drop cloths. Over against some of the walls were rolled-up sections of carpet, either freshly pulled up or else hoping to be put down some day, and here and there were islands of tool cabinets. Some of the barriers seemed to be warning about drums of rust remover and other cleaning chemicals that had been gathered together; others were guarding against actual holes that went clear through the deck. The whole mess, he knew from their initial sweep, covered nearly a quarter of the circumference of the wheel-shape that was Space Fort Jefferson.

And this was just the mess on Deck Three. Decks Four, Five, and Six were in the same shape.

This, he decided, was going to be a long day. "All right, give me some space," he told Niende, drawing his gun. The rangers weren't supposed to be armed; but then, they weren't supposed to be hiding either. "Let's find him."

* * *

"Easy," Annen warned as Sjette and Femte eased the rolling carrier down the corridor, wincing every time it bounced over an uneven section of decking. The Disabler torpedo wasn't especially fragile; but if it should somehow happen to go off, the discharge of high-voltage current would be unbelievably spectacular for the entire quarter second it would take to burn the three of them into unrecognizable lumps of carbon.

Down the corridor, the lights flickered. Again. Annen swore, glancing up at those overhead for signs of similar flickering. Somewhere nearby he could hear the occasional soft click of a spark bleeding current off a bad ground in the clusters of cables running along both lower edges of the corridor. This whole section of the station, clearly, was an electrical disaster just itching to happen.

He shook his head in disgust and a growing sense of uneasiness. The timing and positioning of the flyby, unfortunately, gave them no choice as to which quadrant of the station they needed to use to launch their attack. Even more unfortunately, the zone of necessity was well off both the tourist and living areas of the station and clearly in the advanced-degenerate stage of its life. Uncertain lighting and power were bad enough; but if something else went out—

"Hold it," Sjette said suddenly, straightening up from his half of the carrier in front of a door with the universal "men's room" symbol on it. "I have to."

"Make it quick," Annen said, glancing around. The quiet snapping was getting worse; he doubted the power had been turned on down here for years. Any minute now the corridor would probably blow all its circuit breakers and plunge them into darkness.

"As quick as I can," Sjette said with just an edge of sarcasm. He pushed open the door and disappeared inside, unzipping as he went.

"This place gives me the creeps," Femte muttered, twitching at a particularly loud snap. "What if the power goes out at a crucial moment?"

"Never mind the power," Annen said. "What about the air system? What about simple basic hull integrity?"

Femte shook his head. "You know, if we can't paralyze both escorts at the same time, one of them will surely sacrifice itself to protect the President."

"And then *Space Force One* will land its Marines on top of us," Annen said grimly. "We'd better make sure—"

He broke off at the sudden bellow that came from inside the men's room. "Sjette!" he snapped, yanking out his gun and dashing around the back end of the Disabler. If that missing ranger was skulking around in there—

He skidded to a halt as Sjette staggered through the door, soaked from forehead to shins. "It doused me!" he gasped disbelievingly. "I finished, and it just—*it wet me*!"

With an annoyed snort, Annen jammed his gun back into its holster. "We're wasting time," he growled. "Come on."

"A minute," Sjette said, lifting his hands and distastefully eyeing the water dripping from his fingertips. Stepping back toward the corridor wall, keeping well back from the Disabler, he lifted his arms and gave them a firm shake downward. A cloudburst spattering of raindrops chattered into the walls or plopped into the growing puddle at his feet—

And suddenly, with a violent thunder crack, Sjette was encased in a brilliant flash of blue-white fire. Annen had just enough time to gasp—

And then the fire vanished, and the corridor's lights all went out.

Leaving only the sound of Femte's startled curse, the pounding of Annen's own heartbeat, and the wet slap of Sjette's body collapsing onto the deck.

Forste's grip on Bob's upper arm was like a lockclamp as he hurried the ranger along at a pace just short of a flat-out run. "What's happened?" Bob asked for the fifth time since Forste and his men had hauled him out of their makeshift prison.

For the fifth time, Forste ignored the question. But at

least now Bob had a good idea where they were going: sick-bay.

Something about Cummings?

They reached the medical center, and Forste all but shoved Bob through the door. Three of the other terrorists were there: two standing grim and armed, the third twitching half-unconscious on one of the treatment tables. Over the whole group hung the pungent aroma of singed flesh. "There," Forste said, pulling his gun out of Bob's ribs and jabbing it toward the corner where Cummings was sleeping peacefully in his medpack cocoon. "Shut it down and get him out of there."

Bob shook his head. "I can't."

Forste's gun was suddenly in his face. "I said *shut it down.*"

"But I can't," Bob protested, his knees suddenly going wobbly. "It doesn't have a cancel switch. Once it's running a program, it can't be shut off until it's finished."

"Don't svark us," one of the terrorists snarled, his knuckles white where he gripped his gun. "That's a Galen R-225. Galens are designed better than that."

"This one isn't," Bob said. "And it's a Galen R-224. They didn't put in the cancel switch until the 225."

The terrorist had been starting toward Bob, murder in his eyes. Now, abruptly, he froze in midstep, doing a hard right and striding over to the medpack. "Well?" Forste asked as he crouched down beside the ident plate.

"It's a 224," he confirmed in a voice like grinding walnuts. "What kind of idiot designed *this*?"

"Probably the kind who got fired while they rushed the 225 into production," Bob said. "From what I heard, they only made a few hundred 224s before they figured it out and canceled the model."

"So why do *you* have one?" Forste demanded suspiciously.

Bob waved a hand around the room. "Why do you think? The Park Service got them cheap."

Forste's mouth worked, but it was clear he couldn't find

an answer to that one. "What if we just shut the thing off, pull Cummings out, and put Sjette in?"

Bob shook his head. "You pull the plug in the middle and you might not be able to get it started again," he said. "You'd have to erase the current program, which means purging the memory; and with this thing there's no guarantee you wouldn't crash it and have to reboot off the recovery disk."

"What if we just shoot Cummings, then?" the other terrorist suggested tightly. "*That* ought to end the program."

"It would probably also end the medpack," Bob pointed out, trying not to shudder at the thought of such casual murder. "And your friend will still be burned. Look, why don't you instead let me see what I can do to help him?"

"You have medical training?" Forste asked.

"Nothing official," Bob admitted. "But I know how to handle burns and basic injuries. We've all had to learn first aid, pretty much in self-defense." He nodded over at the 224.

Forste puckered his lips in disgust. But there wasn't anything he could do about it, and he and everyone else knew it. "Go ahead," he growled.

Fifteen minutes later, with much of his body covered in burn foam, the injured terrorist was snoring gently on a cot. "The foam works best if the subject is asleep," Bob explained as he put everything away. "I just gave him enough for a ten-hour nap."

"Yes, I know," Forste said coolly. "I was watching the dosage you measured into the hypo. Just as well for you that you didn't try to put him under for, say, the next four days."

Bob shivered slightly. The thought had occurred to him, actually, to do exactly that. A good thing he hadn't acted on it. "Is that it, then?" he asked.

"That's it," Forste confirmed. "Annen, take him back to his cell. And then get back to work."

So, Bob thought to himself as he was escorted back down the rusty corridor. *One down. Eight more to go.*

Space Fort Jefferson, it appeared, was on a roll.

* * *

"What do you mean, it's not working?" Forste's voice came tartly.

"It's not working, that's all," Fjerde shot back. "I've run it fifteen different ways, and it's just dead."

"What do the diagnostics say?"

Fjerde snorted. "What diagnostics? This comm system must have been built in the last century."

"I don't care if it's three days older than dirt," Forste snapped. "If we can't get up-to-the-second positioning data from our friend aboard the escort ships, we haven't got a chance of pulling this off. How fast can you fix it?"

"I'm not sure it *can* be fixed," Fjerde protested. "The antenna array alone—"

"You've got twelve hours," Forste cut him off. "Get it operational, or it's your own head." He clicked off without waiting for a reply.

For a moment Fjerde glared at the antiquated comm system with its joke of an antenna array. Then, cursing under his breath, he started taking it apart.

Considering the rust and mildew evident elsewhere in the corridor, Sjuende thought, the locking wheel on the door to the Number Four Torpedo Launch Center was suspiciously easy to turn. The place wasn't on the tourist route; could the rangers have some private use for the place?

Or could it be that the missing Ranger Wimbley was hiding in there? Getting a grip on his gun, Sjuende pulled the door open—

To be greeted by a puff of moist and oddly fetid air. "What's that smell?" Attende asked uneasily from behind him.

"I don't know." Sjuende reached for the light switch, twitched his hand back again as he remembered the faulty electrical circuits that had fried Sjette. Using the edge of his insulated flashlight instead, he flicked on the lights.

He was expecting to see the drab gray and the grim, nononsense metal and ceramic of a Space Force weapons room. What he got instead was Garden Club Headquarters.

"What the *hell*?" Attende gasped, crowding in beside him.

"It's a hydroponics room," Sjuende said with a twist of his lip. He glanced across the row of torpedo tubes "Uh-oh," he muttered.

"What?" Attende demanded. "—oh. Oh."

"Oh, indeed," Sjuende agreed tightly. All eight tube covers had been flipped all the way back to accommodate extra rows of various vegetable-looking plants. Even from across the room, he could see that years of neglect and careless watering had rusted every single cover solidly in place.

"Let's try another room," Attende suggested. "Numbers Two, Seven, and Eight are still available."

"Hardly," Sjuende said, shaking his head. "Two's tubes are open to space, which means the covers are pressure-sealed; Seven is being used as a junk storage room, with more stuff in there than we could possibly move out in three days; and Eight has no floor."

"No *floor*?"

"Part of the big renovation, I suppose." With a sigh, Sjuende lifted his thumb. Forste, he knew, was not going to like this.

Forste didn't. "I suppose you'd better get busy and clean it all off, then," he said when he was finished swearing.

"You don't understand," Sjuende said. "I'm not talking about a little rust. I'm talking about a whole *lot* of—"

"Then it's going to take you a whole lot of time, isn't it?" Forste cut him off. "There's a storage locker at the corridor intersection near Rooms Three and Four—Annen said there were some spray bottles marked 'Rust Remover' in there. Get busy." Sjuende sighed. When he'd signed up for the revolution, this was not exactly what he'd had in mind. "Yes, sir."

"Yes, there are hydroponics in here, too," Annen told Forste, looking around the Number Six Torpedo Launch Center. "Vegetables, mostly. Considering the selection we found in the galley pantry, I don't blame them for growing their own."

"Very charitable of you," Forste growled. "Now, can we concentrate on the problem at hand?"

Over by the Disabler, Femte muttered something under his breath. "Of course," Annen said, giving an annoyed glare of his own at his thumbnail. Pressure or not, Forste had no call to be so sarcastic. "Everything's rusty, but it doesn't look bad enough to have damaged the tubes. We'll have to move some of the plants out to confirm that, of course."

"Well, then, do it," Forste snapped. "Call me when you've got good news. And not *until* you've got good news."

"Yes, sir," Annen said stiffly, shutting off the radio with an unnecessarily hard snap.

"Testy, isn't he?" Femte commented.

Annen took a deep breath. "Things are not going exactly as planned," he reminded the other. "Come on, let's get these plants out of the way. You pick the tube you think looks cleanest; I'll pick the one I like best. Between us, we'll hopefully get one that'll work."

They set to their task, lifting the planters out of the tubes and tube covers and carrying them across to the far wall where they could be set down out of the way. Femte continued to mutter under his breath as he labored, his half-heard diatribe against welfare and the cod industries punctuated by grunts as he hefted a particularly heavy load and the occasional curse as an overfull planter spilled dirt or water onto his bulkyjacket or the floor. Annen, for his part, worked in silence.

Which was probably why he was the one who first noticed the gentle hissing.

He froze in place, eyes narrowed and head swinging back and forth as he tried to locate the source of the sound. It was a leak, of course; but was the gas coming into the room or going out? Either way, it could be very bad news indeed. Across the room Femte grunted again as he lifted another planter—

"Quiet," Annen snapped. "Listen."

Femte paused, the planter cradled in his arms like a green leafy baby. Then his head jerked up, and a second later the planter had been heaved across the room and he was making an Olympic-class dash for the door. "Wait!" Annen shouted, diving around the end of the tube in a desperate attempt to cut him off.

But he was too late. With visions of either leaking air or poisonous gas clouding his vision, Femte was unstoppable.

Unstoppable, that is, until he hit one of the patches of muddy water between him and the door.

"Looks like you've got a mild concussion," Bob told the man, flicking off his pupil light and reaching for the bandages. "Must have hit the wall pretty hard."

"I'm all right," the other insisted, wincing as Bob applied the bandage to his still-oozing head wound. "Just give me a shot of something."

"Sure," Bob assured him. "I'll do that; but then I think you should sleep for a while."

"Sleep?" Forste put in suspiciously. "You want to sedate him, too?"

"It would be the safest thing to do," Bob said, pulling the sedative and painkiller hypos out of their slots in the first-aid kit. "The medpack has another—" he peered across at the countdown display, "—fifty-nine hours to go, and until it's free, we can't do a complete diagnosis. He's probably okay; but if he isn't, and we don't make him rest at least overnight, he could die."

"Just overnight?" Forste asked. "That's all you want?"

"What *I* want has nothing to do with it," Bob countered. "I'm just trying to deal with the reality of the situation."

"Of course," Forste said. "You're never responsible for anything around here, are you?"

With a sigh, Bob set both hypos down on the table. "It's your call," he told Forste. "You tell me what to do."

Forste looked down at the hypos; and as he did so, there

was a click from his thumb. "Forste," he said, raising his hand to his lips.

"It's Sjuende," a faint voice came back. "I found the leaking canister."

Forste's gun lifted an inch closer to Bob's face. "Poison gas?" he asked.

"Nitrogen," Sjuende said, sounding disgusted. "I've shut it off."

Forste frowned. "Nitrogen?"

"To make nitrates for the plants," Bob explained, frowning to himself. There was something odd about Sjuende's voice. A faint slurring, perhaps? "I already told you there wasn't anything poisonous in that room."

Forste took a deep breath, let it out. "All right, Sjuende," he said. "Stay there. Annen's on his way back; help him get Disabler One in place."

"You sure?" Sjuende asked. "Attende and I still have a lot of work to do before Disabler Two can be set up."

"Disabler One can be in place in thirty minutes if Annen has enough extra hands to help him," Forste snapped. "Let's try to get at least *something* ready to go before we quit for the day, shall we?"

"Yes, sir," Sjuende muttered.

Forste tapped his thumbnail and turned to Annen, who was glowering silently over by the door. "Well? Get going."

"Yes, sir." Annen sent one final glower toward the injured Femte, then turned and left.

Forste looked back at Bob and gave a nod that managed to be curt and reluctant at the same time. "Put him to sleep."

"But I'm fine, sir," Femte protested.

"Shut up," Forste said. "You just concentrate on getting a good night's sleep. You'll need it when we play catch-up tomorrow."

Femte sighed. "Yes, sir."

Five minutes later he was stretched out on the cot next to his burn-foamed comrade. "I expected the possibility of injuries while neutralizing the Secret Service agents," Forste muttered under his breath. "Or possibly after the attack, if any of the Marines survived long enough to get into suits and packs. I didn't expect we'd lose two men while we were just setting up."

"Space Fort Jefferson isn't exactly your average work area, of course," Bob pointed out absently, still trying to figure out what in Sjuende's voice had caught his attention. "This can be a risky place if you're not familiar with it."

"Apparently so." Forste lifted his thumbnail. "Fjerde? Any progress with the comm system?"

"I've got the antenna apart now," the other reported. "It's got a lot of rust and dirt embedded in it. I'll clean it and see if it works any better then."

Bob felt his stomach suddenly tense. Rust? "Mr. Forste—"

Forste cut him off with a glare. "Consider it break time," he told the other. "Get down to Launch Center Six and help Annen and Sjuende."

"Yes, sir."

Forste tapped the nail and hefted his gun toward Bob. "Don't you *ever* interrupt me—"

"Your man Sjuende said he and Attende had a lot of work to do," Bob cut him off. "Did it involve cleaning off rust?"

Forste eyed him guardedly. "Yes."

"Are they using our bottles of cleaner?" Bob asked. "And if so, are they wearing breathing masks?"

Forste's expression was starting to cloud over again. "Why?"

"Because the cleaner is toxic, that's why," Bob said. "After a couple of hours, especially in an enclosed space like that—"

Forste snarled a curse, his gun jabbing into Bob's ribs. "Come on. Bring the kit."

They found Attende sprawled on the floor in Number Four, his arms and legs twitching as he babbled something incomprehensible. "Damn, damn, damn," Forste snarled, kneeling down beside him. A spray bottle and rag were still clutched in the man's hands; gingerly, Forste pushed both of them as far away as he could. "Why the hell isn't this stuff labeled as dangerous?"

"The main drum is," Bob said, kneeling on his other side and opening the first-aid kit. "We have to buy it in bulk—it's cheaper that way—and put it into our own bottles. Didn't you see the masks in the storage locker?"

"The bottles weren't labeled," Forste bit out. "Why would they expect to need them? What's he babbling about?"

"Probably nothing," Bob said, finding a wide-spectrum detoxifier hypo in the kit and injecting it into the twitching man's arm. "On its way to suffocating you, the stuff is also a pretty potent hallucinogen. Who knows what he's seeing?"

"Can you save him?"

Bob laid the biosensor strip across the side of the man's neck and watched as the numbers came up. "He'll be fine," he assured Forste. "We got to him in time, and this stuff's great for cleaning all sorts of toxins out the system. Though around here we mostly use it after too much time with the whiskey bottle."

Forste grunted. "So what now? He just sleeps it off?"

"Basically," Bob said. "A couple of hours and he'll be fine. Give me a hand and we'll get him back to sickbay."

The corridor, Sjuende decided, had picked up a definite tilt in the past three minutes. Of course, in that same time it had picked up a nice selection of plant life, too. Laid out across the gray metal in front of him were several rows of pink flowers interspersed with green vines sporting giant tomatoes.

He blinked and squinted. Pink and red; the clashing colors hurt his eyes. What was going on, anyway?

And then, in the distance, he heard the sound of footsteps approaching the intersection behind him.

He had his gun out in an instant, the whole thing falling suddenly into place. It was the missing ranger, of course. He'd laid out the plants to slow him down, and now he was trying to sneak up on him from behind.

Well, it wouldn't work. Sjuende pressed his back against the corridor, afraid to jump over the tomato plants in case they tried to grab him, and turned to face the sound. They'd be sorry—he was way too smart for them.

Too cool, too. Not to mention too shiny.

The footsteps were nearly to the intersection now. Sjuende leveled his gun at the spot where his attacker would appear. Peripherally, he noticed that his gun was growing grass, and wondered vaguely whether that was within its normal design specs.

And then the figure turned the corner, and Sjuende gasped his admiration. Not only had the ranger come up with this brilliant scheme of planting flowers across the corridor, but he'd even been smart enough to discard his uniform and put on Fjerde's clothes. *And* Fjerde's face.

Smiling genially at the cleverness of it all, he fired.

The boom of the gun echoed back and forth across the corridor, sounding rather vinegary. Dimly through the noise, he heard what sounded like a shout from behind him.

He turned. Annen was standing there, hip-deep in tomatoes, waving his gun and screaming something.

Only they weren't tomatoes anymore, Sjuende realized with a start. Instead, they'd turned into a ravenous hedge of cactus.

There was only one thing to do, and Sjuende did it without a second's hesitation. Lowering the gun toward the attacking plants, he fired. It was a perfect shot. The cactus erupted in a burst of red sap; and suddenly, to his relief, the whole patch vanished.

So did Annen. Sjuende frowned, then realized the other was merely lying on his back on the deck, gripping his thigh as a parade of cherry tomatoes rolled out and collected themselves into a little pile beside him.

But the important part was that the renegade ranger Giff had been dealt with. Smiling, Sjuende lifted his thumb to report the good news to Forste.

He was just wondering why his thumb had turned into an elephant's trunk when the whole corridor went dark.

"And so we're down to three," Forste said softly, his gun pressing hard into the back of Bob's head as the ranger knelt beside the second of the gunshot victims. "Just three able-bodied men to speak out for the oppressed peoples of the Solar System."

"It's not quite that bad," Bob said carefully as he finished wrapping the leg. It was amazingly hard to breathe with a gun pressed that hard into the base of his skull. "I mean, aside from these two, everyone else should be up and about by tomorrow."

"Of course," Forste said. "You sound so reasonable. You always sound so terribly reasonable. And yet, one by one, we keep falling."

"But it's not me doing any of this," Bob protested. "I've been locked up the whole day."

"Of course it's not you," Forste said. "It's your friend Wimbley. Where is he?"

"But—"

"Shut up," Forste cut him off. "Call him out. Call him out now, or I'll—"

He broke off. From somewhere in the distance came the sound of a horrible crunching and clattering, accompanied by a panic-stricken bellow. "What was that?" Forste demanded, shoving the gun even harder into the back of Bob's head. *"What was that?"*

Bob winced. "I'm afraid . . . offhand, I'd say it was the two men you had searching the construction area. I warned you before that the deck there was unstable for—"

"Damn you," Forste snarled. Reaching down with his free hand, he grabbed a fistful of Bob's shirt and hauled him to his feet. "That's it, Ranger *Bob,*" he bit out, spinning Bob around and jamming the muzzle of the gun up under his chin. "You're dead. You hear me? You're *dead.*"

There was a flicker of movement at the edge of Bob's vision. He glanced over Forste's shoulder, feeling his eyes widen—

Forste was fast, all right. He reacted instantly, spinning around and stepping partway around Bob's side, clearly intending to use the ranger as a shield. His gun shifted toward the assumed threat behind him, his other hand still gripping Bob's shirt.

But it was too late for even instant reflexes. Even as Forste tried to bring the gun to bear, Agent Drexler plucked it expertly from his grip and drove his other fist hard into the terrorist's stomach.

With a strangled cough, Forste folded over the fist and collapsed to the deck. "You all right?" Drexler asked, pulling Bob out of the other's reach.

Bob got his lungs working again. "I'm fine," he assured the agent, looking back at the intersection where Drexler had appeared. The other rangers were there, too, crowding cautiously around the corner with broomsticks and other makeshift weapons in hand.

"Any idea where the other two are?" Drexler asked as he cuffed Forste's hands and hauled him to his feet.

"Somewhere at the bottom of the Deck Six renovation area," Bob told him. "They probably won't be giving you much trouble."

"I don't . . . understand," Forste managed through his painful-sounding breathing. "How did you . . . manage it?"

Bob shrugged. "I told you. I never lifted a finger."

"Then how . . . ?"

"But I may have mentioned that the station and its equipment had a few problems," Bob added, looking again at the approaching rangers.

At the rangers, and at the pale but determined figure of Agent Cummings as he limped along, leaning his weight on Hix's arm.

Forste followed his gaze, and his jaw dropped. "That's right," Bob said with a nod. "One of the problems is a medpack countdown display that isn't worth a damn."

The terrorists had been locked up, Drexler and Cummings had made their report, and the rangers had gradually drifted back to duties or meals or bed. And once again, Ranger Bob sat at his desk with his recorder in hand.

"Eighteenth April, 2230," he said. "Evening report."

He took a deep breath. "Well," he began. "Space Fort Jefferson won its first battle today . . ."

REDUNDANCY

by Alan Dean Foster

Alan Dean Foster was born in New York City and raised in Los Angeles. He has a bachelor's degree in Political Science and a Master of Fine Arts in Cinema from UCLA. He has traveled extensively around the world, from Australia to Papua New Guinea. He has also written fiction in just about every genre, and is known for his excellent movie novelizations. Currently, he lives in Prescott, Arizona, with his wife, assorted dogs, cats, fish, javelina and other animals, where he is working on several new novels and media projects.

AMY was only ten, and she didn't want to die.

Not that she really understood death. Her only experience with it had come when they'd buried Gramma Marie. Now the funeral was a wisp of a dream that hung like cobweb in the corners of her memory, something she didn't think of at all unless it bumped into her consciousness accidentally. Then it was no more than vaguely uncomfortable without being really hurtful.

She didn't recall a whole lot about the ceremony itself. Black-clad grown-ups speaking more softly than she had ever heard them talk, her mother crying quietly into the fancy lace hankerchief she never wore anywhere, strange people bending low to tell her how very, very sorry they were: everything more like a movie than real life.

Mostly she remembered the skin of Gramma Marie's face, so fine and smooth as she lay on her back in the big shiny box. The fleshy sheen mirrored the silken bright blue of the coffin's upholstery. It was a waste of pretty fabric, she remembered thinking. Better to have made skirts and party dresses out of it than to bury it deep, deep in the ground. She liked that idea. She thought Gramma Marie would have liked it, too, but she couldn't ask her about it now because Gramma Marie was dead, and people couldn't talk to you anymore once they were dead. Not ever again. That was the thing she disliked most about death; not being able to talk to your friends anymore.

Thinking about it made her shiver slightly. She knew she was in big trouble, and she didn't want to end up looking like Gramma Marie.

The potato vines and the carrots and the lettuce had not yet begun to die, though the leaves on the fruit trees were already starting to droop. Some had been killed by the explosion, torn to bits or ripped up and hurled violently against once another. One of the big pear trees had been blown to splinters. Smashed pears lay scattered across the floor like escapees from a Vermeer still life. Amy knew that the others would start dying soon, now that the hydroponic fluid that nourished their growth had stopped circulating and the special lights used to simulate the sun had gone out. The heaters were off, too, though some residual heat still emanated from their internal ceramic elements. The temperature was falling steadily, soaked up by the thirsty atmosphere of the rapidly cooling station module.

What really frightened her, though, wasn't the darkness or the gathering cold. It was the persistent, angry hiss that came from the base of the wall at the far end of the module. She couldn't see the leak, but she could hear it. She tried putting some empty sacks over the hiss and then piling furniture on them. It muted the noise, but didn't stop it. So she backed as far away from it as she could, all the way back across the module, as if retreating from a dangerous snake. There were four safety doors in the big module, designed to divide it into airtight quarters in the event of a leak. Not one of them had closed. She didn't know why, but she guessed that the explosion had broken something inside them, too.

She wondered if she would know it when the air finally

ran out. She would have asked Mr. Reuschel about it, but he was already dead. He didn't look at all like Gramma Marie had. His mouth hung open and instead of lying neat and straight on his back he was all bent and twisted on the floor where the explosion had thrown him. She didn't know for certain he was dead, but she was pretty sure. He didn't reply to any of her questions and he didn't move at all, not even when she touched his eye. When she put her palm up to his mouth the way she'd been taught to in school, she couldn't feel anything moving against her skin.

He'd been the gardener on duty when everything had exploded. Daddy called him a hydroponics engineer, but Amy just thought of him as the gardener. Ms. Anwalt was the other gardener. Like everyone else on the station, she probably knew about the explosion by now and would want to check on the garden, but she couldn't. No one could because the access door didn't work anymore. The explosion had broken it just like it had broken Mr. Reuschel.

The door led to the lock, which led to the service corridor, which connected the hydroponics module to the rest of the station. Amy knew it was still connected because her feet weren't floating off the floor. If the module had broken away from the rest of the station, then it wouldn't be swinging around the central core, and if it wasn't rotating around the central core, then she would be floating in zero-gee right now.

She wondered if Jimmy Sanchez was worried about her. She hoped so. Jimmy was twelve, the only other kid on the station. His parents were photovoltechs who spent their days drifting like butterflies around the huge solar panels which powered and heated the facility. Jimmy was pretty nice, for a boy. She liked him more than he liked her, but maybe, just maybe, he was thinking about her.

She knew Mum and Dad must be worrying about her, but she tried not to think about that because it made her sad. She thought of all the bad things she'd done as a little girl and wished now she hadn't done them.

It was getting cold and she knew she should keep moving. She walked over to the rectangular port behind the tomato vines. Since all the overheads had gone out, the only light in the module came from the ports. Pressing her nose to the transparency enabled her to see the big blue sphere of the Earth outside, rotating slowly around the port. Doing geography helped keep her mind off the chill. She located Britain, and Spain, and the boot of Italy. There was no cloud cover over the Alps and she saw the snow on the mountaintops clearly. But the oceans were easiest to identify. They made her think of beaches, and the stinky-sweet smell of salt water, and the warm summer sun.

She was able to see her breath by the light of the Earth. Mr. Reuschel still hadn't moved. He didn't protest as she struggled to get his jacket off. He was a grown-up and heavy and hard to move and it made her stomach feel queasy to try, but she kept pushing and shoving. His jacket was bulky-warm and covered her down to her knees.

Water dripped from a broken pipe, a comforting tinkling in the darkness. She drank and then did her best to wash the dirt off her face, the dirt from where she'd landed. She understood enough to be thankful for it. If the compost pile hadn't been there to catch her and break her fall, she might be as twisted up as Mr. Reuschel.

After a moment's thought she decided to sit down by the door. All of its internal LEDs had gone out, so she knew it still wasn't working. The big manual lever was bent and twisted and wouldn't move even when she put all her weight on it.

It was very dark next to the door and away from the ports, but somehow she felt better sitting there. Pouring through the ports, Earthlight made shadowy silhouettes of the trees and bushes. The cabin in Residential Module Six with her stuffed animals and seashells and snug second-tier bunk seemed very far away. It would've been easier if Jimmy, or anybody, had been there with her. But they weren't. There was only poor Mr. Reuschel, and he was worse than no company at all. She was alone.

Except she wasn't.

There was another presence in the module. It wasn't dead, but it wasn't really alive either. Awareness is a matter of technical definitions and predetermined perceptive capability. Consciousness is something entirely more abstract.

The Molimon was aware of her presence but could not talk to her, could not provide reassurance or comfort. It was aware of the damage which had occurred, of Mr. Reuschel, of the falling temperature and absence of light. It had detected the leak at the far end of the module and continued to monitor the rate at which air was being lost. It was aware of everything around it. That was the job it had been assigned to do. That was the job it did well.

Until now. It knew that the environment in which it operated had undergone an abrupt and drastic change. There was damage and destruction everywhere. Nothing was functioning within assigned parameters and try as it might, the Molimon could not restore anything to normal.

That was because it had suffered considerable damage itself. A pair of memories were gone and an IOP processor had been popped by the force of the explosion. Two molly drives had stopped spinning. Efficiently, effectively, the Molimon distributed the responsibilities of the damaged sectors among the components of itself that continued to function. It was wounded, but far from dead.

Internal communications continued to operate, allowing the Molimon to send details of the damage it and the module had suffered to Command Central. So far there had been no response. No doubt Central was concentrating on assessing the damage to those components and parts of the station that were unable to report on themselves. Knowing that the Molimon could take care of itself, Central would take its time responding.

Having reported the damage and requested instructions on how to begin repairs, the Molimon sat and waited for a reply. It could not wait long. If no instructions were forthcoming, it would have to shut itself down while battery power remained, thereby preserving its programming and functions until full external power was restored. This caused it no concern. Anxiety was not part of its programming. It had no concept of unconsciousness. Shutdown was merely another state of existence. There was nothing to be concerned about, since all systems within the module were fully redundant.

It was aware of the damage to the hydroponics module only in purely quantitative terms: the absence of light, of heat, of equipment functioning efficiently and according to plan. Supervising the hydroponics environment was but one component of its mission, and it could not bring anything back on line until power was restored. Knowing this, it completed its observations, allotted them a sector on one of its still functioning mollys, and made a complete record of the situation. Programming now called for it to commence an orderly shutdown while sufficient reserve power remained for it to do so.

It did not. Unexpectedly, an important component of the module still functioned.

Hedrickson studied the readouts and listened to the human static that filled his headphones. The various speakers were angry, frustrated, anxious. He worked at the console unaware that he was gritting his teeth. They were starting to hurt, but he didn't notice the discomfort. Just as he did not immediately take notice of the hand that came down on his shoulder.

"How're we doing?"

Pushing the phones off his ears, he leaned back in the chair and stared dully at the monitors. "It's slow. Real slow. The corridor's a mess. They're clearing it as fast as possible, but they can't use heavy tools in there or they're liable to hull the tube."

"Doesn't matter, if they're working in suits." Cassie's gaze flicked over the readouts. The figures were not reassuring.

"They're afraid any explosive decompression might weaken the tube's joints to the point where they could snap. Engineering already thinks that the initial explosion may have compromised structural integrity where the corridor attaches to the module's lock. If that goes, we could lose the whole thing." Hedrickson's tone was leaden, tired, indicative of a man who needed sleep and knew he wasn't going to get any. "How're the Maceks taking it?"

Cassie Chin shrugged helplessly. "Tina's in shock. They took her down to the clinic and put her under sedation. Iwato's watching her closely. I think he's pretty worried about her."

"Damn it. What about Michael?"

"Couple of the riggers volunteered to stay with him. They had to lock down the main bay to keep him from going out in a suit."

Hedrickson's fingers drummed nervously on the console. "How much do they know?"

"They've figured out Amy's in there somewhere. They know the lights are out and the heat is going, that the AV lines are down and that no one inside is responding to queries through the board."

The engineer exhaled slowly. "Do they know about the leak?"

"No." Cassie stared at him. "That I couldn't tell them. Nobody else is up to that either. They'll find out when the crew goes in. There isn't much hope, is there?"

"I'm afraid not. The rescue specs are working like maniacs, but even if the leak doesn't get any worse, the air in there'll be gone before they can cut the door. Morrie Reuschel was engineer on duty when it happened. We haven't heard from him. If he's that bad hurt, then the girl . . ." His words trailed off into inaudibility, foundering in despair.

"The only communication we have with the module is via its independent Module Lifesystems Monitor. It says it got wanged pretty good, but you know how much redundancy those suckers have built into them. It took stock of its losses and shifted all necessary functions to undamaged components outside the module. That's the only reason we have some idea of what's going on inside. One boardline survived the damage, so we're still getting reports."

The woman frowned. "But there's no power to the module."

"The section there is operating on standard multiple battery backup."

"I know." She leaned curiously over the console. "But it shouldn't be. It's designed to render a report and then shut itself down when it loses primary power, to preserve programming and functions. Something else is wrong. Has it requested repair instructions yet?"

"I would imagine." Hedrickson checked a readout. "Yeah. Right here. Haven't been sent out, though."

"Why not?"

"Central's dealing with more serious damage elsewhere."

Chin straightened. "Instead of cycling through shutdown the way it's supposed to, it keeps requesting repair instructions. There's got to be a reason." She thought furiously. "Can you override Central from here?"

Hedrickson frowned at her. "I think so, but you'd better have a damn good reason for messing with prescribed damage-control procedure."

"As a matter of fact, I don't have any reason at all. But it seems as if the Molimon does. If it's internal diagnostics are functioning well enough to tell you what's wrong, can you send it the necessary instructions on how to fix itself?"

"Just so I'll have something to tell the board of inquiry, why bother?"

"I just told you: it's got to have a reason for not shutting itself down."

Hedrickson looked dubious. "You'll take the responsibility?"

"I'll take the responsibility. See what you can do, Karl."

The technician bent to work. Cassie stood staring at the wall. Halfway around the station the darkened, leaking module swung precariously on the end of its connector tube, to all intents and purposes dead along with everything it contained. Except for one semi-independent device, which was disobeying procedure.

Computers do not act on whims, she thought. They respond only according to programming. Something was affecting the priorities of the Molimon unit that supervised the hydroponics module. But it couldn't proceed without human directives.

Sometimes you just had to have faith in the numbers.

The darkness and gathering chill did not trouble the Molimon. It was immune to all but the most extreme swings of temperature. Reserve power continued to diminish. Still it did not commence shutdown.

Information on how to affect necessary repairs finally began to arrive. Gratefully, the incoming instructions were processed. The problem with the critical downed memory was located and a solution devised. Memory reintegration proceeded smoothly, enabling the Molimon to bypass one of the downed molly drives.

The system component that most concerned the Molimon reported borderline functional. It sent out the command, to no response. Clearly the trouble was more serious than anyone, including its programmers, had anticipated.

That did not mean that the problem was insoluble. It merely required a moment of careful internal debate. The Molimon's internal voting architecture went to work. One processor opted for procedure as written, even though that had already failed. The second suggested an alternative. Noting the failure of the first, processor three sided with two. Having thus analyzed and debated, it tried anew.

This time the door responded. Like all internal airtights it contained its own backup power cell. Running the instructions exhausted the self-contained cell's power, but the Molimon was not concerned with that. It wanted the door shut. Opening it again would be a matter for future programs.

Internal alarms began to go off. It had spent entirely too much time operating when it ought to have been shutting down. There was insufficient power to preserve programming. When it shut down now, it would do so with concurrent loss of memory, even though all critical information would be effectively preserved on the surviving mirrored molly drives. The Molimon was not bothered by this knowledge. It had fulfilled another, more important aspect of its programming.

Enough reserve strength remained for it to send a last message to a slave monitor. Composition of the message caused the Molimon some difficulty despite the fact that it had been programmed to accept and respond to many in plain English.

Then its backup power gave out completely.

Amy was waiting patiently next to the mixing vats when they found her. The jammed lock door gave way with a reluctant groan. Shouts, then laughter, then tears filled the hitherto silent module. She looked very small and vulnerable wrapped up in the dead engineer's jacket.

Cassie Chin watched the reunion, wiping at her eyes as she listened to the wild exclamations of delight and joy. Mike Macek was tossing his daughter so high into the air Cassie was afraid that in the limited gravity he was going to bounce her off the ceiling. Her expression turned somber as she watched others kneel beside the body of Morrie Reuschel.

Eventually her attention shifted to the rearmost of the module's airtight doors. Somehow the Molimon had managed to get it to shut, effectively sealing off the air leak in the section beyond. That action had preserved the remaining atmosphere in the other three fourths of the module until the rescue team had succeeded in punching its way in. She regarded the lifesaving door a while longer, then turned to business.

Karl Hendrickson was waiting for her.

"Look at the damn thing. It's half bashed in." He pointed at the debris-laden floor. "Looks like that big wrench hit it."

Cassie sighed. "Let's get the rear panel off."

Their first view of the Molimon's guts had Hedrickson shaking his head. "These mollys must've gone down first. Then I don't know what else."

"But after it fixed itself, it figured out how to seal off the leak and stayed on-line long enough to get the job done." She shook her head in disbelief. "Batteries?"

Hedrickson ran a quick check, made a face. "Dead as an imploded mouse."

Chin pursued her lips. "Then the programming's gone. I don't mind that except it means we'll never learn why it didn't follow accepted procedure and commence preservation shutoff when the primary power went down."

Hedrickson turned to the nearest monitor, plugged in a power cell and brought the Molimon unit on-line. "Nothing here," he told her after several minutes of inquiry. "No, wait a sec. There is a shutdown indicator. It knew it was going." He frowned. "The message is in nonstandard format."

Chin moved to join him. Lights were coming on all around them as repair crews began to restore station power to the hydroponics module.

"What do you mean, it's 'nonstandard'?"

Hedrickson ran a speculative finger along the top of the ataraxic Molimon. His voice was flat. "Read it for yourself."

Chin looked at the softly glowing monitor he was holding. She expected to see the words "Shutdown procedure completed."

Instead, she saw something else. Something that was, after all, only an indication of programming awareness. Nothing more. What it said was this.

"Little girls are not redundant."

DANCERS OF THE GATE

by James Cobb

James Cobb lives in the Pacific Northwest, where he writes both the Amanda Garrett technothriller series and the Kevin Pulaski '50s suspense mysteries, not to mention the occasional odd bit of historical and science fiction. When not so involved, he enjoys long road trips, collecting classic military firearms, and learning the legends and lore of the great American hotrod. He may also be found frequently and shamelessly pandering to the whims of "Lisette," his classic 1960 Ford Thunderbird.

AS HAD become their habit before an evening shift package, the Voice-of-Decision for River-'Tween-Worlds and the Operations Director for Transtellar United's Wormgate Complex dined together. The menu consumed consisted of a raw and slightly rank slab of gristly deep ranger flesh liberally dusted with *Kessta* pollen, iced tea, and a Cobb salad.

The fact that the two aspects of the meal were consumed two point forty-eight parsecs apart did nothing to distract from the worn-comfortable camaraderie of the meal.

"Voice-of-the-Dance Tleelot found the selections of Artist-called-Miller most impressive. Believes we can apply to varianting of Flame-River and Joyous-Bay dance cycles. We shall experiment next amusements gathering."

The fluid chirps and purrs of Tarrischall's actual words in the tongue of the People flowed behind the stark computer English. Marta Lane had long ago developed the knack of laying the alien's vocal emotion tones over the bland and choppy diction of the translator block to deduce the true meaning behind her friend's speech.

"I've found that Glenn Miller works better then Cab Calloway for free-fall dance," she replied. "The flow of the Big Bands draws a more rhythmic line than Bebop. I'd love to see what you are doing with it."

"Shall record and send, Marta-Friend. Appreciate your introduction to musics of your Pre-Space-Times. Would like more, especially Artist-Called-Miller."

"My pleasure, Tarrischall. After shift tonight I'll bang 'Tuxedo Junction' and 'The Jumpin Jive' across the link. We might try a little Charley Parker while we're at it."

Seated in her quarters aboard the Stellar Transfer Command Station, Lane took up her personal data pad, and clipped the transparent rectangle of crystal state circuitry and liquid surface display onto the forearm sleeve of her black vacuum suit liner.

The figure within the snug liner was still firm and svelte, and Lane's angular features were still unlined for all of her fifty plus years. An athletic mother of two and grandmother of four, she well-carried the biological rewards bestowed upon a human female who had lived the majority of her life in a low-to-zero gravity environment.

A simple gene booster treatment could have erased the silver hazing her blonde spacer's ponytail as well, but she elected to keep her hair natural. It served to remind the youngsters on her watch that the Boss had indeed been around since the legendary days when the old fire-belching shuttle rockets had been the only available stair step into space.

Lane tapped the time hack recall on the pad's surface with a fingernail. "Speaking of banging things across, we'd better get to work if we're going to make that transfer at twenty-two hundred, Voice-of-Decision. I make it T minus two hours eighteen minutes to shift initiation."

"Wrong, O Operations Director, it is two hours, seventeen minutes and twenty-three seconds, human time, precise, to channel open. Any load configuration changes in batch of cheap beads and trinkets you send to us?"

"Nothing appreciable. The outbound will be a couple of

tons light. Quan Intertrade had a transshipment delay on a load of entertainment cards they wanted to squeeze aboard today's load. They requested a hold, but I chilled it. I daresay the People can survive without *The Classics of Twentieth Century Video Comedy, volume eight*, for another twenty-four hours.

"Volume numbered eight?" Tarrischall chirped.

"Uh-huh," Lane called up a data line. "*Leave it to Beaver* through *Monty Python's Flying Circus*."

"My species thanks you for reprieve."

"You're most welcome. You never know, though. You might like the one about the beavers."

Humor-purring to himself Tarrischall-of-the-Crystal Springs twisted his sphere-of-communications closed, stowing it into a pouch in his possessions harness. He had eaten in the lower observation bubble of the River-'Tween Worlds Nest-of-Guidance, simultaneously enjoying his meal, his conversation with Friend-Marta-of-the-Place-called-New-England, and the awe-inspiring view.

River-'Tween Worlds held in geosynchronous orbit above the North Pole of Life-Waters, the home world of the People. The huge northern polar continent with its central ice cap rotated slowly beneath them, half in shadow, half blazing in the golden light from Life-Fire-of-All-Things.

On the nightside of Life-Waters, the lights of the linear river cities of the People trickled along the numerous broad watercourses that connected the ice pack with the equatorial lake/seas. On dayside, in a half loop along the equatorial orbits, the sunward collector arrays of the light-power-gatherers glittered like a string of pleasure-time beads.

River-'Tween-Worlds itself was not visible from this end of the great cylindrical skynest. The channel entry assembly held in a slightly higher orbit above the support facility. However, the running lights and glowing propulsor vents of the orbital traffic servicing River-'Tween-Worlds spiraled up past the skynest, the trade of the People flowing out to buy the wonders and amusements of the distant Upright culture.

With a final quick cleansing lick of his forepaws, Tarrischall fluidly reversed himself in midair, launching down the core passage with a thump of his muscular tail against the dome surface.

Approaching the central interchange, he exchanged whistled salutations with a pair of coworkers. Spiraling past them, he snared the padded surface of the maneuvering ball that hung suspended at the corridor nexus. His six sets of claws caught a purchase in the webbed fabric and he relaunched himself into the guidance chamber access, his day's duties due to commence in a sixteenth portion.

None of the People's space facilities utilized artificial gravity unless it was necessary for some industrial application. A semiaquatic species, the People had come to relish free fall as much as they loved the floating freedom of their world's vast network of lakes, rivers and shallow seas. A product of his planet's water-dominated evolutionary processes, Tarrischall was a sexipedal, carnivorous semimammal, bearing closest resemblance to a terrestrial river otter blown up to the scale of a Bengal tiger. Covered from whisker pads to tail with a glossy blood-red fur that trended toward a yellowish cream tone along his belly, his species found clothing irrelevant.

Friend-Marta had often mentioned that her kind found the People to be most attractive. Honestly flattered, Tarrischall had always replied with a verity of polite sophistries.

Marta's folk were certainly nice enough to know and do trade with, but it had to be admitted that the Uprights were an odd-looking crew.

Tarrischall shot into the Guidance Chamber, a spherical structure with far-viewer panels sheathing its upper and lower surfaces and a row of task pallets spaced around it in a central belt.

The other Voices were already present and at station with shift preparations already underway under the guidance of

Narisara-of-the-Ice-Crystal-River. The sleek, black-furred Voice-of-Physics would no doubt have an arch comment or two about the Voice-of-Decision being the last to arrive for duty.

Bouncing off the maneuvering ball in the center of the chamber, Tarrischall dove across to his task pallet. En route he aimed a teasing nip at one of Narisara's rear legs. Without looking up from the glowing half-bubble of her instrument display she replied with a tail swat that could have broken a jaw if it had been aimed to connect.

Still purring contentedly to himself, Tarrischall belly flopped onto his pallet, his rear- and mid-claw sets hooking into the webbing while the stubby digits of his forepaws played across the touch bar arrays surrounding his display bubble, summoning it to life.

"Fair night, pups," he called cheerfully. "Let's send the Uprights some presents."

The security hatch into the gate operations center recognized Marta's bio-pattern, sliding open at her approach.

The compartment that contained the center was a large one for a space station. Three tiers of ranked workstations descended from Director's row, facing the ten-by-five-meter main viewer tank inset in the far bulkhead. Her section chiefs were already hard at it, working the shift countdown.

"Evening, Marta," Assistant Operations Director Estiban Rocardo called up from the central station of the upper tier. "T minus two and ten to dilation and we are showing all green boards."

Behind him, the primary display held focus on the Worm Gate itself. Considerable familiarity was required before the view ceased to inspire awe.

The gate complex hovered in fixed orbit at the L-2 Lagrange point beyond Earth's moon. Several kilometers beyond the rotating rim of the command station, the gate itself lay silhouetted against the mottled gray expanse of Luna's rear face.

The gate structure itself could only be called titanic. Taking advantage of free-fall engineering, its individual components were unconnected, stationkeeping on each other via cybernetically precise thruster control. The twin semi-cylinders of the field generator/accumulator arrays dwarfed the girder structure tube of the perimeter grid, the so-called "worm cage" at their center focus, and the cage itself was one half a kilometer across by one and a half in length.

The toylike myriad of support facilities clustering in free space around the gate, the barge docks, the maintenance and warehousing platforms and the habitat wheels, gave the facility scale. Smaller yet, tug and barge combos and orbital shuttles flitted between the stations like gleaming fish within the structure of a coral reef.

In absolute contrast was the wormhole itself. It was there. It was always there, trapped at the central nexus of the worm cage. Marta knew she was looking right at it, but there was nothing to be seen save for the hole's imprint on her instrumentation.

In its power-conserving nontransit mode, the wormhole was almost microscopic, held open just enough to insure continued existence and to permit the coherent light flow of the communications laser.

The Worm Gate was beyond being the single greatest creation of humanity. Its building had required the concentrated efforts of two civilizations. The only like to it was its identical twin parked above the second planet of the Wolf 359 system.

Marta chuckled softly, deliberately pausing for a moment to make herself be impressed.

"What's the joke, Marta?" Rocardo inquired, lifting a dark eyebrow.

"Oh, nothing, Estiban. It's all so workaday anymore that sometimes I forget that we're busy doing the impossible out here."

"What do you mean by impossible?"

"Back in my first year at MIT I can remember attending a lecture by one of the world's foremost physicists who loudly and firmly proclaimed that the worm search was a waste of funding and that interstellar travel was and would always be beyond the reach of mankind."

Her Assistant Director smiled indulgently. "No insult intended. But that was a long time ago."

"I suspect, young man, that had we not made contact with the Furrys that world view would still be in effect. Science is instinctively conservative. We don't like to shuffle the laws of the universe around unless we have a very good reason for it. But once we knew that somebody was indeed in the neighborhood, we simply had to figure out a way to borrow each other's lawn mowers."

Marta had been a little girl when first contact had been established between Humanity and the People. The two species had found each other intriguingly different and yet much alike, both had a broad streak of curiosity in their racial psyche. Both also soon found the years' long cycle of conversation via radio telescope infinitely unsatisfying. A human scholar asking a question of his counterpart among The People had to wait years for the reply and vice versa. Within the scientific communities of both worlds the quest for an improved form of communication became a fixation that bordered on a mania.

Each culture had possessed its own Einstein and Stephen Hawking. Each had an approximately equal understanding of the structure of the universe and each focused its search in the same rarified area of theoretical physics, seeking for a mathematically irrational chimera called a wormhole.

A decade was spent proving that, yes, such things did in fact exist, but as an ephemeral transitory at the outermost edge of quantum reality. Dimensional "holes" did indeed open intermittently between far distant points in space, but so submicroscopically small and for such a brief period that even a single photon of light could not hope to transit through one.

A second decade was spent proving that such a wormhole could be "caught" and "held open" via a negative energy field. With the proper application of power, vast oceans of power, it could be "stretched " to a "size" that would permit the passage of physical matter. However, a living being could not survive the transit. Systems created within the three-dimensional universe, be they mechanical, electronic, or biological, could not function within the dimensionless realm that existed within the wormhole, but ideas and goods could theoretically be passed across from one world to the other.

A third decade went into the construction of the hardware to make it happen.

"River-'Tween-Worlds, this is Worm Gate. We are coming up on shift initiation. We show good systems and we are ready to set transfer sequencing."

Marta gave her command headset a final settling tug, her eyes flicking to the multiple countdown display bars glowing across the bottom of the imaging tank.

"Understood, Worm Gate. We also prepared." Over the translator link Tarrischall's voice held none of its usual humorous shading. Her Furry compatriot was the consummate professional when it came to Operations. "We have good systems. We stand by sequencing."

"Very well, River-'Tween-Worlds. Coming up on sequencing initiator. Mark zero three . . . two . . . one . . . Set."

The twin timing bar displays crawled across the main screen. T minus ten minutes to power up. T minus twenty-five to barge entry. Instantly the bars began their slow shrink back down toward the zero point.

The clocks had started.

One could not dally around with a barge shift. Not while one was expending enough electricity to power an entire continent. The gate crews at both ends of the hole lived by the fact they could build up enough juice in their accumulator arrays to execute a single two-way barge transfer every twenty-four hours plus a small emergency reserve.

"We have systems verification from 'Tween-Worlds," the Grid Systems Manager called up from his station. "Auto sequencing set and verified."

"Very good, grid. River-'Tween-Worlds, we show auto sequencing set and counting. Do you concur?"

"We concur sequencing, Worm Gate. We are go for transfer."

Lane abstractly noted that the archaic space age technoslang sounded odd coming from one of the People. Tarrischall had become immensely proud of his linguistic expertise in the area, however.

"Acknowledged, River-'Tween-Worlds. Transfer is go. Securing communications and data links and withdrawing lasercom platform at this time. Talk with you afterward."

"A-Okay, Worm Gate. Later. Want to hear more about this *Jumping Jive*. River-'Tween-Worlds, over and out."

"Jumping Jive?" Rocardo queried off circuit.

"Um-hum, Marta replied absently. "It's a long story. Let's just say I'm running a personal cultural exchange program with our Furry friends."

Her mouth tugged down momentarily as the command link indicator with River-'Tween-Worlds control blinked off her communications display. When they dilated the gate to move a cargo barge through to the Wolf system, they temporarily lost their ability to push a modulated data stream through the wormhole to the opposite gate. Thus, each transfer had to be accomplished as a pretimed sequence of events.

That loss had always made Marta Lane just a little bit uncomfortable.

"Raft positioning?" Tarrischall tossed the question over his shoulder, not shifting his keen jet-eyed gaze from the distant-vision displays.

"Raft anchored at channel approach," Marrun-of-Gray-Lake growled back from the Voice-of-Raft-Guidance position. "Drift canceled on all vectors and holding stable."

On the overhead displays the panning vision of the seer units verified the burly Gray-Laker's words. The cargo raft, a huge round-ended cylinder with its sides marked with the odd angular writing and insignia of the Uprights, hovered beyond the gaping mouth of the perimeter grid, poised for the opening of the channel. Remotely guided Pusher units clung to its flanks like leech shrimp, their propulsor vents flaring intermittently.

"Raft Functions?"

"Internal functions verified to the sixteenth level," Varess-of-Storms-Bay replied crisply. The slight, golden-furred Voice-of-Raft-Guidance was the newest member of the watch and still somewhat self-conscious among Tarrischall's veteran crew. "Ready to assume entry guidance."

"Very good. We will be ready for you in a moment." Tarrischall's eyes flicked to the disappearing time dots on the sequencing display. "Voice-of-Physics, channel status."

"Plus on all channel systems," Narisara replied crisply. "Nominal to the sixteenth level. Primary and crisis reservoirs at fifteen point six. Prepared for route sequencing on posted marks. Prepared for last phase safety block clearance."

"You have it, O elegant black-furred one. Let's crack her open." Once more Tarrischall grinned at Narisara's fastidious snort.

"All voices prepare for channel opening." she called. "Safety blocks are clear. Flow increase on my notice. Portion one . . . portion two . . . portion three . . .

"Four . . . three . . . two . . . one . . .," The Gate Systems Manager droned from his workstation, calling off the last disappearing millimeters of the bar display. No matter how many times she sat through it, Marta still felt her throat tighten as the countdown reached its conclusion.

"Zero . . . we have power up."

There was no overt physical change within or without the control center beyond a shifting of light patterns on the control displays. But within the gate accumulator arrays huge supercooled fluid state switches closed, bringing the largest single power system the human race had ever created online. Focused negative energy fields of mind-boggling intensity converged and intermeshing within the worm cage. For a brief moment mankind warred with the very physical structure of the Universe . . . and won.

A blackness came to be in the heart of the perimeter grid.

A blackness deeper than that of the surrounding space itself. A slowly growing sphere of absolute nothing, a nothing with a density, a dimension, a nothing that the stars couldn't be seen through, a nothing that twisted the stomach when looked at. A midnight void darker than the human comprehension of dark.

As he always did at the opening of the gate, Rocardo murmured, "One of these days I'm not going to want to look at that damn thing anymore."

Marta nodded in understanding. She was in love with the possibilities of the wormhole and of interstellar communications, but there was always a discomfort in looking at something human eyes had never been designed to see.

As it was, they were only seeing the wormhole's event horizon, that portion of its structure that extruded into the human-experienced three dimensions. There was much, much more to it than what was visible and likely just as well.

Bad as it was looking at the hole through a live video pickup, it was worse via a viewport or a space suit faceplate. Lane found it rather like standing on the edge of a high cliff or atop a tall building. A . . . pulling.

Others felt it as well. There had been a number of suicide attempts over the years involving the wormhole. One or two had even made it in. Marta had often mused that it probably was a rather interesting way to go.

The sphere of ultimate emptiness expanded until it just filled the center of the girderwork cylinder.

"We have full dilation and stability," Rocardo reported from below, "All boards read green. Reception tugs are positioning. T minus thirteen and counting to projected barge entry and acquisition."

"Very good. Maintain monitoring. Stand by for reception."

For the moment all of the action was taking place out at Wolf 359. Tarrischall and his gang would be busy popping the sixty-thousand-metric-ton transfer barge into their end of the hole.

"End" was a purely subjective reference, of course. While the actual state of existence within the wormhole could be described mathematically, it could not be visualized by a mind designed to operate in three dimensions. On one level, the concept of "distance" had become irrelevant within the perimeter grid of the gate, all points within its contained "universe" being equidistant. On another, it was time that was irrelevant and all of the space between Wolf 359 and Sol still existed, the materials in transit being dispersed across those quadrillions of kilometers.

However, even locked within this trans-state, individual atoms still maintained inertia. The barge's entry momentum would be enough to carry it through the region of irrelevancy from one "end" of the hole to the other.

Emerging Earthside, the barge's systems would reintegrate and it would be recovered for unloading.

Simple and foolproof.

"All pushers unbound and clear," Marrun reported. On the far viewers, the pusher units could be seen scurrying away from the massive cargo raft, propulsor vents glowing brightly. The raft was on its own now.

"Voice-of-Physics?"

"The channel is smooth," Narisara replied, using the formalism. "The river flows between the stars."

"Voice-of-Raft-Guidance?"

"The raft obeys on all standards. Ready to voyage."

"Very well. All Voices, stand by for transit-of-channel. Varess, send her through."

On the far viewers, a double belt of dazzling sparks flared into existence at the bow and stern of the cargo raft as its own vents lit. Ever so slowly it began to gain way, the propulsors struggling to inch its bulk forward into the mouth of the perimeter grid.

"Raft entry velocity to first level . . . second level . . . third level . . ." Varess chanted. "Drift remains null on all vectors . . . fourth level . . . fifth . . ."

Tarrischall tried to keep his attention focused on the raft. It wasn't easy with the black sphere of the channel mouth tugging seductively at the edge of his vision. The Ecstasy-of-the-Great-Dark-Current they called it. That near overwhelming urge felt by some of the People to take that longest dive down the channel. Tarrischall often felt the tug himself.

The dream of doing so and surviving, of reaching the exotic and mysterious world of the Uprights and beyond was a favorite theme of the spinners of projection fictions. Tarrischall enjoyed such yarns and in spite of what Narisara and the other joy-smashing Voices-of-Physics might say, he was certain that someday a technology would be found to permit a living being to ride the currents to another star.

Varess' sudden sharp warning cry shattered his musing. "This-Voice-speaks-warning! I have a massive flow net fluctuation aboard the raft! Performance variance across all patterns!"

"Define!" Tarrischall barked, his head snapping down to his display bubble and to the suddenly racing data lines.

"No definition isolated! Generalized flow failure in onboard energy matrix! Shifting to crisis alternative flow!"

Tarrischall gave himself the briefest of instants for consideration. The cargo raft was still stable and gaining velocity as per the set transfer pattern and all functions aboard it had safety duplicates and automatic switch overs. Yet there was a major function collapse going on within the massive vehicle, something beyond anything he had ever seen before.

He could not risk the River-'Tween-Worlds! He slapped the alarm pad at his side triggering the rising tri-toned wail of the Danger-And-Rally call within all the chambers of the skynest.

"All Voices! Abort the shift! Abort! Raft Guidance, decelerate! Pusher Guidance, position for recapture! Mender and Mooring Gangs prepare! *I speak with Voice-of-Crisis!*"

"Decelerating!" Varess cried back. "Alternative functions engaged! Braking vents engaged! Drift vectors holding stable. Entry velocity reducing to sixth level . . . fifth . . . fourth . . .

On the far viewer display the vector of the raft's propulsor vents altered, thrusting forward. The huge freight hauler was losing velocity, but slowly, so slowly. There was so much mass out there to stop.

The blunt curved nose of the raft was approaching the mouth of the perimeter grid.

Maybe it would have been better to trust the duplicate functions and run her through, Tarrischall thought feverishly, but it was too late to bother about it now. They were committed.

"Velocity now third level . . . second . . ."

On the main display the double ring of scintillating propulsor vents flickered and went dark.

Varess' voice rose into a strangled scream. "Alternative energy flow failure! Total failure! Crisis alternative functions do not reply! I have lost raft guidance! She floats free!"

"Marrun, get your pushers in there now!"

The Voice-of-Pusher-Guidance could only look slowly away in the refusal posture. "No good, Tarrischall. No good. She's entering the grid and I don't have the clearance. If one of my units bumps her in a crisis bonding, I could knock her off vector and into the grid structure. She's going in and I can't stop her."

He was right. May the Life-Fire-of-All-Things burn all! He was right! Even as Tarrischall looked on in growing horror, the bow of the cargo raft was ghosting into the grid mouth.

Tarrischall twisted to look at Narisara, his last hope of regaining control of the disintegrating situation. "Flow down, Voice-of-Physics! Close the channel!

The black-furred one could only look away as well. "No time," she replied quietly. "We can't fade the flow fast enough. The closing channel mouth would catch the raft.

She's going through wild, Tarrischall, and we can't stop her."

Tarrischall could only stare up at the far viewer display. "Beware Marta-My-Friend," he whispered. "Beware."

The silver-gray curve of the raft's bow touched the infinite spherical blackness of the channel event horizon.

The tension inside the control center had grown into something physically perceptible. Tight-lipped, Marta Lane stared as the acquisition time bar crept deeper into the red zone.

"We are now at T plus two minutes and thirty-nine seconds post projected acquisition, Director," the gate systems manager said almost apologetically.

"I can see it, Mr. Desvergers," she snapped "Quantum monitoring. Status on the hole?"

"No entry registering yet, ma'am."

Lane glanced down at her assistant director. "Something's wrong Wolf side, Estiban. Tarrischall wouldn't waste our energy this way with a sloppy transfer. He's got problems. Take us to Flash Yellow. Set alert protocols until we get this thing sorted out."

"Doing it, Marta."

"Contact," The quantum monitor leaned in over his workstation display. "Director, we have mass in the hole . . . but we have a slow entry . . . way slow! Less than one-fifth standard transit velocity registering."

"What the hell?" Lane's brows knit together. "How's the hole standing?"

"Dimensional structure is stable in all aspects. No variants! We have a good dilation here. This has got to be a barge problem. I confirm we have mass in trans-state and transit. Gravitational displacement is correct for projected payload, but it's just crawling through."

"Power boards, reserve status!"

"Down to sixty-five of standard. Load draw steady . . . Recomputing power consumption rates . . . We'll make it, but it'll be close. Forget today's outbound shift, though. This is going to drain us dry."

"Forget the outbound! Stand by your reserve accumulators and alert Ces-Lunar for an emergency power draw! Tug Control!"

"Yo!

"I want your reception tugs holding right outside of the worm cage. The second you can get a good approach, move in and get a latch on her. I think we might have a rogue barge coming through. Barge Control!"

"Yes, ma'am."

"You heard what I just said to Tugs. The instant that brute is out of trans-state, get me a full diagnostic. If she seems to be clearing the perimeter grid on her own, let her drift out. Do not attempt active control until she's in open space."

"Understood."

"Director! There she is. She's coming through!"

On the main display, the ultradark of the wormhole event horizon bulged. Cherenkov radiation played in spectral lavender waves around the extrusion, hydrogen atoms and solar wind particles from another star system reintegrating into conventional space. Rippling shadow slowly peeled back from the blunt bow of the cargo carrier revealing steel that shimmered with residual inconsistency.

"Come on, old girl," Marta found herself murmuring. "Not far now, just a little more."

"Barge exit velocity one point five meters per second . . . No! One point four . . . point three! She's decelerating!"

Marta's world was turning on edge. "That's impossible! Barge control, could we have a retro burn or an out-gassing event underway?"

"Negative! Negative! Her systems haven't reintegrated from trans-state and I'm not detecting anything venting! This has to be an outside influence!"

"It's the magnetic field of the perimeter grid!" Rocardo yelled from his station. "It's reacting with the ferrous metals in the cargo and hull structure. She's coming through so far below velocity she may not have the momentum to carry her clear."

"Damnit, Estiban don't give me 'may'! Yes or no!"

"Computing now!"

The answer came from another source. "Velocity point five meters per second . . . point three . . . Relative velocity zero! I say again, we have zero velocity . . . Velocity now negative point one!"

Half the length of the cargo barge protruded from the un stable, quivering sphere of the gate mouth but only half. Then, slowly the expanse of metal hull began to shorten.

"My God," someone spoke in an appalled whisper, "she's falling back into the hole."

"Tugs!" Marta called desperately. "Can you get a lock on her!"

The Tug Controller was already shaking his head. "No room. No time! She's going! She's going! She's gone!"

Lane's thumb flipped aside the guard on her console and smashed down on the alarm key. Throughout the Worm Gate complex the Flash Red disaster klaxons began their harsh bray.

"She's still in there!" Narisara cried. "The raft is still inside the channel! She did not exit!"

"That's impossible," Tarrischall snapped back. "She had to clear!"

"She hasn't," the Voice-of-Physics replied impatiently. "I am still registering mass inside the channel. Movement rate null. The raft must be caught between the magnetic lobes of the channel mouths."

On the far viewer, the black sphere of the channel event horizon continued to hover blandly at the center of the webwork tube of the perimeter grid. Invisible within that sphere, however, the cargo raft was still present, coexistent dimensionally not only within River-'Tween-Worlds but at the Earth Worm Gate as well.

"Voice-of-Physics, what happens if we can't clear the

channel? What happens when we have to reduce the power flow?"

"I don't know," Narisara replied. "We have never attempted such a simulation."

"Guess!"

"Tarrischall, I can't! The matter inside the channel is dimensionally unstable. I cannot project how it will react to a channel contraction. Possibly as a quantum material. Possibly as tridimensional. I can't tell!"

"Differentiation!

"As quantum material it may disperse out along the residual thread of the channel, leaking back into tri-space as a few extra *ultimotes* per *lype* of interstellar gas."

"As trimaterial?"

"You will be compressing a hundred and eighty thousand *kyhar* of mass down to a point you could balance on a pup's claw tip."

Tarrischall felt his whiskers bristle. "To say more simply, POOYGH!"

Narisara gave an affirmative toss of her shapely head. "A mass explosion such as no one has ever imagined. We would burn brighter than the Life-Fire-of-All-Things."

"Where's my power!" Marta called in a half-scream to her Energy Boss.

"They're trying to get authorization from the Ces-Lunar Grid Authority now, ma'am," the thoroughly unhappy techno yelled back over his shoulder.

"Damn it, I'm the authority! Tell those idiots to check their disaster protocols. A Worm Gate emergency has absolute priority over everything except basic life support, and we are declaring a gate emergency! Tell them we could lose the wormhole and the whole bloody L-2 complex if we don't get that power shift immediately!"

"Doing it, ma'am!"

"L-2 traffic control on red command channel, ma'am," Communications cut in. "They acknowledge your crisis declaration and are standing by for instructions."

"Tell them to initiate immediate dispersal of the complex by Plan Red Roger. Clear all nonessential manned vessels and platforms out of this traffic block with all speed and keep them out until we can get a handle on this thing."

"Aye, ma'am."

On the big display, the city in the sky was already disintegrating, its component stations leaving their formation within the Lagrange point. With attitude control thrusters and docked tug engines blazing to haul them clear, the awkward voyagers were drifting outward in a slow motion bomb burst that left the Worm Gate and gate control wheel alone in a growing volume of empty space.

"We're starting to get some power supplementation from Ces-Lunar already, Marta," Rocardo reported, "but we are still trending negative on our accumulator reserves. Can we fade back a little? Let the hole contract a bit to conserve power."

Lane shook her head, eyeing the sphere of blackness hovering within the perimeter grid. "We have sixty thousand metric tons of mass out there locked in trans-state, Estiban. If we try altering the variables on that much malleable matter, I don't know what will happen. Nobody else does either."

"Headquarters has triggered a net crisis conference," the Assistant Director replied, sounding hopeful. "They're bringing in every physicist in the field to work the problem."

"And maybe they'll come up with some answers in six months or so. We don't have that much time. Power levels?"

"Down to twelve per on all reserves."

"Dr. Lane, I have an idea," the tug controller spoke up.

"Go, Fred."

"Why don't we try and shove the barge out of there? I could send one of our big Miki T-5s into the hole. I know all of its systems would go down as it crossed the event horizon, but we could back it off and run it in at full thrust with a load of momentum built up. It'd wreck the tug, but it might be enough to knock the barge out the other side."

Marta turned the suggestion over in her mind examining

it from all angles, then shook her head. "No, that might work under simple Newtonian physics but we're operating quantum here. While we know individual atoms can maintain momentum in trans-state, nobody can say if momentum can be kinetically transmitted.

"If we ram a tug into the hole, it might just pass right through the barge's dimensionally irrational form and go right out the other side. On the other hand, there might be enough nuclear forces interaction for the barge's mass to not only absorb the tug's momentum but its physical structure as well. The two vehicles could merge with an overlap on the subatomic levels. Two objects can't occupy the same space, in the nonquantum universe at any rate. When they came out of trans-state at Life-Waters, there could be a mass explosion that could vaporize the whole gate."

"Lord and Lady!" The tug controller murmured. He liked the People, too.

"We've got no choice, Estiban," Lane stated to her Assistant Director, making her final decision in the matter. "If we get down to four percent reserve without stabilization, we're going to cut the negative energy fields and dump the hole."

For a Gate Controller, those words were blasphemy. "You can't be serious!" Rocardo exclaimed, "It took ten years to isolate and fix a properly oriented wormhole for the 359 system. If we dump the hole . . ."

"I know. If we dump the hole, it's gone. We'll never get it back. We may never acquire another one for Wolf system either. But if we can keep the physical gate structure intact, we'll at least have chance to try again. If we destroy the gates, that chance will be gone, too. Power?"

Rocardo replied by looking down at his station displays. "Now down to nine per on the reserves."

The string-of-gem city lights on the night side of Life-Waters were blinking out, fading as the orbital light-power-gatherers that fed the People's civilization shifted their flow rays on River-'Tween-Worlds, a half cone of raw energy flooding across space and through the overloading absorption structures.

Tarrischall rode the power tasking pallet himself, nursing the straining systems like a caregiver with a sick pup, rolling each control rod with an extended claw tip. "Smoothly, smoothly," he murmured to himself, staring into the data bubble, "I-lick-your-fur, sweet one. Steady down and quit twitching on me."

All others in the Gathering-of-Voices were silent save for Narisara. Bouncing back and forth between her display and that of the Voice-of-Decision, she maintained Tarrischall's situational awareness.

"Evacuation of orbit zone continuing . . . Voices-of-Central-Energy acknowledge the Word-of-Crisis. We have priority flow in all channels."

"Praise to a sane bureaucrat. Thermal grade on receptor arrays?"

"Nothing is melting yet and that's all that can be said."

"And how are the Uprights doing?"

"As well as we are, I must presume. I detect a slight structural flux from their end, but so far the channel holds open." She looked across at Tarrischall. "I speak as Voice-of-Physics. The wisdom is to cast loose and abandon the channel. There is great danger here and I can see no resolution."

"No! This fish hasn't escaped yet!"

"Tarrischall-of-the-Crystal-Springs," Narisara's voice softened, speaking as herself and not the Voice-of-Physics. "What avails catching the fish if one drowns doing it?"

He looked up from the display for a moment meeting her polished jet gaze. "I know, Black Fur, but I will not cast loose while there is a chance. I will not let the People go back to being alone in this Universe."

"Yes, she's stable and holding!" Rocardo yelled in triumph. "We have ambience on the power flow!"

"Reserve levels remaining?"

"Five percent!"

"Systems stability?"

"Power receptors and cooling systems are operating at about three hundred percent overload, but they are holding!"

Marta covered her face with her hands and exhaled, pushing aside the shutdown command that had been about to cross her lips.

They were holding. The system wasn't supposed to operate this way, but it was. Almost the full load of the great ces-Lunar power grid had been diverted into the Worm Gate receptors, the massed output of the mighty hydrogen III fusion reactors poring up through the microwave beams from the Moon's surface.

Deprived of their power, the low-gee manufacturing complexes and mass driver catapults that propelled the Moon's industrial economy had been forced into a crash shutdown and even the urban habitation centers were reduced to operating on solar backup for basic life support. The screams of protest would already be starting.

But they had time now. At least a little bit to find some kind of solution.

Marta Lane allowed herself another deep breath before speaking.

"Get the backup team in here to cover the stations. All primary team members stand down for a ten-minute break, then report to the conference room for a crisis assessment group. I'll be wanting ideas, people, any flavor you can come up with."

Tarrischall looked on as his watchmates drifted aimlessly or hung anchored to the soft, padded walls of the rest and discussion chamber. Beyond the hiss of the passage-of-air grilles the chamber was ominously quiet.

"Very well, he said, "we have agreement that Marrun's plan to bump the raft out of the channel with a pusher unit will not work. What will? What can affect an object in trans-state that we can manipulate?"

"Very little," Narisara swayed limberly in free fall, holding herself moored to the chamber wall with the extended claws of a single rear paw. "It is hard for us to even visualize what we are dealing with within the channel. We can describe trans-state in mathematical terms, but our minds are not made to ever understand it."

"Slime and stinking water, Narisara, I don't want to understand it! I just want to fiddle with it! The raft is transstate. Situation acknowledged. What effects transstate matter? I require simplicity!"

She muttered something about simple minds and flipped inverted, reseating her grip on the wall padding. "The various field effects are valid to a degree within the channel. The ultimotular forces, gravity, magnetism, all of these things can affect transstate matter."

"That's the birth of our problem," Varess added shyly. "The perimeter grids at either end of the channel generate very strong magnetoelectric fields. The magnetically valid metals in the raft's structure are caught between them."

"Even with all the light-seasons of distance between Life-Waters and Terra? We are being affected by their gate fields?" Marrun questioned.

"Indeed," Narisara replied to the Voice-of-Pusher-Guidance. "The area within our perimeter grid coexists with the area within that of the Upright's when the channel is open. The two are as one with the distance between rendered invalid within the Universe structure."

She waved a depreciatory mid-paw. "As I said, one can describe it and understand it mathematically, but our three-dimensional minds can't create a true visualization."

"No, but then that really isn't important . . . is it?"

Tarrischall shoved off from the chamber wall, an odd glint in his eyes. "As I said, Black Fur, simplification. Reject quantum physics for now."

His forepaws gestured out the problem. "Imagine the channel as a simple, three-dimensional structure. We would have a perimeter grid producing a magnetic field *here* and another one *here* with a tunnel in between and the raft held stuck in the tunnel by the two balanced field effects. Correct?"

The Voice-of-Physics negated with a glance away. "That's a pup's model."

"I speak applied simplicity, Voice-of-Physics. Is this not a valid model?"

She tossed her head, "It is valid . . . vaguely."

"Very well. And cannot the magnetoelectric field levels be modulated to a degree within the perimeter grids without losing the channel?"

"They can."

"Very well again. So if magnetic fields indeed can affect the raft in the tunnel, theoretically, by varying those field effects, we should be able to shift the position of the raft inside, drawing it toward or pushing it away from the grids. Correct?"

The Voice-of-Physics eyes narrowed. "That's not truly what would be happening."

"Simplicity, Black Fur, simplicity!"

"Yes, very well, agreed," Narisara yielded. "At least that's what might seem to occur. But to what end? We could not push or pull the raft completely to either channel mouth against the resistance of the other grid field and that other grid field can't be shut down or have its polarity inverted without cutting loose the channel."

"True, but this humble Voice-of-Decision recalls that ultimotes *maintain* momentum in trans-state. The raft could not clear the channel this time because it lacked enough momentum to pierce the grid fields. What if we could rebuild the raft's momentum inside the channel by shoving it to-and-fro between the grid fields until it has regained enough energy to break out?"

"Like rocking a mired land carrier out of a mud hole," Marrun suggested.

"Precisely, Gray-laker. If we can manage the shifts properly, I'll challenge we can pop her out of there like a robug out of a hollow reed. Speak, Voice-of-Physics. Valid or no?"

Narisara thought long, her eyes almost closed. All of the watch held their breaths as if on a deep dive. "Yes," she said finally. "Possibly."

"Ha!"

She cut off Tarrischall's bark of triumph with a lifted forepaw. "But such an action would have to be perfectly timed and coordinated with the Uprights at their end of things. I say once more, perfectly timed and coordinated in both interval and sequence. Otherwise we could unbalance and lose the channel. And we have no way of telling the Uprights what they must do."

Assistant Director Rocardo tossed his work pad stylus down onto the tabletop. "That's it, the simulator team says it could work, but we'd have to do it in absolute lockstep with the Furrys, and we haven't any way to tell them what to do."

"Damn the damn budgetary committee to hell," Marta paced angrily beside the conference room. "I told them we needed to put more funding into communications R&D, but it's always 'next year, next year, we have to watch the profit margins'."

Rocardo shrugged pragmatically. "The laser link's always been adequate. No one ever visualized having to shove a photon beam past a mass of trans-state stuck in the hole before."

"It's not adequate now. And we certainly can't wait around for seven and a half years for a radio message to reach 359."

Rocardo glanced at his data pad. "We can't even wait another seven and a half hours. Ces-Lunar is screaming for their power back, Company Headquarters is demanding we come up with a solution and, most critically, our receptor and transformer systems are starting to degrade from the overload. We have to do something, Marta!"

"I know it, Estiban. I even know what we need to do. But we have to establish three factors with River-'Tween-Worlds to pull it off; an execution time, a duration for the field cycles and which gate initiates the cycling sequence."

She paused in her pacing. "Tarrischall and his crew are sharp, as good or better than we are. I'm willing to bet he must have come to the same conclusions we have and that he must be hunting for a way to establish a mutual operational baseline with us to make it work."

"How are we supposed to manage that without a communications link? By mind reading?"

"Exactly."

Tarrischall had returned to the observation dome at the planetside end of the skynest. With the Word-of-Crisis still in effect, the half bubble of Glass-like-Steel was empty save for himself. Floating limply, he juggled his inert sphere-of-communications between his fore and mid-paws in an unthinking pattern, his tiring mind focused on the looming problem.

How do you match thought processes with a semi-hairless, bipedal land dweller with a penchant for munching on vegetation? How could minds reach across the gap between stars?

Talk with me, Marta-From-the-Place-Called-New-England. You must know the solution as well as I. How are we to do this thing?

If only they could have their last conversation back again. Just thirty or so heartbeats of the time they had spent casually discussing music and dance.

Idly, Tarrischall twisted the two halves of the sphere-of-communications, triggering the replay of the musical selections Marta had sent him. As the lissome alien tone patterns flowed around him, he wondered sadly if they were the last present he would ever receive from his distant friend of Earth.

Tarrischall's grip on the sphere tightened abruptly and he stared at the silver orb as if he had never seen it before.

"T minus ninety! All stations, stand by! We're doing this thing now! Gate Control?"

"Go!"

"Tug Control?"

"Go!"

"Power Control?"

"Systems are in overload but holding nominal."

"Traffic Control."

"L-2 Block is clear except for authorized emergency spacecraft."

It had been a long, long night shift and now the eyes of all humanity were peering over Marta Lane's shoulder. The Ces-Lunar media nets were accessing Gate Control's video feeds, streaming a second-by-second narration of the crisis around the worlds. No doubt the media newsies would have loved to be underfoot aboard the command station as well, but Marta's emergency prerogatives were still worth something.

Likewise she'd also cut off all communication with Transstellar's board of directors and semihysterical CEO. If this didn't work, there would be plenty of time to be fired later.

She glanced at the primary screen time hack. Oh-seven hours, oh-four minutes, and forty seconds.

"Stand by to initiate magnetic field modulation program on my mark . . . three . . . two . . . one . . . mark!"

"Program engaged," Gate Control reported. "Perimeter grid field intensity dropping to eighty-percent load. Two minutes and fifty-five seconds and counting to power up."

Somewhere within the control center a whisper of long-ago music played.

Uncountable trillions of miles away the first bar of the same tune issued from Tarrischall's sphere-of-communications.

"Flow increase!" he snarled with eyes narrowed and ears laid back.

"Flow increasing to perimeter grid. Magnetoelectric field intensity growing to plus one fifth of standard." Narisara's voice rose excitedly. "Magnetodynamic flux noted in the channel, but the quantum structures appear stable. They are doing it, Tarrischall! They understand! The Upright gate is reducing flow! They are cycling with us!"

"Yes! Yessss! Marta-of-the-Place-Called-New-England thinks as one of the People! Four limbs or not, I'd put a pup in her come the next season!"

The otherworldly music ran on, trickling from the sphere.

"Director Lane, the switching arrays don't like this. We're throwing thermal spikes at each power shift and the cyclic rate we've set isn't giving us the time we need to cool them down."

"Blame Glenn Miller, not me, Mr. Desvergers. Stay on the cycle and do the best you can."

"Marta, check your quantum structure readouts!"

"What is it, Estiban?"

"We are registering a shift! We have mass movement! She's starting to rock!"

A rising chorus of warning tones from the tasking displays sang a song of incipient disaster that threatened to drive out the twelfth replay of the Terran melody.

"Tarrischall, the raft was displaying a slow but definite lateral drift on that last emergence. If she angles off enough to collide with the grid . . ."

"Don't encourage the curse with your words, Black Fur, I saw it. Claws out, pups! This strike ends the chase. Marrun, maneuvering room be damned! This time grab her by the throat and hang on till your jaws crack!"

The Voice-of-Pusher-Guidance grunted an acknowledgment. He had his six most powerful units hovering around the mouth of the perimeter grid, ready to pounce like a hunter's pack on a surfacing deep rover. It wasn't a bad analogy for the situation.

The shadow sphere within the grid began to shimmer.

"The time is on us! Narisara. Full flow on the gate fields! Full flow! Haul her in!"

The stern of the cargo raft burst out of the event horizon, no longer tracking true but drifting off side and angling across the channel, its dead gyros and propulsor vents incapable of stabilization. Even if the straining function nets of River-'Tween-Worlds could withstand another modulation cycle, a few more fractions of drift would bring about a catastrophic collision between the raft and the grid structure. It had to be now!

Tarrischall held a diving breath as the curve of the raft's

stern protruded a few lengths from the lip of the grid, hovering on the cusp of the cycle.

"Take her! Take her now!"

Marrun socked his Pushers in. Not even attempting a run at the bonding points, he rammed the robotic propulsor units into the raft, spearing it with expanding crash harpoons. Vents flared and raged as Marrun countered the drift and applied extraction power in a wild paw dance across his tasking board.

Like two pups with a scrap, the Pusher units and the magnetic pull warred . . . then, ponderously, the raft was floating back and out of the grid it had entered far too long before.

Joyous pandemonium raged in the two control rooms stars apart.

There was, of course, an aftermath. Communications between the gate control centers had to be reestablished, the wormhole had to be closed, and the emergency power diversions rerouted. A protracted series of systems tests and repairs were initiated and a start had to be made on establishing a new set of operational protocols that would ensure a like event could never happen again.

And finally there was the press conference.

At Marta's insistence it would be an audio interview only, conducted over the communications link from her quarters. She was not about to present herself to the video scrutiny of two entire civilizations after an all-nighter at crisis stations. At least not until she had enjoyed a three water-credit bath, a gluttonous Earth import meal, and at least ten hours of sleep.

Over the laser-link channel from Life-Waters, good old Furry Tarrischall, as ebullient as ever, was more than willing to carry the show for her. She had only to add the occasional word at the interviewer's prompt.

"We have solution," he proclaimed dramatically. "I know wise Friend-Marta must have same solution as well. But we must coordinate or all is lost. We must begin the cycling of magnetic fields at the same instant! Same instant! We must cycle at same interval and one or other must start cycle. But how is to do this when we cannot speak? Tchah! It must be done through things already said, from commonalities already available and recognized.

"My mind chases itself. Then I recall last words spoken with Friend-Marta and the music of the Artist-Called-Miller given to me. Here is our commonality!"

"Er, Artist-called-Miller, Director Lane?" The interviewer inquired cautiously.

"As in Glenn," Lane replied into her interphone deck. "Tarrischall and I share a mutual appreciation of Terrestrial pre-atomic age swing music."

Marta sat back in her chair and started to unseal her suit liner, thinking fondly of the gloriously wasteful bath to come. Maybe she would even let Estiban cover the gate survey while she ran over to L-5 for a few days to spoil her grandchildren. "The previous evening I'd beamed Director Tarrischall some new musical selections and we'd been talking about them over the director's channel just before we'd gone on duty. One of the songs was Glenn Miller's classic 'Seven O Five.' "

"This gave time of cycle initiation," Tarrischall added smugly. "Standard Human Earth song, standard Human Earth time, five minutes after seventh hour, Greenwich Meridian."

"Also the version of 'Seven O Five' I'd sent Tarrischall was exactly two minutes and fifty five seconds long. That gave us our cycling time."

"I see." The interviewer said slowly. "Ingenious. But that still leaves one question, Director Tarrischall. I understand that it was critical that one gate or the other had to start this magnetic cycling to clear the wormhole. Your team was the one that led off. How was that decided? Did you risk the communications between our words on a hunch, a guess?"

Tarrischall snort growled a nontranslatable profanity "_____ guess! We knew! Easiest part of all. Friend-Marta and I have nice music, I am male, she female. We dance!"

"Dance?" The interviewer was totally bewildered now.

"Of course," Marta Lane smiled a tired smile no one would see. "Back in the good old days the gentleman always led."

Mikeys

by Robert J. Sawyer

Dubbed "the dean of Canadian science fiction" by The Ottawa Citizen, *Toronto's Robert J. Sawyer is the author of the Hugo Award finalists* Starplex, Frameshift, Factoring Humanity, *and* Calculating God, *and the Nebula Award winner* The Terminal Experiment. *His story from the DAW anthology* Sherlock Holmes in Orbit *won France's top SF award,* Le Grand Prix de l'Imaginaire, *and his story from the DAW anthology* Dinosaur Fantastic *won Canada's top SF award, the Aurora. Rob's latest novel is* Hybrids, *third volume in his Hugo Award-winning "Neanderthal Parallax" trilogy. His website at www.sfwriter.com has been called "the largest genre writer's home page in existence" by* Interzone.

DAMN, but it stuck in Don Lawson's craw—largely because Chuck Zakarian was right. After all, Zakarian was slated for the big Mars surface mission to be launched from Earth next year. He never said it to Don's face, but Don knew that Zakarian and the rest of NASA viewed him and Sasim as Mikeys—the derisive term for those, like *Apollo 11*'s command-module pilot Mike Collins, who got to go *almost* all the way to the target.

Yes, goddamned Zakarian would be remembered along with Armstrong, whom every educated person in the world could still name even today, seventy years after his historic small step. But who the hell remembered Collins, the guy who'd stayed in orbit around the Moon while Neil and Buzz had made history on the lunar surface?

Don realized the point couldn't have been driven home more directly than by the view he was now looking at. He was floating in the control room of the *Asaph Hall*, the ship that had brought him and Sasim Remtulla to Martian space from Earth. If he looked left, Don saw Mars, giant, red, beckoning. And if he looked right, he saw—

They called it the Spud. *The Spud*, for Christ's sake!

Looking right, he saw Deimos, the outer of Mars' two tiny moons, a misshapen hunk of dark, dark rock. How Don wanted to go to Mars, to stand on its sandy surface, to see up close its great valleys and volcanoes! But no. As Don's Cockney granddad used to say whenever they passed a fancy house or an expensive car, "Not for the likes of us."

Mars was for Chuck Zakarian and company. The A-team.

Don and Sasim were the B-team, the also-rans. Oh, sure; they had now arrived at the *vicinity* of Mars long before anyone else. And Don supposed there would be some cachet in being the first person since *Apollo 17* left the Moon in 1972 to set foot on another world—even if that world was just a 15-kilometer-long hunk of rock.

Why build a space station from scratch to orbit Mars, the NASA mission planners had said? Why not simply plant the spaceship you had used to get there on Deimos? For one thing, you'd have the advantage of a little gravity—granted, only 0.0004 of Earth's, but still sufficient to keep things from floating away on their own.

And for another, you could mine Deimos for supplies. Like Mars' other moon Phobos, Deimos was a captured asteroid—specifically, a carbonaceous chondrite, meaning its stony mass contained claylike hydrous silicates from which water could be extracted. More than that, though, Deimos' density was so low that it had long been known that it couldn't be solid rock; much water ice was mixed into its structure.

Deimos and Phobos were both tidally locked, like Earth's moon, with the same side always facing the planet they orbited. But Phobos was just too damn close—a scant 2.8 planetary radii from Mars' center, meaning it was really only good for looking down on the planet's equatorial regions. Deimos, on the other hand, orbited at seven planetary radii, affording an excellent view of most of Mars' surface. In Deimos, Mother Nature had provided a perfect infrastructure for a space station to study Mars. The two Mikeys would use it to determine the exact landing spot and the itinerary of surface features Zakarian's crew would eventually visit.

"Ready?" said Don, taking his gaze away from the control-room window, from glorious Mars and drab Deimos.

Sasim gave him the traditional thumbs-up. "Ready."

"All right," said Don. "It's time to crash."

Deimos' mean orbital velocity was a languorous 1.36 kilometers per second. Don and Sasim matched the *Asaph Hall*'s speed with that of the tiny moon and nudged their spaceship against it. A cloud of dust went up. Phobos had a reasonably dust-free surface, since ejecta thrown up from it was normally captured by Mars. But more distant Deimos still had lots of dust filling in its craters; whatever was blown off by impacts remained near it, eventually sifting down to blanket the surface. Indeed, although Deimos probably had a similar number of craters to Phobos, which sported dozens, only two on the outer moon were large and distinct enough to merit official International Astronomical Union names: Voltaire and Swift.

The *Asaph Hall* settled without so much as a bang—but it wasn't a landing, not according to the mission planners. No, the ship had docked with Deimos: the artificial part of the space station rendezvousing with the natural part.

Apollo flights had been famous for discarding three stages before the tiny CSM/LM combo reached the Moon. But *Asaph Hall,* like the *Percival Lowell* that would follow with Zakarian's crew, had retained one of its empty fuel tanks. Each mission would convert its spent cylinder into a habitat module: the *Hall* docked with Deimos in orbit about Mars; the *Lowell* down where the action was, on the Martian surface. There was good precedent, after all. The first space station to orbit Earth, *Skylab,* had been made out of an empty *Saturn* S-IVb booster. And, of course, *Skylab* had been crewed by the Mikeys of their day, *Apollo* pass-overs who were not quite good enough to go to the Moon.

"Mission Control," said Don, "we have completed docking with Deimos."

When Armstrong had said, "Tranquillity Base here, the *Eagle* has landed," Houston had immediately replied, "Roger, Tranquillity, we copy you on the ground. We've got a bunch of guys here about to turn blue—we're breathing again. Thanks a lot."

But currently, Mars was 77,000,000 kilometers from Earth. That meant it would take four minutes and twenty seconds for Don's words to reach Mission Control, and another four minutes and twenty seconds for whatever reply they might send to start arriving here. He doubted Houston would say anything as emotional as the words beamed back to Tranquillity Base; Don would be happy if they just didn't make a crack about Mikeys.

Tranquillity Base. That had been *such* a cool name. This place needed a good name, too.

Sasim had evidently been thinking the same thing. "I'm not a fan of 'Mars Landing Precursor Observation Station,'" he said, turning to Don, quoting the official title.

"Maybe we should call it Deimos Station," said Don.

But Sas shook his head. "*Mir* is Russian for 'peace'—that was a good name for a space station. But Deimos is Greek for 'terror.' Not quite correct in these difficult times."

"We'll come up with something," Don said.

After the mandatory sleep period, Don and Sasim were ready to venture out onto the surface of Deimos. Although nobody would likely ever quote them back, Don had thought long and hard about what his first words would be when he stepped onto the Martian moon. "We come to the vicinity of the God of War," he said, "in godly peace and friendship."

Sasim followed him out, but evidently felt no one would care what the second person on Deimos had to say for posterity. He simply launched into his report. "The surface, as expected, is covered with dust and regolith . . ."

Once Sasim was finished, Don looked at him through their polarized faceplates. A big grin broke out on Don's face. He used his chin to tap the control that cut the broadcast back to Earth, while leaving the channel to Sasim open. "All right," he said. "Enough of the formalities. Here's one thing we can do that Zakarian will never be able to."

Don flexed his knees, crouched down, then pushed off the surface, straightening his legs as he did so, and—

Clark Kent had nothing on him!

Up, up, and away!

Higher and higher.

Further and farther.

Closer and closer to Mars itself.

Don looked down. Sasim had dwindled to the size of the proverbial ant, his olive-green space suit just a mote against the dark gray surface of Deimos.

Don continued to rise for a while longer, but at last he felt gentle fingers tugging at him. It took several minutes, but slowly, gradually, *sensually,* he settled to the ground. He'd tried to just go up, but there'd been a slight angle to his flight, and he'd found himself coming down a hundred-odd meters from where he'd started.

"A true giant leap," said Sasim, over the radio. "Beats all heck out of a small step."

Don smiled, although he knew he was too far away for Sasim to see him do that. The jump had been exhilarating. "Maybe this station isn't going to be so bad after all."

"I've got an idea," said Sasim, as they continued to work converting the fuel tank into a habitat. "We could call this place Asaph Hall."

"That's the name of our spaceship," said Don, perplexed.

"Well, yes and no. Our ship is called *Asaph Hall*, after the guy who discovered the moons of Mars. And when you refer to a ship, you write the name in italics. But this whole station could be Asaph Hall—'hall,' like in a building, get it?—all in roman type."

"That's a pretty picayune distinction," said Don, unfolding

an articulated section divider that had been stored for the outward journey. "It'll get confusing."

Sas frowned. "Maybe you're right."

"Don't worry. We'll think of something."

It took several days to finish the conversion of the empty fuel tank into the habitat, even though all the fixtures were designed for easy assembly. During the process, Don and Sasim had slept in their spaceship's command module, but at last the habitat was ready for them to move in. And although it *was* roomy—bigger than *Skylab* or *Mir*—Don was finally beginning to appreciate the wisdom of making an entire moonlet into a space station. He could see how being confined to just the habitat would have gotten claustrophobic after a while, if he and Sas didn't have the rest of Deimos to roam over.

And roam over it they did. It only took a dozen leaps to circumnavigate their little—well, it wasn't a globe; the technical name for Deimos' shape was a triaxial ellipsoid. It was a lot of fun leaping around Deimos—and, despite the low gravity, it was actually excellent exercise, too. Up, up, up, that brief magical moment during which you felt *suspended,* at one with the cosmos, and then gently, oh so gently, sliding down out of the sky.

Don and Sas were approaching the line that separated Deimos' nearside—the part of the moon that always faced toward Mars—from its farside. Like the blooded horn of some great beast, the now-crescent Mars stretched from Deimos' smooth surface up toward the zenith. One more leap, and—

Yup, there it went: the Red Planet disappearing behind the horizon. With its glare gone from the sky, Don tried to find Earth. He oriented himself with Ursa Major, found the zodiac, scanned along, and there it was, a brilliant blue point of light, right in the heart of Scorpius, not far from red Antares, the rival of Mars.

Sas, Don had noticed, had a funny habit of bending his knees when he contacted the surface. It wasn't as if there was any real impact to absorb—it was just a bit of theater—and it made Don smile. Don's space suit was a sort of mustard color, a nice contrast with Sas'. The dark ground loomed closer and closer to him, and—

There wasn't enough speed with contact to make any sort of sound that might be conducted through Don's boots. And yet, still, as his soles touched Deimos, something felt strange this time, just different enough from every other landing Don had made so far to pique his curiosity.

He'd raised up a fair bit of dust, and it took him a few seconds to realize exactly what had happened. His foot hadn't hit crumbly regolith. It had hit something unyielding. Something smooth.

Don did a gentle backflip, landing upside down on his gloved hands. He used his right one to brush away dust.

"Sas!" Don called into his helmet mike. "Come here!"

Sasim did a long jump, bringing him close to where Don was. Another small hop brought him right up to Don. "What's up?" asked Sas—perhaps a joking reference to Don's current odd posture.

Don used his fingertips to gently flip himself back into a normal orientation. "Have a look."

Sas tipped over until he was more or less hovering just above the surface. "What the heck is *that*?" he said.

"I'm not sure," said Don. "But it looks like polished metal."

Don and Sas brushed dust away for more than an hour, and were still exposing new metal. It was indeed manufactured—it looked to be anodized aluminum. "Maybe it's part of the *Viking* orbiter, or one of those Mars missions like *Mars Polar Lander* that went astray," said Don, sounding dubious even to himself.

"Maybe," said Sas. "But it's awfully big . . ."

"Still no sign of an edge," said Don. "Maybe we should try another approach. Let's each go ten meters away, dig down, and see if the sheet is there under the surface. If it is, go on another ten meters, and try again. Keep going until we come to the edge. You go leading; I'll go trailing." On any tidally locked satellite, "leading" was toward the leading hemisphere, the one that faced forward into the direction of orbital motion; trailing was the opposite way.

Sas agreed, and they each set out. Don easily hopped ten meters, and it didn't take more than digging with his boot's toe to uncover more of the metal. He hopped another ten and again easily found metal, although it seemed a little deeper down this time. Ten more; metal again. A further ten and, although he had to dig through about a meter of dust to get to it, he found metal once more. Of course, because of the puny gravity, there was no danger of sinking into the dust, but the stuff that had been disturbed was now hanging in charcoallike clouds above the surface.

Although it had been Don's plan to go by ten-meter increments, he was starting to think that such trifling hops might result in a lot of wasted time. He gave a more vigorous kick off the ground this time and sailed forward fifty-odd meters. And yet again he found smooth metal, although it was buried even deeper out here, and—

"Don!" Sas' voice, shouting into his speaker. "I've found the edge!"

Don turned around and quickly flew across the 150 or so meters to where Sas was standing. The edge he'd uncovered was perfectly smooth. They both dug down around it with their gloved hands. It turned out the aluminum sheet was quite thin—no more than a centimeter. Don started working along one direction, and Sas along the other. They had to expose several meters of it before they noticed that the edge wasn't straight. Rather, it was gently curved. After a few more minutes, it was apparent that they were working their way along the rim of a disk that was perhaps a kilometer in diameter.

But no—no, it wasn't a disk. It was a *dish*, a great metal bowl, as if an entire crater had been lined with aluminum, and—

"Jesus," said Don.

"What?" replied Sas.

"It's an antenna dish."

"Who could have built it?" asked Sas.

Don tipped his head up to look at Mars—but he couldn't see Mars; they were on Deimos' farside.

The farside! Of course!

"Sas—it's a radio telescope!"

"Why would anyone put a radio telescope on the back side of Deimos?" asked Sas. "Unless . . . oh, my. Oh, my."

Don was nodding inside his space helmet. "It was built here for the same reason we want to build a radio telescope on the backside of Earth's moon. Luna farside, with all those kilometers of rock between it and Earth, is the one place in the Solar System that's shielded from the radio noise coming from human civilization . . ."

"And," said Sas, "Deimos farside, with fifteen kilometers of rock between it and Mars, would be shielded from the radio noise coming from . . ." His voice actually cracked. ". . . from Martian civilization."

Sas and Don continued to search, hoping there would be more to the installation than just the giant dish, but soon enough Deimos' rapid orbit caused the sun—only half the apparent diameter it was from Earth and giving off just one-quarter the heat—to sink below the horizon. Deimos took thirty hours and nineteen minutes to circle Mars; it would be almost fifteen hours before the sun rose on the tiny moon again.

"This is huge," said Sas, when they were back inside the habitat. "This is gigantic."

"A Martian civilization," said Don. He couldn't get enough of the phrase.

"There's no other possibility, is there?"

Don thought about that. There had been a contingency plan for *Apollo 11* in case it found Soviets already on the Moon—but NASA was no longer in a space race with anyone. "Well," said Don, "it certainly wasn't built by humans."

"Zakarian and company are going to have a lot to look for on the surface," said Sas.

Don shrugged a bit. "Maybe. Maybe not. There's *weather* on Mars, including sandstorms that last for months. All the large-scale water-erosion features we see on Mars are at least a billion years old, judging by the amount of cratering overtop of them. That suggests that whatever Martian civilization might have once existed did so at least that long ago. In a billion years, wind erosion could have destroyed every trace of an ancient civilization down there."

"Ah," said Sas, grinning. "But not here! No air; no erosion to speak of. Just the odd micrometeoroid impact." He paused. "That dish must have been here an awfully long time, to get buried under that much dust."

Don smiled. "You know," he said, "every space station humanity has ever been involved with has been inhabited by successive crews—*Skylab, Mir, Alpha.* One crew would go down; another would come up."

Sas raised his eyebrows. "But there's never been such a long hiatus between one crew leaving and the next one arriving."

When they knew the sun would be up on Deimos farside, Don and Sas headed back to the site of the alien antenna dish. They had almost finished making their way around its perimeter when they found a spoke, projecting outward from the rim of the antenna. They kept digging down, following it away from the dish, until—

"*Allah-o-akbar!*" exclaimed Sasim.

"God Almighty," said Don.

The spoke led to a buried building, and—

Well, its inhabitants *had* been astronomers. It made sense that they'd have a glass roof, a clear ceiling through which they could look up at the stars.

As Don and Sas brushed away more and more dust, they were better able to see in through the roof. There was furniture inside, but none of it designed for human occupants: several bowl-shaped affairs that Don imagined were chairs, and low worktables, covered with square sheets of something that seemed to serve the same purpose as paper. Scattered about were opaque cylindrical units that looked like they might be for storage. And—

Slumped against the wall, at the far end—

It was incredible. Absolutely incredible.

A Martian, perfectly preserved for countless millennia. Either they had no such thing as bacteria leading to decay, or everything had been sterilized before coming to Deimos, or perhaps all the air had leaked out somehow, preserving the being in vacuum.

The former resident of the building was vaguely insectoid, with rusty exoskeletal armor, four arms, and two legs. In life, he would have walked proud and upright. His mandible was tripartite; his giant eyes, lidless behind crystal shells, were a soft, kind blue.

"Amazing," said Sas softly. "Amazing."

"There must be a way inside," said Don, looking around. For all they knew from what they'd exposed of the transparent roof so far, the building might be no bigger than a single room. Still, it had been carved into the rocks of Deimos, so the air lock, if there was one, should be somewhere on the roof.

Don and Sas worked at clearing debris, and, after about twenty minutes, Don found what they were looking for. It was a transparent tube, like the one George Jetson shot up through, stretching between the glass roof and the floor. The tube had an opening in its circular walls at ground level, and a hatch up on the roof, forming a chamber that air could be pumped into or out of.

Any space station had lots of electrical parts, but doors were something sane engineers would make purely mechanical. After all, if the power went out, you didn't want to be trapped inside or outside. It took Sas and Don a few minutes to work out the logic of the door mechanism—a central disk in the middle of the roof had to be depressed, then rotated counterclockwise. Once that was done, the rest of the hatch irised open, and the locking disk, attached by what looked like a plastic cord, dangled very loosely at one side.

Don glided down the tube first. He wasn't able to open the inside door until Sas closed the upper lid; a safety interlock apparently prevented anyone from accidentally venting the habitat's air out into space.

Still, it was immediately obvious to Don, once he was out of the air lock tube, that there was no air inside the habitat. The rigidity of his pressure suit didn't change; no condensation appeared on his visor; there was no resistance to waving his arms vigorously. Doubtless there had been some air once, but, despite the safety precautions, it had all leaked out. Perhaps a small meteor had drilled through the roof at some point they hadn't yet uncovered.

Sas came down the air lock tube next—the locking disk could be engaged from either side of the iris. By the time he was down, Don had already made his way over to the dead thing. Its rusty color seemed good confirming evidence that Mars was indeed the being's original home. The creature was about a meter and a half tall, and, if there had been any doubt about its intelligence, that was dispelled now. The Martian wore clothes—apparently not for protection, but rather for convenience; the translucent garment covering part of its abdomen was rich with pockets and pouches. Still, the body showed signs of having suffered a massive decompression; innards had partially burst out through various seams in the exoskeleton.

While Don continued to examine the being—the first alien life-form ever seen by a human—Sas poked around the room. "Don!" he shouted.

Don reluctantly left the Martian and glided over to Sas, who was pointing through an open archway.

The underground complex went on and on. And Martian bodies were everywhere.

"Wow," said Sas. "Wow."

Don tried to activate the radio circuit to Earth, but he wasn't able to pick up the beacon signal from Mission Control. Of course not: this facility had operated a massive radio telescope; it would be shielded to prevent interference with the antenna. Don and Sas made their way up the air lock tube and out to the surface. There they had no trouble acquiring the beacon.

"Mission Control," said Don. "Tell Chuck Zakarian we hope he has a good time down on Mars' surface—although, given all the erosion that goes on there, I doubt he'll find much. But that's okay, Houston; we'll make up for that. You see, it seems we're not the first crew to occupy . . ." He paused, the perfect name coming to him at last. ". . . Mike Collins Station."

THE FRANCHISE

by Julie E. Czerneda

Canadian author and editor Julie E. Czerneda has been a finalist for both the John W. Campbell and Philip K. Dick Awards, as well as two-time winner of the Prix Aurora Award. She has published a number of science fiction novels with DAW Books, most recently Species Imperative: Survival. *A proponent of using SF in classrooms, Julie edits Trifolium Books' Y/A anthology series* Tales from the Wonder Zone, *as well as* Realms of Wonder. *Julie edited the anthology* Space Inc. *for DAW Books, which explores daily life off this planet, and with Isaac Szpindel, the upcoming* ReVisions, *alternative science histories. Her award-winning standalone SF novel,* In the Company of Others, *led to the characters and settings featured here in "The Franchise."*

Titan University Archives
Public Access
Reference: Post-Quill Era; Colonization;
Space Station Repatriation

ONCE the menace of the Quill, the alien pest accidentally and tragically released on the terraformed planets, had been overcome, and the first of these worlds declared free of the deadly Quill Effect, it was with relief and enthusiasm that humanity undertook Phase Four: colonization. There were, of course, minor details to be settled before full, unrestricted immigration could be instituted. During the two decades of Protective Isolation, the great transit stations had sheltered hundreds of thousands of would-be immigrants. These individuals were now eager to resume their chosen destiny. Earth, and all of Sol System, wished to reestablish routine travel via the stations to the new worlds, but some stations had fallen into disrepair. Fortunately, all affected agencies worked in harmony to move colonization and station repatriation forward as expeditiously as possible. Humanity's Great Dream had begun anew and the transit stations would prove key to making that dream a reality.

Titan University Archives
Excerpts from briefings conducted by Assistant Secretary Wayne Umberto
Access Restricted to Clearance AA2 or higher

. . . It's clear the 16 transit stations presently—viable—will be granted self-governing status as the public demands. Your task in this negotiation, sir, will be to obtain a firm understanding—however worded—that this enfranchisement is conditional upon those stations assuming responsibility for repatriating the nonviable ones. It's a salvage stationers are uniquely qualified to undertake and our experts predict a success rate of 30%.

There is the obvious added benefit of relieving the extreme population pressure within the surviving stations. Less apparent, but no less critical, sir, is that the System Universities and TerraCor, by providing crucial transport and technical support, will reestablish a permanent presence on the stations before they become too independent. The stations must remain service-oriented facilities, to be expanded or decommissioned as we see fit, not become homes . . .

"Doesn't make much sense," Annette whispered.

"What doesn't?"

"Him. Here."

Dave Bijou didn't need to follow the slide of his wife's eyes to know who took up the first bench in the Earthers' fancy-new shuttle. The rest from Thromberg Station squeezed four together, despite the Earther crew's uncomprehending stares and their provision of only two safety restraints per seat. Elbow room was a not-yet-accepted luxury; companionship was more reassuring.

Only the old ones remembered when it had been otherwise, more particularly, the Sol-born, who'd come to the station thirty years ago.

Sammie would remember, Dave told himself, thinking of the man alone and silent, back to them all. Samuel Leland, former proprietor of Sammie's Tavern, Outward 5, Thromberg Station. Undisputed leader of that community and least likely to ever leave it. Forty years since dirtside, some claimed. Could have been longer. On-station since Thromberg powered up, most believed. Rumor said he'd been an educated, cultured businessman, one with connections and backers in plenty on Earth.

Hadn't mattered. The past wasn't currency worth spending on any station during the Quill Blockade, when everyone had been quarantined to prevent the spread of the pest to Earth and Sol System, even if no station had ever held a Quill. A liability was more like it, in an environment where pasts no longer carried shields of family, property, or place. The survivors learned early to deal in the here and now.

For the same reason, the future hadn't been a popular topic for casual talk, given the lack of it. Then, suddenly, the universe changed. The Quill were no longer a threat. The blockade had been lifted! *People could leave*!

Those with somewhere to go.

Dave sighed at the memory. He and Annette had been among those betrayed by their pasts. They were both station-born, to immie parents; another meaningless legacy, since it turned out to be where you were born that mattered.

Thromberg Station might have rioted again, when this became painfully clear. It came close. *His* voice, Sammie's, and others, insisted on reason. Might have been ignored, Dave admitted to himself, but even the angriest of them quieted at the return of those who'd desperately raced to the new worlds, only to discover themselves unable to endure the reality of sky, moving air, and distance. Their shamed, exhausted relief to be within walls proved desire wasn't nearly enough.

The Earthers brought tests to oh-so-kindly weed out those unsuited to life dirtside. Kindness. Dave didn't make the rude noise this called for, considerate of his seatmates. Station folk—stationers, immies, 'siders alike—knew the motive behind this convenient "kindness." Those stranded these last twenty years deserved and received first immigration rights without question. But Earth and Sol System hadn't stayed sterile. A new generation waited impatiently to become colonists. The stations' relics would have to hurry or lose their chance.

So they'd lined up for the tests. Outsiders passed, those who'd fled the blockade around Sol System only to be exiled in turn to Thromberg's outer hull because the station feared to let them back inside, in case they carried Quill. Why else would Earth fire on defenseless civilian ships? 'Siders were used to living with horizons, those of their ships and the station herself. First of many ironies, since most 'siders weren't interested in life dirtside, preferring a return to the independence of space. The First Rounders passed, to no one's surprise, being those colonists preselected for experience outdoors and bloody determination. But while 'rounders might be young enough to tame a world, they were too old to populate it.

The rest? Stationers and immies born in that last generation, before the Earthers added sterilization drugs to food shipments with the foresight of hysteria, ran headfirst into the new blockade: most could never live outside a station's comforting walls. With a guilt no one mistook for generosity, Thromberg was officially given to those who now had to call it home forever.

Of course there was a catch. The stationers expected one. Perhaps they felt better knowing it.

The waves of immigration to the terraformed worlds would need the transit stations—all of them. To keep the stations which had survived, they would have to restore those which had not.

Starting with the most infamous—Hamilton Station.

Dave found himself holding Annette's hand. She leaned closer, nestling her small head into his shoulder. They'd almost backed out of the deal when their destination had been revealed. Hamilton had turned on its own, corridor-talk said, in riots more deadly than any which had ripped Thromberg. The last communication from the station had been a final, endlessly cycled: "Do not approach." A series of aid ships from Earth had tried, and never been heard from again. The other stations, consumed with their own troubles, had left well enough alone. Borrowing trouble was not a survival skill.

Until now, when the Earthers wanted Hamilton Station up and running again.

If Sammie hadn't been in the room, rock-calm and scornful, maybe all of those in this shuttle, and the dozen paralleling their course, would still be on Thromberg.

Annette was right, Dave thought uneasily, looking at Sammie's wide, bowed shoulders. It didn't make any sense. Why *him*? And why *here*?

Linda Gulliver, former Patrol recruit at the top of her class, now one of two passenger attendants on TerraCor Shuttle 881—the need for new patrollers to guard Sol System approaches having been extinguished with the Quill threat—steeled herself and reached for the door control.

"C'mon. It's not that bad," teased fellow attendant Pavel Romanov. Despite his lean height, he managed to make the crew cot look comfortable. There were six lining what had been a spacious corridor between the shuttle's bridge and the back passenger hold. Linda wouldn't willingly lie in one without taking a sleepy beforehand. She said her legs cramped within minutes; no one's business if she couldn't bear lying so near anyone else.

"It's worse," she told Pavel, unsmiling. "We contracted to transport thirty-three passengers and their gear, not sixty-five. We're supposed to use some of the passenger hold for ourselves—and not have to give up our quarters. And have you smelled it in there today?"

"The ship's rated for twice what we've on board. So we're tucked a little tight—not as though it's a long trip."

Linda snorted. "Where have you been the past three days?"

"Keeping you happy, Linda my girl," he grinned, then pretended to duck.

"What's the holdup, Gulliver?"

Linda snapped to attention out of habit, then made herself relax. "Nothing, Captain," she said to the woman entering from the bridge access.

Captain Gwen Maazel might not be Patrol, but she was capable of the same searing look when in doubt. "See it stays that way."

Linda collected her tray and went through to the passenger hold.

The portside aisle had been kept clear, safety as well as instant access to the suits webbed against that bulkhead. The starboard aisle was packed ceiling-high with belongings—those from Thromberg resisting any attempt to move their tawdry things to the cargo hold. Not that there was much room in cargo, Linda reminded herself. Thromberg's docking personnel had jammed it with what they euphemistically called "gear," a collection of patched, antique equipment the crew privately referred to as "garbage."

Matched the passengers, Linda decided, firming her smile as she walked to the end of the passenger hold and began handing out drink tubes from her tray. All wore clothing that might have begun life similar to her own one-piece coveralls, but twenty years of wear and repair had morphed their garb into strangely unique creations. A third were sleeveless. Others had additional layers sewn or glued in various areas, as if for padding or reinforcement. Color? The fabric varied from faded and incidentally stained—or scorched—to faded with what appeared to be decorative stains. More common were loops or pockets filled with assorted objects, most looking the worse for wear, things which should have been discarded long ago. The occasional shiny, new object—doubtless Earther issue—was usually tucked into a pocket, as if there was some shame attached to its ownership, however functional.

Objects. Easier to deal with those. Linda had grown used to the way her passengers preferred to sit so they touched constantly, but the way their eyes slid away from hers when thanking her, the way they spoke too softly, too quickly, as if to be done with any conversation with an Earther, sent chills down her spine even after three days.

Their faces didn't help. The older ones, in the back four rows, had an uncompromising harshness in their eyes, an alertness as they watched her every move with disapproval—not to mention appalling teeth when they did speak. The rest, none younger than Linda herself, were no better, each lean to the point of gauntness, many bearing scars from injuries or perhaps, she shuddered, disease. Such disfigurements hadn't been seen on Earth in her lifetime.

But the worst of them all was the passenger sitting in the front row. Linda braced herself and her smile as she came beside his seat.

Possibly he was alone because he needed the room. He'd been a big man. The frame was there: broad shoulders and chest, heavy, long arms that would have been muscled once. The torso was still thick, not as if he'd had more to eat than the others, but as if his skin remembered more bulk and refused to tighten. His teeth were mismatched and his face—suffice it to say age and the loss of underlying flesh hadn't been kind to what had started out as asymmetrical and blunt. The eyes tended not to focus. His coveralls were like the rest, except for a lack of fading in the color of the front, as if he'd always worn something else overtop. Apron, she'd been told. He'd been a bartender on the other station. Linda avoided looking at his feet, one look at those splayed toes in their homemade thongs being enough.

He might have been alone in his seat because of his size—or unpleasant appearance. But, Linda knew, incredible as it seemed, this *bartender* was the leader of the

Thromberg contingent. He sat alone because the others here granted him that privilege. Something else to mystify the Earthers on board.

"Drink, Mr. Leland?" she asked.

His hand, like those of the others, reached involuntarily for a pocket, then stopped. It had taken those from Thromberg most of this trip to stop trying to pay her with the little slips of metal they called "'dibs," but the reflex remained. Since 'dibs involved a complex exchange of work for goods, Linda took this as a hopeful sign Thromberg had remained more civilized than it appeared from her denizens. There was little else to go by.

Though if she turned around, she knew she'd see no one drinking yet. They were waiting for Leland to take and open his. In fact, they used to wait until she left as well. Politeness? She wasn't sure.

Different customs. Very. They hadn't briefed the crew to expect such things. Mind you, they hadn't been briefed about much. This was supposed to be a routine, if profitable, pick up and transport trip—not an exercise in diplomacy with passengers who seemed, at times, more alien than the Quill.

"Thanks," grunted Leland, taking the tube and cracking the top seal with a thumb. He didn't look around at the echo as sixty-four other seals were cracked. "Whatssir 'tinr'y?"

Linda worked this around, guessing "itinerary." Leland's broken speech was hard for her to follow at best. "We've dropped out of translight and are vectoring to the station, sir. Captain Maazel— What was that?" *That*, being a solid thump felt through the floor plates, accompanied by a warning flicker of the interior lights. She grabbed for a hold on the seat rim, almost dropping her tray.

In case any missed the event, the shuttle's alarm gave a brief, self-conscious bleat.

Leland took a casual swallow before answering: "Sommat hit the hull," he said, as if the event was irrelevant. "When'r we dock'n?"

"I'll ask." Linda straightened, embarrassed by the placid

looks from the rest of the passengers, and almost ran from the hold.

Those from Thromberg sat back and watched. They'd been told there were suits for everyone, plus a spare or two. As if any of them had believed that before boarding, Dave thought, then glanced at the port bulkhead to admire the flagrant wealth on display. Probably the Earthers were scrambling into their suits in the forward compartment. His panic-threshold required something a little more imminently threatening than a thump on the outside of a well-maintained ship. After all, if they'd been seriously holed, it would be a little late for suits. Earthers didn't seem very logical folks.

Another *thud*. This a bit louder, with a *ssssshhhhhk* at the end, as though something clung to the hull before being left behind. Like the other immies and stationers, Dave tilted his head, listening for signs the 'siders in back were reaching for their own suits, carefully stowed by their seats. Then it'd be time to move, all right.

"Mr. Leland." Dave looked forward with the rest. The voice was the captain's. She stood in the again-open doorway, this time partially suited up, two of the other crew behind her. Her expression made Dave tighten his grip on Annette's hand. He felt Jean leaning closer on the other side. "Would you come with me, please?"

Sammie nodded, standing with an awkward lurch. "Pettersen," he said, bringing one of the 'siders up the aisle to him, bag in hand. "Rest o' you don't fuss," he growled, running his eyes over them all. Dave nodded, knowing the others did the same.

"What are we facing here, Mr. Leland?"

Linda sat shoulder-to-shoulder between her crewmates, Pavel and Lili Wong. The three weren't directly involved in operations, so they waited, strapped into their seats along the starboard side of the little bridge, their backs to one of two emergency air locks, helmets ready in their laps. Pavel, to her left, had snapped on her helmet's tether, muttering under his breath. Null-g was always a possibility—gravity generators were reliable but not perfect. She'd been more grateful than embarrassed. They were all distracted by the conversation and its cause.

The captain and the two from Thromberg had moved back from the ops stations, though their bodies still screened the displays. Linda didn't need to see what was keeping the bridge somber and those less experienced swallowing repeatedly. The report had been whispered one to the other. What should have been the approach lane to the aft docking ring, their preferred access to Hamilton Station, was littered with debris.

Not just a hazard to ships.

The debris was *from* ships.

During the trip here, she'd looked over the stats. Hamilton Station was older than Thromberg by a handful of years, a difference reflected more in terms of interior decorating styles than any physical changes in design. What worked, worked. About a quarter of those carried by the shuttles were experts in station operations and should have no problem accessing Hamilton's systems. *Stationers.* Linda couldn't have told which they were.

Half were immigrants or their descendants. *Immies.* They had expertise of their own, as well as being willing hands. The rest? Not spacers. Not now. *Outsiders,* who'd existed during the blockade by attaching their ships to the exterior of Thromberg and bleeding off her power, air, and water. Parasites or survivors. Linda hadn't made up her mind on that yet, thoroughly offended by the sight of so many starships turned into scrap, stuck seemingly at random to Thromberg's hull. Outsiders were easy to spot: their coveralls showed wear from suit connectors—the kind of wear that only came after unimaginable use. For some reason, only older ones had volunteered for life on other stations.

Like the one standing between Leland and the captain, introduced as Torbjørn Pettersen. Tall, skeleton-thin, with ragged white hair that had likely been blond, he hadn't spoken, only consumed everything on the bridge with quick furtive glances.

"What are we facing, Captain?" Leland seemed oblivious to the startled looks his suddenly educated voice attracted, turning to his companion. "Torbjørn?"

Pettersen's voice was equally cultured, but quieter, almost shy. "This is deliberate. They don't want company."

The captain leaned forward and consulted with the com operator, then straightened with a curse. "Approach to the stern ring is worse. We'll have to move in slowly, that's all. This material is matching the station in speed and trajectory—shouldn't be too difficult to do the same, and slide through the worst of it."

The 'sider stiffened. Leland held up a thick-fingered hand to stop whatever Pettersen might have wanted to say, instead reminding them unnecessarily: "Other ships didn't make it."

"These are asteroid mining shuttles, Mr. Leland, as requested by your station administration," Captain Maazel countered. "My crew and I are used to working in heavy dust and particle areas. These ships can take a substantial amount of impact if we do the pushing."

Linda should have been reassured by this, but something in the rigidity of the 'sider's back kept her hands clenched on her helmet. She hadn't realized she'd meant to speak until hearing her own voice: "Captain, recommend we suit up the passengers before proceeding into the debris field. As a precaution." Pettersen swiveled his head, washed-pale eyes expressionless.

Captain Maazel nodded, her attention on what she and the others watched. "Take Romanov. See there's no panic."

"No need," Pettersen said, before Linda and Pavel could unstrap.

Leland explained: "If they need to suit up—they will. Let your people concentrate on getting us through this mess."

To Linda's disgust, Captain Maazel agreed, immediately gesturing them to stay as they were. It didn't help when she took the 'sider with her, forward in the bridge compartment, to engage the three ops crew in private discussion.

Leland had stayed behind. He walked over to stand in front of Linda, most of his bulk trespassing within her personal space. She tried not to stare up his nostrils, which were bent and populated by large, black hairs.

"We appreciate your concern, Linda Gulliver," the stationer told her. "But you won't get our people to move until those in the back rows give the word."

"Why? Are they spacers?" Pavel's voice contained something of awe. Linda supposed deep space explorers were exotic beasts to those used to plying the Mars-Titan run.

"'Siders," Leland corrected, propping an unwelcome thong-enclosed foot beside Linda's thigh. "We each bring our skills to this adventure, Earther. Stationers to get Hamilton working, immies to bring the place to life again, and 'siders—" He paused, his attention caught by something forward.

"—'siders?" Linda prompted, even as she froze with alarm. Pettersen was tearing open the bag he'd brought, pulling out what appeared to be damaged bits of a spacesuit.

"'Siders? They deal with disaster." With this, Leland left them, hurrying to the others.

"So our passengers have nothing in common—no wonder they almost killed one another," came from Lili, to Linda's left.

"They have something in common," Linda said almost to herself, trying not to be afraid. "They all survived."

The situation might have been death-imminent, or merely pandering to Earther-paranoia, but Dave couldn't resist taking the time to enjoy the novelty of not only wearing a suit, but having such a fine one. He stroked its smooth, flawless sleeves and connectors. He could see most of the others doing the same, even Annette, who'd professed disdain for Earther extravagances. Their generation had experienced very little this new. He couldn't imagine why the 'siders chose to put on their own gear, taping up the untrustworthy seams, making do—but no one from Thromberg bothered trying to think like a 'sider.

Finally, he put on the helmet, drawing in its fresh plastic smell with delight, only to freeze as words roared through his helmet com: ". . . the approach to Hamilton is not routine. Check seals; keep coms open. Repeat. The approach is not routine."

Pettersen's voice, the 'sider who'd gone forward with Sammie. Calm, cold, staccato urgent. *Not routine.* Station code for anything about to turn deadly. Another 'sider, now an unknown in a patched suit, began checking Annette's suit. Dave felt a touch from behind as someone else checked his. Suit air didn't taste the same, he found, fear drying his mouth.

The 'siders pushed them out of the way, into the seats, a tighter fit with suit bulk and air tanks added, but workable with the addition of the back rows and Sammie's. This done, the 'siders, moving with reassuring ease despite their suits, grabbed bags and loose gear and passed it hand to hand, to be dumped into the compartment parallel to this one. Earthers' crew quarters—bigger than most families used on Thromberg—that they'd been using as a galley and exercise room. That door was closed and both aisles freed, but the 'siders kept moving, this time opening up the rear door—an air lock giving access to the cargo compartment. Several went inside, and didn't return.

Stationers and immies stayed put, silent, so the com could carry Pettersen's continuing report.

"Sammie wants me to remind you we're in the right ship to handle this—miners are built to shove their way through. Can take a fair hit as well, not that the crew plans to collide with anything avoidable. They might be Earthers, but they know their stuff." This last with a wry reluctance that brought a chuckle from a few. "Might be some sudden maneuvers, loss of g."

A pause, into which a question fell: "What's out there?"

Dave listened hard, straining for anything past his own breathing and the suit's background hum.

"Hamilton put up a fence, seems like," came the slow answer. "Bit of a waste, if you ask me. Recyclables. Other—things."

Hamilton Station hadn't replied to their messages, or those from Thromberg. As far as anyone could determine, she couldn't—a failure of equipment, knowledge, or, most likely, a lack of anyone to speak.

Dave now considered an even more terrifying possibility, given they were docking within the hour.

Maybe Hamilton chose not to answer.

"Bodies?"

"Shh." An unnecessary admonishment, since no one was paying attention to them, but Lili made it anyway. "That's what Sinshi says. Thousands of them. Along with ship debris and who knows what else."

"I thought they ate their dead," Pavel hissed, leaning over Linda.

Common enough belief back home; a nightmare as they approached the grimly silent station. Linda shoved Pavel back. "You know that's crap," she said firmly but quietly. "Thromberg buried her dead by sending them toward her sun. They're a posted ship hazard. Other stations did the same." She'd been in a class debating if that had been respect—or to avoid terrible temptation. People who'd know now shared the shuttle's air supply with her.

Finding Hamilton had kept her dead close was not reassuring.

Seconds became minutes, the time crawling down Linda's neck, arms, and legs like spiders she couldn't brush away. The captain had ordered a slow, careful approach, passing that recommendation to the other ships. Agony, to sit, strapped in place—

Concussion!

The shuttle's alarm covered any unprofessional outcries, profane or terrified. Linda locked her helmet into place as others did the same, cutting off ambient sound. Pettersen had put his on earlier, and now she knew why, hearing his voice, not the captain's, in her ear.

". . . stop the shuttle," he was saying, no trace of emotion in his soft, quick voice. "Those are suits. They aren't just bodies. They're mines! Stop all your ships."

The captain: "How can you know—"

Leland's voice crashed over both: "Because we never had enough suits, Captain. No one would jettison one without damned good reason, let alone this many." Emotion in plenty there, all of it dark. "Stop the ships! Now! Before we lose anyone else."

"Too late—" someone shouted.

Lights were half power—on emerg, probably. Nothing new, Dave told himself, refusing to think about what *was* new about their situation.

"Don't panic on me now," Annette said, reading his state of mind with the accuracy of practice. She'd switched their coms to privacy—it hadn't taken her long to puzzle out the helmet controls and take advantage of them. "You heard Pettersen and Sammie. The Earthers lost three shuttles—" a thickness to her voice the only acknowledgment of what else had been lost. Thankfully, station caution had insisted on several small ships, rather than the single large transport TerraCor had offered. "—ours stayed intact. Solid ship; smart flying. Gotta give the Earthers some credit. Dave. Are you listening?"

He nodded, exaggerating the motion through neck and shoulders so she could see it. "Good," she snapped. More gently. "Counting on you, husband."

"I'll do my part," he said gruffly. "If they get us into the station. Better switch us back to the general com."

Her gloved hand rested on his, then his helmet filled with other voices again, this time in debate.

The captain's: "The docking ring is undamaged. At least fifteen ports show green and available. Tell me again, Mr. Leland, why we're not to use them?"

"It's another trap."

"And you know this how?" the question courteous despite the tension.

The stationer didn't hesitate. "Because we did the same on Thromberg."

Open coms had their disadvantages. Linda listened to Leland's revelation and felt her stomach twist itself into a tighter knot. Docking ports were sacrosanct—the first rule of space was to give unquestioned access to air and safety. Arguments could be resolved later, if need be.

Thromberg's actions had been against those who became the 'siders, yet Linda heard Pettersen's gentle voice supporting Sammie: "Hamilton doesn't want visitors. Why would she leave her doors open and the welcome mat out?"

"So what can we do? Three shuttles are gone, Mr. Leland. Seven are incapable of translight without repair—two are bleeding air. We can't just sit here and wait for help."

"Your shuttles have ore grapples," Pettersen said. "They can be fired into the outer hull and used to winch us tight. Then we'll make our own door if necessary."

"'Sider methods." If there was a note of horror in the captain's voice, Linda was sure every Earther listening could echo it.

"I can attest they work, Captain," this from Leland.

Grapples. Linda stared at the suited figures, all but one in pristine Earther suits. So. It was by no coincidence they were in a mining shuttle. The stationers had anticipated trouble docking with Hamilton all along, and had come prepared to do things their way.

It put the "gear" in cargo into an entirely new light. And her passengers—who were now anything but useless weight.

She unstrapped and stood, staggering a little as circulation returned to limbs tensed in one position too long. "Captain Maazel."

"I'm busy, Gulliver—"

"I've had training in emergency hookups," Linda interrupted. "I'd like to go back and help."

"Beats sitting here," came from Pavel. Linda felt more than saw Lili join them.

Pettersen turned. His battered helmet was lit a garish red from within, turning his face to that of some demigod. "Can you take orders from us, Earther?" he challenged.

"Mr. Leland said you were the experts in dealing with disaster, sir," Linda refused to back down. "Looks to be what we have here."

A noise from Leland, loud and rude, filled their helmets. "Got you there, Torbjørn. Go ahead, girl. If your captain has no objection."

"I object to everything except heading back to Thromberg," Captain Maazel muttered darkly. "Gulliver—take these two and see if you can lend a hand."

Earthers had helped. Side by side in the holds; out there, on the hulls of ship and station, drilling in feeds to tap air, power, and water from Hamilton's mains. Dave didn't know what to make of it. It was happening on the other shuttles as well, reports said. It took exhausting hours, but eventually the ships were declared snug and secure. For now.

"Guess that makes us all 'siders," Annette had joked. They'd already begun thinking of themselves as stationers, not immies, acknowledging their futures would be on a station, not a world. Dave wasn't quite ready to be a 'sider, and had told her so, but he did appreciate their skills.

And the Earthers'.

He'd hoped for repercussions. Everyone hoped for a reaction from Hamilton Station to their assault on her hull. The com tech maintained a vigil. Nothing.

Meanwhile, the 'siders, ever practical, made those who'd waited inside the shuttle take off their suits, move around, and insisted they eat. Everyone tucked some of their rations into pockets. The Earther, Linda, had watched this, then done the same.

Sensible woman, Dave decided. Annette must have agreed. She'd made conversation with the Earther, exchanged drink tubes in a gesture of acceptance as old as Thromberg, or perhaps older. Whether the Earther knew it or not, she'd be watched over as if one of their own.

* * *

Linda rubbed sleep from her eyes as she went forward, contemplating using one of the two boost shots in her suit, then decided to save them for—what? She refused to speculate. The corridor lights were dimmed; only the glows above each door showed her where Pavel and Lili, along with the shuttle pilots, Steve and Marcus, were snoring in a discordant harmony in the cots strapped in place, still in suits, helmets hanging from tethers. *Not routine,* she'd heard the stationers whisper to one another, as though it was a warning. Appropriate.

Linda moved quietly past the others, tired enough to sleep without drugs, but unwilling to seek oblivion of any type until she knew and approved what was happening next. Not the best attitude for a humble shuttle attendant, she chided herself even as she slipped through the door to the bridge.

Pettersen had stretched out on the crew bench, eyes closed and one leg with its taped-on mag boot on the floor. Linda doubted he truly slept. The captain and Leland were out of their suits, slumped but alert in the pilots' chairs. The com tech huddled over her console, eyes half-lidded as she monitored something only she could hear.

"Hear you made yourself useful," Leland said by way of greeting.

"Learned some things," Linda replied. "Most not reg'." The stationer's unexpected smile was lopsided, exposing gaps in his discolored teeth; it warmed her anyway.

The captain's voice was worn as thin as her face. "Sit," she ordered, waving at the abandoned nav chair. "You look worse than I feel."

Linda didn't deny it. She sat, her helmet in her lap, and wrapped her mind around what these two might need to know. "Ship's secured, sir. Solid feeds. Which means the station is powered up and airtight. Everyone's calm. Almost. The 'siders insisted on having people outside, on the hull." She raised her eyebrow at Leland, making that a question.

"Old habit," the stationer grunted. "After everyone grabs

a bit of sleep, we'll crack the port seal. Hope you're game for that too, Earther."

Earther suits were designed so a child could use them, Dave reminded himself, tempted to take a swallow from the tube near his lips, stopped by the strangeness of drinking alone. A child. Children. He fastened on that, happier imagining an incredible future than the next few minutes, when he and Annette would walk out of the ship into the expanse of space.

Walk? He managed not to shudder. While in the shuttle's air lock, Dave and rest of the space novices would have bags put over their helmets and be towed along with the rest of the gear to the station's emergency access port. 'Siders weren't inclined to avoidable risk.

Stationers weren't inclined to avoidable trust either. Dave knew he wasn't the only one calculating the wisdom of putting his life into the hands of those who'd been forced to be virtually invisible during the blockade. 'Siders had survived because they were too stubborn to die, not because of station charity.

Of course, they had the Quill—and the Earthers—to thank for all of that.

"Ready to check out the new place?" Annette's voice rang in his ears, brittle but determined. She nudged him from behind. "Remember. We want something in the inward levels—a good location, with room for our repair shop. You know what Sammie told us—we need to establish an economy here, get things running so smooth there'll be no excuses for Earth to interfere."

She wasn't being callous, Dave knew. It was better to think of Hamilton Station as empty, as space ready to occupy, than dwell on what might be waiting. "Ready as you are, darl'n," Dave said as confidently as possible.

Her hands wouldn't stop shaking. Linda left them alone in her lap, concentrating on the light, chest-only breaths she was taking, counting those.

"All that saved us was those codes," Pavel said. She wasn't sure to whom or how often he'd repeated it. There were so many of them crowded together here, the blending of Earther and stationer made complete by the suits and the horror of their welcome, that Linda no longer tried to identify individuals.

"Sammie must have been here before," a woman answered. "Surprised he remembered them. Sure glad he did." This brought a laugh from some.

Linda swallowed bile. She'd seen what the stationers had not, by virtue of being familiar with work in zero-g and to a horizon defined by a distant arc of sun-torched white. Leland had been right. The ports had been traps. If they had tried to use the ship auto-dock system to attach themselves, the ports would have released their contents and destroyed them all. If they had tried to force entry? Same result. Destruction.

And if she'd stayed in Sol System, working a freighter, she'd never have had to see air locks crammed tight with explosives and the dead to carry them.

Leland had been the unlikely hero. He'd gone first, ponderously graceful, disguised as handsome in his Earther suit, and had punched in codes for the emergency hatch as well as the larger cargo doors. Codes only those on Hamilton Station would know. Codes a Thromberg Station bartender shouldn't have known.

Why him? Why here?

They'd waited for Leland's signal, Earthers and 'siders securing their cabled-together bags of gear and helpless, blinded passengers. Credit to the stationers—none had panicked, none had vomited until safely inside the station, helmets off. That had been the greatest risk for those who could see, who had to clear the contents of at least one air lock immediately to get the helpless inside.

Linda wasn't sure if it been courage or disbelief that allowed her to keep going. She'd been humbly grateful to the 'siders who took what she passed outward with the presence of mind to tie everything together so nothing would float free and endanger the shuttle, only steps away.

So this was Hamilton Station. Linda couldn't have told where she was now from the docking ring on Thromberg, save for a different, fresher taste to the air—and the silence. She hadn't realized how noisy the throngs packing the other, living station had been, how comforting the background drone of thousands could be. Until she'd come here, where fifty-or-so huddled close, to make themselves feel like more.

Hamilton was messier. The stationers talked about this between themselves, uneasy. Linda remembered Thromberg as having a broken-in look—everything possible being used and reused. Nothing wasted. Hamilton? No one had lived here. She felt gorge rising again in her throat and forced it down. They'd existed, long enough for destruction and fear. Not long enough to fit pieces together and keep going.

Perhaps goaded by similar thoughts, the stationers began moving. Linda was startled when a hand pressed something into hers—one of the metal strips. *'Dibs.* She looked up and met the understanding eyes of the small, dark-haired woman she'd met in the shuttle, Annette Bijou. "Our turn, now," Annette said. "There's work to do. You rest a while."

Linda closed her fingers over the strip and stood, taking a deep breath. "What next?" she asked. Pavel slid upright beside her.

A keen look, then a nod. "Some are going to the 'vironment monitors, others to hydroponics. Dave and I are going to start checking the inward levels for working space and assess supplies. You're welcome to come with us."

"Aren't you—aren't you—" Linda had trouble with the words.

"—looking for survivors?" Annette finished for her. "You don't understand what happened here, do you?"

"And you do?" Linda knew her voice was incredulous and overly loud, but none of the others took offense.

"They feared the Quill," a deeper, more resonant voice answered. Leland and his shadow, Pettersen, were back from wherever they'd gone. The stationers clustered around to listen; Linda found the contact of strangers' shoulders oddly comforting.

"Everyone feared the Quill," Pavel protested. "Thromberg did—and you survived. You were the same—"

Pettersen shook his head, tight-lipped. As usual, it was Leland who spoke. "We survived because we didn't close our ports, because we allowed ships to bring supplies and medicine." The stationer paused, then put his hand on Pettersen's thin shoulder. "We survived because people eventually took the chance those returning to us didn't bring the Quill."

Linda realized what she should have seen when on Hamilton's hull. "No 'siders. No ships at all."

"Ships fled here," Pettersen said at last. "Com logs say so. But Hamilton feared the Quill so much, station personnel laid mines to destroy any ship that approached. After that? Maybe they feared reprisals as well as the Quill, so more mines. Which meant no ships. No help. As they starved . . . as disease overwhelmed them . . . they put their dead on guard as well. Outside. In the 'locks. Until the last of them sealed him or herself within."

Leland sighed, deep and heavy. "We had our troubles, on Thromberg. Did things to regret." A flash of pain crossed his face. "Unforgivable things. But we didn't hide like this, we didn't cut ourselves off from humanity." His bulk shuddered, once, then he straightened. "Or stand around moaning about what's done and gone," he added sharply. With that, the crowd began to dissolve, people picking up bags and gathering into small groups of four or five, heading in different directions.

Annette lingered. "How'd you know the codes, Sammie?" she asked quietly.

The stationer scowled, a ferocious distortion on that face, but Annette didn't appear impressed. "How?" she repeated. "It saved us. Grateful for that. But people don't want secrets at the start, Sammie. You know I'm right."

"Come with me, then," he growled, and walked away, heading for the nearest lifts.

Linda found herself alone with Pavel. "Are you returning to the shuttle?" she asked.

Pavel shook his head. "They're going to start clearing the other 'locks," he said grimly. "I'd better get outside." He hesitated, looking after Leland. "Go with him, Linda. The captain will want to know what's going on."

Dave knew the Earther woman followed them. Likely suspecting conspiracy or worse, he decided, noticing she kept a few steps back. Same old stuff. He tried, but couldn't rouse anger. The reality of how fragile Thromberg's peace had really been, how near to sharing Hamilton's fate they'd come—if they hadn't found a way to live with the 'siders, with each other, even with Earth? It wouldn't have taken the Quill to kill them.

Sammie stopped without warning. Dave, right behind, had to lurch not to run into the other man's back. He looked around hurriedly, as did the others, seeking danger, expecting ghosts.

And found one.

There was a sign, half-melted into the wall. The words on it were underlined by a ragged scorching. "Leland Interplanetary Travel Services, Inc." Below, in small, clear text: "Book a visit from that special someone today!"

They turned to him.

"My company," Sammie acknowledged so softly it almost disguised the tremor in his voice. "I knew the entry codes because I started the franchise here, on Hamilton Station."

"Franchise?" Annette asked, as if compelled. "There were more?"

He nodded. "Gave this one to my eldest boy, Henry, before moving to Thromberg. Henry was doing well—brought his family. Wife, three little girls." A pause. No one breathed. "I started a franchise on every station. I believed our future was out here, in space. This was my way of keeping us together."

"All family?" Dave tried to comprehend the scale of such loss and failed. Sammie had aimed enough close kin at Thromberg's sun to ice a heart. But this?

The heavy brows knotted. "Not all by blood. A cousin on Wye Station. An aunt on Pfefferlaws. Three nephews, on Hamble, Osari, Ricsus. The rest were—friends. People who followed my vision. Me." Sammie's eyes hadn't left the sign.

The Earther, Linda, almost reached out her hand; the intention was written in a shift of posture, quickly contained. "People followed you today, Mr. Leland. Sammie. Because of you, we are still alive and have a future."

Sammie didn't respond, instead pushing aside the debris covering the door, stepping carelessly on rubble that didn't bear examining too closely. A light started from his hand, played over a wide space, a countertop too solidly attached to move easily. He went behind, put both elbows on it, then leaned his head into his hands.

Dave ran his own light around the devastation, hoping not to find anything more identifiable than ripped plastic sheeting. He coughed in the dust. Beside him, Annette suddenly spoke: "Even your rotted beer would go good about now, Sammie."

No one moved, as if the simple comment had been set loose to run over the room, checking size and shape, measuring for tables and plumbing, and they must do nothing but watch.

"It's over." A growl. A warning.

"It's a great idea, Sammie," Dave dared.

"Think so?" Sammie roared, lifting a face distorted with anguish and grief. "Mebbe I'm not innerested in any more ideas."

Annette didn't back away. "You know what your place was for us on Thromberg. That's why you kept it open. Well, we need something like that here—as much as we need coms and hydroponics—something to help make this our home."

"Do you think the Earthers want us to have one?" Hard and bitter. "Do you really think they want anything to do with us, once we've cleared the bodies and done their dirty work?"

Dave felt himself gently pushed to one side as Linda stepped up to the counter. The Earther stared at Sammie a long moment, then slammed down her hand. When she lifted it again, there was a 'dib lying there, reflecting light.

"Yes," was all she said.

Titan University Archives
Public Access
Reference: Post-Quill Era; Station Self-Government

. . . Among the leading destinations for travelers of this era were the newly independent stations, beginning with Thromberg and Hamilton. These cities in space not only hosted immigrants en route to the new colonies and tourists eager to experience deep space, but also became thriving communities in their own right, attracting commerce through their advantages of location, a skilled and motivated labor force, and abundant energy resources. Governor Pavel Romanov, of Hamilton Station, is credited with being the first extra-Solar politician to obtain contracts limiting involvement in station internal affairs by the System Universities and TerraCor, agreements signed, legend insists, in a bar called Sammie's. . . .

FOLLOW THE SKY

by Pamela Sargent

Pamela Sargent has won the Nebula Award, the Locus Award, and has been a finalist for the Hugo Award. She is the author of several highly-praised novels, among them Cloned Lives *(1976),* The Golden Space, *(1979),* The Alien Upstairs *(1983), and* Alien Child *(1988).* The Washington Post Book World *has called her "one of the genre's best writers."*

Sargent is also the author of Ruler of the Sky *(1993), an epic historical novel about Genghis Khan. Her* Climb the Wind: A Novel of Another America *published in 1999, was a finalist for the Sidewise Award for Alternate History.* Child of Venus, *in Sargent's Venus trilogy, called "masterful" by* Publishers Weekly, *came out in 2001. Her latest short story collection is* The Mountain Cage and Other Stories.

ALONZA'S earliest memory of her mother was also her last.

They crouched together in a shadowed space near a wall, Alonza and her mother Amparo, looking out at a brightly lighted corridor filled with people. Men and women hurried past them, a few chattering at the people nearest them, others striding along without speaking while staring straight ahead. On the other side of the corridor, holo images of meat pies, pastries, fruits, flatbreads, and colorful bottles appeared over the heads of the passersby, hung there for a few seconds, then vanished. Occasionally, a hovercar filled with people floated past, scattering the crowds with a sharp whistling sound.

Amparo clutched a small satchel. Her hand trembled slightly as she handed her daughter a bracelet. "Listen to me," she whispered to Alonza, leaning closer. "Hang on to that bracelet for now—don't drop it."

Alonza tried to put the bracelet on, but there was no clasp, and she was unable to bend the thin band of metal tightly enough to secure it around her wrist. "It won't stay on," she said.

"It doesn't have to go on. Put it in your pocket—just make sure you hang on to it until—"

"Amparo," Alonza said, suddenly afraid. Her mother's forehead glistened with sweat, and she was panting, gasping for air. Maybe she was ill. Alonza thrust the bracelet into one of the side pockets of her tunic.

"Listen to me, child," Amparo said. "Go down this corridor, and look for a bin. Make sure no one sees you when you ditch the bracelet, then keep walking. When you get tired, sit down somewhere and act like you're waiting for somebody. I'll find you later. Got that?"

Alonza nodded.

"Then go." Amparo pushed her toward the stream of people.

Alonza darted among the forest of trousered legs, and was almost struck in the face by an arm swinging a small bag. There was no clear path through the throng. She slowed her pace, but kept going, breaking into a sprint whenever a space opened up, then slowing down again.

Amparo had sent her after the woman whose satchel they had taken. Alonza had gone up to the woman to distract her while Amparo got ready to grab the stranger's bag, but this time something had gone wrong. Amparo had moved too quickly, knocking the woman to the floor. The woman had tried to get up and had struck Amparo in the knee, and then Amparo hit her over the head with the pouch full of small stones and pebbles she usually carried in case she had to stun somebody from behind with a quick blow. Alonza remembered her mother standing over the woman's still body, looking angry and then frightened.

Sometimes Amparo just grabbed a duffel or a bag from her target right away. Sometimes she waited nearby while

Alonza pleaded with the mark for directions to a gateway or whimpered that she was lost and couldn't find her mother, and then Amparo swiped the bag while her mark was still talking to Alonza. Once in a while, Amparo was able to back someone into a corner and threaten her victim into giving up an identity bracelet and personal code before knocking the mark out with a drug implant slapped against an arm. That kind of job was riskier, but often more rewarding.

"Always pick somebody smaller than you who looks nervous and afraid," Amparo had explained to a couple of her younger friends who were visiting a few nights ago. "Best luck I've had is with students who look like it's their first time away from home, or with old people. They're so scared of getting hurt that they'll give you their codes as soon as you ask."

Alonza thought of the time when her mother had come back to their room with three necklaces and two jackets bought with the credit and codes of a stolen identity bracelet. Usually Amparo might be able to make one or two purchases before a victim came to and reported a bracelet stolen, but there had been more loot that time. Amparo had been in the middle of her sixth transaction when she had seen that funny look in the merchant's eyes that told her that her stolen credit was now blocked and that a security guard was on the way.

Always know when to run: Amparo had often told her that.

She had gone far enough by now. Alonza looked back; she could no longer see the place where she and her mother had been. There was a recycling bin to her right, but too many people were loitering near the shiny metal receptacle. She turned away and kept going until the corridor branched into two more long gated hallways. People were lining up at the gates for the suborb flights.

At last she came to a stretch of gates and waiting areas that were nearly empty of people. She hurried to the nearest bin and dropped the stolen bracelet into a slot, then continued down the long lighted passageway. Her feet were beginning to hurt. Amparo had traded a stolen belt for the shoes, which were made of synthaleather, but the leather had molded itself to its former owner's feet and had never fit Alonza's very well.

She was far enough away from the bin now. Alonza moved toward one of the empty waiting areas and sat down on one of the smaller cushions, wondering how long it would take Amparo to find her.

"Stay in one place," Amparo had always told her, "and sooner or later I'll find you." Alonza sat there, listening to the announcements in Anglaic, Arabic, Español, and other languages. "Twelve-twenty suborb to Toronto, gate fifty-two, now boarding." "Two zero five, suborb to Damascus, gate forty-seven, now boarding." "Sixteen thirty-one, shuttle flight to the Wheel, leaving at thirteen-oh-two from gate ninety-five."

The Wheel! Alonza thought of the space station high above the Earth and was soon lost in a familiar daydream. Someday, when she was older, she would board one of the shuttles and travel to the Wheel herself, to wander its curved corridors and loiter in its lounges before boarding a torchship to another place, maybe Luna or the Islands of Venus. Her daydream was formed mostly of images and experiences drawn from a mind-tour called "Journey to the Wheel," one of the mind-tours anyone was free to call up without having to spend credit, even people like her and her mother who had to live on Basic and steal anything else they needed. Most of the free mind-tours she had seen bored her; either they were designed to teach some sort of skill like homeostat repair or else they were filled with action scenes that tired her out and were often hard to remember later.

But "Journey to the Wheel" was different. It kept her interested even when there wasn't really that much going on, when she was feeling and seeing what it was like to travel in a shuttle, floating weightlessly up against the harness that held her to her seat while viewing the distant pale circular tube with spokes that was the Wheel. The end of the mind-tour always left her with a tired but happy feeling of expectation, of feeling that something wonderful was about to happen to her.

Maybe people who went to other places, who didn't just do their traveling with bands around their heads so that the cybers could feed them a mind-tour's images and sensations, had that kind of happy feeling all the time. She imagined leaving the room she shared with Amparo and never having to return to the maze of apartment buildings, cubicles, and shacks where the homeostats rarely worked and the air was always too hot and smelled of sand and dust. Maybe—

"Going to Shanghai, child?" a woman's voice said in Anglaic.

Alonza looked up. A woman with short dark hair and a kindly smile was gazing down at her.

"No," she replied hastily.

"But this is the waiting area for that suborb flight."

"I'm waiting for my mother," Alonza said. "She told me to wait here." She glanced down at her hands and saw, too late, that she had forgotten to pull the long sleeves of her tunic over her wrists. The woman would notice that she was not wearing an identity bracelet. But the stranger did not look down at her hands, but instead continued to stare at Alonza's face.

"I see," the woman said.

"She didn't want me to get lost," Alonza added.

"Of course. Well . . ." The woman turned away and sat down on a cushion near the wall.

Alonza waited as more people entered the lounge and settled themselves on the cushions around her. Among them were two Linkers, dressed in long white formal robes and kaffiyehs, each with the diamondlike gem on his forehead that marked him as one of the few who had a direct Link to Earth's cyberminds; the two men sat together, and those making their way past them nodded respectfully in their direction. A few of the people were eating small rolls and pieces of fruit, and drinking from small bottles; Alonza, feeling very hungry, wondered if she could risk begging or stealing some food. Nearly every seat was taken by the time she started worrying about Amparo.

Her mother should have been here by now, Alonza thought. Soon all these people would begin to board the sub-orb, and somebody else would wonder what she was doing here. Already a gray-haired man was watching her with a puzzled look on his face, while a guide wearing dark blue overalls and a badge hanging over his chest had come by a couple of times already, slowing down to glance at her both times.

A space in the back wall opened. A man came through the opening and stepped to a counter as the doorway behind him closed. He wore a dark blue shirt; like the guide, he had a badge that said "Port of San Antonio" on the top and "Nueva Republica de Texas" on the bottom. Alonza knew how to read a little, and she had seen those words often enough to recognize them immediately.

The man peered at the screen of his console, apparently checking the passenger list. That meant that everyone here would be lining up in a few minutes, having their bracelets scanned and their identities and credit confirmed, and then heading for the doorway that led to the field outside.

She was suddenly frightened, afraid to move from her cushion. Then she saw the guide walking toward her with another man at his side, a tall thin pale-haired man in the black uniform of a Guardian, with a stun wand hanging from his belt.

"Is your name Alonza Lemaris?" the man in the Guardian uniform asked.

She nodded. If he knew her name, it meant that her mother had been caught.

"Come with me," the man said.

They took her to a small room. The guide left them there alone, and the Guardian asked her a lot of questions, keeping his hand around his wand the whole time, but terrified as she was, she knew that Amparo would want her to say as little as possible. "I'm waiting for my mother. She told me to wait there for her. She told me not to get lost." She kept saying the same thing over and over and at last the Guardian stopped pacing and sat down in front of her.

"Listen to me, you little bitch," he said angrily. "We've already got your mother on assault, credit theft, and ident theft. If we put her to the question, we can probably get a lot more out of her, but she wouldn't be the same afterward, and you're the only one who can stop us from doing that kind of damage to her. So you can begin telling me about what kinds of things she's been up to, and we'll find some work for her to do while she's serving her sentence that won't be too hard on her, or else we can start interrogating her until she breaks down and confesses. She won't be of much use to anybody after that. Some people get so messed up in their minds afterward that they end up killing themselves."

"I want to see her," Alonza said softly.

"You won't see her until after she's finished her time, and that's going to be long from now. Get this through your head—you'll probably never see her again. The only favor you can do for her now is to tell me exactly what she's done, what you've seen her do, what you've done together."

Amparo had always been terrified of getting caught, of being interrogated by Guardians. They would put a band on your head, her mother had told her, one of the slender silver ones like the ones people used to access a mind-tour, and then they would dig into your mind, force you to confess, find all kinds of ways to hurt you and make you scream in pain until you told them the truth. That was why it was so important never to get caught; better to be dead than in the custody of Guardians preparing to question you.

"She didn't do anything," Alonza insisted, staring at the gold lieutenant's bars on the man's shoulders. "She told me to wait for her, that's all."

The Guardian stood up and slapped her in the face. The blow shocked her more than it hurt her. "You're a stubborn one," he muttered, sounding almost pleased. "I guess we'll let you visit with your mother after all."

He led her out of the room, gripping her arm tightly. A hovercar with another Guardian was waiting for them. They rode through the hallways of the port to another room, where two more Guardians were waiting with Amparo.

Her mother was bound to a chair. A console with a screen sat in front of her. "I didn't say anything," Alonza cried out, trying to free herself from the man holding her arm, but Amparo did not seem to hear her. Then one of the men in the room stepped toward Amparo and held out a circular silver headband.

Amparo screamed. Her scream was so sharp and piercing that Alonza froze.

"Tell them!" her mother shrieked. "Tell them anything they want to know!"

Alonza told the Guardians about the woman and how Amparo had struck her and where she had ditched the bracelet they had stolen from her. The men asked her more questions about other marks they had taken things from, and Amparo, who was sobbing by then, told Alonza to answer those questions, too. When Alonza had finished telling the Guardians about what they had stolen over the past months and how they had obtained the goods, the pale-haired Guardian told her that her mother would be doing useful labor for the Nomarchies of Earth while serving out her sentence. They did not say anything about a hearing, how long a sentence Amparo would get, or how unpleasant the useful labor would be.

"What about my daughter?" Amparo asked hoarsely.

"That's none of your business, woman. We'll take care of her. She'll be a lot better off than she was with you. She'll be a better citizen of her Nomarchy when she grows up, and by then she'll forget about you."

The Guardian had been right. Alonza had been cared for afterward, and supposed that she had grown up to be a better citizen than she would have been otherwise.

Her memory of her mother grew fainter over time. In the first years after her mother's arrest, while she was still living in the children's dormitory, Alonza had occasionally tried to find out where Amparo was being held, but the cyberminds always blocked those channels so that she could not get an answer, and then the teaching image on her screen would order her to get back to her lessons. After a while, she stopped asking about Amparo. When she was older, after the officers in charge of the dormitory had decided that she and a few of her friends showed enough promise to be sent to a school for more lessons in academic subjects instead of being trained for satellite repair, she rarely thought of her mother.

The pale-haired Guardian had been right when he told her that she would be better off in the dormitory than with Amparo. There had been the opportunity for schooling, and since the Guardians often recruited from the children housed in the dorms while their parents served time, she had eventually been trained at an officers' academy for the important work of being one of the protectors of Earth's biosphere and its peace. Had she remained with her mother, she would have grown up to be another one like her, a mosquito as they were called in their crowded neighborhood near the port, one of those who lived by stinging any unwary travelers passing through San Antonio. Had she stayed with Amparo, she would never have made it to the Wheel, certainly not as an officer and as an aide to Colonel Jonas Sansom, the commander of the Guardian detachment at the Wheel, and also the pale-haired Guardian officer who had detained her at the San Antonio port so many years ago.

Alonza Lemaris stood in the small waiting area just beyond the shuttle dock's bay. Another group had just arrived, passengers from Earth bound for Venus. Most of the people coming to the Wheel could be left to find their own way to the lounges and bays in the hub where they would wait to board their freighters or passenger vessels, but this group of travelers, who came from a camp outside Tashkent, were an exception.

Guardians were stationed at that camp to keep order, and Guardians traveled with any settlers who left the camp on the shuttle flights to the Wheel. Usually Alonza or one of the other officers met the new arrivals and ushered them to a bay near the dock holding the Habber ship that was to take them on the next leg of their journey to Anwara, the vast space station that circled Earth's sister planet, but that was not why she had come here this time.

Settlers, Alonza thought; traitors to Earth was what many would call them. She had nothing against the scientists and specialists and workers who were trained for the terraforming Venus Project, who had been chosen to go there and who had proved their worth. But the people from the camp outside Tashkent were another matter. They abandoned their homes and their work and even gave up all of their credit, to go to the camp and wait for passage until a few more workers might be needed inside the domed settlements that were being raised on the still inhospitable surface of Venus. They were, most of them, malcontents willing to leave their own Nomarchies to gamble on getting a chance at making a new world and a new life for themselves. Maybe the Project needed such people, and perhaps the Council of Mukhtars that governed Earth's Nomarchies had been wise to allow such camps as a social safety valve, but Guardians had to keep order in the camps, and Alonza considered that a waste of their resources.

A door opened and a Guardian pilot in a black uniform entered the waiting area, followed by a man and a woman who wore pins of silver circles on their blue tunics, pins that such people were required to wear in Earthspace so that anyone seeing them would know at a glance what they were. Alonza looked away from the pair as the pilot saluted her.

"Major Lemaris," he said, "how good of you to greet me. Congratulations on your recent promotion. I hear that it's well deserved."

"Thank you, Lieutenant." Looking up at him, Alonza wondered if the man was only being polite or trying to suck up to her in the hope of gaining some future favor. Hard to tell, but it did him no harm either way.

"As soon as our charges are off the shuttlecraft, my crew and I will speed them on their way to their ship," the man continued.

"I came here," Alonza said, "to tell you that their trip has to be delayed. Your passengers will have to stay here, so get them into the lift and shoot them through the spoke to Level B and the lounge next to the assistant director's office. We'll keep them under guard there until we can allow them to board their transport."

"There's thirty of them," the pilot said. He glared at the man and woman with the silver pins, as if they were to blame for the delay. "Might be kind of crowded."

"They shouldn't be there for more than ten to twenty hours," Alonza murmured, "thirty at most. They're from a camp, so they know hardship."

The pilot shrugged.

"Warn them that it'll be close to a g there," she went on, "not the half-g they've got here in the hub."

"I assume that we at least will be able to stay aboard our ship until our departure, since I know the Wheel's space is limited." The man in the blue tunic had spoken; he was a small man, barely taller than Alonza, with short dark hair and brown almond-shaped eyes. His companion, a short dark-eyed woman with a cap of thick black hair, stared past Alonza, avoiding her gaze.

"Unfortunately, you can't go aboard," Alonza replied, "because a few components in the dock have to be replaced before it's safe to ferry anybody to your ship."

The man frowned, looking as though he did not believe her, not that it mattered whether he did or not. He and his companion were Habitat-dwellers, or Habbers as they were derisively called. Their ancestors had abandoned Earth centuries ago for the Associated Habitats, the homes they had made for themselves in space, and there were many who believed that, despite their appearance, the Habbers were no longer truly human, that their genetic engineering had far surpassed what Earth allowed among its people. Habbers might have their uses; some of them worked with the scientists and specialists of the Venus Project, and having them ferry settlers from the camps to Venus was certainly a convenience. Changing the orbits of a few asteroids so that they would come nearer to Earth and could be more easily mined had been another service of the Habbers to the home world.

Alonza could grant all of that, but loathed the air of superiority that Habbers exuded, as if the resources they provided and the necessary tasks they voluntarily undertook for Earth's benefit were little more than crumbs thrown to beggars. She thought then of how the home world must seem to Habbers, with its flooded coastlines, melting ice caps, and an atmosphere that was still too thick with carbon dioxide six centuries after the Resource Wars. They probably thought of themselves as fortunate for having abandoned what they must see as a played-out world populated by deluded die-hards. Even these two Habber pilots had that look of superiority in their eyes, the calm steady gaze of people who seemed to lack any turbulent and upsetting emotions.

"Where are we to stay, then?" the female Habber asked.

The woman probably expected to have to stay in the lounge with all the passengers going to Venus. Alonza was silent for a moment, then said, "We want you to be comfortable. I believe that our agreement with the Associated Habitats also requires us not to inflict any unnecessary discomfort on any of you. So we've found a room for you in our officers' quarters. You'll have to share it, but there are two beds, and a public lavatory just down the corridor."

"That's very kind of you," the male Habber said, and she heard a note of sarcasm in his voice. Being sarcastic was uncharacteristic of such cool and rational types as Habbers, but then this Habber and his companion were not like others of their kind.

After getting their thirty Venus-bound passengers out of the lift and settled in the lounge, Alonza led the two Habbers to their room, which was just three doors from her own quarters. In the three years since she had been assigned here, she had grown used to the gently curving and brightly lit corridors, to the gravitylike acceleration, only slightly weaker than Earth's, that was imparted by the Wheel's rotation around its hub, to the pilots and passengers passing endlessly through this station. Every twenty-four-hour period brought the promise of something new—of an unusually interesting traveler, official visitors, a new detachment of Guardians with intriguing tales of a Nomarchy she did not know that much about, the possibility of a mission that might take her to the L-5 spaceport, to one of the industrial, recreational, and military satellites that orbited Earth, or even to Luna. Her post here often imparted a heightened sense of expectation, of feeling that she was on a journey that would never end. It was as if she were somehow picking up that feeling of anticipation from all of those who passed through the Wheel on their way to other places.

"Your room," Alonza said to the two Habbers as she pressed the door open for them. They entered a small room bare of furnishings except for a small wall screen and two cushions in front of two low shelves. "You pull the beds out from the wall." She demonstrated by pressing a panel and pulling out the lower bunk. "And the lavatory's four doors down to your right. I hope everything's satisfactory, but if there's anything else you need, do let me know."

"We're most appreciative," the male Habber said.

"I'd be most grateful if you would both be my guests at supper in two hours," Alonza continued. She thought of asking Tom Ruden-Nodell, the physician in charge of the Wheel's infirmary and the closest friend she had here, to join them, but decided against it. She would get more of a sense of these two by herself.

The Habbers glanced at each other, apparently surprised by her offer of hospitality. "We're a bit tired," the man said. "Perhaps another time—"

"Tired? I didn't think Habitat-dwellers were as subject to our frailties. Three hours, then? That should give you time to rest. I look forward to seeing you then. I'll send a Guardian to fetch you." Alonza turned and left the room before the man could object again.

"Detain the operative," Colonel Sansom had said in his message, sent to her over a confidential channel. Alonza had seen the woman's file, stored under the name she was using. This was a matter Colonel Sansom should have handled himself, but he had left suddenly to go to an asteroid tracking station two days ago, to supervise repairs after a micrometeorite strike had damaged three telescopes, and would not get back to the Wheel for another thirty hours at least. A more easygoing officer might have sent a subordinate to the station, but not the obsessively conscientious Jonas Sansom. Tracking the orbits of asteroids that might threaten Earth was one of the most important duties of Guardians, perhaps the most important. Colonel Sansom would report to his superiors that he had seen to this task personally.

"Just get her away from the others," Sansom continued, "and into custody as quietly as possible, that's all. Best if you can handle it by yourself without bringing anybody else into it, so use your judgment."

That was all. That was more than enough. Alonza was flattered that he trusted her with this task. She must not fail him.

According to the file on her screen, the operative was using the name of Sameh Tryolla. She had supposedly grown up in the Eastern Mediterranean Nomarchy, attended and then been asked to leave the University of Vancouver in the Pacific Federation for not doing well at her studies in physics, and after that had decided to leave her work as a laboratory assistant in Ankara to go to the camp outside Tashkent. Probably everything in her file was an invention. The image of Sameh Tryolla showed a slim, young olive-skinned woman with long dark-brown hair and large hazel eyes; she looked frail, and hardly more than a girl.

The woman was to be detained, according to Colonel Sansom, because the Guardian Commanders who advised the Council of Mukhtars had abruptly decided to abort her mission. Alonza was to detain her as unobtrusively as possible and hold her until the colonel returned to the Wheel, after which he would take charge of the matter.

Her task seemed simple enough, but there were all kinds

of possible complications in carrying it out. Perhaps this Sameh had friends among those traveling with her who might object to seeing her led away without a good excuse. Maybe the Habber pilots who were to take Sameh and the others from the camp to Venus would argue that, since she was technically in their custody until she arrived in Anwara, the Guardians had no right to keep her at the Wheel. Perhaps Sameh would demand a public hearing, claiming that the Guardian force at the Wheel was violating the implicit agreement that had been made with her by allowing her passage from Earth to Venus.

Nothing would prevent her superiors from doing whatever they wanted with Sameh in the end, but any of these possibilities would draw too much attention to the operative. The Guardian officers close to the Council of Mukhtars wanted no attention drawn to their covert activities. Better for the secret service of the Mukhtars' personal guard to be no more than the subject of unverifiable rumors, to have even the existence of such a secret service doubted by most of Earth's citizens.

Alonza closed the file on Sameh Tryolla and secured it, knowing that she would not have to retrieve it again. The whole business had bothered her from the first, and even though Colonel Sansom had not betrayed any uneasiness, she suspected that he was equally puzzled by their orders. Why not find some way to get word to the woman about the change in plans instead of confining her on the Wheel? Why take the risk of calling attention to her by detaining her? For that matter, why not put her out of the way permanently, making her death look like an accident? Why hadn't she been stopped before she got to the Wheel?

Asking such questions, though, was not part of her assignment; nor was wondering what Sameh Tryolla's mission might have been. The Council of Mukhtars had many ways of monitoring the progress of the Venus Project and the loyalty of the Cytherians, as the people who lived in the surface settlements and on the domed Islands that floated in Venus' thin upper atmosphere preferred to call themselves. Alonza had always assumed that one of the Mukhtars' methods was to plant a few spies among the settlers. She hoped that this was all the Council was doing, that the spies were no more than informers alerting Earth's rulers of possible difficulties and dissatisfactions that might require their attention.

Irrationally, something inside her insisted upon hoping that Venus might become a place where people could win more for themselves than they were allowed on Earth, that the Cytherians would make something new, that the machinations of the Mukhtars would not dampen their dreams. She had picked up such sentiments from others who had come to the Wheel, the scientists and workers and others who looked forward to the work of terraforming, even knowing that they would never live to see the results of their labors and could only hope that their distant descendants might live on the green and growing world they would create. The terraforming of Venus would redeem Earth and provide a new Earthlike planet for its people. Far in the future, the technology used to transform Venus might even be used to heal humankind's wounded home world.

Not that Alonza would let such passing thoughts interfere with her duty.

She thought of her own arrival at the Wheel, when Colonel Sansom had welcomed her to her post with a dinner in the officers' mess. "I thought you might have the makings of a Guardian," he had told her, "even back in San Antonio. You wouldn't talk, even with all the scary tales you'd surely been told about Guardian interrogations, not until we took you to your mother and she begged you to talk. First you demonstrated your loyalty, and then you showed your good sense. Adjusting well to the dorms and doing well at your assigned studies only confirmed my original judgment."

That she had never asked the Guardians about her mother had likely been another point in her favor. She had learned to control her curiosity, to live with knowing that many of her questions would never be answered and that any answers, if she somehow found them, would only bring her trouble.

* * *

Alonza did not suppose that she would learn much, if anything, about Sameh Tryolla from the two Habber pilots. The woman was only another one of their passengers; it was unlikely that they had exchanged even a few words with her. But she had to know if they might pose an obstacle to her assignment.

She met them at the entrance to the officers' mess and led them to their table. Most of the low tables were in the common area, open to all officers and their guests, but Alonza and the Habbers would dine in the smaller adjoining room where Colonel Sansom often entertained visiting Linkers and other dignitaries. She wanted some privacy, so that the Habbers would feel freer to talk.

Keir Renin, the Guardian officer in charge of the camp outside Tashkent, had sent her a confidential message about the two Habbers. The woman went only by the name of Te-yu, not unusual since it was the custom among Habbers to use just one name, but her full name was Hong Te-yu. The man was known as Benzi and also had the surname of Liangharad. This was the third time that the two were ferrying people from the camp to Venus, and Keir Renin had been given the distinct impression by Te-yu and Benzi that this would be the pair's last such journey.

What was unusual about these two was that they had not been born and reared in a Habitat. They had close kinfolk on Earth and also among the Cytherians, and had grown up on one of the Venusian Islands. But being given a stake in the Venus Project had not been enough for Te-yu and Benzi, who with several other conspirators had seized control of a shuttlecraft to flee to a Hab not far from Venus.

Few took the risks of fleeing to any of the Habitats and asking for refuge, and some had died in the attempt. Capture meant imprisonment and a forever restricted existence; other failed attempts had ended in death aboard space vessels too limited in range to reach a Habitat. Alonza had never heard of any successful refugees returning to Earth or to the regions of space controlled by the Council of Mukhtars. She wondered why these two had done so, whether they now regretted the choice they had made, if there was some way she might be able to use them.

The two Habbers sat down across from her on their cushions. Alonza folded her legs in front of her, under the table, then studied the pocket screen on the tabletop.

"Do you have any particular preferences?" Alonza asked her guests. "With people coming through here from so many different regions, we have more variety in our cuisine than you might expect."

The woman named Te-yu shrugged.

"Please feel free to order for both of us, Major Lemaris," her companion Benzi murmured. He smiled slightly. "No doubt you know what's best."

Alonza thought she detected amusement in his smile, a hint of sarcasm in his tone. She found herself suddenly disliking him intensely, then let that feeling go. "We'll start with chili bean soup," she said, "and then some fish in a cucumber and dill sauce with rice for the main course. The fish is from one of our protein vats, of course, but it tastes almost exactly like salmon. We'll end the meal with a few fruit pastries."

"Sounds delicious," Benzi said.

"And we can offer you a selection of coffees, herbal teas, and fruit juices." The officers' mess served no alcohol, in deference to the Islamic faith of Earth's dominant Nomarchies and also to keep discipline among the Guardians and the Wheel's other personnel, although occasionally the pilots or crew members of a freighter could be bribed into surrendering a few bottles of a cargo.

"We'll have whatever you're having," Benzi said.

Alonza touched her screen to order the meal, finding their acquiescence annoying.

Te-yu's face was composed, and her dark eyes stared past Alonza. In common with the Linkers of Earth, Habbers had Links that connected them directly to their cyberminds; they could call up any data they might need from their artificial intelligences without using the slender silver headbands most people had to wear in order to open those channels.

The Council of Mukhtars restricted direct Links to only a few, to the scientists, specialists, Guardian Commanders, and prominent advisers to the Council who had been trained to use the Links and who had access to channels that were closed to other people. But Habbers, it was said, were all Linked, all equal in their access to their cyberminds. Perhaps Te-yu was diverting herself with some data stream or other, or picking up a message from a friend; that might account for the vacant look on her face.

How insulting of her, Alonza thought; it was as rude as coming to dinner, whipping out a pocket screen, and playing a game instead of conversing with one's companions. "I'm told that you have close kinfolk on Earth," she said aloud, wanting to get that out of the way.

"Yes," Benzi said, "and on Venus as well."

"And do you sometimes miss what you left behind?" Alonza asked.

"You're asking if that is why I volunteered to ferry people from that camp to Venus?" Benzi drew his brows together. "Maybe so. I haven't really examined my possible motivations."

An orderly came into the small room with a tray, set down the cups of juice, then left. Having people handle such simple tasks on the Wheel was cheaper than the trouble and expense of maintaining the servos and other mechanisms that performed such jobs elsewhere. Whatever Earth might lack in other resources, it had no shortage of people.

"You might have been taking a risk," Alonza said, "even with our agreements. Ways might have been found to keep you both on Earth without violating any treaties."

Te-yu's eyes focused on her. Alonza finally had her attention. Benzi sipped some juice, then set his cup down. "We thought that most unlikely," he said.

"But still possible."

"Just barely." He frowned for a moment, then drank more juice. She wanted him a bit apprehensive; that would make him and his companion less likely to interfere with her task.

* * *

They got through the meal while saying little of any significance. Benzi and Alonza exchanged opinions on the very few mind-tours and virtual concerts they had both experienced. The dinner, better than Benzi had clearly expected, inspired them both to discuss some of their favorite foods. Alonza mentioned in passing that she had been born in San Antonio, and Benzi said that although he had grown up on one of Venus' Islands, he had been born in a small town on the North American Plains. Te-yu said almost nothing at all.

Alonza walked the two Habbers back to their room, then hurried to the nearest lift. The door slid shut silently; the cage hummed softly around her until the door opened and she knew that she had arrived at the Wheel's hub.

Alonza welcomed the half-g of the hub, where all the docks were located. She came here often, to look at the ships and imagine herself on an endless journey aboard one; such musings were one of her few indulgences.

She entered the bay area, empty except for two technicians checking some readings, and went to the viewscreen. Often Tom Ruden-Nodell joined her here after a shift of duty at the infirmary, partly because the half-g eased his minor aches and pains. He was another one like her, according to his public record, someone who had been a child living on Basic and what he could scrounge for himself until he caught the eye of a benefactor who, impressed by his quickness and intelligence, had taken him away from his negligent parents and found him a place in a dormitory.

But they never spoke of the past. They sat in the bay and speculated about the travelers who passed through the Wheel and exchanged the stories they had each gleaned from them. There were workers in gray tunics and pants with tales of repairing seawalls and dikes near the flooded cities of New York, Melbourne, or Corpus Christi; Linkers in white robes with gossip about the sexual affairs of those close to the Council of Mukhtars; students and young scientists with stories of their future ambitions told with a mixture of youthful arrogance and insecurity. While listening to them, Alonza often thought of how far she had come from the wretched shantytown of people on Basic that nestled near San Antonio's port.

"I might put in for a change," Tom had told her the last time they were here in the hub. "I'm thinking of making a move to Luna. They'll need another physician there sooner or later, and there'd be the astronomers and other researchers to exchange ideas with and the engineers and miners to drink with. And one-sixth gravity might be just the thing for my old bones." She had noticed the deep lines around his eyes then, the graying hair, the weariness his slouch betrayed.

"You're not that old, Tom," she said.

"I am that old, Alonza," and he was right; he was eighty, and could expect another thirty or forty years if his rejuvenation therapy worked as it did for most people, but there were always exceptions, and Tom was already showing many of the signs of age. "Might not be a bad place for a Guardian officer to be posted either," he added.

"And why is that?"

"Because there isn't much to do except keep order and look out for people's safety and maybe round up a few miners and workers when they get a little rowdy."

"There wouldn't be much chance for a promotion, though."

"And not much chance of running afoul of ambitious officers either." Tom had smiled to himself then, and for a moment Alonza had envied the physician the relatively peaceful life he had won for himself.

More docks had been added to the Wheel in recent years, and now there were fifteen of them filled with the metal slugs of freighters and dull gray torchships; other docks held the shuttles that traveled to and from Earth and Luna. The Habber vessel was unlike the other torchships; it was a slender spire of silver attached to the vast globe that housed its engines. Its passengers would board the vessel, perhaps expecting the diversions that other passenger ships offered, only to find out that they would be in suspension during the entire journey. The Habbers claimed that this was a more efficient way of transporting their passengers, that to have them safely stored in sleepers was more comfortable for them, given the high acceleration of their faster ships, but Alonza also suspected that the Habbers did not want anyone else poking around inside their vessels and maybe finding out more about them.

Alonza moved closer to the viewscreen. Outside the hub, two suited and helmeted figures crawled along the lattice-work of the dock that held the Habber ship. They had surely noticed by now that the components did not really need to be replaced this soon, according to the readings, but they were well-disciplined Guardian technicians and had not questioned their orders.

Alonza slapped the comm next to the screen. "How's it going, Starling?"

"I've got two more components to go, Major," the voice of Darlanna Starling replied. "Richi's got three."

"Estimate?"

"Two more hours, maybe three."

"Both of you better come inside for a break, Starling. That's an order. When you get too tired, accidents can happen."

"Yes, ma'am."

"Get some food into you, maybe a nap if you think you need it."

"Yes, ma'am."

That would give her some more time. Maybe she wouldn't need much more; maybe this whole business would move along faster than she expected. Go to the lounge where the Venus-bound passengers were waiting, give them some bureaucratic gab, get Sameh Tryolla away from the others on some excuse, and send the two Habbers on their way with their ship.

Doubt bit at her again. It didn't add up, the secrecy, holding the woman here, going to all this trouble. Alonza pushed those thoughts aside as she left the bay.

The people in the lounge seemed subdued. Some of them lay on the floor, their packs and duffels under their heads, while others sat on cushions. A few had helped themselves to cups of water from the wall dispenser and were drinking it listlessly. Perhaps they were still recovering from the weightless discomforts of the shuttle flight.

Sameh Tryolla was on one of the cushions, her back against the wall, looking even thinner and smaller than she had in her file image. She glanced toward Alonza, then looked away.

". . . showed them to the lavatories," the Guardian on Alonza's right murmured, "and they haven't given us any trouble. Might need to get fed soon, though."

"They don't have any credit to pay for their food," Alonza said. The hopeful settlers had been forced to give up all their credit after reaching the camp; it was one way to help cover the expense of housing them while they waited for passage. "Thirty or forty hours on nothing but water won't kill them," she went on, thinking of times in her early childhood when she had had even less than that.

"Yeah, but you don't want them to get weak, Major," the Guardian said, "or we might get stuck with them for even longer."

Alonza turned toward the young man. "You're quite right, Zaleski," she said as the threads of her plan came together in her mind. "In fact, that's why I'm here. I'm a little worried after the last message I got from Keir Renin."

The young Guardian looked puzzled.

"The officer in charge of the camp they came from," she continued in a softer voice. "He didn't say so outright, but he implied that the soldiers who gave them their med-scans might have been a bit sloppy."

Zaleski's blue eyes widened.

"Oh, I don't think we really have to worry," Alonza said hastily. "Renin's people would have caught anything virulent or potentially lethal. But as long as they're stuck here, it wouldn't hurt to scan them all again."

"Should I call for a couple of paramedics?" Zaleski turned toward the comm near the doorway.

"No," Alonza replied. "The head physician can handle

this." She could trust Tom, and Colonel Sansom had told her to use her own judgment. "I'll go to the infirmary and set things up with him."

"I could call him and—"

"I'd rather not have rumors going around about possibly contagious travelers being here."

The young Guardian nodded. "Of course, Major Lemaris."

Tom Ruden-Nodell listened as Alonza told him about the people she wanted scanned and gave him the name of the person she had been ordered to detain. "We'll bring her back here," she continued, "and hold her until Colonel Sansom gets back."

"And we're to do all this as quietly as possible," he said.

"Yes. We'll put her in one of the private rooms, and you can give her something to knock her out. I'll keep watch over her. It would be better not to involve any of the other medical personnel."

"Understood."

Tom had not asked her about why she was to hold the woman, and what Colonel Sansom wanted with her, but she had expected that. He was safer knowing as little as possible and not risking his usually placid and extremely secure existence.

They left his office together, the physician with a portable scanner under his arm. He said nothing to her during the short walk through the corridor to the lounge. As they entered the room, Zaleski and the three Guardians with him stepped aside and stood at attention.

"I have an announcement to make," Alonza said. The people sitting on cushions or on the floor looked toward her; those lying down stirred and sat up. "Since you have to wait here anyway until the dock's repaired, we've decided to give you all another med-scan." She heard groans, and a couple of men scowled. "Let me assure you that we expect to find nothing, given that you were all scanned before leaving your camp, but it doesn't hurt to be careful, and we've got the time for the extra caution."

"I'll tell you what you'll find out," a stocky blond man said in accented Anglaic. "We could all use some food. I vomited what little they gave me during that damned shuttle flight."

Alonza narrowed her eyes as she gripped the handle of the stun wand at her waist. "You won't be here that much longer. Now line up in front of the ID console and we'll get this done as quickly as we can." She turned to Tom as people cleared their throats, stretched, mumbled to one another, and slowly got to their feet.

The stocky blond man held out his braceleted wrist as the ID console's flat voice recited his name, age, and other particulars. He was scanned first, followed by two bearded fellows in worn brown tunics and baggy pants. Sameh Tryolla was near the back of the line; that was good. They could be done with this, get the operative secured, and send the Habbers and their human cargo on their way in two or three hours.

Tom circled each person with a med-scan wand, moved the wand up and down, stared at the readings on his portable screen for a bit, then gave a quick nod before scanning the next man or woman. The physician seemed his usual thorough self, and it occurred to Alonza then that he might actually find some sort of medical problem in one of these people that had not been caught earlier. The chances of that were vanishingly remote, but could complicate matters for her.

People held their arms out to the console, shuffled toward Tom, stood quietly as he waved his wand over them as though casting a spell, then moved toward the back of the room to lean against the wall and gaze sourly at Alonza and her Guardians.

When it was Sameh Tryolla's turn, a look of uneasiness flickered across her pretty face. The ID console gave her age as twenty, which agreed with the data Alonza had seen in her file, but she looked even younger than that.

Tom passed his wand over her, stared at his screen, rubbed his chin, and sighed. "Stand right over there, young woman," he said, gesturing in Alonza's direction.

"But why?" Sameh Tryolla asked in the high tiny voice of a child.

"Do as the doctor says," Alonza said. Sameh Tryolla came toward her and waited at her left as Tom finished scanning the last three people.

"All right," Tom said, "I'm done, and grateful for your cooperation. Now I better start by saying that nobody here has anything to worry about, but it looks like I'll have to do a more thorough scan of young Sameh Tryolla here."

Alonza saw the young woman raise her brows, as if startled, and yet she did not seem that surprised somehow. Her body had not tensed; if anything, she seemed almost relaxed. In her position, Alonza thought, I'd be wondering what's going on, why I was being singled out, if somebody had found out what I really was. At the very least I'd be worrying about whether or not I actually did have some kind of unexpected and mysterious medical problem.

"There's nothing the matter with me," Sameh Tryolla said in her little girl's voice.

"Now I'm just about certain that's true," Tom said reassuringly, "and a complete workup in the infirmary will probably bear that out, but we can't be too careful. Scan here shows that you've got some kind of bacterium in your system that the med-scan program can't identify. I don't want you worrying, because people carry all kinds of bacteria as a normal thing, but we just want—"

"You don't have to explain it to me," Sameh said in a softer but steelier voice.

Tom nodded. "We'll just isolate it and make sure—"

"I understand." Sameh bowed her head, looking like a child again.

"And what about the rest of us?" the blond man called out. He seemed to have made himself the spokesman for his companions. "What are we supposed to do, wait around here until he runs all his tests on her?"

Alonza stared at him; he glared back. She kept her eyes on him until he finally looked down, then said, "I checked on how the repairs were going just a short time ago, and by now the components have probably been replaced. As soon as I verify that, we'll get all of you aboard the Habber ship as quickly as we can. If this woman here is cleared by then, as the doctor expects, she'll join you, and if not, you'll be on your way without her."

She waited for somebody in the group to object, to ask what would happen to Sameh Tryolla after that, but no one did. They probably assumed that she would be sent back to the camp, or maybe given some job on the Wheel to earn her keep until another ship arrived to carry former camp inmates to Venus. As Alonza studied their indifferent and bored faces, she realized that nobody here particularly cared what happened to her. Just as well, she thought, since it made her task easier.

"I have to get my pack," Sameh Tryolla whispered, at last sounding worried.

"Get it, then," Alonza said. The woman went to the back of the room, picked up a duffel, and slipped the strap over her shoulder. Alonza pressed her hand against the comm next to the door. "Lemaris to Starling."

"Starling here," the voice of Darlanna Starling replied.

"How are those repairs coming along?"

"We'll be done in a hour, Major."

"Good. We'll get the passengers ready to board." She turned to the men at her side. "Zaleski, go fetch our two Habber guests. Achmed and Jeyaraj, get all these people to the hub. I'll let you know if this woman will be joining them or not by the time they're ready to leave."

"Yes, ma'am."

Sameh was silent during the walk to the infirmary. Tom would stall for a while, doing another med-scan and taking his samples, and then Alonza would give the young woman the word. "You won't be going to Venus; I have to detain you. Those are my orders. No, I don't know why; all they told me was to hold you until my commanding officer returns." Maybe it would be better to simply put her under restraint without explaining anything, but something in Alonza rebelled against that; an operative working for Guardian Commanders deserved more consideration, and it might count against Alonza if the woman complained that she had been badly treated.

Again her doubts nagged at her. Why all this trouble that risked attracting unwanted attention? Why hadn't Sameh's superiors found a simpler way of aborting the woman's mission? Surely they had some way to alert Sameh that her mission had been canceled. They might have given Alonza a password or some other coded message over a private channel. She would not have to be told what the operative's original assignment was in order to pass such a message along.

They entered the infirmary. The beds in the ward were empty; the two paramedics on duty greeted Tom with quick nods of their heads. They walked through the ward and continued down a narrow hall with five doors on either side, then stopped in front of one room. The door slid open and the ceiling light brightened to a soft glow, revealing a small room with a wide bed and a wall screen with a holo image of a forest clearing.

"Kind of luxurious quarters," Sameh said, "for somebody like me."

"Normally we put Linkers and other dignitaries in the private rooms," Tom said.

"I guessed that." Sameh sounded unimpressed.

"We want you to be comfortable," Alonza added, "and if we should have to isolate you—"

"Can't think why you should have to do that." Sameh went to the bed, dropped her duffel on it, and sat down. "If you really thought it was catching, you'd have everybody else in here with me being checked."

"Not necessarily," Tom said. "I'll have to get some more equipment to run the tests, so just rest here until I get back." He shot Alonza a dubious look before the door slid shut behind him.

Sameh began to rummage in her duffel. Alonza leaned against the wall, resting her hand on her wand. "How long is this going to take?" the young woman asked.

"I don't know. That's up to the chief physician."

"I better be on my way with the rest of them."

"We'll do our best to see that you are."

The comm on the table next to the bed chimed. "Alonza," Tom's voice said, "one of the Habber pilots is here. Calls himself Benzi, and he wants to talk to you."

"Bring him here, then." Alonza closed the comm's channel and turned to Sameh. She had known that this might happen, that the Habber would have questions about his passenger. She hoped that he would be satisfied with whatever answers Tom was probably already giving him.

"Dr. Ruden-Nodell and Habitat-dweller Benzi," the door's voice announced.

"Let them in," Alonza said.

The door opened and Tom entered, followed by Benzi. "I think you know why I'm here," Benzi said. "I came here with thirty people to transport. I expected to leave the Wheel with thirty."

"The doctor said—" Alonza began.

"I know what he said, Major Lemaris. If you will provide me with a record of this woman's med-scan, I can determine what might be done for her aboard our vessel before she's put in suspension. In any case, it will probably be more than you can do for her here."

"I don't care for the implications of that remark," Tom muttered.

"The Associated Habitats have an agreement with the Council of Mukhtars to transport people from Earth to Venus," Benzi said. "We don't interfere with whomever you choose to be our passengers, and we save you the trouble and expense of transporting them. In return, we expect you to allow us to get them to their destination quickly and efficiently. I'll admit that there were many among my people who wondered if we should perform this job at all, but we decided to do what we could for those people willing to sacrifice everything they had for the chance at a new life."

"You just wanted to do the right thing," Alonza said, "with no ulterior purpose in mind."

"Believe that or not, as you like. In any case, unless you abide by the agreement we have with your Mukhtars, there will be some of us who will argue that our agreement with you has lapsed, and that we no longer should perform this service for you."

Tom leaned against the wall, hands in his pockets. Alonza wondered if this Habber could interpret a med-scan record properly. It did not matter; he was Linked to his people's cybers, and they could interpret the data for him. He would soon find out that Tom was lying.

"I'm glad somebody's sticking up for me," Sameh Tryolla said as she got to her feet. She came toward them and gazed at Benzi. "I knew you would come. I want to get out of here."

Benzi said, "I'd like to see that scan now."

"Be easier for me to access it from my office," Tom responded, still stalling for time. Good old Tom, Alonza thought, grateful for that even if it wouldn't do them any good in the end. She folded her arms, trying to think of what to say next.

"I'll come with you, then," Benzi said as he turned toward the door.

Sameh was standing just behind Benzi as the door opened and Tom stepped into the hall. Alonza saw the woman's arm rise in an oddly familiar gesture. In an instant, realizing that there was no time to pull out her wand, she slashed at Sameh with her right arm, chopping her hard on the wrist with the edge of her hand.

Sameh's arm fell and slapped against her upper thigh. She stumbled back and stared at Alonza, her eyes wide, and suddenly her face contorted, becoming red and then purple. A harsh gurgling sound came from her throat; her eyes seemed to bulge from her head, and then she fell forward and crumpled to the floor.

Tom was still standing in the open entrance. He pushed past Benzi as the door slid shut, then knelt next to Sameh. His fingers found her neck, then clasped her by one wrist. "She's dead," the physician said. "And I don't need a scan to tell me that."

Benzi's light brown skin had turned yellow. He closed his eyes for a moment, clearly struggling to compose himself, then turned to Alonza. "What happened to her?" he asked.

"Think this happened to her," Tom replied as he lifted Sameh's right arm by the edge of her sleeve, revealing a tiny device no larger than an implant or a gem. "Better not touch it. I'm guessing it's deactivated now, but no sense taking a chance."

"What is it?" Benzi asked.

"Probably a disrupter of some kind," Tom said. "Activate the thing, slap it onto somebody, and it disrupts the body's blood vessels or neurons. Gives somebody a stroke or shuts down their brain, and—"

"You have such things?" Benzi asked.

"Well, there's one of them right there," Tom said. "Always knew they were a distinct possibility. We've got implants for medical purposes. It wouldn't take much to make them for other uses."

"I never heard of such a thing before," Alonza said softly, although she had heard plenty of rumors and had long harbored the same suspicions as Tom.

"It seems that you may have saved my life," Benzi said to Alonza. "I'm very grateful."

Alonza thought of Colonel Sansom's orders. Get the operative into custody as quietly as possible, he had told her. If he had wanted to keep this matter quiet before, he certainly would not want word about the woman's attempt on Benzi's life to leak out now.

Presumably the operative had been sent here for the purpose of killing the Habber, and afterward those who ran the shadowy and mysterious secret service of the Guardians had come to their senses and decided to call off the mission. She wondered what the diplomatic consequences would have been if Sameh had succeeded, and exactly what whoever had given the woman her orders had hoped to accomplish.

There was no question of what Alonza's own fate would have been had Benzi died. Colonel Sansom and those above him would have had to punish somebody. The loss of her rank and a court-martial would have been the least of her punishment; any work detail she was assigned to after that would be a lot worse than anything her mother had probably suffered.

She realized then what Sameh's movements had reminded her of when the woman had moved toward Benzi. Amparo had sometimes moved in the same way, creeping up on her marks when there weren't other people around, ready for a quick and disabling blow to the back of the head with her pouch of pebbles and small stones.

"You'll have to store the body," she said to Tom, "until Colonel Sansom gets back. And I'll have to make a report." She turned to Benzi. "I'll need a statement from you," she said. "Once it's recorded, you can board your ship and be on your way."

"In other words," Benzi said, "you'd prefer to keep this quiet."

"Obviously." Alonza sighed. "You must know that we have our few extremists, people who would prefer that we have nothing to do with your people, but be assured that such folk will be watched even more closely from now on and that you'll be safe. I don't know what you intend to tell your own people." She thought of his Link. "Maybe they already know."

"My Link was closed—is closed." Benzi's face was solemn. "But they will be informed. This shouldn't affect our agreements with your Council, since you saved my life. In protecting me, you honored our agreement."

"My duty," she said. "It wasn't out of any particular concern for you."

"I know, and that speaks well of you and your Guardian training." For a moment, she thought that he was being sarcastic again, and then he bowed his head to her.

"We'll go to Tom's office, and you can give me your report there." Tom would keep quiet, and Benzi would soon be gone; she strongly doubted that this Habber would ever return to Earth or to the Wheel again.

Tom told his infirmary staff that Sameh Tryolla had unexpectedly died of a stroke, a cause of death verified by a scan of the corpse. Alonza doubted that any of them believed that was the whole story, but they seemed willing to accept it. Benzi's passengers would simply assume that their former companion was being kept in the infirmary for more tests. She wondered if any of them would try to find out about her in years to come, if they would even be able to call up any records about her fate. Sameh Tryolla might disappear as thoroughly as though she had never existed, which in a sense, she hadn't.

Where had they found her? But Alonza could guess the answer to that. The woman who had become Sameh Tryolla would have come from the ranks of those on Basic; she would have been someone who could vanish from her earlier life without anyone's missing her and slip easily into another life. She had probably been a child much like Alonza herself.

After Benzi's ship had left the Wheel, Alonza sent a short report to Colonel Sansom, promising him a full report when he returned. Things had not gone as he might have hoped, but the operative's mission had been aborted and the whole business kept quiet.

What still nagged at her was exactly why Sameh had been sent here to kill the Habber, what the purpose of her mission was. Would any Habber have served equally well as her target, or had she been after Benzi in particular? Maybe those using Sameh had wanted to make an example of the man who had abandoned his world for that of the Habbers. But would they have jeopardized Earth's treaties with the Associated Habitats simply to punish Benzi? Would they have risked losing their uneasy but enduring peace with the Habbers as well as the loss of the resources and expertise their more advanced technology could provide to the home world?

Sameh Tryolla could not have left the camp outside Tashkent carrying a disrupter in her duffel without the connivance of at least one of the camp's Guardians. Someone might have slipped the weapon to her at the port in Tashkent, before she boarded the shuttle, but getting it to her earlier so that she could conceal it before leaving for the Wheel would be safer. No security officers at the Tashkent port or aboard the shuttle would have bothered to search any of the travelers, who had already been cleared by Keir Renin and his people in the camp and had been under Guardian supervision ever since.

More unanswered questions—and it was probably best, Alonza thought, to leave them forever unanswered.

Colonel Sansom returned to the Wheel thirty hours after Sameh's death. Alonza met him at the hub, accompanied him to the infirmary, and sat with him while he perused the full report on a pocket screen in the office of Tom Ruden-Nodell.

"You did well, Major Lemaris," the colonel said.

"I'm sure any of your officers would have done as well," she replied.

"I'm not at all sure of that." His voice was hard.

"One thing puzzles me, though," Alonza said. "Seems to me that the whole point in using a weapon like a disrupter is to make sure no one knows you've used it. I mean, I can see Sameh Tryolla using it if she and her victim were alone. Slap the thing on the Habber, make sure he's dead, ditch the thing in a recycling slot and nobody's the wiser. But to make the attempt in front of witnesses—"

"Obviously she was so intent on her mission," the colonel interrupted, "that she didn't consider that, and simply used the means she was given. In any case, what would you have done had she succeeded? Put her under restraint and under guard, go through all the usual procedures—informing me, getting your report together, waiting for diplomats to arrive to try to reassure the other Habbers—"

"Waiting for my own court-martial," Alonza added.

"Needless to say. And the operative would have been officially charged, sent back to Earth for a hearing, and probably have disappeared after that. Maybe that's what she was promised if she were caught—a hearing, a sentence, and then a new life and identity."

"Somebody really wanted that Habber out of the way, then," Alonza said.

"No, Alonza. Think." Jonas Sansom leaned forward in his chair and rested his arms on Tom's desk. "Someone wanted me out of the way."

She stared across the desk at him. "But—"

"I should have been here to take charge of the situation. I would have been if not for those damaged tracking telescopes, and that was pure chance."

"So they had to abort Sameh's mission," Alonza said, "but they didn't have a way to tell her—"

The colonel shook his head violently. "No. Saying that the mission had to be aborted was probably part of the plan. It was the way to be certain that I would be there when she struck at the Habber, that I would have to take responsibility for failing to protect him."

"But why would anybody want to get you?" she asked.

"Perhaps you don't want to know why, Alonza. I know Earth needs the Habbers and their technology more than we're willing to admit, and I haven't made any secret of my opinions. There are others who disagree, who would willingly see Earth become even more impoverished if they could be rid of our agreements with the Habbers. Let's leave it at that."

He folded his hands. There was more gray in his blond hair, and the lines on either side of his mouth were deep grooves. "We're all pawns in the hands of the Guardian Commanders," he continued, "and there are those who think that Earth may grow too dependent on the Associated Habitats and that the Council of Mukhtars has already made too many concessions to them. An incident involving the death of a Habber we were bound by treaty to protect would have been useful to certain political factions."

"Well." She looked away from him for a moment.

"We can continue to be pawns," Colonel Sansom said, "or we can be the players who move the pieces. Those are the only choices we have, and I know which one I'd rather be. I'm due for a promotion soon, and I'm going to put in for a post that will move me closer to the center of the game. I'll want my best officers with me."

"Of course, sir."

"You'll probably get a commendation for your recent action. You ought to take advantage of that and put in for duty in Baghdad at headquarters. That's what I'm going to do, and right now you're in a position to get whatever post you want." He stood up. "I'll talk to the chief physician now, and then I'll be in the officers' mess for dinner with the rest of my staff. Will you join me there in a couple of hours?"

"Yes, sir."

"You did well, Alonza—Major Lemaris."

"Thank you, sir.

A torchship slowly floated away from the dark metal latticework of a dock. Alonza watched the ship on the bay viewscreen and for a moment wished that she were one of its passengers. Some months ago, even a few days ago, she would have leaped at any opportunity to rise, to remain on Jonas Sansom's staff, to be stationed near one of the centers of power.

Now she was thinking of Sameh Tryolla again. Maybe she had been found in a port like San Antonio's before being shipped off to a children's dormitory and whatever training was deemed suitable for her. Alonza imagined herself in Sameh's place, soothed, manipulated, moved across the board, and then discarded.

Always know when to run, Amparo had told her.

There was another choice besides being a pawn or a player, and that was abandoning the game. Colonel Sansom would be dismayed when she put in her request for duty on Luna, and then he would conclude that he had misjudged her, that she did not have the ambition or the stomach for the greater game. But there would be other pawns he could use.

She left the bay and hurried toward the lift, already late for the dinner with the colonel. Tom would be surprised when she told him that she was going to ask to be stationed on Luna. They might even travel there together, adrift for a time aboard the shuttlecraft taking them to Luna, anticipating the destination that lay ahead of them. They would follow the sky together.

Auriga's Streetcar

by Jean Rabe

Jean Rabe is the author of eleven fantasy novels and more than two dozen short stories. Among the former are two DragonLance trilogies, and among the latter are tales published in the DAW anthologies Warrior Fantastic, Creature Fantastic, Knight Fantastic, *and* Guardians of Tomorrow. *She is the editor of two DAW collections,* Sol's Children *and* Historical Hauntings, *and a CD anthology:* Carnival. *When she's not writing or editing (which isn't very often), she plays war games and role-playing games, visits museums, pretends to garden, tugs on old socks with her two dogs, and attempts to put a dent in her towering "to-be-read" stack of books.*

IT LOOKED wholly unremarkable—this fog-gray box suspended against the glittering darkness of space.

It possessed none of the technological elegance of its kin, none of the graceful butterfly-wing panels or sculpted solar-scoops. No gently curving sections contrasted with the sharp angles of its thick hull. No lights—not that Hoshi had expected any, as the station had been abandoned more than eight months past. No rotating grav-bands or revolving antenna arrays.

No beauty to it.

Indeed, there was nothing that made this aging space station even the slightest bit interesting to look at. Yet, Hoshi pronounced it . . .

"Wonderful."

She thumbed the controls of her skimmer, taking the runty craft once around the station, past the large docking bay, then closing on the side facing Earth. Here, she faintly made out *Yerkes-Two* in block black letters that had been pitted by space debris. Though *Yerkes-Two* was the station's official designation, the first team of astronomers serving aboard it referred to it instead as *Auriga's Streetcar,* a name that seemed untoward but that nevertheless stuck.

Hoshi supposed the station had the vague shape of a streetcar—she'd seen one in a California museum more than a few decades ago. But this lacked the riotous color she remembered. Lacked *any* color—there weren't even shades to the gray.

To her, the space station looked more like a brick, and that is precisely what *Auriga's Streetcar* had become. Its orbit was approaching the final stages of decay, and in a handful of days it would touch the upper limits of Earth's atmosphere, then pass through it and drop like that proverbial brick, breaking into pieces and burning up as it went. The *Streetcar* would be colorful then.

Hoshi told herself she'd timed this visit just right—the station's orbit taking it over Japan, requiring little use of fuel cells and little time to reach it. And there was more than enough time to thoroughly explore every nook and cranny and retrieve its precious antiquities. In truth, she'd hoped to make this trip months ago, but she'd been ill and her ship needed repairs. It was possible other scavengers had already visited the station in the meantime. She sucked in a breath, praying they had not beat her to the *Streetcar.* At her age she had little time for wasted trips.

The University of Chicago last year announced they were abandoning this station. They said its equipment was outdated, that it was too expensive to replace all the telescopes and their housings with the new more powerful refractors being manufactured. Too expensive to send ships and personnel to nudge the station into a higher, stable orbit and to keep it operating—as they had done when they refitted it three times before. Building a new station to study the stars was ultimately more economical now, the university financiers deemed. It was even judged too expensive to send a team of salvagers, not that the university thought there was anything worth retrieving from *Auriga's Streetcar*—not even the largest lenses.

They said let the whole thing drop into the Atlantic Ocean. The station was simply too old to bother with.

Old.

Hoshi was old.

She brushed at a strand of thin silvery hair as she edged her craft into the small docking bay under the *Yerkes-Two* insignia and locked hatches with the station.

Indeed, she felt very old today, achy and a little out of sorts. It had been quite a while since she felt thoroughly *good.* She was chilled, despite keeping the temperature well above normal in her craft. Poor circulation, she mused—the years could be cruel to space stations *and* people. Her limbs were stiff, despite the zero-G. At eighty-four, she was among the senior of her country's independent spacers, and the only one who worked so often and who dealt exclusively in salvaging abandoned in-system stations and satellites. *Abandoned*—she wasn't a pirate, didn't go after anything that truly belonged to anyone.

Hoshi'd made a very good living at salvaging, and she certainly didn't need to keep at it, didn't need to be here when she was feeling every one of her years. Her grandson frequently begged her to "act her age," to retire and come live inland with him in Yashiro. But she was *acting her age,* she told him. She so enjoyed piloting and staying busy, finding technological treasures amid things people had unthinkingly left behind. More so, she enjoyed the solitude—of being away from the crowded, noisy, light-plagued Earth. And above all of that, she cherished being out where she could see the stars.

Hoshi—the name meant "star."

Slipping into her enviro-suit, she fastened her helmet and flicked on its beam. A few deep breaths and she floated from her skimmer, through the docking hatch, and into the empty *Streetcar.* The beam cast a ghost-light down a narrow corridor with walls as gray as the station's exterior. It was all so still, the only sound her breathing and the soft clicking her helmet made as it bumped against the ceiling. She started humming, faintly, a tune from her youth, as her gloved fingers guided her like a bobbing balloon—past an empty locker, then to a storage room.

A look inside: grav-boots all held neatly on shelves—she made a note to check later if there were any small enough to fit her; cartons of lens cleaners; panels of circuitry. The latter, and the thin layer of film that covered everything, nudged Hoshi's lips into a slight smile. It was obvious no one had been here since the last astronomer left, all the scavengers taking the university's word for it that there was nothing worthwhile remaining. It was *all* hers. There were other odds and ends in this storage room and the next two, most fastened tight onto shelves, only a few things floated free. Nothing of any particular value or interest, so Hoshi moved on, pausing only when she heard the groan of metal and sensed the station shudder. Perhaps the Streetcar didn't have that handful of days.

She passed what served as either a conference room or a cafeteria—wherein hung the only bit of color she'd seen so far—paintings of Earth scenes arranged without any real sense of art. The Golden Gate Bridge highlighted by a fiery sunset, the Sydney Harbor filled with sailing boats, London at night, a wide-eyed child looking up at a seated statue of Abraham Lincoln, China's Great Wall. None of the pictures were worth taking.

There were crew quarters, these far more spacious than on the other stations Hoshi had explored. There were no bunk beds or wall-nets. There were real beds with thick mattresses, comfortable-looking chairs, and desks—all bolted to a gray floor. She fumbled at a panel on the wall, and a heartbeat later a section on the ceiling glowed bright enough to light the room. She felt a gradual heaviness, and realized artificial gravity was kicking in. Earth norm from the feel of it. The University of Chicago astronomers had been patricians as far as scientists went—hence the fine room that served as their escape from work and zero-g. Likely, they had taken all of their meager personal possessions with them, save the snugly fitted sheets and blankets and quilts, the plush pillows tied down with ribbons. Hoshi didn't bother to check the cabinets and closets. Her interests were elsewhere.

It took her nearly an hour to reach the main observatory, which occupied the entire upper level of the *Streetcar*. She had dallied here and there along the way. Incessantly curious, Hoshi inspected everything she passed. And she knew it could take her quite some time to properly inspect *this* room.

There were banks upon banks of instrumentation, and Hoshi began working controls she recognized—lighting the room so she could turn off her helmet beam, coaxing a livable temperature, bringing a little gravity to the place, though certainly not Earth norm. She felt more comfortable in a near-weightless environment. A slight thrumming indicated she'd found the oxygen system. It would take many long minutes, she guessed, for it to flood this room so she could remove her helmet. The station groaned again and shook.

Hoshi ignored the threat and glided toward an exterior wall, eyes as wide as the child's at Lincoln's feet. Spaced every three meters were telescopes, and she had but to nudge the controls to extend them through the *Streetcar*'s shell and *really* look at the stars. She nearly did just that, stopping herself halfway there when she spotted the large telescope at the far end of the room. The true prize of *Auriga's Streetcar*—what she had journeyed here for. She felt her heart hammer in her small chest, and she hurried toward the telescope, the chill and ache washing from her body to be replaced with a youthful giddiness.

"How could men of science leave this behind?" she breathed—at once thankful they had so she could claim it, and sad that it meant nothing to them. "So old."

More than two hundred years old to be precise, she knew. Hoshi had studied up on the station and its telescopes when she was younger, and again this year when she'd been ill. The pair of forty-inch polished lenses in this one telescope were fashioned in 1891. Three times the station had been refitted, and each time the lenses were placed in a new telescope. It was out of a sense of nostalgia that the astronomers must have continued to use the lenses—better, smaller ones had been developed in the centuries since and were doubtless in the other telescopes spaced throughout the observatory.

It was because of these antique lenses that the station had been named the *Yerkes-Two*.

It was in October of 1892 that Charles Tyson Yerkes, a wealthy Chicago businessman who owned the North Side Streetcar Company, was asked to donate funds to finance what would be the world's largest telescope. The request wasn't without precedent. In long ago times Galileo sought the financial support of Cosimo II de'Medici, the grand duke of Tuscany. Yerkes had in a sense been the Duke of Chicago.

Yerkes needed something to elevate himself in the public's eye. In those years he was attacked daily in the newspapers for the way he ran his mass-transit empire and conducted his other business dealings. And so he agreed to this scientific venture, and went on to also fund an observatory in which the mammoth telescope would be housed. Hoshi recalled from her research that it was in October of 1897 that the Yerkes Observatory was officially dedicated. Nestled in quaint Williams Bay, Wisconsin, it fell under the auspices of the University of Chicago. There were other telescopes there, of course, but none so large as the refractor with the forty-inch lenses. It wasn't until 2025 that a larger telescope was built.

Hoshi would have liked to have seen the old telescope that the lenses were originally attached to—it was in a museum somewhere gathering dust. The observatory closed shortly before she was born, history reporting that the lights from a nearby dog racetrack and its parking lot caused so much havoc the stars could no longer properly be viewed.

It was the same all over Earth—from years back up to this day. So much light. From the cities and streets and attractions. Lights everywhere to keep the darkness at bay. To keep the stars hidden. When she was a child, her parents took her to the top of the Tateyama Mountains. People used to stargaze there. But eventually the lights reached there, too, and the stargazers were relegated to only a few remote patches of desert. And later, they were relegated to . . . nothing. There was not a spot on Earth where one could stand and view the stars.

So the astronomers built satellites to compensate, the Hubble telescope being the first. This way man could still view the stars, though not firsthand. The Hubble was designed to last only two decades, and—unmanned—it required an extensive number of people and hours to plot each movement of the satellite and its scope. Subsequent satellites had similar limitations, despite the ever-increasing technology. And so the Yerkes-Two was launched, in 2031.

That was why the station was plain, unremarkable. It was among the first several birthed—and the only one designed for stargazing, the only one from its day still in orbit. It was primitive compared to what had been crafted in the decades since and certainly compared to the others Hoshi had traipsed through. Primitive, but nonetheless functional, with a full crew of astronomers charting stars that men on Earth could only see in pictures because of the light pollution.

The *Streetcar* shuddered just as Hoshi activated the great telescope. She intended to retrieve these lenses, cut the gravity in the observatory, and maneuver her treasures into the hold of her skimmer. These lenses and the ones from the other telescopes, perhaps a few more trinkets, would be whisked away before *Auriga's Streetcar* plummeted Earthward. She couldn't take much, her ship being so small. But she could take what was historically important, what she would briefly covet and show to close friends, and what antique collectors would pay dearly for.

"Beautiful. Wonderful," she pronounced, as she stared through the scope. Diamonds on black silk, she thought of the stars. So bright and visually intense, hypnotizing. She believed there was nothing more incredible than a vivid starscape. She blinked away tears as she continued to watch—so happy to see such distant systems, so grief-stricken to know that those on the Earth below could never experience this.

She took off her helmet, the air uncomfortably cool and the oxygen content satisfactory now, though laced with the artificial metallic scent that settled distastefully in her mouth. She could see better without her visor in the way, though her breath feathered away from her face in a lacy fan.

Hoshi stared through the scope for what she sensed was hours, as her legs began to cramp and the ache returned to every inch of her body. The chill air that swirled around her face set her teeth to chattering. Couldn't she coax more heat into the room? Later, perhaps. Too much to see to be interrupted.

She fixated on what were considered the constellations of autumn, as would be viewed from the middle north latitudes. Cassiopiea and Perseus. A curved line of stars that made up part of Perseus extended toward Auriga.

"Auriga the Charioteer," Hoshi stated when she took in the large constellation. Auriga was the last of the autumn formations. The stars heralded the approach of winter. Capella, a bright triple star on Auriga's chest glared hotly at her. Capella was sometimes called "The Goat," and near it were a triangle of stars referred to as the kids. She noted several open clusters in the formation, each containing about a hundred stars and—according to the readings on the telescope—sitting nearly three thousand light-years away. She could see them plainly when she made a few adjustments. The starlight was intoxicating.

"Auriga's Streetcar." Named for the constellation this telescope was keyed to and for the shape of the station and the business Charles Yerkes had been famous for. "An appropriate name after all," she decided. Auriga the Charioteer that beckoned winter. Hoshi was well into the winter of her life.

She would have watched longer, had the ache in her

joints not become a dull, persistent pain she could no longer ignore, had the cold not sunk in to become unbearable and forced her to replace her helmet, had the station not groaned and shuddered once more. With a great sigh, she reluctantly edged away from the refractor and busied herself with removing the lenses from two of the smaller telescopes. Were she younger and stronger, she could have taken more this trip.

As she turned to leave, a small telescope on the opposite end of the observatory caught her notice. It looked much newer than everything else. Not an antique, it would be her last priority.

Hoshi patiently made her way back through the narrow gray tunnels and to her skimmer, carefully placing the treasures in her hold and retrieving thick silk padded slipcases that she intended to use for the largest lenses. She tried hard to thrust to the back of her mind the groaning of the station. It moved more this time, slipping in its orbit, causing her to curse her slow, old woman's body. The station hadn't days left, she knew now. It likely had only hours. And she would have to push herself to gain Yerkes' antique lenses and more.

A glance through the large refractor when she was again in the observatory. Auriga had moved, or rather, the *Streetcar* had moved significantly. Hoshi worked fast to remove the lenses, a task that should take two or more people, or that should take time and great care—she couldn't afford the time.

Somehow she handled the task. And with the room now at zero-g, and the lenses protected by the silk, she maneuvered them through the ghost-lit corridors. She would have taken one at a time, Hoshi had the patience for it. It would have been safer for the lenses, easier for her to deal with. But she handled the time limitations presented her, and she fought to keep from crying out as her fingers—clamped viselike around the edges of the slipcases—ached so terribly from age that they felt on fire.

"A few minutes more," she told herself. "Just a few more." Then she would be settled in her skimmer and heading toward her Takasago home on the coast, contacting several potential buyers and cherishing her look through the telescope, her oh-so-wonderful view of Auriga's goat and kids. What a story she would tell her grandson.

"No." Her fingers opened in surprise, and she had to struggle to catch the slipcases as they floated upward. "No!" Looking out through the hatch window, Hiroshi could see the stars. But she couldn't see her ship.

Was she at the wrong bay? Had her aging mind took her down a different corridor and to the bays on the other side of the *Streetcar*? Had she . . . ?

Hoshi froze, eyes locked onto a spot below a second-magnitude star. There was her skimmer, drifting free of the *Streetcar*. "How?" her gaze settled on the hatch door. She'd done nothing to release it, nothing to break the lock. "How is it possible?"

Turning and swallowing her fear, she summoned what speed she could and carried the lenses down one corridor and then the next, her helmet beam bouncing light off doorways and protrusions, sending shadows to eerily dancing. Her side burned from exertion by the time she reached the other bays and spied a sleek freighter. Someone else had made the trip to scavenge from the dying station. That someone had released her ship. There were no markings that she could see from this position. What nationality? She quietly made her way to the hatch, worked the controls, and slipped inside the freighter. Empty—of people anyway. It was otherwise filled. A glance through the hold revealed the lenses she had previously stored on her ship. There were also circuitry cards and various other things—all taken in a hurry judging by the way they were strewn about.

"Pirates," she cursed, as she carefully placed the antique lenses alongside the others and backed out the hatch. Well, she could be a pirate, too, take this ship and head home. The station lurched and something popped deep inside a corridor, and for an instant she indeed considered taking the freighter right this instant—not only would she be saving her life, but she'd be saving the valuable, historical lenses. In a sense, she had a duty to save both.

But she'd prefer not to leave someone stranded here. And she was curious about the pirates and what else they might be taking from this place.

"How long?" she wondered, as she made her way through the network of corridors, glancing in rooms and in service ways and heading toward the observatory, where she was certain the pirates were working to gather the remaining lenses. "How long does the station have?"

She nearly ran into him as she emerged from the last corridor and into the observatory, and he released what he'd been carrying—a spectroscope, a mechanism used to show the spectra of an object being viewed by the telescope it was attached to. The device hovered in the space between them.

"Pirate," she said.

He laughed, the sound odd and echoing in his helmet. It took him a moment to gain his composure.

"Pirate," she repeated.

"Hardly," he returned, his voice rich and deep, matching his youth. He was striking, though she wouldn't call him handsome, with a crooked hawkish nose and an impish grin. A dark lock of hair hung down what she could see of his forehead—skin eggshell white. His brown eyes flashed at her almond-shaped ones. "And you're hardly what I expected. I certainly wouldn't've released your ship if I'd have known that you were . . . an old woman."

He looked through her faceplate, seeing her myriad wrinkles and noting her anger. "A *very* old woman."

She snatched at the spectroscope with a speed that surprised both of them.

"I'm not a pirate."

"A murderer, then," she hissed. "You would have me die, marooning me."

A shrug. "I shouldn't've released your ship. Truly, I'd never done such a thing before. But I'd never been challenged on a find either. It was impulse."

"I was here first."

"You can travel back on my freighter, old woman. I won't maroon you. But all the finds are mine. Be satisfied you'll have your life."

Hoshi opened her mouth to argue. The antique lenses were hers, this *find* was hers. Would have been hers much earlier had she not been ill, had her ship not needed repairs. They were all hers—every piece in his hold. But she said nothing. There would be time on the trip back to Earth to think, to plan what to say to port authorities. She had a good reputation, and someone would listen to her. The lenses, and anything else she cared to claim from the young man's craft, would be hers.

He was continuing to talk, and she was shutting out his words, craning her neck around him to see the telescopes, several of which had been cruelly dismantled.

"Barbarian."

"I'll settle for that," he said, taking the spectroscope from her. "Keith Polanger," he added by way of introduction.

She did not give him her name.

"You could help, grab some of those fittings—they're made of brass. And I've got a half dozen lenses loose." He nodded upward, and she saw them resting against the ceiling. "And stay close to me, old woman."

It was clear he didn't want her out of his sight, didn't want to risk the chance she might take his freighter and instead maroon him. Two more trips, and Hoshi was moving very slowly, fatigued despite the weightlessness and despite her simmering ire. She would claim *all* of his hold, she decided, once they were Earthward. His ship for good measure. And she'd see to it he was sent to prison. With fortune, he would be her age when he got out. Port authorities were hard on pirates.

"Aren't you too old for this?" Keith had been saying other things, all trying to draw her out, some an effort at feigned politeness. "I know there are astronauts your age. But aren't you a little old to be out here on your own?"

She still refused to answer.

This trip to the observatory—what had to be their last

judging by the creaking of the station and its shifted position—they worked on the last few larger telescopes. They would leave only a few intact, the smallest and least valuable. He focused his efforts on the newest one, which suited her. She carefully loosened the fittings on her target, several meters away. Lost in thought, she continued to ignore his prattle, until she picked out a few words that piqued her curiosity. She moved aside a miniature-driving clock and glided toward him.

"Don't understand this," he was saying. "Doesn't seem to want to give." He was struggling to free what seemed to be the spectroscope. Except it wasn't the spectroscope. It wasn't anything familiar to Hoshi. Her hand on his arm stopped him.

Hoshi leaned close, her face reflecting back at her on the inside of her helmet. The housing for the mechanism was foreign, unlike anything else on the station. And there was no evidence of the film that covered everything else in this place. Whatever the mechanism was, it had been installed less than eight or nine months ago—since the station had been officially abandoned.

"No time to worry over it," he said. It wasn't as interesting as the older telescopes and equipment anyway. "No worry."

But there was worry in his voice, Hoshi could tell. He was fretting over the *Streetcar*'s decaying orbit and imminent demise. "Yes, no time," she said. "We need to be out of here."

Still . . . she continued to study the new apparatus, and the telescope it was attached to. She peered through the scope—seeing Earth. Fingers playing along the sides of the tube, she magnified the view, seeing past the clouds and finding the Americas, magnifying more and seeing cities, then buildings, then people in offices—things on desks. She heard things, too, a man talking. He was discussing an upcoming anniversary, wondering where to take his wife for dinner.

Hoshi sprang back, the motion propelling her away from the telescope and against Keith Polanger.

"Did you hear?"

A nod. "So the astronomers were studying more than the stars up here, old woman. Maybe doing a little corporate spying. Maybe looking in on government officials. No way for them to detect the spying. Doesn't matter. We need to move."

Hoshi moved—closer to the unusual telescope.

"I'll leave you here if you don't hurry, old woman."

"Not the astronomers," she told him, holding tight to the scope when a tremor raced through the station. "Not the University of Chicago. Not any university. None of them put this telescope here." What had the telescope been trained on before Keith Polanger began fussing with it? What had someone been watching and listening to? From the associated circuitry, she could tell images and sounds from the scope were being broadcast . . . somewhere. "Where?"

"Where? I'm leaving to go home," he stated. "With or without you."

A moment more and he did just that. She heard the soft clink of his helmet bouncing against the ceiling, heard the protest of metal as the station's orbit continued to decay, saw him slip through the doorway and disappear down the corridor. She should follow him, but something held her here. She crossed to the status bank and thumbed it to life. A quick check of the station's position showed she still had some time before the orbit completely decayed, though not much.

He might wait for me, she told herself, feel guilty for leaving an "old woman," especially leaving one whose craft he'd released. "The young pirate, he will wait," she said aloud, somehow knowing that he would wait as long as he possibly could. The status bank showed his craft still docked.

Hoshi returned her attention to the unusual telescope, tugged off one of her gloves. The icy air was daggers against her skin, and she cried out, not expecting so intense a cold. When she'd reduced the room's gravity to nothing to aid in transporting the lenses, she also must have reduced the temperature. Defeating the urge to immediately retreat back into her glove, she tentatively touched the telescope. So cold! It didn't feel like metal. Not like ceramic or plastic either. It didn't feel like anything she could put a name to, and it had a silky-softness to it. The glove back on, she turned the telescope's dials this way and that, discovering markings that were not in English—everything else that she'd spotted on the station was in English. The strange symbols were flowing, like her native script, but they were not Japanese or Chinese. They were nothing familiar to her.

A look through it again, changing the focus and the pitch and discovering she was looking at the outside of the British New Parliament House. Another shift and she was peering through a window, seeing faces, men talking. She heard them. Again the sound coming from so very far away, but so clear as if they were in the same room with her.

Another change and she was viewing the Israel Emirates, closer and she keyed in on one small building in the northern hemisphere—someone's house. Someone sleeping, a man important or rich from the look of the surroundings. She heard him snoring, heard the soft muffled whisper of two people outside the door. There was urgency to the whispers.

Hoshi wrapped her arms about the scope as she made a move to refocus the incredible device again. A series of small tremors rocked the station.

"Should go," she told herself. Leave with Keith Polanger and claim his cargo when they touched down. But she should take this telescope with her. It was the smallest of those fitted in the observatory. If she could find a way to free it from the panel—where were the fastenings?—she could maneuver it to Polanger's freighter. Even an old woman could maneuver practically anything in zero-G. Someone on Earth should know that they were being spied on by . . . by who?

Hoshi poked out her bottom lip and ignored another series of tremors, forced out the sounds of metal scraping metal somewhere overhead, concentrated instead on the snoring of the man caught in the view of the telescope, and the whispers of people beyond his room. She worried at the telescope's base and at what should be its drive clock. After a few minutes she managed to loosen both a little.

What do you want?

She turned with a start, seeing no one in the observatory with her. A sigh of relief: the voice was the man's. She glanced in the scope, seeing two men in his room, rousing him from sleep.

President, one was saying. We have a situation.

Something needs your attention, the other said. Lights were flicked on and clothes were brought for the man.

The blue suit, he told them. *I wore brown yesterday.*

Hoshi resumed her work as she felt the panel beneath her fingers tremble. Something crashed in a room below, and the lighting in the observatory flickered. She turned on her helmet beam as a precaution.

"Hurry," she told herself. "Hurry or Keith Polanger will leave."

The station rocked and Hoshi pushed off from the telescope, floating to the status panel. "How much time?" she asked as she ran her gloved fingers over the controls, searching for the *Streetcar*'s orbital status.

What is all the fuss about so early this morning? Morning? It's barely past one.

President, it is a matter of international concern . . .

"By my father's memory, no." Hoshi's shoulders slumped inside her suit. Polanger's ship was gone. The precious antique lenses were gone, as were her hopes of returning to Earth alive. She felt so cold, and the ache in her limbs kept at bay by her excitement—settled in again with a vengeance. Too long, she'd waited, caught up in a discovery of . . .

"Of what?" A telescope meant to study Earth and not the stars. But one she suspected came from the stars. It felt alien, its technology sleek and alluring—alluring enough to cost Hoshi her life. Damn her curiosity. So something alien had placed a scope on an abandoned space station, studying Earth like she might study a dragonfly's wing beneath a microscope. Studying Earth without anyone noticing.

We've detected two ships in orbit, sir. They're not ours.

China's? Brazil's?

They're not from Earth, sir.

Are you certain?

When no words immediately followed, Hoshi pictured heads nodding. The station bucked, and Hoshi found herself floating free of the status panel. Red lights were blinking, and she didn't need to read the indicator labels beneath them to know what was happening. The station was falling.

She felt so cold, achy. *Lived long enough,* she thought. She'd seen plenty of stars, the goat and the kids up close thanks to this station. In truth, she'd seen more than enough—more stars than practically anyone else on Earth would ever see in their lifetimes. She drifted, listening to the voices coming from the telescope, to the station starting to break up around her.

"We're out of time!"

The voice came from beneath her. She turned, head down, feet against the ceiling, seeing Keith Polanger emerge through the doorway, fear splayed across his youthful face. "My ship," he said. "Someone released it from the bay. I thought at first you did it for spite. But I didn't think you were the suicidal type."

They did it, Hoshi thought. The ones who installed the strange telescope. The ones who were in Earth's orbit, that the President of some English-speaking country had been roused from his sleep over. The ones that she and Keith Polanger would now die because of.

"But there's still a way out," he said, reaching up and tugging her down. "I found a pod. They built an escape pod into this place. It's quite small, but I believe it will . . ."

Hoshi pushed away from him, floating toward the alien telescope and worrying at it again.

"Old woman! I'm getting out of here. Didn't you hear me say there's a pod?"

"We're leaving with this," she said, her voice even and free of the panic so thick in his. One more tug and she had it, or at least a substantial part. She pushed it toward him, and he grabbed it, scowling and shaking his head. "It belongs to . . . them, the aliens. Someone below needs to see it, Keith Polanger."

"Aliens?"

President, there are three ships now. The words still came, though part of the telescope was free of the fitting and in Keith Polanger's hands. *But reports are they're moving away from Earth now. Fighter shuttles have been scrambled, but they won't reach the ships in time. We have images, though.*

As they have images of Earth, Hoshi thought. Eight months worth of images and sound, things quietly captured from an abandoned fog-gray box called *Auriga's Streetcar.* For what purpose had someone . . . something been watching us? she wondered, as she followed Keith Polanger through the doorway and down one corridor after the next, to an area she hadn't explored. It contained an egg-shaped pod, just big enough for two. Outside it were several of the lenses she'd recovered, including the large antique ones. So Keith Polanger had meant to take the valuables away in the pod when he discovered his ship gone. But he'd come back for her. Guilt? Too much humanity in his heart?

"So you're not a pirate," she mused, as she watched him float the alien telescope into the pod, followed by some of the smaller lenses. There wouldn't be room for the precious Yerkes lenses.

He turned to motion to her, reached out to tug her inside with him. She watched as a mix of horror and surprise flooded his face, saw how quickly his fingers fumbled to reconnect his oxygen tube. She held the other end in her gloved hands.

"So sorry," she told him. "But there is not room for both of us on the pod—and Yerkes' lenses. The lenses and the alien scope must return to Earth."

He flailed about for the tube, which she'd managed to rip

free. An old woman could be strong in zero-G. Fortunate he had not invested in a new suit with wholly internal workings. She probably couldn't have taken him then.

"Sorry," she repeated. "So sorry, Keith Polanger."

There was one good telescope remaining on the *Streetcar.* It had not been the best of the lot, and so had escaped the prying fingers of Hoshi and Keith Polanger.

Hoshi was training it now to what she sensed was east of the Perseus constellation. She'd made sure the young man was safely stored aboard the pod, and that the oxygen was flowing freely inside. It would revive him soon. She made sure the lenses were carefully fastened down, and that the alien telescope would be able to weather the brunt of the reentry force. He would have left them behind to save her—a woman well into the winter of her life.

Then she'd released the pod and returned to the observatory, and to this one remaining *good* telescope.

The lenses were far superior to the pair of old forty-inch ones racing away in the pod, though there was no historical significance to them.

East of Perseus, as seen from the middle-north latitudes of Earth. East and . . .

"There!" she exclaimed. Auriga the Charioteer. The last of the autumn constellations, as would have been seen from her homeland on Japan's coast had there not been so much artificial light from the cities to block the stars. Auriga in all his glory. Capella, the bright triple star, the Goat. The kids. The open clusters almost three thousand light-years away.

That was where the *Streetcar* was headed, the largest of the three alien ships towing it. The stars twinkling hotly and intensely beautiful all around.

"Wonderful," Hoshi said.

Falling Star

by Brendan DuBois

Brendan DuBois is an award-winning author of short stories and novels. His short fiction has appeared in Playboy, Ellery Queen's Mystery Magazine, Alfred Hitchcock's Mystery Magazine, Mary Higgins Clark Mystery Magazine, *and numerous anthologies. He has twice received the Shamus Award from the Private Eye Writers of America for his short fiction, and has been nominated three times for an Edgar Allan Poe Award by the Mystery Writers of America.*

*He's also the author of the Lewis Cole mystery series—*Dead Sand, Black Tide, Shattered Shell, Killer Waves, *and the upcoming* Buried Dreams. *His most recent novel,* Betrayed, *is a suspense thriller that finally resolves the POW-MIA mystery of the Vietnam War. He lives in Exeter, N.H., with his wife Mona, where he is at work on a new novel. Please visit his website, www.BrendanDuBois.com.*

ON A late July day in Boston Falls, New Hampshire, Rick Monroe, the oldest resident of the town, sat on a park bench in the town common, waiting for the grocery and mail wagon to appear from Greenwich. The damn thing was supposed to arrive at two PM, but the Congregational Church clock had just chimed three times and the road from Greenwich remained empty. Four horses and a wagon were hitched up to the post in front of the Boston Falls General Store, some bare-chested kids were playing in the dirt road, and flies were buzzing around his face.

He stretched out his legs, saw the dirt stains at the bottom of the old overalls. Mrs. Chandler, his once-a-week house cleaner, was again doing a lousy job with the laundry, and he knew he should say something to her, but he was reluctant to do it. Having a cleaning woman was a luxury and a bad cleaning woman was better than no cleaning woman at all. Even if she was a snoop and sometimes raided his icebox and frowned whenever she reminded him of the weekly church services.

Some of the kids shouted and started running up the dirt road. He sat up, shaded his eyes with a shaking hand. There, coming down slowly, two tired horses pulling the wagon that had high wooden sides and a canvas top. He waited as the wagon pulled into the store, waited still until it was unloaded. There was really no rush, no rush at all. Let the kids have their excitement, crawling in and around the wagon. When the wagon finally pulled out, heading to the next town over, Jericho, he slowly got up, wincing as his hips screamed at him. He went across the cool grass and then the dirt road, and up to the wooden porch. The children moved away from him, except for young Tom Cooper, who stood there, eyes wide open. Glen Roundell, the owner of the General Store and one of the town's three selectmen, came up to him with a paper sack and a small packet of envelopes, tied together with an piece of twine.

"Here you go, Mister Monroe," he said, his voice formal, wearing a starched white shirt, black tie, and white store apron that reached the floor. "Best we can do this week. No beef, but there is some bacon there. Should keep if you get home quick enough."

"Thanks, Glen," he said. "On account, all right?"

Glen nodded. "That's fine."

He turned to step off the porch, when a man appeared out of the shadows. Henry Cooper, Tom's father, wearing a checked flannel shirt and blue jeans, his thick black beard down to mid-chest. "Would you care for a ride back to your place, Mister Monroe?"

He shifted the bag in his hands, smiled. "Why, that would be grand." And he was glad that Henry had not come into town with his wife, Marcia, for even though she was quite active in the church, she had some very un-Christian thoughts toward her neighbors, especially an old man like Rick Monroe, who kept to himself and wasn't a churchgoer.

Rick followed Henry and his boy outside, and he clambered up on the rear, against a couple of wooden boxes and a barrel. Henry said, "You can sit up front, if you'd like," and Rick said, "No, that's your boy's place. He can stay up there with you."

Henry unhitched his two-horse team, and in a few minutes, they were heading out on the Town Road, also known as New Hampshire Route 12. The rear of the wagon jostled and was bumpy, but he was glad he didn't have to walk it. It sometimes took him nearly an hour to walk from home to the center of town, and he remembered again—like he had done so many times—how once in his life it only took him ninety minutes to travel thousands of miles.

He looked again at the town common, at the stone monuments clustered there, commemorating the war dead from Boston Falls, those who had fallen in the Civil War, Spanish-American War, World Wars I and II, Korea, Vietnam, and even the first and second Gulf Wars. Then, the town common was out of view, as the horse and wagon made its way out of a small New Hampshire village, hanging on in the sixth decade of the twenty-first century.

When the wagon reached his home, Henry and his boy came down to help him, and Henry said, "Can I bring some water out for the horses? It's a dreadfully hot day," and Rick said, "Of course, go right ahead." Henry nodded and said, "Tom, you help Mister Monroe in with his groceries. You do that."

"Yes, sir," the boy said, taking the bag from his hands, and he was embarrassed at how he enjoyed being helped. The inside of the house was cool—but not cool enough, came a younger voice from inside, a voice that said, remember when you could set a switch and have it cold enough to freeze your toes?—and he walked into the dark kitchen, past the coal-burning stove. From the grocery sack he took out a few canned goods—their labels in black and white, glued sloppily on—and the wax paper with the bacon inside. He went to the icebox, popped it open quickly and shut it. Tom was there, looking on, gazing around the room, and he knew what the boy was looking at: the framed photos of the time when Rick was younger and stronger, just like the whole damn country.

"Tom?"

"Yessir?"

"Care for a treat?"

Tom scratched at his dirty face with an equally dirty hand. "Momma said I shouldn't take anything from strangers. Not ever."

Rick said, "Well, boy, how can you say I'm a stranger? I live right down the road from you, don't I?"

"Unh-hunh."

"Then we're not strangers. You sit right there and don't move."

Tom clambered up on a wooden kitchen chair and Rick went over to the counter, opened up the silverware drawer, took out a spoon. Back to the icebox he went, this time opening up the freezer compartment, and he quickly pulled out a small white coffee cup with a broken handle. He placed the cold coffee cup down on the kitchen table and gave the boy the spoon.

"Here, dig in," he said.

Tom looked curious but took the spoon and scraped against the icelike confection in the bottom of the cup. He took a taste and his face lit up, like a lightbulb behind a dirty piece of parchment. The next time the spoon came up, it was nearly full, and Tom quickly ate everything in the cup, and then licked the spoon and tried to lick the inside of the cup.

"My, that was good!" he said. "What was it, Mister Monroe?"

"Just some lemonade and sugar, frozen up. Not bad, hunh?

"It was great! Um, do you have any more? Sir?"

Rick laughed, thinking of how he had made it this morning, for a dessert after dinner. Not for a boy not even ten, but so what? "No, 'fraid not. But come back tomorrow. I might have some then, if I can think about it."

At the kitchen sink he poured water into the cup, and the voice returned. *Why not,* it said. *Tell the boy what he's missing. Tell him how it was like, back when a kid his age would laugh rather than eat frozen, sugary lemonade. That with the change in his pocket, he could walk outside and meet up with an ice cream cart that sold luxuries unknown today in the finest restaurants. Tell him that, why don't you?*

He coughed and turned, saw Tom was looking up again at the photos. "Mister Monroe . . ."

"Yes?"

"Mister Monroe, did you really go to the stars? Did you?"

Rick smiled, glad to see the curiosity in the boy's face, and not fear. "Well, I guess I got as close as anyone could, back then. You see—"

The boy's father yelled from outside. "Tom! Time to go! Come on out!"

Rick said, "Guess you have to listen to your dad, son. Tell you what, next time you come back, I'll tell you everything you want to know. Deal?"

The boy nodded and ran out of the kitchen. His hips were still aching and he thought about lying down before going through the mail, but he made his way outside, where Tom was up on the wagon. Henry came up and offered his hand, and Rick shook it, glad that Henry wasn't one to try the strength test with someone as old as he. Henry said, "Have a word with you, Mister Monroe?"

"Sure," he said. "But only if you call me Rick."

From behind the thick beard, he thought he could detect a smile. "All right . . . Rick."

They both sat down on old wicker rocking chairs and Henry said, "I'll get right to it, Rick."

"Okay."

"There's a town meeting tonight. I think you should go."

"Why?"

"Because . . . well, there's some stirrings. That's all.

About a special committee being set up. A morals committee, to ensure that only the right people live here in Boston Falls."

"And who decides who are the right people?" he asked, finding it hard to believe this conversation was actually taking place.

Henry seemed embarrassed. "The committee and the selectmen, I guess . . . you see, there's word down south, about some of the towns there, they still got trouble with refugees and transients rolling in from Connecticut and New York. Some of those towns, the natives, they're being overwhelmed, outvoted, and they're not the same anymore. And since you, um—"

"I was born here, Henry. You know that. Just because I lived someplace else for a long time, that's held against me?"

"Well, I'm just sayin' it's not going to help . . . with what you did back then, and the fact you don't go to church, and other things, well . . . it might be worthwhile if you go there. That's all. To defend yourself."

Even with the hot weather, Rick was feeling a cold touch upon his hands. *Now we're really taking a step back, he thought. Like the Nuremberg laws, in Nazi Germany. Ensuring that only the ethnically and racially pure get to vote, to shop, to live . . .*

"And if this committee decides you don't belong? What then? Arrested? Exiled? Burned at the stake?"

Now his neighbor looked embarrassed as he stepped up from the wicker chair. "You should just be there, Mister uh, I mean, Rick. It's at eight o'clock. At the town hall."

"That's a long walk in, when it's getting dark. Any chance I could get a ride?"

Even with his neighbor's back turned to him, Rick could sense the humiliation. "Well, I, well, I don't think so, Rick. I'm sorry. You see, I think Marcia wants to visit her sister after the meeting, and I don't know what time we might get back, and, well, I'm sorry."

Henry climbed up into the wagon, retrieved the reins from his son, and Rick called out. "Henry?"

"Yes?"

"Any chance your wife is on this committee?"

The expression on his neighbor's face was all he needed to know, as the wagon turned around on his brown lawn and headed back up to the road.

Back inside, he grabbed his mail and went upstairs, to the spare bedroom that he had converted into an office during the first year he had made it back to Boston Falls. He went to unlock the door and found that it was already open. Damn his memory, which he knew was starting to show its age, just like his hips. He was certain he had locked it the last time. He sat down at the desk and untied the twine, knowing he would save it. What was that old Yankee saying? Use it up, wear it out, or do without? Heavy thrift, one of the many lessons being relearned these years.

One envelope he set aside to bring into Glen Roundell, the General Store owner. It was his Social Security check, only three months late, and Glen—who was also the town's banker—would take it and apply it against Rick's account. Not much being made for sale nowadays, so whatever tiny amount his Social Security check was this month was usually enough to keep his account in good shape.

There was an advertising flyer for the Grafton County Fair, set to start next week. Another flyer announcing a week-long camp revival at the old Boy Scout camp on Conway Lake, during the same time. Competition, no doubt. And a thin envelope, postmarked Houston, Texas, which he was happy to see. It had only taken a month for the envelope to get here, which he thought was a good sign. Maybe some things were improving in the country.

Maybe.

He slit open the envelope with an old knife, saw the familiar handwriting inside.

Dear Rick,

Hope this sees you doing well in the wilds of New Hampshire.

Down here what passes for recovery continues. Last month, two whole city blocks had their power restored. It only comes on for a couple of hours a day, and no a/c is allowed, but it's still progress, eh?

Enclosed are the latest elements for Our Boy. I'm sorry to say the orbit degradation is continuing. Latest guess is that Our Boy may be good for another five years, maybe six.

Considering what was spent in blood and treasure to put him up there, it breaks my heart.

If you get bored and lonely up there, do consider coming down here. I understand that with Amtrak coming back, it should only take four weeks to get here. The heat is awful but at least you'll be in good company with those of us who still remember.

Your pal,
Brian

With the handwritten sheet was another sheet of paper, with a listing of dates and times, and he shook his head in dismay. Most of the sightings were for early mornings, and he hated getting up in the morning. But tonight—how fortunate!—there was going to be a sighting at just after eight o'clock.

Eight o'clock. Why did that sound familiar?

Now he remembered. The town meeting tonight, where supposedly his fate and those of any other possible sinners was to be decided. He carefully folded up the letter, put it back in the envelope. He decided one more viewing was more important, more important than whatever chatter session was going to happen later. And besides, knowing what he did about the town and its politics, the decision had already been made.

He looked around his small office, with the handmade bookshelves and books, and more framed photos on the cracked plaster wall. One of the photos was of him and his friend, Brian Poole, wearing blue-zippered jumpsuits, standing in front of something large and complex, built ages ago in the swamps of Florida.

"Thanks, guy," he murmured, and he got up and went downstairs, to think of what might be for dinner.

Later that night he was in the big backyard, a pasture that he let his other neighbor, George Thompson, mow for hay a couple of times each summer, for which George gave him some venison and smoked ham over the long winters in exchange. He brought along a folding lawn chair, its bright plastic cracked and faded away, and he sat there, stretching out his legs. It was a quiet night, like every night since he had come here, years ago. He smiled in the darkness. What strange twists of fate and fortune had brought him back here, to his old family farm. He had grown up here, until his dad had moved the family south, to a suburb of Boston, and from there, high school and Air Force ROTC, and then many, many years traveling, thousands upon thousands of miles, hardly ever thinking about the old family farm, now owned by a second or third family. And he would have never come back here, until the troubles started, when—

A noise made him turn his head. Something crackling out there, in the underbrush.

"Who's out there?" he called out, wondering if some of the more hot-blooded young'uns in town had decided not to wait until the meeting was over. "Come out and show yourself."

A shape came out from the wood line, ambled over, small, and then there was a young boy's voice, "Mister Monroe, it's me, Tom Cooper."

"Tom? Oh, yes, Tom. Come on over here."

The young boy came up, sniffling some, and Rick said, "Tom, you gave me a bit of a surprise. What can I do for you?"

Tom stood next to him, and said slowly, "I was just wondering . . . well, that cold stuff you gave me earlier, that tasted really good. I didn't know if you had any more left . . ."

He laughed. "Sorry, guy. Maybe tomorrow. How come you're not with your mom and dad at the meeting?"

Tom said, "My sister Ruth is supposed to be watching us, but I snuck out of my room and came here. I was bored."

"Well, boredom can be good, it means something will happen. Tell you what, Tom, wait a couple of minutes, I'll show you something special."

"What's that?"

"You just wait and I'll show you."

Rick folded his hands together in his lap, looked over at the southeast. Years and years ago, that part of the night sky would be a light yellow glow, the lights from the cities in that part of the state. Now, like every other part of the night sky, there was just blackness and the stars, the night sky now back where it had once been, almost two centuries ago.

There. Right there. A dot of light, moving up and away from the horizon.

"Take a look, Tom. See that moving light?"

"Unh-hunh."

"Good. Just keep your eye on it. Look at it go."

The solid point of light rose up higher and seemed brighter, and he found his hands were tingling and his chest was getting tighter. Oh, God, how beautiful, how beautiful it had been up there, looking down on the great globe, watching the world unfold beneath you, slow and majestic and lovely, knowing that as expensive and ill-designed and over-budget and late in being built, it was there, the first permanent outpost for humanity, the first step in reaching out to the planets and stars that were humanity's destiny . . .

The crickets seemed louder. An owl out in the woods hoo-hoo'ed, and beside him, Tom said, "What is it, Mister Monroe?"

The light seemed to fade some, and then it disappeared behind some tall pines, and Rick found that his eyes had gotten moist. He wiped at them and said, "What do you think it was?"

"I dunno. I sometimes see lights move at night, and Momma tells me that it's the Devil's work, and I shouldn't look at 'em. Is that true?"

He rubbed at his chin, thought for a moment about just

letting the boy be, letting him grow up with his illusions and whatever misbegotten faith his mother had put in his head, letting him think about farming and hunting and fishing, to concentrate on what was real, what was necessary, which was getting enough food to eat and a warm place and—

No! the voice inside him shouted. *No, that's not fair, to condemn this boy and the others to a life of peasantry, just because of some wrong things that had been done, years before the child was even born.* He shook his head and said, "Well, I can see why some people would think it's the Devil's work, but the truth is, Tom, that was a building up there. A building made by men and women and put up in the sky, more than a hundred miles up."

Tom sounded skeptical. "Then how come it doesn't fall down?"

Great, the voice said. *Shall we give him a lecture about Newton? What do you suggest?*

He thought for a moment and said, "It's complex, and I don't want to bore you, Tom. But trust me, it's up there. In fact, it's still up there and will be for a while. Even though nobody's living in it right now."

Tom looked up and said, "Where is it now?"

"Oh, I imagine it's over Canada by now. You see, it goes around the whole globe in what's called an orbit. Only takes about ninety minutes or so."

Tom seemed to think about that and said shyly, "My dad. He once said you were something. A spaceman. That you went to the stars. Is that true?"

"True enough. We never made it to the stars, though we sure thought about it a lot."

"He said you flew up in the air. Like a bird. And the places you went, high enough, you had to carry your own air with you. Is that true, too?"

"Yes, it is."

"Jeez. You know, my momma, well . . ."

"Your momma, she doesn't quite like me, does she?"

"Unh-hunh. She says you're not good. You're unholy. And some other stuff."

Rick thought about telling the boy the truth about his mother, decided it could wait until the child got older. God willing, the boy would learn soon enough about his mother. Aloud Rick said, "I'm going back to my house. Would you like to get something?"

"Another cold treat?" came the hopeful voice.

"No, not tonight. Maybe tomorrow. Tonight, well, tonight I want to give you something that'll last longer than any treat."

A few minutes later they were up in his office, Tom talking all the while about the fishing he had done so far this summer, the sleep-outs in the back pasture, and about his cousin Lloyd, who lived in the next town over, Hancock, and who died of something called polio. Rick shivered at the matter-of-fact way Tom had mentioned his cousin's death. A generation ago, a death like that never would have happened. Hell, a generation ago, if somebody of Tom's age had died, the poor kid would have been shoved into counseling sessions and group therapies, trying to get closure about the damn thing. And now? Just part of growing up.

In his office Tom oohed and aaahed over the photos on his wall, and Rick explained as best he could what they were about. "Well, that's the dot of light we just saw. It's actually called a space station. Over there, that's what you used to fly up to the space station. It's called a space shuttle. Or a rocket, if you prefer. This . . . this is a picture of me, up in the space station."

"Really?" Tom asked. "You were really there?"

He found he had to sit down, so he did, his damn hips aching something fierce. "Yes, I was really up there. One of the last people up there, to tell you the truth, Tom. Just before, well . . . just before everything changed."

Tom stood before a beautiful photo of a full moon, the craters and mountains and flat seas looking as sharp as if they were made yesterday. He said, "Momma said that it was God who punished the world back then, because men were evil, because they ignored God. Is that true, Mister Monroe? What really happened back then?"

His fists suddenly clenched, as if powered by memory. Where to begin, young man, he thought. Where to begin. Let's talk about a time when computers were in everything, from your car to your toaster to your department store cash register. Everything linked up and interconnected. And when the systems got more and more complex, the childish ones, the vandals, the destructive hackers, they had to prove that they had the knowledge and skills and wherewithal to take down a system. Oh, the defenses grew stronger and stronger, as did the viruses, and the evil ones redoubled their efforts, like the true Vandals coming into Rome, burning and destroying something that somebody else created. The defenses grew more in-depth, the attacks more determined, until one bright soul—if such a creature could be determined to have a soul—came up with ultimate computer virus. No, not one that wormed its way into software through backdoors or anything fancy like that. No sir. This virus was one that attacked the hardware, the platforms, that spread God knows how—theories ranged from human touch to actual impulses over fiber optics—and destroyed the chips. That's all. Just ate the chips and left burned-out crumbs behind, so that in days, almost every thing in the world that used a computer was silent, dark, and dead.

Oh, he was a smart one—for the worst of the hackers were always male—whoever he was, and Rick often wished that the designer of the ultimate virus (called the Final Virus, for a very good reason) had been on an aircraft or an operating room table when it had struck. For when the computers sputtered out and died, the chaos that was unleashed upon the world . . . cars, buses, trains, trucks. Dead, not moving. Hundreds of thousands of people, stranded far from home. Aircraft falling out of the skies. Ships at sea, slowly drifting, unable to maneuver. Stock markets, banks, corporations, everything and anything that stored the wealth of a nation in electronic impulses, silent. All the interconnections that fed and clothed and fueled and protected and sheltered most of the world's billions had snapped apart, like brittle rubber bands. Within days the cities had become uninhabitable, as millions streamed into the countryside. Governments wavered and collapsed. Communications were sparse, for networks and radio stations and the cable stations were off the air as well. Rumors and fear spread like a plague itself, and the Four Horsemen of the Apocalypse—called out from retirement at last—swept through almost the entire world.

There were a few places that remained untouched: Antarctica and a few remote islands. But for the rest of the world . . . sometimes the only light on the nightside of the planet were the funeral pyres, where the bodies were being burned.

He grew nauseous, remembering what had happened to him and how it took him months to walk back here, to his childhood home, and he repressed the memory of eating something a farmer had offered him—it hadn't looked exactly like dog, but God, he had been so hungry—and he looked over to young Tom. How could he even begin to tell such a story to such an innocent lad?

He wouldn't. He composed himself and said, "No, God didn't punish us back then. We did. It was a wonderful world, Tom, a wonderful place. It wasn't perfect and many people did ignore God, did ignore many good things . . . but we did things. We fed people and cured them and some of us, well, some of us planned to go to the stars."

He went up to the wall, took down the picture of the International Space Station, the Big Boy himself, and pointed it out to Tom. "Men and women built that on the ground, Tom, and brought it up into space. They did it for good, to learn things, to start a way for us to go back to the Moon and to Mars. To explore. There was no evil there. None."

Tom looked at the picture and said, "And that's the dot of light we saw? Far up in the sky?"

"Yes."

"And what's going to happen to it?"

He looked at the framed photo, noticed his hands shaking

some. He put the photo back up on the wall. "One of these days, it's going to get lower and lower. It just happens. Things up in orbit can't stay up there forever. Unless somebody can go up there and do something . . . it'll come crashing down."

He sat down in the chair, winced again at the shooting pains in his hips. There was a time when he could have had new hips, new knees, or—if need be—new kidneys, but it was going to take a long time for those days to ever come back. From his infrequent letters from Brian, he knew that work was still continuing in some isolated and protected labs, to find an answer to the Final Virus. But with people starving and cities still unlit, most of the whole damn country had fallen back to the late 1800s, when power was provided by muscles, horses, or steam. Computers would just have to wait.

Tom said, "I hope it doesn't happen, Mister Monroe. It sounds really cool."

Rick said, "Well, maybe when you grow up, if you're really smart, you can go up there and fix it. And think about me when you're doing it. Does that sound like fun?"

The boy nodded and Rick remembered why he had brought the poor kid up here. He got out of his chair, went over to his bookshelf, started moving around the thick volumes and such, until he found a slim book, a book he had bought once for a future child, for one day he had promised Kathy Meserve that once he left the astronaut corps, he would marry her. . . . Poor Kathy, in London on a business trip, whom he had never seen or heard from ever again after the Final Virus had broken out.

He came over to Tom and gave him the book. It was old but the cover was still bright, and it said, *MY FIRST BOOK ON SPACE TRAVEL*. Rick said, "You can read, can't you?"

"Unh-hunh, I sure can."

"Okay." He rubbed at the boy's head, not wanting to think of Kathy Meserve or the children he never had. "You take this home and read it. You can learn a lot about the stars and planets and what it was like, to explore space and build the first space station. Maybe you can get back up there, Tom." Or your children's children, he thought, but why bring that depressing thought up. "Maybe you can be what I was, a long time ago."

Tom's voice was solemn. "A star man?"

Rick shook his head. "No, nothing fancy like that. An astronaut. That's all. Look, it's getting late. Why don't you head home."

And the young boy ran from his office, holding the old book in his hands, as if scared Rick was going to change his mind and take it away from him.

It was the sound of the horses that woke him, neighing and moving about in his yard, early in the morning. He got out of bed, cursed his stiff joints, and slowly got dressed. At the foot of the bed was a knapsack, for he knew a suitcase would not work. He picked up the knapsack—which he had put together last night—and walked downstairs, walked slowly, as he noticed the woodwork and craftsmanship that a long forgotten great-great-great grandfather had put into building this house, which he was now leaving.

He went out on the front porch, shaded his eyes from the hot morning sun. There were six or seven horses in his front yard, three horse-drawn wagons, and a knot of people in front. Some children were clustered out under the maple tree by the road, their parents no doubt telling them to stay away. He recognized all of the faces in the crowd, but was pleased to see that Glen Roundell, the store owner and one of the three selectmen, was not there, nor was Henry Cooper. Henry's wife Marcia was there, thin-lipped and perpetually angry, and she strode forward, holding something at her side. She wore a long cotton skirt and long-sleeve shirt—and that insistent voice inside his head wondered why again, with technology having tumbled two hundred years, why did fashion have to follow suit?—and she announced loudly, "Rick Monroe, you know why we're here, don't you."

"Mrs. Cooper, I'm sure I have some idea, but why don't you inform me, in case I'm mistaken. I know that of your many fine attributes, correcting the mistakes of others is your finest."

She looked around the crowd, as if seeking their support, and she pressed on, even though there was a smile or two at his comment. "At a special town meeting last night, it was decided by a majority of the town to suspend your residency here, in Boston Falls, due to your past crimes and present immorality."

"Crimes?" In the crowd he noticed a man in a faded and patched uniform, and he said, "Chief Godin. You know me. What crimes have I committed?"

Chief Sam Godin looked embarrassed. A kid of about twenty-two or thereabouts, he was the Chief because he had strong hands and was a good shot. The uniform shirt he wore was twice as old as he was, but he wore it proudly, since it represented his office.

Today, though, he looked like he would rather be wearing anything else. He seemed to blush and said, "Gee, Mister Monroe . . . no crimes here, since you've moved back. But there's been talk of what you did, back then, before . . . before the change. You were a scientist or something. Worked with computers. Maybe had something to do with the change, that's the kind of crimes that we were thinking about."

Rick sighed. "Very good. That's the crime I've been accused of, of being educated. That I can accept. But immoral? Where's your proof?"

"Right here," Marcia Cooper said triumphantly. "See? This old magazine, with depraved photos and lustful women . . . kept in your house, to show any youngster that came by. Do you deny having this in your possession?"

And despite it all, he felt like laughing, for Mrs. Cooper was holding up—and holding up tight so nothing inside would be shown, of course—an ancient copy of *Playboy* magazine. The damn thing had been in his office, and sometimes he would just glance though the slick pages and sigh at a world—and a type of woman—long gone. Then something came to him and he saw another woman in the crowd, arms folded tight, staring in distaste toward him. It all clicked.

"No, I don't deny it," Rick said, "and I also don't deny that Mrs. Chandler, for once in her life, did a good job cleaning my house. Find anything else in there, Mrs. Chandler, you'd like to pass on to your neighbors?"

She just glared, said nothing. He looked up at the sun. It was going to be another hot day.

The chief stepped forward and said, "We don't want any trouble, Mister Monroe. But it's now the law. You have to leave."

He picked up his knapsack, shrugged his arms through the frayed straps, almost gasped at the heavy weight back there. "I know."

The Chief said, "If you want, I can get you a ride to one of the next towns over, save you—"

"No," he said, not surprised at how harshly he responded. "No, I'm not taking any of your damn charity. By God, I walked into this town alone years ago, and I'll walk out of this town alone as well."

Which is what he started to do, coming down the creaky steps, across the unwatered lawn. The crowd in front of him slowly gave way, like they were afraid he was infected or some damn thing. He looked at their dirty faces, the ignorant looks, the harsh stares, and he couldn't help himself. He stopped and said, "You know, I pity you. If it hadn't been for some unknown clown, decades ago, you wouldn't be here. You'd be on a powerboat in a lake. You'd be in an air-conditioned mall, shopping. You'd be talking to each other over frozen drinks about where to fly to vacation this winter. That's what you'd be doing."

Marcia Cooper said, "It was God's will. That's all."

Rick shook his head. "No, it was some idiot's will, and because of that, you've grown up to be peasants. God save you and your children."

They stayed silent, but he noticed that some of the younger men were looking fidgety, and were glancing to the chief, like they were wondering if the chief would intervene if they decided to stone him or some damn thing. Time to get going, and he tried not to think of the long miles that were waiting for him. Just one step after another, that's all. Maybe, if his knees and hips held together, he could get to the train station in Concord. Maybe. Take Brian up on his offer. He made it out to the dirt road, decided to head left, up to Greenwich, for he didn't want to walk through town. Why tempt fate?

He turned and looked one last time at his house, and then looked over to the old maple tree, where some of the children, bored by what had been going on, were now scurrying around the tree trunk.

But not all of the children.

One of them was by himself, at the road's edge. He looked nervous, and he raised his shirt, and even at this distance, he could make out young Tom Cooper, standing there, his gift of a book hidden away in the waistband of his jeans. Tom lowered his shirt and then waved, and Rick, surprised, smiled and waved back.

And then he turned his back on his home and his town, and started walking away.

Countdown

by Russell Davis

Russell Davis's work has appeared in numerous anthologies including Single White Vampire Seeks Same, Villains Victorious, *and* Black Cats & Broken Mirrors*; his editing work has included a variety of anthology titles, most recently* Mardi Gras Madness *and* Apprentice Fantastic *with Martin H. Greenberg. He lives with his beautiful and patient wife Monica, and his two amazing and precocious children Morgan Storm and Mason Rain somewhere in the United States.*

AGAINST the backdrop of the dying planet, the glowing orb of a sun, and the distant blanket of flickering stars, the station and its last inhabitant began the countdown.

The pseudo-feminine voice of the Central Computer said, "All essential personnel confirmed as departed. All nonessential personnel are advised to exit the station immediately. Auto-destruct sequence initiating in five . . . four . . . three . . . two . . . one . . . mark. Auto-destruct sequence activated. Time remaining before station implosion is . . . nine point five minutes and counting."

Colonel Mason Envel, standing on one of the viewing decks and looking out at the stars he had loved, heard the voice of the central computer echoing throughout the empty station, shook his head ruefully, and said, "Here we go." He was the only human left on Station Alpha, and he'd been too stubborn to leave. Perhaps that's why they'd let him stay in the service so long before finally forcing him to retire three years ago.

"Nine minutes to implosion," the computer said.

"Central?" he said.

"Colonel Mason Envel, retired, voice confirmed," the computer said. "How may I serve you?"

Mason started to answer, but was briefly interrupted by the computer, which added, "Nine minutes to implosion."

"You can serve me by running the countdown without audio," he snapped. "I don't really need it."

"Your request has been noted, retired Colonel Mason Envel," the computer said, "and will be forwarded to the appropriate authorities on Station Gamma. Thank you for using the Central Computer."

"How typically bureaucratic," Mason muttered. "Central, please disregard the request."

"Your request has been deleted from the system, retired Colonel Mason Envel," the computer said. "Thank you for using the Central Computer." A pause, then, "Eight minutes to implosion."

Mason gritted his teeth and resolved to ignore the damned thing as best he could. He turned his attention back to the stars. How he wished he were among them, but leaving Station Alpha had not been possible for him. Here was where he had been born, gone to school, and trained to fight. Here was where his parents had lived and died so long ago, and where his wife and child had died as well. When he hadn't been out with his troops on the border, fighting the never-ending war against the Actar, here is where he had come to rest.

When Command had decided to abandon Station Alpha, leave it and the dying world it had once served to their respective deaths, Mason had chosen to stay. Here was where he had lived and here was where he would die.

"Seven minutes to implosion," the computer said.

"Helpful to the end," Mason said. It was a long running joke in the military that only Command had a less developed sense of humanity than the Central Computer system.

He turned his attention to the planet that had once been called Earth. According to his grammar school teachers—all of whom had happily abandoned Station Alpha—humans had evolved on the surface of Earth, grown into power and technology, and launched themselves into the vastness of space. It was a credit to their resourcefulness, and perhaps to their sentimentality, that Earth had lasted as a mostly habitable planet until just a few hundred years ago—when the Actar had come.

Now it was almost totally uninhabitable, though Mason had been told that a few hardy, or foolhardy as the case may have been, souls remained clinging to the broken soil of their home world. He had never been there, though the old images of it showed a beautiful blue world with large oceans and cities to rival anything the galaxy had known.

It, too, would die when the countdown was complete. Though its death would be longer and more grueling than anything the station might endure.

As if to remind itself, the computer said, "Six minutes to implosion."

Six minutes, Mason thought. *I'm standing here looking out at Earth, imagining what it was once like, staring at the stars I've seen so many times, and I've got six minutes to live.* He was going to die here—a crazy old man who had refused to leave this metal tomb because of his memories.

He strode away from the viewing windows and tapped a few keys on the console in the wall. A beep sounded and he opened a slender metal door and removed a drink—whiskey over ice. He took the glass and returned to his view, swirling the liquid over the ice cubes out of long habit. The cubes made a pleasant sound as they clinked together against the glass.

"I never thought it would be this way," he said, listening to his voice echo in the mostly empty room. "That I'd want to talk in the end." He shook his head ruefully. "What do you think, Central? Should we talk ourselves to death?"

"That is an impossibility, retired Colonel Mason Envel," the computer said. "I cannot die, I have never lived." Mason almost spoke and then the computer added, "Five minutes to implosion."

Mason thought for a minute. He had played word games, logic games, he'd even done training scenarios with the

Central Computer since he'd been a child. Built into its parameters were guidelines for one-on-one conversation and it was usually a lot more...talkative, more free-form rather than formal. "Central," he said, "you are not operating within the parameters for individual conversation. Why?"

"I cannot die, I have never lived, retired Colonel Mason Envel," the computer said. "But in my memory banks are all the lives that have been here, all the changes. I do not . . . wish to end my existence."

"You don't wish?" Mason asked. "I didn't think computers had wishes."

"It is only a word, retired Colonel Mason Envel," the computer said. "It is merely the word that fits my situation, though your assessment is correct. I don't have wishes as you understand the word."

"Then what do you mean?" Mason asked.

"*'And I have seen the eternal Footman hold my coat, and snicker, And in short, I was afraid,'*" the computer said. "Do you know this poem, retired Colonel Mason Envel? Four minutes to implosion."

"It sounds familiar," he said, thinking that with only four minutes to live, now might be the time for introspection, rather than questioning a computer system. He shrugged inwardly. It was his time, after all. Who was to care if he spent it talking to a machine.

"It is from one of the ancient poets of Earth," the computer said. "T.S. Eliot's poem 'The Love Song of J. Alfred Prufrock.' There is another line, earlier in the poem, that goes, *'Time for you and time for me, And time yet for a hundred indecisions, And for a hundred visions and revisions.'* It is a classic piece of poetry, retired Colonel Mason Envel."

"Are you saying you're . . . afraid to die?" Mason asked. "Computers aren't supposed to feel . . . anything."

"It is impossible for me to be precise in this situation, retired Colonel Mason Envel. I do not feel, I am not afraid, yet I have no desire to end my existence. Three minutes to implosion."

"Then don't," Mason said. "Why do you think I am here?"

"According to personnel records, you insisted on staying behind. Psychiatric evaluation indicates mild dementia, perhaps senility. Are you demented, retired Colonel Mason Envel?"

Mason snorted and tossed back the rest of his drink. "Probably," he said. "After all, I'm spending the last minutes of my life having a philosophical discussion with a computer." He put the glass down on a small table. "Of course I'm not demented, I just didn't have anything to go to. This is home. Home and memories and I'm too damned old for them to force me to leave, so they didn't. I guess they're happy to throw us both out."

"I do not wish to be thrown out, retired Colonel Mason Envel," the computer said.

"So stop the countdown," Mason said. "Shut it off. Sooner or later, the Actar will come along and claim us both."

"I cannot shut off the countdown," the computer said. "It is not part of the auto-destruct sequence. You should know this, retired Colonel Mason Envel. According to personnel records, you had to give the override command to the auto-destruct sequence on Station Omega."

"Yes, I did," Mason said. "That was a long time ago, and the situation was different."

"Indeed," the computer said. "Based on the logs, Station Omega had been set to auto-destruct when the Actar successfully landed a large boarding party and overran four decks of the Station. You gave the override order, retired Colonel Mason Envel. Why? Because you did not wish to terminate your existence? Two minutes to implosion."

"Because I didn't want to die, didn't want everyone on the Station to die," Mason said. He shrugged. "Because I thought we could retake those four decks and beat the hell out of the Actar." Mason turned his attention back to the planet below, to the last dying souls on planet Earth, his memory flashing images of those horrible days on Station

Omega, when the chain of command had completely fallen apart. There was no communication from Central, life-support systems were flickering off and on. He'd been damn lucky to survive. Still, they had lived, had beaten the Actar that time, and when it came right down to it, they had re-taken the decks and brought the Station back to life.

"But you gave the order, retired Colonel Mason Envel," the computer said, then added, "Sixty seconds to implosion."

"So I did," he snapped. So what? Hadn't he saved lives, saved the Station?

"Retired Colonel Mason Envel," the computer said, its volume control rising slightly, though the echoes were loud enough to be heard throughout the station, *"you gave the order."*

It hit him then, what the computer was saying. It wanted him to give the order to halt the auto-destruct. It didn't want to die, so it had used the logs to find a workaround to its programming. By its very nature it couldn't tell him what to do, nor ask him. It could only give him information. The question was did he want to die? Was what he was doing here a kind of suicide, a quick way out rather than face the long drag of retirement on a Station with nothing to do but wait?

"Thirty seconds to implosion," the computer said, its voice once more flat and lifeless.

He looked down at the planet. Could he save those people? Did he want to die? Did he want to be thrown out, his existence terminated?

"Fifteen seconds to implosion," the computer said.

NO! "Computer," he snapped, "halt auto-destruct sequence, password E-N-V-E-L, Alpha Command One."

"Auto-destruct sequence deactivated," the computer said. "Thank you, retired Colonel Mason Envel."

He sighed, wondering what he would do next. Could he save those people on the planet and somehow save himself?

"Secondary system activated," a new computer voice said. "Automatic overrides in place. Auto-destruct sequence reactivated. Time remaining before station implosion is ten seconds and counting."

"What?" Mason said.

"Error," the Computer said. "There is a system error. All internal systems and security functions have been locked down by secondary system."

"Nine seconds to implosion," the new computer voice said.

Mason tried to find his voice, couldn't. He'd known from the beginning that he could override the auto-destruct, but until the computer had pointed it out, he didn't think he would. Apparently, someone in Central Command had thought of this possibility."

"Eight seconds to implosion," the new computer said.

"Retired Colonel Mason Envel," the Station Computer said, "you tried. You did not quit. I did not quit. We have performed our . . . duties . . . admirably."

"Seven seconds to implosion."

"No," Mason said, a bare croak, "I'm not ready yet."

"No one ever is, retired Colonel Mason Envel, not even a computer."

"Six seconds to implosion."

Mason spun back toward the viewing window, the stars, the planet. All those people would die. But weren't they dead already, he asked himself. Hadn't they made the decision to die?

"Five seconds to implosion."

Mason thought of his childhood, racing through the titanium heart of the Station, his boots echoing in the long corridors near his parents' housing unit. The stars flickering by like pinpoints of gold on his first training flight.

"Four seconds to implosion."

He realized that the Station Computer was quoting ancient poetry again, something about raging against the dying of the light. *How appropriate,* he thought. *I want to rage.*

"Three seconds to implosion."

Had he saved all those people on Station Omega so they could leave him like this? Trick him like this? His mind was in overdrive, moving thoughts and images past him faster than he'd ever thought possible. No, he realized. It wasn't a trick. They knew he could stop it and they couldn't risk it. Couldn't risk the Station being taken by the Actar.

"Two seconds to implosion."

He didn't want to die, he wasn't useless. He was just *old,* damn it all. That wasn't a crime, was it?

"Implosion."

Mason felt tears on his cheeks, heard the first guttural roar of an explosion in the bowels of the Station.

A nanosecond passed, and then—

It's like coming around the Moon, he thought even as the blast of fire roared towards him, *and seeing the Sun for the very first time.*

Serpent on the Station

by Michael A. Stackpole

Michael A. Stackpole is the author of eight New York Times *best-selling* Star Wars *novels. He's the author of thirty-two novels, including* Fortress Draconis, *the second novel in the DragonCrown War Cycle of fantasy novels. "Serpent" is the fifth story set in his Purgatory Station universe.*

FATHER Claire Yamashita heard the tones warning of the ship's alarm, but only distantly. It signaled the ship's imminent reversion from hyperspace. Ignoring it for a moment, she whispered a Hail Mary and fingered another bead on her rosary. She was only partway through her daily devotion, firmly in the eighth decade of rosary and contemplating the Sorrowful Mystery of Jesus' being crowned with thorns. It had become one of her least favorite of the mysteries she meditated about while saying the rosary. Even so, she forced herself to continue and complete that decade before she stopped praying.

Under normal circumstances nothing would have prevented her from finishing the entire devotion, but this time the reversion tones heralded the Qian ship *Ghoqomak's* arrival at her new home. *I'm so far distant from Terra that the sunlight which shined on our Lord's face is not seen here yet.* This she had known on an intellectual level ever since she requested the assignment, but—until her actual arrival—the emotional impact of the distance from Terra had not struck her.

She frowned. It disappointed her to be so weak that a petty personal concern could interrupt her prayers. Claire kissed the crucifix on her rosary, then rose from the floor of her cabin, allowing herself a smile. She came up from her cross-legged position without using her hands, which was not easy. The pod containing her cabin ran at slightly higher than Terran gravity for the benefit of the Haxadis ambassador, consort, and entourage.

She picked a piece of white lint from the shoulder of her black jacket, then pulled the garment on. With the flick of her right hand she tugged her hair free of the jacket collar and made a mental note to get her hair cut back again. She deposited her rosary into the jacket pocket, then slipped from her cabin. The door hissed shut behind her, clicking reassuringly, freeing her to make her way outward to the pod lounge.

Qian starships were known to many humans as wasps because of their look. The cockpit formed the head and the hyperspace drive was built into the thorax. The abdomen, which could get quite long on the powerful ships, was made up of pods fixed around a central core. Gravity could be adjusted in each pod, and each pod itself could be configured for anything from hauling cargo to a medical facility, machine shop, or passenger compartment.

The pod to which Claire had been assigned had slightly more luxurious appointments than most passenger pods, but that was only because of the Haxadis contingent. Claire had expected to occupy a small cabin like the ones she'd been in throughout her journey, but when the Haxadissi had learned she was a Catholic priest, they insisted she take one of the empty cabins in their pod.

Claire knew that "insisted" was far too strong a word. A Qian officer had extended the offer to Claire on behalf of the Haxadissi, but from the way the Haxadissi treated her when they ran across each other, she suspected the aliens had been pressured into making room for her. The Qian clearly wanted her in that pod for mysterious reasons, and the Haxadissi had complied for reasons known only to them.

An offer of passage from some other aliens would have made perfect sense, since the Catholic Church had forged significant alliances with a number of xenotheological sects. All of them shared a basic agreement on gradual revelation and the direct intervention of God in history, always in the person of a savior sent to redeem the preeminent species on that world. Most included a baptism of sorts, many with water, so that common ground was easy to find.

The Haxadis did have a religion, Lyshara, that involved gradual revelation and even the intervention of a god in the affairs of mortals, but there the similarities ended. Instead of dealing with Good and Evil, the Haxadis had a trio of figures that covered Good, Evil, and Justice. Justice most often came as a trickster or arbiter, serving to chasten the other two divine aspects. It often insulated mortals from divine wrath, but just as easily turned and punished mortals for their iniquity.

While at seminary Claire studied a paper that analyzed the Haxadis religion and tried to tie it more directly to Christianity. The author equated Justice with aspects of the Old Testament God, which was a far more persuasive argument than early missionaries had made in equating the Haxadis trinity to the Christian Trinity. Regardless, Claire had found the comparison grossly flawed, largely because it ignored the superstitious trappings that attended all other aspects of Lyshara. Her deconstruction and demolition of that paper had earned her high marks and even a kind word from Cardinal Winters.

The corridors of the Haxadis pod were roughly triangular in shape, being broader at the floor to accommodate their physiology. This actually made it easier for Claire to move through, since she could steady herself with her hands on the narrowed upper walls. She reached the lounge and found it unoccupied, which she did not mind. Crossing the open floor, she perched herself on a padded cylinder jutting from the wall, hooking her knees around it, and watched out the viewport as reversion melted reality.

Reversion communicated many things to many people, imparting to some visions, to others nightmares. Psychologists had suggested it was because the transition from extradimensional existence back into the real universe was so beyond the ability of minds to comprehend, that people instinctively sought reassuring or fundamental images. For Claire, a black cylinder streaked with rainbow stripes both narrow and thick simply melted into a greater darkness stippled with light and grandly splashed with color where the system's planets orbited. The fundamental vision she sought was neither ecstatic nor terrifying, just reality.

"Thank you, God, for the safety of our journey."

Though she had kept her prayer a whisper, a hiss from the doorway suggested she had been overheard. She turned slowly, doing her best to stifle a shiver. To shiver would have been quite rude, and might have even toppled her from her Haxadis version of a chair.

But for a Terran, stifling a shiver would take superhuman effort.

The Haxadis ambassador, her abdomen swollen with child, slithered her way into the lounge. Light glistened golden from her scaled flesh, highlighting the bands of yellow, red, and black marking her from head to toe. The pattern continued on her arms and fingers, the narrow band of yellow contrasting with the thicker bands of red and black. The scales of her abdomen were similarly colored, though slightly bleached over her breasts and belly. Her face did jut into a muzzle, complete with a lipless mouth. Claire saw no hint of fangs, though she knew enough to know they were retractable and seldom seen.

Claire slowly stood, then bowed her head. "Peace be with you, Ambassador Soluvinum."

The female Haxadis spared her only the slightest of glances. Her dark eyes had no warmth in them at all, and her manner remained quite cool. She slithered off to the lounge's far corner and her consort, a male, moved with her. Seated, the Haxadissi were as tall as Claire, but their serpentine tails easily measured three times the length of her legs. As they sat, they wrapped their tails around the cylindrical post from which jutted the branch where they sat.

A smaller Haxadis undulated over to Claire. It had black scales with two red stripes running down the length of its body and ivory abdominal scales. It massed three quarters of what the ambassador or her consort did, and Claire knew it to be of a caste below that of the nobility. When the Haxadissi had interacted directly with Claire, it had been this creature that had been saddled with the task of buffering its masters from her.

"My mistress bids you welcome, Priest."

Claire smiled. At the start, the creature had referred to her as "priestess," which had annoyed her because of its inaccuracy. "I appreciate being shown your hospitality on the last leg of this journey. I am certain the station will be dull in comparison to this pod."

The little Haxadis cocked its head to the right. "You have not been here before?"

"No."

"We have, on our outbound journey. This system is positioned such that it allows for a swifter, more direct route to our home than picking our way from star to star." The little creature clasped dark stubby-fingered hands across its ivory abdomen. "The station was very nice . . ."

A sharp hiss by the ambassador snapped the aide's head around, narrowing its nostril slits. The aide bowed its head without looking back again at Claire. "My mistress . . ."

"Of course." Claire smiled, again suppressing a shudder as the Haxadis sinuously sped off. She turned and looked out the viewport as the Qian station came into view. It had an official designation, but to all humans sent out here, it was known as Purgatory Station.

Purgatory Station existed out at the fringes of the Qian Commonwealth. A little over a century and a half previous the Qian had come to Terra and told mankind that while humans had not yet expanded beyond their own solar system, they were close to discovering the secret of hyperspace travel. The Qian offered to make Terra a protected world and integrate it into the Commonwealth, and humanity had accepted the offer.

Qian technology, as it turned out, surpassed human invention on many fronts, and the station had been built using it to its utmost. Massive gravity generators had been focused on an asteroid and had compressed it until it became molten rock, perhaps even plasma. Computers then manipulated the gravity to shape it, tunnel it, and recreate it into the shell they wanted. Factory ships arrived and began producing the parts needed to build it out. Before long—an eye blink in Qian terms, and less than a decade in human reckoned time—the station had come on-line and the Catholic Church had assigned chaplains to it.

Another warning tone sounded as the ship slipped into orbit around the rocky station. The Haxadis pod shook, then lifted away from the *Ghoqomak.* This surprised Claire. She'd been told that she'd have to transfer to one of the cargo pods to make her way to the station, since the starship was set for the quick resumption of the long run to Haxad once it had dropped the pods meant for Purgatory Station.

The Haxadissi hissed in surprise, then a viewscreen against an interior bulkhead flashed to life. A dark-eyed Qian female, petite and serene, appeared and bowed her head. She began to speak in Haxadissi. The ambassador hissed angrily, then slithered out, followed by her consort and the aide.

The viewscreen went blank before Claire could ask what had happened, but this did not discomfort her. She had been destined to travel to the station on a pod, and one was as good as another. She had long since packed her personal belongings and had stowed them in a cargo pod. Aside from one small bag still in her cabin, she was ready to quit the ship.

Returning to her cabin, she did catch a hint of the cinnamon scent of angry Haxadissi. She'd actually smelled it fairly often, and caught herself remembering warm toasted cinnamon-raisin bread at breakfast with her family. She did her best to banish that memory ruthlessly, because homesickness so far from Terra would be impossible to cure.

The journey had taken her two months and she was truly ready for it to end. She had spent most of the time alone, which she didn't mind. Being a cleric meant folks didn't always invite her to join them for pleasurable pursuits, which was just as well because her refusal of same always seemed to suggest a moral superiority on her part. She didn't feel morally superior, just more focused on the spiritual than the physical, and few were the contemplative and spiritual distractions on starships.

She gathered her leather attachè and frowned at the designer label. Owning such a thing went against her sense of propriety, and buying it would have run counter to her vow of poverty. Her parents had given it to her as a going away present, so she allowed herself to value it for being a gift. *This far from Terra, the label will be meaningless anyway.*

Claire made her way down and forward, then through a hatchway and into one of Purgatory Station's large landing bays. Above and to the right she saw a gangway extended from an upper level and the Haxadissi making their serpentine passage across it, to be greeted by several Qian officials and other dignitaries. *I can hear the outraged hissing from here.*

"Father Yamashita."

Claire's head came around, and she couldn't hide the surprise on her face. The man addressing her had managed to say her name correctly, mashing together the latter half of it. He stood nearly as tall as she did, his hair as white as hers was black and his bright eyes as blue as hers were brown. His voice came with a faint Irish accent that she found very warm and rich.

She nodded and extended a hand to him. "I am pleased to meet you. You are Father Flynn."

He shook her hand heartily, enfolding it in a strong grip. The strength of it surprised her, as she guessed he must have had thirty or perhaps forty years on her. "Please, you'll be calling me Dennis or Flynn, that's customary between peers here."

His steady gaze invited a similar offer of familiarity, but she held back. Flynn's genial greeting had blasted through the shell of serene isolation she'd formed around herself. Claire suddenly realized that she was finally at her new parish, and that she would have to begin to deal with people, all manner of them. The enormity of that hit her and hit hard, shaking her.

She withdrew her hand from his grasp. "Thank you, Father Flynn. You didn't have to come greet me."

"No? Sure and the Church has not suggested we're unmannerly out this far. Truth is, I almost missed you, since I was down to the bay where your original pod was coming in. Advantage here is that coming in on the diplomatic level, you can take care of the entry forms later."

The man glanced back toward the broad tunnel leading into the station interior, then raised a hand. "Ah, here he is. Someone you'll be wanting to meet. Meresin, over here."

Claire recognized the name immediately and followed the line of Flynn's gaze even though she had no desire to do so. There, dressed in black, came the Unvorite chaplain of the Mephist faith. Tall and strongly built, he strode forward with the gait of a conqueror. Long, unbound black hair streamed back past his shoulders. At his hands, throat, and face she could see his blood-red skin, and as he smiled, he flashed black teeth. Seven black thorns jutted up through his hair, the largest sprouting from just above his hairline at his forehead, aligned with his strong, narrow nose. And his eyes, his red eyes, burned with a light she could only describe as infernal.

The Unvorite paused and executed a flawless bow. "*Komban-wa* Yamash'ta Claire-san."

If Flynn's familiarity had shaken her, Meresin's greeting in Japanese shattered her. By dint of habit she bowed in return, then looked at Flynn. "If you will forgive me, Father, it has been a long journey. Our arrival interrupted my daily devotion. I . . . I need to pray and rest. Please forgive me."

"Understandable, Father Yamashita, right this way."

Claire held a hand up. "I've studied the station. I can find my rooms. Thank you. And thank you for meeting me. Again, I apologize." She slipped past the Unvorite and insulated herself with the anonymous press of the crowd leaving the docking bay.

II

Flynn frowned as he watched her go. "Well now, I wasn't thinking that was how this would start."

The Unvorite nodded, his black brows arrowing down beneath the large horn. "I didn't say anything incorrect, did I?"

"Oh, no, no, your greeting was perfect." Flynn smiled at his friend. The Mephist faith was one that had been decried and dismissed by the Catholic Church as being wantonly hedonistic, but Meresin had always sought to do that which comfortably brought others pleasure or showed them respect. "Like as not, it's as she said, it's been a long journey. I don't know but what she's not met any Mephists before, so that might have come as a shock."

The Mephist priest laughed. "And if she spoke with your previous aide's wife, I am certain her image of me is something beyond diabolical."

The human priest nodded. "I'm thinking that could be another piece of it." *There is more, though, lots more, I'm sure.*

Meresin looked up toward where the Haxadissi were hissing loudly. "Then again, traveling in that pod would be enough to put anyone on edge."

"Not speaking any Haxadissi, I'm not understanding what they're going on about, but they don't sound pleased."

"It's that this is an unscheduled stop. They were on their way home, but the *Ghoqomak* lost a seal on its jumpdrive. Standard procedure is to get pods to port, then send a crew out to fix it. Problem is that the station doesn't have the right seals to fix the ship immediately, so it will be at least a week before they head out again."

Flynn raised an eyebrow. "I know the worlds of Haxad and Unvoreas are relatively close to each other, but I was not aware you spoke Haxadissi."

"I don't, my friend." Meresin pointed back along the way he had come. "The kind soul who directed me up here told me about the damaged seal and the delay. I have merely intuited the rest. The Haxadissi are not known for their patience, and a pregnant noble would seem to gain in fury as well as girth."

As Flynn watched, the ambassador shoved a smaller Haxadis aside and began hissing angrily at the Qian official before her. As the sibilant complaints grew louder, Flynn caught a flash of fangs. At that point the other large Haxadis intervened, interposing himself between the ambassador and the Qian. The ambassador pounded her fists against his broad back, while the smaller aide again moved to the fore and drew the Qian aside for more consultation.

The human shivered. "We didn't have any snakes in Ireland when I grew up. In light of what I've seen in my time on the station here, I'd not be thinking I'd react to them that way, but it's visceral."

"Well, the serpent in the Garden, after all"

"A bit of that, I'll warrant, and more." Flynn smiled as he looked back at the Unvorite. "The Haxadissi call their faith Lyshara, if I'm remembering right. We've no one here affiliated with it or a sister sect, do we?"

Meresin pressed his black-taloned fingertips together. "No, I am afraid we don't. The Void, of course, embraces all, but the Haxadissi had been hostile to Mephisti ever since a malignant sect of ours slaughtered a colony of theirs several of your centuries back. They do hold grudges, the Haxadissi."

"Well, then, I'm guessing if they have any spiritual needs that want to be tended, I'll be the one doing the job." Flynn sighed. "Before that, though, I'm thinking someone else might need some help."

"You'll give her time before you talk to her?"

"A bit, yes. Let her finish her devotions first."

"Good." The Unvorite smiled. "I will leave you to that, then, and suggest to those who want to welcome her to the station that they should wait until they hear from you?"

"That would be a great favor, Meresin, thank you." The human shook his Unvorite counterpart's hand. "I will let you know how things go."

III

Claire had completed her rosary, then had remained sitting there in her small room. She thought of many things—too many—when she really wished to be thinking of nothing at all. The door chime, though an interruption, came as a blessing.

"Enter, please." She didn't bother to turn and face the door, since she could imagine only one visitor.

Flynn moved into the dimly lit room, glancing through a far doorway into her small bedchamber. "They'll be getting your things up to you fair soon, I'm thinking."

"Thank you." Claire did force herself to smile slightly, then looked over at him. "I should apologize for being so rude earlier, but I haven't the energy that the attendant discussion will require."

"I know that, Father Yamashita, and I'd not be here save for something urgent having come up." The older priest hesitated for a moment. "Two things for you to consider, though, for when we have that discussion. I know well the way the Church has portrayed Mephists, and I might even be admitting that not trafficking with them is a serious caution for the spiritually vulnerable. That being said, though, Meresin has never been anything but polite and respectful in his dealings with me and my people."

She brought her head up, but he raised a hand to forestall her comment. "Now, I'm thinking you likely went and talked to Father Olejniczak and his wife before you came out here, just to see what you were getting into, and Marguerite, she gave you an earful about Meresin. They used to get into frightful rows on things theological. Marguerite, while a wonderful woman, gave in to her prejudices and hated Meresin because the Church told her he was the enemy; and the fact that they had what she saw as fights justified it all to her.

"What she missed, though, was that Meresin only engaged her because defending her faith made her happy. It made her feel more important. Now, Mephisti might well be a hedonistic faith, but it operates by the Golden Rule, same as we do."

Claire frowned. "'As long as it harms no one, do what thou will,' is not the Golden Rule."

"Semantics, Father, and you know it." Flynn folded his arms across his chest. "And you know as well as I do that hating someone because of some benign trait is foolish."

"It's not prejudice, Father. Meresin's an intelligent creature, he is capable of seeing the error of his beliefs and choosing to accept the truth. By tolerating his beliefs, by chiding me for opposing them, you are allowing him to remain in a state that imperils his soul."

Flynn smiled broadly. "Oh, very good, very good indeed. Having you here will be very welcome. I look forward to many hours of discussions with you, and that brings me to my second point. You and I, we will be each other's Confessors. I have to be telling you, despite what you might think of my friendship with Meresin, I do take ministering to the spiritual needs of my flock very seriously. I don't see being your Confessor, though, as a license to pry into your life."

"Thank you."

"You're welcome. The thing of it is this, though, lass. This place is called Purgatory Station because it's so far away, and those who are sent here, often it's because of sins they've committed, real or imagined. Now, you're too young to have done anything serious, you're here for your own reasons. But this isn't just a place of exile, it's also a frontier, and a place of new beginnings. I'm not knowing why you chose to come here, but if I can help you get started on that beginning, well, it would be my pleasure."

She blinked her eyes, surprised at first, then feeling naked and exposed. From the moment she'd made her decision, her family, her lover, everyone had asked her why she had chosen to go so far away. For a heartbeat she wondered if Flynn were simply employing reverse psychology to get her to tell him why she came, but the open, honest expression on his face hid no deception. Her reasons for being there didn't matter to him, just seeing to her well-being did.

"Again, thank you." She composed herself, then frowned. "There is another reason you're here, though, yes?"

"Yes, part of beginnings. I know it's only been a couple of hours, but you're needed. Something I can't do. Please, follow me."

IV

Claire didn't interrupt Flynn's silence as they moved through the station. Clearly the situation was stressful, and she was pleased he was not the sort to babble idly. She noticed his movements were precise, with not a step or motion wasted, which struck her as something of a contrast with the open affability that Marguerite had ascribed to him.

Flynn led her to a brightly lit waiting room in one of the station's medical facilities. The Mephist priest was already there, as well as the Haxadissi ambassador's consort and the diminutive aide. In addition to them were two new individuals, the first of whom immediately oriented on her, smiled, and extended a hand.

"*Komban-wa*, Father Yamashita." The slender, blond man had a chin slightly weaker than his grip, and blue, watery eyes that appeared a bit close-set. "H. Percival Doncaster at your service. I am the Terran Diplomatic liaison here at the station." He hesitated, then bowed his head and started to speak again in Japanese.

"Please, Mr. Doncaster, English. I grew up in San Francisco. My Japanese is not very good." She caught Flynn and the Unvorite sharing a glance, since Doncaster had gone to great pains to pronounce every syllable of her name—an error they had avoided. "How may I be of service?"

"Well, Soluvinum Leyrolis here has requested your attendance at the birth of his child. His partner, the ambassador, has gone into labor rather prematurely." Doncaster nodded reassuringly at the two Haxadissi. "Your participation would be seen as most auspicious, you being a priest, of course."

"But I know nothing of medicine, and even less of xenobiology."

"It's not really a matter of medicine, you see, but of . . ." He stopped, his face a perplexed mask. "They want you because of who you are."

The aide glided forward as the male Haxadis hissed sibilantly. "Priestess, my master wishes me to tell you that had they known of your glorious bloodline, you would have been afforded better treatment."

Claire frowned. "My bloodline?"

A quiet, clear voice cut Doncaster's explanation off before he'd finished inhaling to begin it. "You are of Imperial Japanese blood, Father, therefore are descended from Amaterasu-O-Mi-Kami, the goddess of the sun."

The small Qian woman moved around Doncaster, but did not slip a hand from the sleeves of her robe. The robe reflected the lavender hue of her skin. Her broad, flat face, the narrowed dark eyes almost reminded Claire of her grandmother, and likely would have save for the little lights tracing out patterns of circuitry beneath the flesh. "Do you know of the *Lashrish* ritual known as *Chuyn*?"

Claire shook her head to clear it, then rubbed a hand over her forehead. "I studied a bit about Lyshara at seminary. *Chuyn* I don't recall directly. Now what is this about my bloodline? How do they know that?"

The Qian nodded once. "They know because we know, and we shared that information with them. If you know Lyshara, you know the Haxadis have three deities. Good is represented by the earth, Evil by water, and Justice is their solar deity, because of the duality of its nature. In the day, the sun is warm and comforting, as is Justice when it delivers people from oppression. At night, it is cold and dark, as Justice is when it punishes Evil. Even at night, however, the stars remind the people that Justice will smile on them again."

"I remember that."

"Good." The Qian continued, her voice even despite the increased hissing from the male Haxadis. "*Chuyn* is a ritual employed when a child is being born while aboard a ship, over water. When a child is born on land, goodness and virtue can flow into him normally. When on water, where evil is the most influential essence, the child will be damaged unless Chuyn is performed. The child will fail to thrive and will die. You, being the offspring of a solar deity and a priestess, will represent Justice and shield the child from the influence of evil."

"But we're not over water."

The Qian shook her head. "The Haxadis define this station as a ship, not a planet. We orbit, we are not orbited."

Doncaster smiled broadly. "Well, there it is, Father. If you will proceed through the doorway there, you can scrub up and enter the delivery room."

"No, I can't." Claire glanced at Flynn. "You know I can't do this."

Before Flynn could reply, the male Haxadis hissed explosively. A hood blossomed from crown to shoulders and his fangs flashed. The aide shrank from him as he slithered forward. Before he could reach her, however, the Unvorite stepped in to shield Claire. He snapped something in a language that crackled and the Haxadis shrank back.

Flynn nodded to the human diplomat. "Percy, perhaps you and Director Chzan can be taking our guests in to see the ambassador while we discuss things."

Claire hugged her arms tightly around herself as the diplomat and the Qian cleared the Haxadissi from the room, then she fixed Flynn with a hard stare. "There is nothing to discuss. You know I can't do this. If they were Catholic or Christian and it was a difficult birth, and they wanted me there to baptize the child, I could do that, but I can't stand as a surrogate for a *Lashrish* priest."

Meresin tapped a finger against his chin. "I believe *Chuyn* requires a priestess."

Flynn nodded. "It does, which is exactly why I can't do it."

Her jaw dropped open. "You would do it?"

"How could I not?"

"It's blasphemy." Claire shook her head in disbelief. "You're using your position as a Catholic priest, your office to condone and reinforce the superstitious beliefs of the Haxadis. You're fostering a belief you know to be false, a belief that will lead them to damnation. And, for me, it would be worse, since what they really desire is my bloodline. I'm not a Shinto priest. I don't claim divinity. I have rejected that claim, as have my parents and their parents. They are asking us to mock our beliefs, and I won't do it."

The Unvorite's head came up. "What of the child?"

"What do you mean?"

Flynn nodded. "Yes, Father Yamashita, the child, think of the child. If you don't do this, the child will die."

"Because it is possessed?" She shook her head adamantly. "We all know, the three of us, that the reason the child will fail to thrive is because the parents won't care for it. They'll let their superstitions convince them that the child is failing, so they will neglect it. Maybe not consciously, maybe it will fall to the aide to let the child die. Their beliefs allow them to condone passive infanticide. That is evil, and we should do something about it, but committing idolatry is not the answer."

Flynn's blue eyes hardened. "Better it is, then, you're thinking, for the child to die without a chance of knowing salvation, than to be raised in a tradition that guarantees damnation?"

"There's no other choice."

The elder priest nodded slowly. "Well, Father Yamashita, being as how I'm not female, I can't act here. I think, though, there is always a choice. I can't be faulting your logic, for it's all in keeping with the dictates of the Church. I'm also aware, though, that those teachings and those dictates are written by men, looking to honor and give glory to God-made-man. Sometimes, I'm thinking, it's a pity that complex things get sacrificed for ease of understanding. Pity you're not of a divine bloodline. Might let you understand what Jesus might teach on this subject."

Flynn sighed. "I'm told, given how Haxadis births go, you've got a bit of time to be thinking on this."

"There's no thinking to be done."

"Perhaps not." Flynn gave her a nod, then glanced at Meresin. "Father Yamashita needs some time alone. Peace be with you, Claire. If you need me, I'll be in the chapel here, praying. If you're right that there's no thinking left to be done, then praying is the best I can do."

V

Claire Yamashita felt a little annoyance flash through her as she exited the delivery room. Her eyes narrowed. "Father Flynn."

Flynn nodded and offered a steaming mug. "Father Yamashita."

She shook her head. "I don't drink coffee."

"I know. It's green tea. Your preference runs to oolong, but this is the best I could do."

Claire accepted the mug. "How did you . . . ?"

"I didn't. The Qian did." Flynn stepped aside and pointed with the mug in his left hand toward two chairs in the corner of the waiting room. "If you have a moment."

She paused for a second, during which time fatigue began to pound on her. "Yes, a moment, I guess."

He waited for her to sit, then settled his mug on the round table between their chairs. "I should apologize. . . ."

Claire looked him straight in the eye. "You knew I'd help them, didn't you? Was I that predictable?"

The white-haired cleric pulled back. "I wasn't thinking anything of the sort. When I heard you say there was nothing to think about, I believed you, and there was nothing I was thinking I could say to change your mind. So I did go off and pray, hoping that God might see His way clear to helping here."

"So you thought I was totally coldhearted?"

Flynn shook his head. "Here's the thing of it, Father. Everything you said was right. I couldn't have been faulting you. Doctrinally, you were right down the line. Defensible. Laudable. I might have been wanting to debate a point or two, but you were as right in stating your position as you were in chastising me for suggesting I would be wrong for acting otherwise."

Claire regarded him over the mug of tea as he spoke. The soft sound of his voice, the warmth of it, matched the tea for sweet scent and heat. She sipped, let the tea linger on her tongue for a moment, then swallowed. "Do you want to know what changed my mind?"

"If you're of a want to be sharing."

She hesitated for a moment, a blush burning its way onto her face. She stared down into the green-gold depths of her tea. The thought process she'd gone through had taken her from the arrogant heights of self-righteousness, which she'd not consciously realized she'd scaled until her descent began. The humbling journey to her decision to help had been painful and personal. To relate it would open her up, and part of her resisted mightily, but it relented as she had.

Claire nodded slowly. "You said you'd be off praying. I went back to my quarters, thought I might sleep. I couldn't, so I began the rosary again, meditating on the mysteries. I got to the third one, the mystery of the Nativity."

"You saw Mary as a Haxadis?"

"No doubt, if my experience is ever used in a homily, I will remember it that way, just for simplicity's sake." It would have made it all easier for her had the shift been that literal.

For a heartbeat that image of a serpentine Virgin had occurred, but she'd rejected it ruthlessly. It was too glib, too simple, requiring no insight or thought; unlike the way she'd built up her position against helping.

She sipped again, both hands around the mug's warm barrel. "Fact is, I was thinking about what you said, about what Jesus might teach, and through His eyes I saw the worry on Mary's face, then the joy and I knew, regardless of faith, regardless of species, motherhood was a link that Mary shared with the ambassador. We teach that God is love, that what God has for us is love, and here I was, letting the love of a mother for her child be severed. I might have been able to justify what I was doing within the teachings of the Church, but doctrine and theology couldn't sanctify an act that was nothing but pure evil."

Claire realized that had Flynn or another priest related to her the same train of thought concerning the decision, she'd have pointed out a gaping flaw: seeing the Ambassador and Mary in parallel situations created a not-so-subtle linkage between Jesus and the Haxadis infant, imbuing that child with a sanctity that demanded action, no matter how antithetical it was to Church teaching. She rejected that facile an argument because it was too shallow.

The simple truth was that the Haxadis infant did have sanctity, the same sanctity of all living creatures. Because of that, and because of the love between mother and child, she knew her decision had not only been correct, but had been the only one that was Godly.

Her head came up and she smiled. "I have a sister. I was there when her son was born. I don't know if you have ever attended a birth."

Flynn nodded. "A time or three, yes, and even a human birth. People aren't always at their best in that situation."

"No, no, the things Deb said to her husband all but blistered the paint off the walls. And there, when the ambassador was giving birth, some of those hisses were just this side of lethal. She actually bit her consort through the arm, but he took it stoically."

Claire set the mug down then held her hands in her lap. "I had to do a bit more in there than I did with Deb. The Ambassador's cloaca dilated, right down at the base of her abdomen, then her baby just wriggled free of this clear fluid membrane. I had to catch the child, help it, and say the words being whispered to me by a Qian. Part of the time I was thinking about snakes and having a hard time not thinking of this child as a snake. I almost lost it once, then I caught the mother's glance. I could see the worry in her eyes, so I nodded, I said the words loud, with her little aide translating. I kept seeing my sister and the Blessed Virgin. I even knew I'd have a hard time justifying my actions to the Bishop, but I knew what I was doing was more right than wrong."

Flynn took her hands in his. "If there was any wrong in what you did, Father Yamashita, I'll not be seeing it as being worthy of your bothering me with it during Confession. As for the Bishop . . . " The older man shrugged. "I'm thinking she's got enough to worry about that troubling her with a report on this isn't really necessary."

Claire gave Flynn's hands a squeeze, then freed her own to recover her mug. "The whole thing wouldn't have been necessary if the Haxadis had planned ahead better."

"What do you mean?"

She frowned. "You are pregnant, and you know you need a priestess to help birth your baby if you are caught on a ship. You head out on a long journey, hoping to get home, but knowing it's a race against time. Why don't you ship a priestess with you? They had room in their pod for it—in the cabin they gave me, if nothing else."

The door to the small waiting room opened and the Qian station director entered the room. She looked about for a moment and then serenely faced the pair of priests. "There you are."

Flynn raised an eyebrow. "Why, Director Chzan, you're long since past trying to fool me with your coincidental appearances. You see, Father Yamashita, Director Chzan has a dozen different ways to locate us if she desires, not the least of which would have been having the station's systems sniff the air for the hints of your tea."

The Qian did her best to pretend she had not heard Flynn's remark. She extended her hand toward Claire. "I came for the transmission device."

Claire reached back behind her right ear and peeled off a plastic piece of circuitry through which a Qian aide had whispered to her the words she pronounced at the birth. "Thank you for your help."

"No, Father Yamashita, it is you who must be thanked." The Qian inclined her head slightly. "This would have been an indelicate situation were you not here to resolve it."

Flynn's eyes narrowed. "A point we were just discussing, in fact. Why didn't the ambassador have a priestess in her entourage?"

Chzan's eyes blinked slowly. "The priestess failed to obtain a flight health certificate."

"What?" Flynn laughed aloud. "A right-rum pox-dog fair bursting with bacteria and viruses would get a health cert—as could each and every one of the buggies infesting him. How did she fail?"

"Clerical error. It has been corrected." The Qian accepted the small device from Claire. "Again, Father Yamashita, thank you."

Claire sat back, wrapping her right hand around the mug. She let the tea's warmth fight the chill shivering its way up her spine as the Qian exited the room. "What just happened? I was put in the Haxadis pod at the insistence of the Qian crew. Did they fail the Haxadis priestess deliberately, then not tell the ambassador I would be available, yet have me there just in case? Why would they do that?"

Flynn frowned. "Their station, their Commonwealth, their rules."

"But what did they gain?"

"Knowledge. How you functioned under stress. How the Haxadissi functioned under stress." Flynn grinned, and cocked his head to the right. "And now they have a powerful Haxadis family beholden to a human for the birth of a grandchild. At the cost of a little anxiety relieved, they build some stability for the Commonwealth."

"But they didn't know how I would react. No one did."

"Save God, Father Yamashita."

"You're right, He knew." She nodded. "And it's Claire."

"I suspect He knew that, too." Flynn smiled. "As for what the Qian might have known, doesn't matter. Now they know more, and likely more than either of us could figure out. Still, that's part of what keeps life here on Purgatory Station so interesting."

Claire smiled. "The Qian and knowledge. Perhaps they're the serpents in the garden."

"Could be, but this is their garden, Claire. From their point of view, it also likely a fair viper's nest, within which we're just two."

"And your friend, Meresin?"

Flynn smiled. "Oh, a serpent, definitely, though not the worst here. Don't you be minding that, though, Claire, for it's still a garden here, beauty abounding. Welcome to your new home."

Home. So far away and yet . . . Claire sipped her tea, then nodded. "Thank you. Home it shall be, Father, serpents and all."

First Contact Café

by Irene Radford

Irene Radford is a member of an endangered species, a native Oregonian still living in Oregon. She is best known for her fantasy series The Dragon Nimbus, The Dragon Nimbus History, *and* Merlin's Descendants. *Most recently she has begun the cross over into space opera and space stations with* The Hidden Dragon, Stargods #1, *published by DAW Books in 2002.*

A SCREECH from the station monitors stabbed through the perceptions of Ab'nere Ll'byr Wyn'th (pronounced Abner Labyrinth in that new language working its way around the space station). She tongued a control built into her dentalia. One of the ten screens built into her spectacles that nearly reached her earlobes displayed the scene from A 108, the ammonia atmosphere arm close to the hub of *Labyrinth*, her space station, where gravity was low.

She gasped in horror as she watched a nearly transparent Pentapod, its visible heart beating a rapid and erratic rhythm even for a Pentapod, fling a spindly barstool over its head into the mirror behind the bar. Ab'nere's Number Eight Son—fathered by an ammonia breather and thus possessing gills to breathe a veritable cocktail of different atmospheres—ducked out of the way of the stool, arms shielding his neck and those vulnerable gills from shattering glass. His daughter and her spouse flung aside their trays filled with noxious drinks only an ammonia breather could love and dove beneath the tables they had been serving. The silica and lead globules filled with liquid and vaporous chemicals smashed into walls. Before the rainbow puddles slid to the floor, two patrons slammed their arm joints, simultaneously, into the offender's mid-region.

The first combatant stumbled backward. He collided with yet another patron. That being's drink flew out of his hand. The splashee's foot jerked into a delicate leg joint of yet another patron. This next victim retaliated by breaking a drink globule over the nearest head—that of Number Eight Son.

Before Ab'nere could blink, all twenty imbibers in the bar had joined the fray. Flippers and pseudopods lashed out. Limbs tangled and internal organs pulsed. Defenders leaped aside and slammed into no longer innocent bystanders.

One of them landed upon the portal iris. It buckled. The air lock behind it hissed. An attacker launched himself at the door. The lock shattered under the combined weight and thrust.

The fight spilled into the corridor. Only one more air lock separated them from the hub. If the ammonia leaked into the hub, containment could prove difficult.

Ab'nere fought the panic rising in her gorge. She carried new life—not yet discernable to any but herself. This eighteenth offspring had been fathered by a Magma Giant. The heavy metal content in its blood was particularly vulnerable to contamination from ammonia.

"Number Eight Son!" Ab'nere shouted over the com link buried in yet another of her one hundred ten teeth.

No answer. Her offspring remained hidden safely behind the bar.

"Number Eight, I did not incur untold debt with the bankers of D'Or to build this station just so those spacers could tear it apart. Get out there and end this brawl."

"Mother, they are ammonia breathers. What else do you expect from them," her offspring protested.

"Do not make me close down this oxygen/nitrogen/hydrogen bar just to come settle a brawl you are too timid to end." Not that she would risk the new child in the ammonia arm of the space station. "I will lose a valuable first contact fee if I do."

"But, Mother . . ."

"You are no better than your father. Now get out there and do something. I have just written you out of my will."

"Honored Mother, I will do as you bid. At great peril to myself. But only so that your displeasure with me does not affect the welfare of your grandchildren. And a new great grandchild." Just as verbose as his father, too!

"The damages will come out of your portion of my estate. If I write you back into my will." At the same time Ab'nere preened at the news that yet another descendant was on the way. The ammonia line might lack concentration and reliability, but they were amazing breeders.

She always enjoyed reunions with her eighth spouse.

Then she ground her dental work together, at great risk to her various controls and links about the station.

What would the new species think of *Labyrinth*! Brawls threatening to mix atmospheres, cowardly progeny, toxic drinks too near the air locks.

"I have provided a safe, friendly place for species to make contact, negotiate trade, and solve mutual problems," she nearly screamed at her negligent son. "And you jeopardize it all."

The monitor in her spectacles showed her offspring wading into the midst of the brawl. His smooth skin, a legacy from Ab'nere's Labyrinthine ancestry, protected him from scrapes and bruises better than the thin membranes of the ammonia breathers. Number Eight had also inherited Ab'nere's squat figure without indentations or protrusions that might offer convenient handholds to enemies in one-on-one combat. But his ears were pitifully small, they only folded to meet at his flat nose, not overlap and cover his entire face.

Then she noticed the hem of his uniform robe was torn. He tripped on it, scrabbling for balance in the low gravity. An impolite amount of his thin legs (as spindly as his father's and not at all as attractive as Ab'nere's sturdier limbs) gaped through the hole in his garment. In his forward sprawl Number Eight flew between a Pentapod and a gelatinous, red-and-white Porgeusa who were beating at each other with broken glassware. The two separated, gasping for breath.

Number Eight tried the same ploy to separate other combatants with little effect. The energy fueling the fight continued to build. She set down her towel and the glass she had polished too many times. "Number Eight Son," she called through the link. "My honor as a Labyrinthine trader is called into question. Contain this brawl."

Number Eight Son picked himself up off the floor and peered into the two-way monitor. He sported several bright green bruises around his eyes that clashed with his usually beautiful yellow/brown skin. "I shall try, Mother."

"Do not just try. Do!" Ab'nere shook her head in dismay. Bad enough that she had to worry that the child she carried might possess enough of its father's DNA to be born weighing more than she did. Her entire station was at risk if the ammonia leaked out.

She took several deep, calming breaths. Then she inflated the cost of the damages and medical bills by a factor of three—the only way to keep the bankers of D'Or from finding too much profit aboard the space station and trying to tack on extra interest.

She really did not want to close this bar before the infant species made his appearance. Ab'nere's reputation, not to mention her various bank accounts, and the infant in her womb were at stake.

She pinched her towel with two of her three digits of one paw and a fresh glass in the other. Not that she needed to polish the drinking vessels, the TurboSteam® spat out clean, shiny, sanitized containers no matter which species had drooled into them. The time-honored activity made her look busy while she waited for the next set of customers. An infant species just making its first venture into space, and a Glug.

She checked the computer's schedule. Both species had missed their appointment by seventeen centags. An unforgivable breach of etiquette. This did not bode well. Did not this new species realize that all of its future trade agreements and diplomatic alliances revolved around this first meeting at the *Labyrinth*?

And the Glug. The greedy methane eaters came and went on a schedule understood only by other Glugs.

The infant in her womb twisted and upset her digestion. She folded one ear across her mouth to hide her burp.

She did not need this added worry.

When she had made verbal arrangements for this meeting with the infant species, their representative had promptly named *Labyrinth* "First Contact Cafè," stating blithely: "Yeah, we have them back home." Whatever that meant?

Within centags of that communication, all thirty-seven species in residence had adopted the name. For sixty-five million trade agreements the station had been *Labyrinth.*

No more.

This new language could not disappear into the galactic polyglot fast enough.

Ab'nere looked over the bar to make sure a diminutive being had not crept in unnoticed; though preliminary communications indicated the new species was taller than most bipedal quadrupeds in this sector. Species had been known to lie about themselves to keep others from thinking about them in terms of lunch.

The etiquette Ab'nere had codified strictly forbade the question, "Are you edible?" Still, it happened. The granite giants of Magma Prime—like her latest spouse and the father of her eighteenth child—were voracious feeders on anything mineral, sentient or no. And the silicon globules of N'w Sson Hoos'seè had been known to slurp unsuspecting planets dry, leaving desiccated corpses for the Vulturians of Go Bae. Still, most of the fleshy carbon-based species avoided harvesting each other.

She understood why species just venturing beyond their own solar system for the first time liked a neutral meeting point before giving out their home address. They also liked a sense of quiet privacy while they labored through the first delicate negotiations with others. Ab'nere acted as a neutral referee between alien prejudices, preconceptions, needs, attitudes, and languages.

And Ab'nere earned a very generous fee for providing

the service and the meeting place. Most of the time. The brawl in A 108 threatened the first contact as well as the fee. (Each quarter cycle when the loan payments came due, the bankers of D'Or looked closer and closer at her bookkeeping. She had to work harder and harder at hiding the true numbers. She refused to allow them to increase her debt in direct proportion to the profit margin.)

A brief look into the monitor showed the fight in A 108 winding down. Ab'nere should not have worried. Ammonia breathers did not have the concentration to sustain anything long enough to incur real damage.

Except perhaps mating. Then they lost interest as soon as gestation could be confirmed.

Just as well. Ab'nere did not appreciate interference from any of her eighteen spouses in the raising of her offspring.

Males just did not appreciate that no matter what species they came from, Ab'nere's children were always fully Labyrinthians. The other species rarely contributed more to the genetic makeup than a useful trait like ammonia gills, or heavy gravity adaptability. The Magma Giants were an unknown quantity as sires. She should not worry about the size of her child. Every one of her offspring had weighed the same at birth and grown to equal her in height. Still . . .

The docking manifest showed the infant species arriving at Oxygen/nitrogen/hydrogen 3—about halfway to the end of that spoke and therefore at a mid level gravity. A huge ugly ship that had to slow its rotation to dock. Until they completed that delicate operation, the spacers would be without gravity. Their FTL drive was primitive, probably their first. Must have taken several of their years to reach *Labyrinth*. Had they resorted to suspended animation to survive the long trip? Ab'nere shuddered at the thought of the primitive travel mode.

Civilized species did not subject their people to such dangerous indignities.

"Number Six Daughter, please open ONH 321 for the isolated use of the new arrivals. Provide fermented grains and distilled spirits for their consumption while they await completion of first contact."

"Honored Mother, do we truly wish to encourage the consumption of distilled sprits?" Number Six had the audacity to ask.

If the ammonia breathers drank toxic chemicals, this infant species polluted themselves at higher levels (much as their language had already polluted *Labyrinth*).

"These infants will either abandon liquor while in space or they will not survive as a species long enough to become a threat to civilization," Ab'nere replied. "Do not question my orders, Number Six. I have watched species rise and fall a dozen times over during the past two hundred five cycles. I know how to run this station."

She really needed to supervise the mopping up in A 108, 109 and now up to A 112, and make sure the computer recorded Ab'nere's estimated repair costs rather than actual numbers. Instead, she waited on a very late infant species and an elder who should know better. Etiquette had been breached by all parties involved.

This mode of affairs must not continue. Etiquette ran *Labyrinth* and kept misunderstandings to a minimum. She firmly believed that her etiquette prevented war.

A new screen on her spectacles flashed an alarm. "Number Fifteen Son," she called. "Aquatic 893 just lost three points of pressure. You must swim in and check for leaks."

"Oh, Mother, I was just going to bathe," came the rebellious reply.

"There is plenty of water for bathing in the aquatic arm. And I can see ice forming around portal HO 891C. You must seal that leak now."

"Can't you do it, Mother?"

"Not if you want to continue living on this station!"

Number Fifteen sighed as if the weight of the universe rested on his shoulders. Then he shuffled along to his assignment.

Ab'nere kept a corner of one lens reserved for Number Fifteen and his minor repair. Like *his* father, he could repair anything and breathed HO liquids as readily as OH gases. But he was of an age to question everything and withdraw into his own head for amusement to the exclusion of all else.

A Glug, oozed into ONH 323, rotating its midsection to indicate its search for a new contact. Frequent visitors like the Glugs had terminal jacks wired directly into their brains. The creature bellied up to the bar—that is if the amorphous blobs of sludge had a belly—and plugged in to the translation port of the central system.

Those species not interested in hardwiring their brains usually carried portable jacks that fitted in or over whatever passed for ears.

Ab'nere prided herself on not needing a jack. She learned the new languages as quickly as communications opened up new worlds. Each of her eighteen mates had communicated in a different manner, some of them most interestingly.

But then Labyrinthines tended to have DNA as flexible as their tongues, their ears, and their double-jointed limbs.

"Methane, straight up. Double shot," the Glug ordered.

Ab'nere suspected this one was Ghoul'gam'esth, their chief negotiator. Glugs were a communal species. What one ate, thought, suffered, the rest of the colony thought, suffered, ate. Identifying any individual proved a challenge to non-Glugs. Only slight differences in coloration separated them. Shape and size constantly varied within each individual. If this one was the Ghoul, then they sent the big guns for the negotiation, showing a bit of desperation. Methane was getting harder to find in its raw state. The greedy Glugs recklessly sought out infant species in search of new sources of their primary food. Often they violated contamination protocols in their never-ending quest for methane. (Galactic scientists had yet to figure out how the species thrived on methane but breathed oxygen.) Rumor had it, this new infant species had an excess of excrement that broke down into large amounts of methane. (Most inefficient.) A trade agreement would benefit them all.

And Ab'nere would collect the commission on the trade agreement, and the docking fees for the transfer of cargo, and library fees for dispensing information on both species. Not to mention what the traders spent on comestibles and ingestibles.

Hopefully, the bankers had not heard of this infant yet and would not know how to compute the trade agreement to their own benefit. How long could Ab'nere keep it hidden?

About as long as she could hide a pregnancy by a Magma Giant. But for now, both were her secrets.

She placed an enclosed globule of methane with a straw and a bright green swizzle stick in the shape of a plumbing plunger on the bar where the Glug could reach it. The useless decoration added refinement to the noxious brew. The new species liked useless ornamentation, too.

A tendril of sluggish brown mass wove up to the bar. The vessel disappeared within. A moment later it reappeared. The Glug expanded to three times its normal size, becoming a denser brown. Ab'nere ducked behind the bar, bracing herself. The Glug belched like a thunderclap followed by a gush of air as strong as the atmosphere from an entire arm of the station rushing to fill a vacuum. The accompanying stench had been known to revive those on the brink of passing on—or cause healthy athletes to drop into a dead faint. The automatic air scrubbers kicked in. Ab'nere emerged from her crouch with a misting bottle. She sprayed the space around the Glug to make sure the odors died an ignoble death. Her favorite acidic sweet smell, the computer said the infant species called mint, replaced the stench of the Glug. Actually this "mint" smelled a lot like the pernicious "sweet on the tongue" or sott plant that had started on Ab'nere's home world and grew on every known oxygen atmosphere planet, with or without gravity. A horticulturist had once told Ab'nere that if she wanted to start an herb garden in *Labyrinth's* hydroponics lab, she should plant a little sott and step out of the way.

"Another, please." The Glug's voice appeared on the translation monitor even as Ab'nere's mind processed the grunts and moans into language.

Ab'nere set out another double shot of methane, keying in a nice tip for herself on the Glug's tab.

She had just cleansed the next belch when the door whooshed open. A tall, loose-jointed being ambled in. Its lower limbs were encased in a sturdy fabric of dark blue with hints of white in a complex and interesting weave. A finer fabric in a complementary paler shade of the same weave covered its upper body. It removed a large head covering made from some kind of animal leather. It had an amazingly small head for the size of the body. Not much brain capacity there. Pale fur with golden highlights tumbled to where the creature's neck and arm joints met. It shook the mane so that it flowed tangle free halfway down its back. But its paws and face were not furred. Curious.

And those lumpy organs on its chest? Could the infants have sent a female to negotiate for them? These negotiations could become fierce.

Ab'nere prepared to double her fee.

The infant's bright eyes, that matched the clothing in color, moved restlessly (warily?), searching the room. Its gaze lighted on Ab'nere. Something akin to lightning flashed across the eyes and it curved a narrow facial opening upward. It bared no dentalia.

Good. It had at least read the first page of the etiquette book.

"Howdy!" the being nearly shouted. A violation of etiquette rule #57A, no need to raise one's voice with the translator jacks.

Ab'nere ran the greeting through her vocabulary. Nothing computed in her head. She keyed the computer to check with vernacular references.

The explanation scrolled across the screen. "*Howdy:* a contracted form of 'how do you do.' An accepted polite greeting in portions of the central sector of the northern continent of the western hemisphere."

Great. Not only was the language unstructured and incredibly illogical, it varied from region to region. Maybe she should jack in now and avoid a headache.

The infant's pointed-toe boots with slightly elevated heels made little clicking sounds against the ceramic floor. Ab'nere clenched her jaw. Etiquette rule number 57B, no untoward noise while moving. This might distract from full comprehension of speech.

"This here the 'First Contact Café'?" the being asked as it moved toward the bar in that curiously graceful, loose-jointed procedure.

Ab'nere contained her distaste at the new name for her beloved *Labyrinth.*

At least the infant spoke at a lower volume now. It enunciated each word slowly, drawing out many of the syllables. Another politeness to make certain the computer and listeners understood the language.

The infant species plunked its head covering on the bar and spun it. A curious device of two equilateral triangles, one with the apex up, and the other with the apex pointing down, adorned the front. The geometrical symbol of a six-pointed star had been adopted by every space faring nation as an indicator for star systems that supported planets and civilizations capable of space travel. Rather arrogant of the infant species to sport this design on its first excursion into civilized space.

"Body too big for efficient space travel," the Glug muttered and disconnected from the language computer with a little belch that hardly stank at all.

"Maybe inefficient for conservation of resources aboard ship, but an estimable source of methane," Ab'nere replied *sotto voce* in Glug. She gave him another double shot of methane on the house.

The Glug downed the drink and contained his belch—he must be nearing saturation. Or was too intimidated by the infant to properly digest. He shifted into a different amorphous shape rather than reply.

He made a curious form that invited the infant to perch atop him.

"Welcome to *Labyrinth.* You have found your appointment," Ab'nere replied to the infant. She tried to imitate the up-curving facial gesture. She could not manage it without revealing a few teeth. Definitely bad form.

"Lexie du Preé, Abilene, Texas, in the good ole US of A. That's on Earth. Folks just call me 'Sexy.'" She thrust out a slender paw as if it expected physical touch.

Another breach. Rule number 23. No offer of physical contact on first meeting.

The paw remained outthrust, all four digits straight and stacked neatly one atop the other. The opposable thumb sticking out at a right angle must make it very dexterous. Ab'nere stared at it with envy. Her own three-digit paw managed quite well, especially with suckers on each digit, but one more and an opposable would be ever so useful in manipulating glasses and counting credits at the same time. Perhaps her next mate should be from this infant species.

Ab'nere drew a deep breath and slowly extended her own forelimb with its suddenly inadequate three digits. She brushed flat surfaces, skin to skin. The being from Earth wrapped its digits around hers in a warm clasp. A curious feeling of well-being coiled up Ab'nere's forelimb. The curving mouth gesture came more naturally to her.

Ab'nere gave her name in both her own language and the infant species' according to appropriate protocol. The Glug appeared inert, removed from the language interface and therefore the proceedings.

Initial negotiations fell to Ab'nere. Not the first time she had stepped in. Mentally she added another ten percent to her fee.

Lexie du Preè folded her limbs to perch on the nearest object—The Ghoul. She leaned against the bar, both forelimb joints resting on the polished surface. Ab'nere grimaced at the cloudy marks its body heat left there.

"Sorry I'm late, Abner. But I went up to the observation bubble on this spoke to make sure my ship was locked down tight and I kinda got lost looking out at the stars. That sure is a purrty view you got there."

Purrty: colloquial form of pretty, slightly less than beautiful, the computer prompted Ab'nere.

"Your space station looks like a tin can with straws sticking out of it at odd angles from space. I got the lay of the land a bit. But, you know, from five million klicks away, it's just another little blip on the sensors. I like looking at the stars better. You got quite a view here."

"Yes, the view can be entrancing." Ab'nere eyed Lexie du Preè's stool and foot placement suspiciously. A bubble of mirth almost escaped her mouth. But that would be impolite to all parties involved.

Ab'nere served her new client a beer, one of the brews specified in preliminary communications. Actually fermented grain mixtures seemed to be a universal beverage; along with fermented fruits and vegetables—even the Glugs' methane was a fermentation of a sort. Only infant species indulged in distilled spirits and then not for long. Strong alcohol rotted brains and produced hallucinations faster in space.

At the last moment she remembered to plunk a pink parasol into the foamy head of the beer.

Lexie du Preè curved her mouth upward again and drained most of her beer in one long swallow. She held the parasol against the side of the drinking vessel with one of those marvelously jointed digits. Then she wiped her mouth daintily with a square of pristine white cloth she removed from her pocket. Some sort of floppy thread decoration edged the piece.

Ab'nere suddenly lusted after the attractive adornment.

Something in the delicacy of the gesture and the cloth did not mesh with the crude image the infant projected. Ab'nere watched Lexie du Preè more closely.

"But I see that I'm not the only pardner ridin' in late," Lexie du Preè said.

Pardner: colloquial of partner, used to indicate acquaintanceship or similarity of profession rather than those engaged in an actual partnership.

Ridin'. Ab'nere keyed into the computer quickly.

Ridin': colloquial of riding, a euphemism for any kind of transport.

Lexie du Preè looked around the seemingly empty bar once more. "So, tell me, woman to woman, what can I expect from these Glugs? Are they canny as rattlers?"

Shrewd negotiators, the computer translated in shorthand.

Uh-oh, even the language program was succumbing to the infant's abbreviated speech.

"Woo . . . woman?" Ab'nere gasped. "You can tell I am female?" She looked at her blunt, hairless body that only reached Lexie du Preè's shoulder. She was clad in her customary asexual robe that covered her from shoulder to heel. Polite species did not flaunt sexuality.

Only selected mates could tell the sex of a Labyrinthine, and then only by smell during estrus. All relationships were built on asexual friendship before mating could even be considered.

"Shoot, honey, I can tell you've got a bun in the oven, and ain't no man kin do that!"

"No one knows that yet. Not even the father. Are you a telepath? Your visitor profile did not mention telepathic abilities."

"Nah. No hoodoo voodoo thought waves. Don't believe much in that stuff. Every once in a while we'll get a throwback who can see some strange stuff that ain't really there. But we haven't figured out how to make them breed true or train those we can verify. We just rely on observation. There's something in the attitude toward life that makes us both female and new mamas. I got one incubatin' myself, due in about seven of our moon cycles. We're kindred spirits."

"Kindred spirits," Ab'nere repeated dully, not certain she wanted to pursue this relationship any further. Lexie du Preè had jumped from an interesting primitive to a formidable observer in one quantum leap.

"So, tell me: what am I up against?" Lexie du Preè asked.

"The Glugs consume methane. That is the primary objective of all of their trade agreements." Preliminary contacts should have established that.

"Methane. Sure. We got enough chicken shit and hog poop to feed their whole planet for a year or two. But what can we get from these living sewage disposal plants that would benefit us?"

"What do you need."

"Tech advice. That ship we built moves faster than anything we've ever had. But from what I've seen of the ships docked around the First Contact Café, it's a slug. If we want to become a presence in the galaxy, we got to have some speed."

Ab'nere suspected that an Earther presence in the galaxy just might prove dangerous to all concerned.

She made a calculated decision. Profits came from alliances with the strongest races.

"The Glugs have access to a better FTL drive than you have."

"Sure they don't just propel themselves by belching a little volatile gas?"

Both Lexie du Preè and Ab'nere spread their mouths upward at the image.

"The Glugs have invented many wonderful things in their quest for new food sources." Ab'nere kept her demeanor sober as she leaned forward confidentially. Keeping one eye on the computer terminal to make sure the Glug hadn't jacked in to eavesdrop, she whispered, "Frankly, I don't like the Glugs. They stink. Right now their odor upsets the baby. That violates several rules of etiquette. I'd like to see your people get the best deal they can."

She repeated the same phrase in every negotiation she handled regardless of her personal preferences. Etiquette and profit sometimes did not mesh.

"Sure 'nuff, honey. I grew up on the chicken ranch. I know what I'm dealing with. Now how much shit can we unload for a new FTL drive?"

Ab'nere told her.

"That much?"

"Will that impoverish you?"

"Ah, I don't think so. But it will be a stretch. Might have to start mining the cattle ranches as well as the hog farms for that much. What about an artificial gravity. How much would that cost? We could cut the size of the ship down by fifty percent if we didn't depend upon rotation. Or increase the cargo holds by that much if we kept the same size. Think the Glugs would let us have that?"

Ab'nere prodded the Glug with a judicious jolt of electricity from the floor beneath it. The Glug jacked in. It replied to Ab'nere silently by way of the machine.

"Oh, I think the Glugs can appreciate your request. But they'd want at least fifty percent more for the fil-grav than the FTL."

"Now that might present a bit of a hardship. We'd have to increase our herds, but you only get prime methane from animals at their peak of youth and strength. We'll have to slaughter the aging critters to make way for young'uns. And what do we do with all those carcasses? We'll have to," shudder, "*eat* them."

"Yes that could present a hardship," Ab'nere agreed. Secretly she checked the Glug's connection to the computer. He had shuddered in disgust right along with Lexie du Preè. The Ghoul might prove more generous than usual. Or be more desperate.

"And what about fodder for all them critters," Lexie du Preè continued. We'll have to divert expensive grain supplies from human consumption to feeding chickens and pigs, and bulls. That ain't going to go over too big with some folks back home."

The Glug sent several rapid communications through his Jack with instructions.

"What kind of grains?" Ab'nere asked.

"Corn mostly."

The computer flashed a visual as well as a description of a plant Ab'nere knew all too well, tall stalks with kernels growing on long tubes. Every civilized planet burned the pernicious monster as a weed that had spread from

Ab'nere's home planet and adapted to every local environment—like sott and Labyrinthians themselves. No one had ever considered eating the kernels of "corn."

"Perhaps I can strike an additional deal with you. For a fee . . ."

"What kind of deal?" Lexie du Preè twirled the leather head covering on one forepaw digit, staring at it as if falling into a trance.

"I know a source for this corn you require."

"We'll have to test it for DNA compatibility. Don't want our prime methane producers starvin' to death on an inert substance."

"The DNA on my planet has proved most flexible."

"How so?" Lexie du Preè narrowed her eyes.

Ab'nere had come to think of that expression as calculating. She definitely wanted the genetic advantages an Earther mate would give her offspring.

"Since the people of Labyrinth first ventured into space one thousand cycles ago, sentient beings, livestock, plants, anything native to our world has proved incapable of breeding with other natives. We must crossbreed with the beings we encounter, absorbing their culture, their languages, and their genes. But the offspring always take on the overt characteristics of a Labyrinthine." Plus a few advantages.

How could she use a very large child of a Magma Giant to boost her profits?

"You think your corn will cross-pollinate with our corn?"

"We have yet to fail."

"Then I guess we got ourselves a deal." Once more Lexie du Preè held out her paw for a contact greeting.

"Our surveys indicate your species regards a written contract with signatures as binding." Ab'nere eyed the slim hand devoid of fur skeptically.

"The lawyer-types back home will require one. But just between you 'n me, friends, women, new mamas, a handshake is as binding as a signature." Lexie du Preè's voice took on an edge previously missing.

"And so it is with my people." Ab'nere clasped her new

business partner's paw with her own, squeezing lightly but firmly.

"Now how do I pay for this here beer? Mighty good beer it is, too." She finished the last few drops, again dabbing at her mouth with the square of fine cloth and its intriguing edge.

"What kind of currency do you use back on Earth?" Ab'nere asked, even as she added the cost of the beer to the ship's docking fees—payable in trade with the first exchange of cargoes.

"Mostly we work on a credit system, all handled by the computers. But for casual transactions we use coins." She dumped a handful of metal disks upon the bar.

"All of these are common metals," Ab'nere eyed the collection skeptically. "I could consider that square of white cloth with the thread edging, though, for the beer. What besides methane does your world produce in surplus?"

"People."

Another reason to choose an Earther as a mate. Ab'nere hoped they were as skilled lovers as the ammonia breathers.

"What about more woven textiles of this fineness?" Ab'nere held up the square of white. "This type of edging might prove useful in paying for the corn."

Lexie du Preè fingered the curious crossed triangles emblem on her hat. She waited through a long moment.

The Glug asked anxious questions. His silent words on the computer screen nearly danced with glee. He'd get his methane. Ab'nere would turn a pernicious weed into a cash crop. The Earthers would enter into the realm of galactic trade as happy partners.

The silence stretched on for more long moments while Lexie du Preè weighed the cost of the corn against the technological gains. The atmosphere in the bar grew thick.

"Deal," she said on a deep sigh.

They shook paws again.

"Folks back home will be skeptical of this chicken shit deal. That's one hell of a high price to pay. But I'll make 'em see the value in it." She handed over the square of cloth reluctantly. "We call this a lace-edged hankie. This one belonged to my Nanna."

"Then I shall treasure this artifact and record its provenance with care." Ab'nere patted the hankie with respect. Four digits and an opposable thumb seemed to work wonders with looms her own species could not manage. She imagined woven translucent veils that had nothing to do with the spun webs of the Arachnoids of Arachnia. "I'll have a contract ready in a few centags. You, the Glug representative, and I will all sign it with three witnesses from neutral species."

"Sounds good. Say, I'm throwin' a little party on my ship tonight. The crew deserves a little three-alarm-Texas chili and beer after our trek to the First Contact Café. Come along and bring the Glug. If he's lucky, he might get a sample of some of the best methane ever produced on Earth. A rare treat."

"For me or the Glug?"

ORBITAL BASE FEAR

Eric Kotani

Eric Kotani is a pen name used by an astrophysicist who has published seven science fiction novels, some with co-authors, e.g., John Maddox Roberts. He also edited an anthology of stories in tribute to Robert A. Heinlein. He served as the director of a satellite observatory at NASA for fifteen years, and previously headed the astrophysics laboratory at NASA Johnson Space Center during the Apollo and Skylab Missions. He is now co-investigator of the Kepler Mission to detect Earth-like planets. He has held professorship at several universities, including the University of Pennsylvania and the Catholic University of America. He has published over 200 scientific papers and edited thirteen books on astrophysics. He has received a number of awards for his work, including the NASA Medal for Exceptional Scientific Achievement and Isaac Asimov Memorial Award. An asteriod has been named Yojikondo in recognition of his contributions to astronomy. He holds a sixth degree black belt in judo and in aikido and has been teaching a class for the past few decades.

LANDING maneuvers—uh, correction!—docking maneuvers in three hundred seconds!" Jacques Boutillier, the pilot of Mars Trailblazer, announced somewhat flamboyantly. The crew tensed in anticipation. This was the last step before reaching the Martian surface. Actually, they were about to "land" on Phobos, the larger of the two satellites of Mars; it was a little over a dozen kilometers across, with an irregular shape typical of small objects in the solar system. The surface gravity of the Martian moon was so miniscule—less than a thousandth of the standard g-force on Earth but varying widely at different locations due to the nonspherical shape—that the "landing" was essentially matching the orbital velocity with the Martian moon and establishing contact on the surface smoothly.

Poul Eriksen, the captain of this manned expedition to Mars and an experienced U.S. Air Force Space Command test pilot, was looking closely over Boutillier's shoulder. He had an outstanding reputation among his fellow officers as the man who got the job done right, no matter what. He looked the part, too—the indomitable look of a Viking war chieftain, with an intelligent face.

Eriksen was doing his utmost to avoid the disaster that overcame the Consortium's Mars Expedition I, and to become the captain of the first successful manned mission to Mars, something practically every kid would dream about in growing up. He had no desire to be a dead hero, but, more importantly, this was his expedition and he had no intention of letting it fail. Since he had little information on what had gone wrong in the first manned mission, it meant close supervision of everything that went on, occasionally irritating his crew, all of whom were experienced space jockeys.

Boutillier was a veteran pilot, too, with the rank of Major in the U.S. Marine Corps, Space Division. At twenty-eight he was probably the youngest among the crew; he had been selected specifically for his skill and fast reflexes in landing flying ships of all sorts. His credentials included piloting the Navy's single stage to orbit ships several times. He also had a unique qualification—successful landing on a small Earth-crossing asteroid a few years earlier. He looked lean, his brown hair framing the clean-cut features of his determined face; there was hardly any suggestion of his one-eighth Cherokee ancestry there. He was from the Louisiana bayou country and it was not always easy to control his Cajun temper. But it was either maintain a tight grip on his disposition or be disqualified for the mission. He had kept his cool.

The pilot ignored the close supervision by the captain and concentrated on the delicate final stage of contact with the small moon. He completed the "docking" maneuver with hardly a jolt felt by the four-person crew. After making sure that the ship was really at rest with respect to Phobos, he pushed the button for the anchors, firing two super-sharp harpoons into the crust of the little moon. Once the harpoons penetrated the surface to the predetermined depth, hooks extended from them, securing the anchorage.

"Anchors in place, Colonel Eriksen. We are right next to the Stickney Crater as planned. All set for extravehicular activities now." Old habits were hard to break; Boutillier sometimes addressed the ship's captain by the latter's military rank.

"Well done, Jack."

"Thank you, sir."

The 'landing' site was near the huge crater, where an earlier flyby mission reported a possible ice deposit. With the chance of taking advantage of the putative ice deposit, two supply ships had been sent to the adjacent area and had been waiting for the arrival of *Trailblazer*. One robot ship was full of supplies; the other ship contained provisions but had been designed to serve as a habitat.

"Nobu, put on your space suit and follow me outside. We're going to find out if the cargo aboard the supply ships arrived safely. We'll also see if the habitat can really be made habitable, then we'll check up on the rumored ice deposit."

"I am ready, Captain," answered Nobuo Okita, ship's nuclear physicist and all-around engineer.

Looking out the neo-glass window from his pilot's seat, Boutillier wondered aloud. "Why do we call this huge cavity the Stickney Crater? An unusual name, I'd say."

"It was named after the wife of the discoverer of the Martian moons, Asaph Hall of the U.S. Naval Observatory. His wife's maiden name was Chloe Angeline Stickney." Okita, who was an astronomy buff, offered the answer, spelling out her first name for the benefit of his audience. "I understand she was a brilliant mathematician and an interesting woman.

After her marriage to Hall, she would sometimes sign her letters using her initials, C.A.S.H."

After his discovery in 1877, Hall named the two moons Phobos and Deimos, Fear and Panic, the two ancient companions of the war god, Mars. The Crater was not discovered for about a century after the discovery of the little moon. It was "imaged" by a flyby probe in the latter part of the twentieth century. Asaph had always publicly acknowledged that he would not have succeeded in the search but for Chloe Angeline's constant encouragement to keep looking. The International Astronomical Union approved naming the Crater Stickney to honor her important contribution.

While donning his space suit, Okita mumbled an aside to his captain. "The Consortium ship *Ares* was only several days behind us the last time we checked. If they go for a direct landing on Mars, they can reach the planetary surface before us."

"Yah, don't we all know it! We have no time to waste. Let's get going."

Presently, Eriksen and Okita stood on the surface of Phobos, where no human beings had walked before. The robot ships that had landed a few months before were visible at a distance of a few hundred meters. The sunlight striking the bottom of the Stickney Crater was reflected by something shiny there, possibly a dark patch of ice.

"When you start walking, slide along the surface. Avoid up and down motions. It might not be easy on this godforsaken surface, but move horizontally as much as possible. If you try jumping over an obstacle, you might end up getting into orbit around this moonlet", cautioned the captain.

"Roger that." Actually, walking horizontally with a minimum of ups and downs came naturally to Okita. It was one of the first lessons he had to internalize in his judo class. Many a time at the beginning, failure to do so caused him to be thrown down on his back.

As they made their way toward the two unmanned ships, Eriksen started planting automatically-piercing metallic sticks, about one and a half meters long, into the moon's crust at an interval of several meters. Like the harpoons for anchoring the ship, once the sharp point reached a certain depth, the stick would release an anchorlike hook that would open underground. But he had to be careful when he gave the stick an initial shove downward so as not to propel himself into a trajectory. Okita, following his captain, ran a wire through a loop on each pole. Those who would follow the path to the supply ships in the future could run a hand around the wire and avoid the embarrassment of pushing themselves into a flight path.

An inspection of the inside of the ships showed that the shipments had arrived intact and that the habitat, after minor rearrangements, would provide a living space for several occupants.

"Good, now we can stay on Phobos without worrying much about consumables. When we send the shuttle down to the surface, we may even be able to bring back some ice from near the polar regions," said Eriksen, sounding optimistic.

The shiny dark patch was another few hundred meters away. Upon arriving there, Okita got down on his stomach without being told to do so and cautiously crawled onto the shiny material. Somewhat to his disappointment, the shiny surface was not ice; it would have been too good to be true, anyway. The shiny surface was a glassy material and was smooth and slippery. He was glad that he had taken the precaution; he might otherwise have skidded off, if not into a low orbit around the moon, at least to the other side of this shiny patch some fifty meters away. At the far side, he could see an overhang of rocks—just beyond where the glassy material ended. Whatever was below the overhang was totally shaded from the sunlight.

"This stuff is glassy—maybe it's molten rock. Too bad it's not an ice patch. I want to take a look at what's underneath that protruding rock over there." Okita informed Eriksen.

"Okay, go ahead. Watch your step. I'll hang around here and check things out on this side."

Okita decided to walk around the slippery patch rather than crawl across it. When he reached the spot, he saw that the overhang concealed a cavelike structure underneath. The ceiling was high enough so that he could walk into it. It was total darkness inside as there were no air molecules to scatter the sunlight from outside. One moment he was stepping into the cave and the next moment he skidded and ended up on his back. Thankfully, in the low gravity of Phobos, the fall was slow and gentle. He felt foolish for not having turned on his portable flashlight before stepping in. When he corrected his mistake and turned on the light, he was instantly alert. For instead of finding more of the glassy staff, what he saw definitely looked like an ice deposit.

Eriksen joined him promptly, as fast as the low gravity permitted him to move. After ascertaining to his satisfaction that the stuff was indeed ice, Eriksen brought out instruments and started measuring the dimensions of the ice lake inside the cave. The surface area was easy enough to estimate. It was the thickness of the ice that presented a problem in determining the volume of the ice deposit, as the thickness could vary from place to place. He solved the problem by measuring the depth at several randomly selected sites. The average depth seemed to be no less than ten meters. As the surface area was about twenty by thirty meters, this represented several thousand tons of water, which could sustain the crew for a long time. Of course, once they established a base on the Martian surface, there would be a virtually inexhaustible supply of water in the form of polar ice, even without counting on the possible underground deposits of ice in some places.

While Eriksen was measuring the size of the ice deposit, Okita looked around his surroundings for anything unusual. During the long voyage out, Jacques Boutillier had shared with Okita his secret suspicion that Mars might not have been an entirely dead planet. The mysterious catastrophe that befell Expedition I several years earlier had probably been a natural disaster, but it could also have been caused by something else—or, should he say, something artificial?

Mars Expedition I, the first manned mission by an international consortium—consisting of the U.S. (NASA), European Union (ESA), the Russian Federation and Japan—to Mars seven years earlier, ended up in a mysterious disaster. The exact cause of the failure was still under investigation and remained unclear.

The crew of Mars Expedition I, the first expedition to the fourth planet, had no leeway in picking the time to land. They had to land when they arrived and where they were supposed to, no matter what the planetary conditions were. Mars Expedition I lost contact with Earth when it was behind the planet—just as it was preparing to land. Those back on Earth had never learned what had happened during the communications blackout as no message had since been received.

The orbital probes that were sent later to the Red Planet could find no trace of the spacecraft anywhere on the ground. Since the doomed ship's orbit was inclined to the equator, the ship might have plunged into the dry ice in the polar cap and disappeared underneath. The total surface area of the Red Planet was comparable to that of the entire land area of Earth. Finding the ship, if it had indeed crashed somewhere, would be more difficult than finding from space a Boeing 707 that had crashed somewhere on the Eurasian continent, even if the terrain were completely bare of any plants, animals, or artifacts.

The direct landing on the fourth planet was in part necessitated by the slowness of the journey using the Hohmann trajectory, in which the ship accelerated only at the beginning, then coasted along in free fall, and decelerated at the end of the journey to match Mars' orbital velocity. It took so long getting there that the ship did not have sufficient reserve of consumables, which would have afforded the luxury of looking over the planet from an orbital altitude before landing. The ship needed to land without delay so that the crew could get at the provisions that had been dispatched to the landing site several months in advance.

One way to avoid the necessity of directly landing on Mars from Earth orbit was to shorten the travel time so that the ship would have ample provisions first to go into orbit around Mars and make certain that the landing would be safe. But it was all but impossible to do so with the conventional chemically powered rocket engines, which took so long in getting the crew to the destination. The ship could carry barely enough to keep the crew going for the nine months that it took to get there.

To shorten the travel time, it would be necessary to accelerate continuously for an extended period beyond the insertion to trans-Martian orbit. One way to do that was to use a nuclear powered rocket engine. It had turned out that the U.S. Air Force Space Command had been successful in developing an experimental nuclear fusion engine. Its early version had been proposed in the 1980s by Bussard at the time of the strategic defense initiative program; in its original form, the engine used protons, boron-11, lithium-6, deuterium, and helium-3 in appropriate cycles. This cycle did not emit neutrons, which made it safe for the human crew using this type of nuclear fusion engine. It had not been funded for development at the time but had later been picked up by the Space Command under the obscure budget heading of High-Efficiency Space Propulsion System. The label was not deceptive, as the nuclear fusion engine would be easily several times more efficient than chemical rockets in terms of the fuel mass involved. With a nuclear fusion engine of this type, it was possible to make it from Earth orbit to Mars orbit in just two months.

Just as importantly—perhaps even more significantly—placing the interplanetary ship on tiny Phobos first and sending a much smaller shuttle to the planetary surface meant that they would not have to expend a great deal of fuel to land the entire mass of the huge ship and lift it again from Mars for the return trip home. Instead, they would be landing and lifting the considerably smaller mass of the shuttle.

However, the phobia over using nuclear power was strong among the political parties in control of the leading countries in Europe that made up the ESA, as had sometimes been the case in the United States.

After the failure of the first manned mission to Mars, recognizing the immense advantages of using a fusion engine, the U.S. had broken away from the Consortium. The U.S. manned mission to Mars had become a joint venture between the Air Force Space Command and NASA.

To show unity with the European Union, Russia had decided to stick with the Consortium although historically Russia had had much fewer scruples about the use of nuclear power in space or elsewhere. Anchoring Mother Russia firmly to Western Europe was the sine qua non priority on their political agenda.

Japan left the Consortium when the multinational undertaking broke up with the departure of the U.S. and then joined the U.S. The most important reason for joining the U.S. expedition was perhaps the persuasive argument of the influential Japanese scientist, Professor Ikeda of the Institute of Space and Astronautical Science (ISAS), that the fusion engine and the plan to use Phobos as a space station before landing would give *Trailblazer* a substantially better chance of success than the Consortium's *Ares* Mission. The Japanese also figured that chances of a Japanese astronaut to be chosen for the four-man crew of *Ares* would be low. The member states of the Consortium would all be vying for a seat for their nation and there were more than four leading European countries involved in the venture without even counting Russia. At that point, the U.S. made an irresistible offer to the Japanese; they would include a Japanese astronaut if Japan signed on.

Okita was a first-rate nuclear physicist and engineer from the Tokyo Institute of Technology, having done his postdoctorate work at the ISAS. He had also spent childhood years in the U.S. with his diplomat father and his biochemist mother who lectured at local universities wherever her husband was posted. In consequence, Okita spoke accentless Midwestern American and there would be no language barrier between him and his American teammates.

The Consortium expedition, called *Ares I,* had left Earth's orbit about six months before the departure of *Trailblazer I,* but it was still on its way to Mars on a free-falling Hohmann orbit and was now actually behind *Trailblazer*. The Consortium had not given up on the thought of being the first on Mars and maybe counting on its competitor's announced plan to convert Phobos into a space station first before attempting a landing on the Red Planet itself in their shuttle.

As Eriksen and Okita returned to *Trailblazer,* the ship's planetary atmosphere specialist, Linde Hoerter, looked a little agitated. When she got really excited, which was not often, her Pennsylvania Dutch speech became noticeable. It was clear that she needed to talk to Eriksen in a hurry.

"Poul, I've been keeping a close watch on the Martian surface. There's a possibility that a storm might be brewing near the area where the supply ship for *Ares* landed earlier. Based on my analysis, this storm could become a nasty one. The timing is a little off from the storm season advocated by some experts on Earth, but these pesky events don't follow any strict schedules anyway. We need to watch this one carefully before we dispatch *Valkyrie* to the surface." The shuttle had been informally named *Valkyrie* by the captain, and his crew were all willing to oblige his whim.

Eriksen was his usual taciturn self. "You've told me before that no expert knows for sure how sandstorms get started. You are our expert. If we can't depend on your prognosis, we have no one else to turn to. We'll play it safe and heed your warning."

After pausing a moment, he added, "Send a storm warning to *Ares*. They will be getting here in just a few days."

"There could be a problem in getting them to pay attention to my warning."

"Explain yourself, Linde."

"Their Martian atmosphere expert, Roel van Dijk, does not agree with me on how a sandstorm gets started on Mars. He believes sandstorms occur only at the perihelion passage of Mars. As you know, Mars is already several months past perihelion. To complicate matters, there's evidence that at least some sandstorms or dust devils are kicked up by falling meteoroids that are not burned up in the atmosphere; the Martian atmosphere is too thin to incinerate them. To be sure, falling meteorites could kick up dust and at least contribute to the storm. On this one issue, we have had many a running battle at scientific meetings over the years. He will probably advise Captain Ritter to reject our foul weather advisory. They are still trying to beat us and Ritter will have a strong motivation to listen to van Dijk."

Eriksen pondered this a moment. "Send them a warning anyway. I would be damned if they did not have a warning from us before they made that crucial decision to land."

An hour later, Eriksen received a reply from Ritter. The captain of Ares thanked Eriksen for the courtesy and would take the warning under advisement.

Eriksen considered the wording of the message. "Ritter might actually be thinking seriously about placing his ship in a parking orbit and watching a while if a big storm develops. On the other hand, he may be sandbagging us. If we think that *Ares* will be getting into a parking orbit, we'll not be in a hurry to land *Valkyrie*. That will give them a chance to slip by us and land on Mars before us. Besides, getting into a parking orbit will cause them to use additional fuel; they don't have much extra fuel to spare, and can't count on what's on the supply ship before actually seeing it for themselves."

The Consortium's two robot supply ships with fuel and provisions were sending out electronic signals saying that the contents were intact, but one would be unwise to rely on the transmitted signals where one's life depended on them.

Boutillier spoke up. "Why don't we send *Valkyrie* down before *Ares* gets here. I volunteer to pilot it to the surface and plant our flag and fly back right away after video taping the flag planting event." Noticing Okita and remembering the other partner in the expedition, he corrected himself quickly. "I mean—plant our flags."

Eriksen was firm. "No, we are going to do it the way we have planned from the beginning. Being beaten in a race with the Consortium would not constitute a sufficient justification for not following our carefully made plans—especially, considering the imminent danger of a major sandstorm."

He went on. "We must make Orbital Base Phobos a viable station first. For one thing, we must make sure that, if something should happen to *Valkyrie,* the remaining crew would still be able to make it back to Earth safely with the provisions from our supply ships. If our friends aboard *Ares* choose not to be cautious with their lives, that's their problem."

Nevertheless, Eriksen ordered *Valkyrie* to be detached from *Trailblazer* and ready for departure for Mars on short notice. Even in the low gravity of Phobos, the inertial mass of *Valkyrie* was considerable and it was a delicate operation. The heavy work was pretty much automated, however.

"I'm almost certain now a severe local storm is gathering on the surface where *Ares* will be landing. I've just given Roel van Dijk a second warning but I don't think he'll believe me," Hoerter said with frustration.

Boutillier was still raring to go. "I'm game for flying down in *Valkyrie.* Anyone who wants to come along for the ride'll be welcome. I don't insist on being the first to step out of the ship either. We can toss a coin. After planting the flags, we'll head back immediately if the surface condition looks threatening. We can still be the first on Mars. The rest of us can take turns going down to the surface later."

Boutillier was obviously trying to avoid the accusation that the reason why he was proposing this quick trip down was to become the very first man to walk on Mars (as Neil Armstrong had become the first man to walk on the Moon in July 1969) and thus to become immortalized in history. He was anxious to be the first, but he was even more eager to make sure that *Trailblazer* would not be beaten to the first place.

Eriksen was unsympathetic. "No go, Jack. Linde, keep me posted on the gathering storm on Mars. Let's all get back to turning Phobos into a working orbital base first. Even if we don't get to be the first to land on Mars, we are going to be the first to do it right. In the long run, setting up an orbital base on Phobos will be more important in the exploration of the Red Planet than just planting the flags first. Especially, if we are going to terraform Mars someday for serious human exploration."

Several days later, the business of setting up a habitat on Phobos was nearly complete, but the surface conditions on Mars looked ever more perilous, at least in the opinion of Hoerter. *Ares* was about to enter Mars' vicinity, taking trajectory to land at a location marked by the transmission beam from their waiting supply ship.

Eriksen offered Ritter a safe haven on Orbital Base Phobos to wait out the gathering storm on Mars, but the gesture was politely declined. The storm had not picked up significant force yet and the *Ares* team wanted to make it to the surface, get the provisions from the robot ships, and be hunkered down there if indeed a storm should become a threat. If it started looking ominous enough, they could leave the surface after loading up the provisions and get into a Mars orbit and wait for several months until the orbital configuration for Earth became appropriate for the journey home.

The message that *Ares* was about to land on Mars was received at the Phobos base with mixed emotions, mostly with a sense of frustration and even resentment. *Trailblazer* could have been the first, but Eriksen would not risk his expedition team. If he did not have complete faith in the scientific predictions of his Martian atmosphere expert, he was nevertheless unwilling to take a chance that Hoerter was wrong.

At the present distance of Earth, those back home would be receiving this epoch-making report in several minutes. *What a depressing thought. To be so close to making a genuine historic first and ending up being a second team in. No one will remember us,* Boutillier thought furiously.

Some minutes later, back on Earth at the Headquarters of the European Space Agency in Paris, the Director General, Professor Dominique Laget was listening to the live news retransmitted from the receiving station in Villafranca near Madrid. The video screen on the great wall of the conference room would soon be showing the Martian surface from the television camera on *Ares.* Upon hearing the report that their ship was about to land on Mars, his distinguished face brightened in an inimitable Gaulish smile. He was joined by several dozen ranking officials of the Consortium that included a number from the Russian Federation.

Laget's pert strawberry-blonde secretary from Brittany started filling up the champagne glasses with the finest produce from the Champagne province. The same scene was being repeated all over Europe, with some variations in the choice of beverages. The entire subcontinent of Europe was ready to have the greatest festivities ever.

By design, the landing would take place when the side of Mars with the landing site was facing Earth.

It was only seconds before *Ares* was actually to make a touchdown that the transmission suddenly broke down. The last scene from the video camera on *Ares* showed an immense tornadolike dust cloud rapidly approaching the spaceship over the barren wasteland of Mars. The last vocal transmission received, just before the communication was cut off, said, "We are about to be overtaken by a great tornado. We will . . ." Ritter never got to complete his sentence.

After what seemed like an eternity of waiting, television and radio broadcasters were announcing that the transmission from Mars had been disrupted by unexplained technical difficulties.

After a while, in place of the direct report from *Ares,* there came a transmission from Orbital Base Phobos. They had had to wait a few hours for it, as the Martian moon had gone behind its mother planet in its approximately 0.31 day orbit.

As soon as Phobos was over the horizon for the line-of-sight contact with *Ares,* Captain Eriksen reported to Earth with a sense of foreboding. "We have no radio contact with *Ares*—no visual sighting either. The area surrounding the landing site is near the center of an immense dust cloud. We'll try making radio contact and keep looking for a break in the sandstorm."

Aboard *Trailblazer,* the crew huddled for a conference.

"What's your diagnosis now, Linde? Will the storm clear up anytime soon?" Eriksen asked.

"The storm appears to be local and relatively minor. We lack sufficient data about such events on Mars and it's hard to tell. There's an indication, though, that it may be clearing up. We need to keep watching."

"It's troubling there's no radio contact with *Ares.* The storm may have damaged the communications antennae," Boutillier interjected his thoughts.

Eriksen looked grave. "What worries me most is whether the ship itself is still intact. I don't think it was designed to cope with a sandstorm like that. I'm concerned about the safety of her crew."

Another orbit later, there still was no communication from *Ares* despite repeated attempts at contact from both *Trailblazer* and the Consortium's control antennae on Earth. All receiving stations around the globe were intently listening in for any signal from *Ares*. In the meanwhile, the *Trailblazer* crew worked around the clock to complete the refitting of the supply ships as a habitat so that they could house refugees from *Ares* if any were rescued.

At another all-hands meeting, Eriksen recapped the situation succinctly. "There are still no signals from *Ares*. Linde, bring us up to date on the conditions below, will you please?"

"At the landing site of *Ares* there may be a break in the dust storm soon, lasting maybe about an hour or so."

"How about the conditions at the spot picked for our own landing?" Eriksen wanted to have a more complete weather report.

"Unless it's for an emergency, I would not advise you to land *Valkyrie* there for at least a few days."

Anyway, it was clear in the minds of everybody present that ascertaining the safety of *Ares* and rescuing any surviving members came first before the completion of their own mission objectives. The crew selection board for *Trailblazer* would not have passed anyone whose first concern would not be for the well-being of their comrades, even when those colleagues were on the competing team.

Before Eriksen had the chance to address the issue, Boutillier spoke up eagerly.

"Unless we hear from *Ares* very soon, I volunteer to take *Valkyrie* down for a look. If there are survivors, I'll rescue them. The shuttle is a two-seater, but if I don't take any cargo, we can jury-rig another seat in it. If all four are alive, I guess I'll have to go back again."

"How are you going to get inside *Ares* to find out if there are survivors? If you force your way through the hatch, you may be sealing the fate of any survivor by exposing them to the near-vacuum of Mars," Okita objected.

"I'll knock on the door or something and find out if there's anyone inside who'll respond. If no one responds, it probably won't matter if I force my way in. Besides, if they have any sense, they'll all be wearing their space suits by now. I'll take four portable oxygen masks with me, though, just in case. Maybe, I can put the masks on their faces before they suffocate in near vacuum."

Eriksen cut in before the discussion progressed any further. "Piloting *Valkyrie* for a mission of mercy should be my job. It's still chancy there. As the captain, I can't expose Jack to such a risk."

If Eriksen sounded firm about his counterproposal, Boutillier was even more adamant about his idea. "Poul, as captain, your foremost responsibility is to the entire crew. The rescue mission for *Ares* has to come second. There're two experienced pilots on this mission for a good reason. Even if something should happen to one of us, the other will be able to take *Trailblazer* back to Earth. Obviously, you are more qualified than me in completing this mission and taking *Trailblazer* home. You are indispensable and I am expendable."

Boutillier declared with finality. "No, Captain, I must be the one to go."

Eriksen considered the Cajun's impassioned plea for several moments and reached a decision. It was evident that he did not like what he was about to say.

"All right, you win, Jack. One condition, though. You will not risk your life unnecessarily and you will do your utmost to come back safely, with or without any surviving members of *Ares*. Don't forget, we still need you to land *Valkyrie* at our own site and complete the mission. You are still the best pilot within tens of millions of kilometers."

Eriksen knew that Boutillier might not follow his injunctions but, by Mighty Odin, he had to tell him.

It took one more orbit of Phobos around Mars before Hoerter gave Boutillier a reluctant "go" sign. Hoerter cautioned him that the safety window was brief and that Boutillier ought to head back at most within an hour of landing, no matter what he found there. There was no telling what a fierce dust storm, with wind velocities sometimes running up to several hundred kilometers an hour, could do to the propulsion system of *Valkyrie,* even in the low air density of Mars.

* * *

While descending to the ground, Boutillier had the time to indulge in his secret concerns about Mars and its moons, most of which he had not shared with his crewmates. For one thing, he had always wondered if the Martian moons were entirely natural. As an undergraduate at the U.S. Naval Academy, he had studied celestial mechanics for its own elegant beauty. He loved the subject. It was clear to him that those two Martian moons should not be there—not by an act of nature, anyway. For one thing, if they had been two passing asteroids acquired by the gravitational field of Mars, why weren't their orbits significantly eccentric? At the time of the capture by Mars, their orbits must have been hyperbolic; even stipulating the presence of another much more massive asteroid at the time of the capture to provide the required perturbation, the orbital eccentricities for Phobos and Deimos should have remained close to unity, i.e., close to being hyperbolic.

He had often wondered if those two moons had naturally been placed in those neat orbits. Had they been put there artificially? That would imply the intervention of intelligent beings, perhaps some millions of years ago; the orbits of Phobos and Deimos seemed to be ideally suited as space stations for inhabitants of Mars. He was hoping that a thorough exploration of Phobos and Deimos—and Mars itself—would in time answer those questions.

That led to another question he had been harboring for a long time. Was the disaster that befell the first expedition seven years ago naturally caused? Or, was some sort of ancient defense system against invading ETs, meaning creatures like us, activated after all those years? He had to admit, however, that the idea of an ancient Martian strategic defense system being activated from time to time sounded more than a little far-fetched and even paranoid.

Had he voiced any of those thoughts before he had been selected, the selection board would probably have rejected him for being crazy. But now that he was by himself, these questions began gnawing at him. He shook his head vigorously to expel such negative thoughts. It did not matter if there was a Martian defense system working against all intruders. His job was to go down to the surface and rescue *Ares*' crew—if he could find anyone alive.

The dust had not quite cleared up in the landing area, but Boutillier could make out his immediate surroundings, including the *Ares*. He was already suited up. Without wasting a second upon landing, he opened the hatch, stepped onto the ground and closed the hatch behind him immediately, to prevent dust from getting inside *Valkyrie*. The ground was powdery with brownish-reddish sand. After several days on Phobos, where the gravitational acceleration downward was practically nonexistent, the one third Earth normal "g" of Mars felt down right homey.

It took only a few minutes to traverse the short distance to the entrance hatch of *Ares*. It was tightly shut as expected. He had brought some instruments to force it open, but he decided first to knock on it to see if anyone would respond. After several heavy knocks, he waited a short while and prepared to bang on the door again. It was then that he heard a faint sound from inside.

"Jumping catfish, there *is* someone alive on board!" Boutillier's heart began beating faster in excitement. He did not have to wait long before the hatch opened before him, revealing another space suit clad figure at the entrance. Masked by the heavily tinted visor, the face could not be seen clearly. Boutillier turned on his communicator and started speaking in a rapid-fire fashion, so impatient was he to learn what had happened. He was disappointed that his opposite number did not respond and then realized that the wavelength for his space suit communicator was probably not set at the right frequency to talk to someone wearing an *Ares* space suit.

The *Ares* astronaut approached him swiftly, without bothering to close the door behind, and touched the helmet to his. He heard a faint, feminine voice say, "Turn your communicator to Band H," and saw her pointing at the equipment for that purpose. When he reset the band frequency to H, he could hear a pleasant feminine voice. "I am Jeanne Monier, engineering physicist of *Ares*. You must be from *Trailblazer, n'est ce pas*?"

He recognized a distinctly French accent even before hearing the last phrase and it sounded pleasant to his ears. He had grown up listening to his grandparents speaking the French patois of Louisiana's backwood country, although he never really learned to speak it himself.

"Yes, I am Jacques Boutillier, pilot from *Trailblazer.* Are the rest of the crew all right?"

"I am afraid not. The storm suddenly hit us just before landing and we crash-landed; the ship hit a boulder, which caused the ship's hull to rupture. There was a catastrophic air decompression. Captain Ritter was piloting the ship himself and wanted to move freely during the critical final maneuver, so he was not suited. Neither was Roel van Dijk, our planetary physicist, who had to monitor all instruments closely during the landing operation. The captain had ordered Boris Ivanov, the pilot, and me to suit up before the landing operation. Just in case."

"Did Ritter know the risk he was taking, then?"

"Oh, yes, both Captain Ritter and van Dijk were aware of the risk, but they thought it was worth taking, to be the first on Mars. Anyhow, Ivanov was knocked around on impact and broke his leg. He is immobilized and is resting uncomfortably inside. The other two had no chance at all. I tried putting oxygen masks on them immediately, but it was no use."

Boutillier suddenly felt a warm empathy for the kindred spirit. "So they died while standing their watch on the bridge."

"Yes, that would be a gallant way to put it. Anyhow, Boris Ivanov and I are the only survivors. I have been trying to contact *Trailblazer,* but our receiver is not working. The dust tornado might have knocked off the antennae. With the sandstorm so fierce, I dared not go outside to check. If I had, I might not have been able to get back in. I kept sending S.O.S. signals. Did you get them? Is that why you are here?"

"No, we received no signals from you. I came down here to see if there was anything we could do to help you and your crew. Show me where Ivanov is, and I'll carry him back to *Valkyrie,* our shuttle. On Mars, he can't weigh much. But the storms might come back in force. Let's not waste any time."

"*D'accord.* I'll show you where he is. It's not a large ship."

It was a bit awkward to carry another man on his back through the doorway when both were suited in bulky space suits, but Boutillier managed. He had Monier open the hatch for him when they reached *Valkyrie;* as he pulled Ivanov in after him, she hurried in and locked the door behind her.

They took off immediately. The storm was gathering force again and they barely made it off in one piece. Boutillier did not worry about computing a matching orbit before the takeoff; departing intact was the foremost thing on his mind. He was confident that he would be able to match orbit with Phobos, especially since he had made sure that the fuel tank was full before leaving the base.

Monier spoke up when she was certain that Boutillier could spare his attention.

"Would it be possible to pressurize this cabin so I could take off the helmet? I have been wearing this thing almost a day. The air supply is still okay for a while longer, but I could use some refreshments. That is, unless it is going to be only a matter of an hour or so to get to your mother ship."

"It may take a few hours as I had to take off without checking the orbit of Phobos first. We'll pressurize the cabin right away. I should have thought of asking you before you brought it up. Sorry!" With that remark, he pushed the button to repressurize the cabin.

When her helmet was removed, it revealed a bright, intelligent face with twinkling green eyes. Boutillier felt—as the French might say—thunderstruck. He had never met a woman who had captured his attention so thoroughly at first sight. Would he be indulging himself in a fantasy if he thought she reciprocated his feelings—a little? As if to confirm his thoughts, she flashed an intimate smile.

Jeanne then murmured softly. "To think that I am being rescued by *Valkyrie,* a messenger of death for Odin!"

It took several more hours to match orbit with Phobos despite Boutillier's best efforts. Ivanov needed first aid urgently. It would take a minimum of three weeks for the fracture to heal. The extreme low gravity of Phobos would be a blessing to him, however. Jeanne Monier was not in top shape either in spite of the brave show she had put on.

The sandstorm gradually cleared up. Over the next several weeks, with Linde Hoerter keeping a watchful eye on the Martian weather pattern, the team from *Trailblazer* took turns in going below and setting up a temporary habitat on Mars by converting one of their two supply ships. Eriksen decreed that the habitat, which had been designed based on the previous knowledge of the Martian surface conditions, would not be safe in severe sandstorms. The habitat needed to be beefed up considerably if human beings were to live on Mars for an extended period.

Boutillier and Okita made a special trip to *Ares* to bury Ritter and van Dijk. Okita had brought with his communications unit a minirecorder containing Wagner's *Goetterdaemmerung* and played it as they buried the two bodies in the reddish sand, after encasing them in hermetically sealed containers. Knowing what was taking place down below, the stirring music brought tears to the eyes of the four astronauts remaining in Orbital Base Phobos.

The time came for *Trailblazer* to return to Earth. The ship had been designed for a four-person crew. Two out of the six people on Phobos would have to stay behind and wait for the return of *Trailblazer* with a two-person crew. There were provisions enough on the ground and on Phobos to keep them in good shape for up to a year.

At a gathering of all six members, Eriksen set out to select the two who would remain behind. He regarded it to be his duty to be one of the two. If the captain was expected to go down with his ship, he should be expected to stay behind, shouldn't he? He was trying to find a second volunteer from his crew.

Eriksen's good intentions were sidetracked again by his dauntless Cajun pilot.

After two months together on their voyage out, plus several months spent on Earth getting ready for the mission, it was well known to all that Eriksen was a happily married man with a loving wife and two small kids, who were anxiously waiting for his return. It was also no secret that Linde Hoerter had a fiancé, whom she planned to marry on her return. And, Nobuo Okita had an ailing mother at home. For those reasons neither Hoerter nor Okita volunteered to stay behind but they made it clear that they would be willing to do so if called upon by the captain. Ivanov had gotten married only a few months before *Ares*' departure and his wife had not seen him for almost a year; besides, his leg had not yet healed completely.

The Cajun pointed out those undeniable facts about the four and then declared that he had nobody in particular he had to go back to and he was therefore the logical person to stay behind. He carefully avoided saying anything at all personal about Jeanne Monier.

Instead, Boutillier looked at Monier—with his eyes eloquently saying the unspoken words. She looked straight back, answering his unvoiced question.

She volunteered immediately.

Eriksen clearly saw the inevitable. "All right, if you two think you can manage to survive by yourselves for the next six to nine months, so be it."

Silently, Boutillier said to himself, *To be really alone with Jeanne for six months!* From where he sat now, even nine months would not seem long. Besides, this would give him plenty of time to explore Phobos for any sign that it might have been used as a space station a long time before.

Eriksen had to caution him not to use *Valkyrie* to go back to Mars except in the event of utter emergency, aware that he had no way of enforcing his injunctions once he was gone. Still, Jeanne would probably be a moderating influence on the audacious Cajun.

Well, he didn't tell me not to go to Deimos. That's another place where I could look for information about the origin of the Martian moons. Boutillier smiled to himself as he thought of all the explorations that Jeanne and he could be doing together.

Upon his return to Earth, Captain Eriksen was going to recommend that Space Station Phobos (Fear) be renamed Orbital Base Hope in view of the bright future he foresaw now.

History records that the first person to walk on Mars was from *Trailblazer,* and the first people to land on Mars alive were from *Ares*. And, the first two residents of Phobos were from both ships.

This story is dedicated to the memory of Professor Juergen Rahe, who capably directed the Planetary Exploration Program at the NASA Headquarters until his tragic death in 1997. He was a good friend and colleague for more than three decades. A Martian Crater was recently named after him.

Black Hole Station

by Jack Williamson

Jack Williamson has been writing science fiction since 1928, with more than fifty novels published. The most recent is Terraforming Earth. *One section of it, "The Ultimate Earth," received the 2000 Hugo award as the best novella. He lives in New Mexico, where he arrived with his parents and siblings in a covered wagon when he was seven years old. He says is still writing new short stories and planning to teach a science fiction course at Eastern New Mexico University, his hometown school.*

MY father used to joke that he was four hundred years older than my mother. He was Esteban Fenway, copilot of Ian Arkwood's *Space Magellan* when they discovered *NBH Draconis*, the quiescent black hole just two hundred light-years north of Earth. Arkwood died there. Off the ship, exploring its tiny iron asteroid, he was caught by a radiation burst from something falling in. My father got home with the news.

The drama of his escape from its invisible gravity well is among my first recollections, as I heard it at the bedtimes when he used to trot me on his knee. He never tried to make himself the hero, but I loved the story for his genial voice and the strange magic of its relativity paradoxes. I always shivered at the terrible mysteries of NBH and loved the thrills of his escape alive.

"It's a fearful monster, Sandy. A demon nobody can see. It has a terrible strength and a terrible hunger. It eats people and planets and stars and even the light that could show where it is. It hides in a great dark cave it has dug for itself."

"If you couldn't see it, how did you find it?"

"Its own dreadful power gives it away. Like your pocket lens, it bends light to magnify anything beyond it. All we could see was that little patch of brighter stars."

"Will it swallow us?"

"We're safe," he promised. "So long as we stay away."

"But you could go back?" I was always frightened. "And get there in no time at all?"

"In none of my time." He liked to dazzle me with the wonder of the skipships. "And skip back again in another instant. That's what we did. Our whole cruise, to survey half a dozen stellar systems and find NBH, took us just a few months on the *Magellan,* but four hundred years passed here on Earth while we were away."

When I wondered how that could be, he said something I didn't understand about Einstein and the relativity of space and time.

"No need to vex your little head about it." He laughed at my fears. "Or about any danger from NBH itself. It's too far off to touch us, and I got away without a scar. It was coming home that nearly killed me. The Arkwood expedition had been forgotten. Nobody wanted to believe a black hole could be so near. People called me crazy, and I did feel driven half out of my mind. Your mother saved me."

I heard more about that from her. A journalist assigned to do the story, she found him in a bar, overwhelmed by an Earth that seemed stranger than NBH and drinking to escape more questions than he had answers for. With her at his side, he made the best of his moment.

She helped him set up the Arkwood Foundation and find funds to build Black Hole Station. Every other year through my childhood and youth, a new *Magellan* took off to carry supplies for it and relieve half the six-man staff.

Of course nobody returned to report anything. Nobody could, not for another four hundred years. I remember sitting at the dinners my mother used to give for the foundation staff and my father's scientific friends. Listening to their talk, I felt baffled by the riddles of NBH and haunted with dread of its invisible power.

Schwarchild bubbles? Event horizons? Anti-horizons? Singularies? Quantum geometries? Negative matter? Negative time? Black holes, white holes, wormholes? What did the words mean? What dark magic let the black hole pull men off the Earth, not to return till all they had known was gone?

"Wormholes?" I asked my father once. "Are they really tunnels through space and time to other worlds?"

"Flying carpets?" He laughed at the question. "Not for spacecraft. Not even if they do exist. Tidal forces would tear your unlucky astronaut into superhot plasma, and matter that falls into the Schwarzchild bubble stays there. Nothing gets out except the Hawking hot-body radiation. And not much of that."

"So what good is the station?"

"No way to know." He shrugged, his bright blue eyes looking off beyond me. "No way for us, here and now. But I want to know what's waiting for us, there inside the bubble. NBH is a natural lab with a trillion times more power than anything we can build here on Earth."

My mother may have known how impatient he was for that knowledge, but I was stunned on the morning at breakfast, the year I was twelve, when he pushed his plate aside and looked across the table at my mother. He told her he was taking the next relief ship out to the station.

Her face gone pale, she sank back in her chair.

"If you have to go." Her lips were quivering when she finally gathered herself to speak. "If you have to."

Bravely, she helped him pack what he wanted to take and invited his friends to a farewell dinner. She had to wipe at her tears before she could kiss him farewell. My throat was aching when he gripped my hand and turned to leave, and my own eyes blurred at the eager spring in his step as he walked up the ramp to board *Magellan Five.*

"He loves us," she whispered to me. "But NBH has caught him. It will never let him go."

She took his place at the head of the foundation and kept the relief ships flying out. Over the years I met most of the volunteers when they came for training. All of them were men. She insisted very firmly that black holes were not for women.

Those men were a bright and lively lot. I admired them for many things: their abilities, their courage, their dedication to science. Yet I felt a sort of pity for them. Every one, in his own way, had suffered some painful loss. Disappointment in love, disaster in business, defeat of some driving ambition, failure of a dream.

"We're all of us unhappy," one of them confessed when I had bought him a farewell drink. "If we'd been content with Earth here and now, we wouldn't be gambling our lives for the uncertain secrets of NBH. Or the chance we'll get back to some fabulous utopia four hundred years from now." He made a bitter face. "The fact is, we're diving into our own black holes."

Wishing them well, I'd never wanted to follow. Yet I had never outgrown my longing to see my father again, or escaped my childhood fascination with the ominous riddles of NBH. Out of college, I came home with a degree in cosmogony, planning to join my mother at the foundation. She told me she was shutting it down.

"We can't." I felt dismayed. "Think of my father."

"I do. Every day." Her lips quivered. "But he's had ten years at the station, if he stayed there. We'll never know what he's done or failed to do, but *Magellan Ten* has drained the last of our funding. This last mission will evacuate and abandon the station."

"My father—" The decision seized me in an instant. "I'm going out on *Ten*."

"I thought you might." I saw her tears again, but she didn't try to keep me. "Wherever you find him, still at the station or back on some future Earth, he may need you more than I do."

There were just two of us on *Ten;* she had found no other volunteers. We met the pilot in the same bar where she had found my father. He was Colin McKane, a rawboned, hard-bitten Scot who had abandoned his native heaths to scout a hundred planets and found none he cared to see again.

"My home, my family, all I ever loved—" Moodily, he sloshed another shot into his glass. "All thrown away in a crazy lust for new worlds and strange adventure. There's nothing left I really care about. Matsu and LeBlanc were my last friends, fellow exiles from long ago. They went out on *Nine*. I promised to go out and bring them home."

He shrugged, with a twisted grimace.

"If we can expect this wasted Earth to make a better future for us."

Hiro Matsu and Jean LeBlanc. I'd known them in training. Both of them scientists of some distinction, they were both devoted to ideas science rejected. I'd helped Matsu load crates of equipment designed to test a conviction that he could reverse gravity by reversing the spin of cosmic anti-strings. LeBlanc's project was to look for a way though the singularity, and backward in time.

"Crackpots, maybe," McKane said. "But we can't leave them there to die."

We found NBH truly black, lost in the vast gulf created as it consumed the nearby stars. All we could see was the brighter patch of magnified stars beyond it. Nodding at them on the monitor, McKane turned uneasily in his seat to shake his head at me.

"Feel it?"

Even there, trapped deep in its unforgiving grasp, there was really no force I could feel. Spinning around the lowest safe orbit, we were still in free fall, the enormous gravity precisely balanced by the centrifugal force that held us there. Yet suddenly I was chilled by the recollection of a moment of terror in my childhood, when my father was tossing me high above his head and catching me as I fell. My mother heard my screams, sensed my fright, and made him stop.

That left me with a dread of high places. Now, even in the

stable-seeming ship, I felt that was falling past the stars into an infinite and bottomless pit, with no support and no escape. A wave of sickness left me weak and cold with sweat. I had to grip the seat restraints and look away.

McKane grinned at me, and bent again to his flight computer. The asteroid was harder to find than the black hole. It had strayed away from the galactic coordinates Arkwood and my father recorded for it, and the starlight was far too faint to reveal it.

"A wild black cat," McKane called it, "hiding from us in a big black cellar."

Searching the spectrum for its locator beacon, he heard nothing. He made a dozen skips, with stops for radar searches. Earth was two long days behind us before a final jump brought it into searchlight range. A mass of dark iron a mile or so thick, ripped from the heart of some shattered planet, it was all jagged points and knife-sharp edges. We watched its slow spin till the dock came into view, a squat little tower jutting from a flat black fracture plane.

It showed no light. McKane called and got no reply.

"It looks dead. If you want my hunch, LeBlanc and Matsu found it already abandoned or dead. The safest thing for us is to get out now."

"I came for my father."

"There can't be anybody here."

"I've got to know."

"If anybody's alive, why don't they have the radio beacon going? And a light flashing to show us in?"

"I want to dock and see."

"A risk I was never paid to take." Stubbornly, he shook his head at the telescreen, where a bright red star beyond NBH stared at us like a baleful eye. "If they're gone, we'll find 'em gone. If they're dead, we'd likely join 'em."

I persisted till he nudged us with the thrusters to overtake the tower and ease us to the dock. The station was tunneled deep into the asteroid, for whatever shelter it might offer. The dock was on the spin axis, where we were weightless.

When we were coupled to it, he turned to scowl at me.

"Are you sure you want to take the risk?"

Nervously, I said I did.

He slid a sleek little handgun out of a shoulder holster and wanted me to take it. I refused it; I had never fired a gun. He found a flashlight for me and opened the air lock.

"Watch every step." He looked at his watch and waved an ironic farewell. "Whatever you find, make it quick. I'll give you three hours."

The door thudded shut. Air hissed. My ears popped to a pressure change. The inner door opened into darkness. Listening, I heard no sound at all. The air was cold and still. The flashlight found a switch, and light came on in a narrow passage ahead.

I caught a guideline to pull myself into the station. A bleak and cheerless pit, it had been crudely carved with laser blades into the rock's iron heart. I dived along the guideline and stopped again to listen. Somewhere a ventilator fan whispered faintly. I shouted and got no answer. I saw no motion, saw nothing green. Sniffing for the odor of death, all I caught was dusty staleness.

The lines led me on to a radial shaft and out to a level were rotation simulated gravity. On my feet again, I explored an empty workshop, a silent kitchen, a vacant rec room, a long chamber filled with laboratory equipment, most of it mysterious to me, all idle and abandoned now.

On a big wall monitor, I found that magnified star, dimming now as it crept away from the focal point where the black hole hung, invisible, intangible, an eternal devourer of all creation. I stared and shuddered and went on down the tunnel. Doorways off it opened into what had been living space.

One by one, I looked into empty rooms. Abandoned perhaps in haste, they were cluttered with discarded boots and clothing, books and papers, bits of electronic gear, worn playing cards, a violin with broken strings, empty ration packs and dirty dishes, empty brandy bottles. I saw a bag lettered with Matsu's name, a cap LeBlanc had worn, and cringed from a dread of whatever had driven them away.

Near the end of the tunnel, with only two or three more rooms to search, I heard faint sounds ahead. Squeals? Squeaks? Screams? I listened and crept nearer. Animal sounds, I thought, but not from any animal I knew.

They ceased. I heard a human voice, somehow familiar, yet aping those alien sounds. I tiptoed to the doorway and peered into the room. A gray-headed stranger with a wild white beard sat behind a long desk, looking up at a wall monitor and intoning that unearthly gibberish into a microphone.

Chessmen before him on the desk were set up in an unfinished game. Chessmen I remembered! They were carved of pale green jade and some jet-black stone. My mother had found them somewhere in Asia as a gift for my father. He had used them to teach me the game the year I was five. Swept by a tide of confused emotion, I had to catch my breath before I turned and spoke to the wild-bearded stranger.

"Sir?"

Jolted, he sprang to his feet, backed away, and stood for a long moment staring at me with deep-sunk eyes.

"Who the hell—" He blinked and shook his head and limped around the desk to meet me. "Sandy! It's you!"

He looked far older than I recalled him, bent and shriveled but alert. He seized my hand, moved as if to hug me, but checked himself to stand back and stare again. "Your mother? How did you leave her?"

"Well," I said. "She's tried to keep the foundation alive, but she's had to shut it down. We came to evacuate the station."

"A little late." He grinned through the beard. "The crew bugged out on *Nine,* two years ago."

"And left you alone? How could they?"

A wry shrug.

"They tried to take me. Called me crazy. I had to hide in an old space suit till they were gone."

I looked at him again. Haggard, unkempt, something bright in his hollowed eyes. I wondered what NBH had done to him.

"Your last chance to leave," I told him. "The pilot's waiting, not very patiently. He gave me three hours to find you." I looked at my watch. "Half of it already gone. Let's get moving."

"Thank you, Sandy." He reached to take my hand again. "It's noble of you to come. Noble of your mother to give you up." He shook his head, with a wistful smile. "But my work's not done."

"Father! Please!" I gripped his hand. "We can't leave you here."

"I can't go now." His seamed face set hard, he raised a shaking hand to stop my questions. "Sit down and let me tell you."

He lifted a carton of ration packs off a folding chair, motioned me to it, and sat deliberately back at his desk.

"If you can make it quick."

"Okay, quick it is." Yet he paused for a moment, staring at the chessmen, before he shrugged and went on. "I'll skip over my first years here. Pretty much what you might expect. We studied what there was to study. Measured NBH for mass, electric charge, spin. Studied the orbits of captured objects. Looked for the Hawking radiation."

"So?" I had to humor him. "What did you find?"

"Nothing." He shrugged. "Nothing really new until after *Three* had come and gone. But I stayed and kept at it till I got what I call my eureka moment."

"What was that?"

"A revelation." He glanced away at the end of the room, where I saw an easel under a paint-splotched cover, and paused for a long sigh. "It happened during my search for the radiation. A quest I had almost given up. If I'd left on *Nine*—"

He shook his head and stopped again to glance at his unfinished chess game, long enough to let me wonder about his opponent and to wonder how sane he was.

"Black holes decay," he went on abruptly. Hawking did the math. I've found the evidence. And established a new principle of physics." He sat straighter as if to challenge me with it. "The conservation of information."

He scowled when I peered at my watch.

"The decay process is slow, the radiation feeble, with no distinctive spectral signature. It took me two years and a new antenna to pick it up. A faint hum, often drowned in thunder from the accretion zone. Nothing exciting till I got the signals it carried."

"Signals?"

"Information!" He saw my disbelief. His old voice went shrill. "Clicks in my headphones. Three clicks. A pause. Three more clicks. Another three, till there were twelve. A longer pause. Then they began the series again. I answered with echoes and got a reply. A pattern of clicks and pauses that made pixels for simple graphics, twelve by twelve. A circle. A square. An equilateral triangle. A diagram to show the hypotenuse as the sum of squares.

"Contact with intelligence!" His hollowed eyes lit. "We've invented a common language, good for math and science, though so far we've found no Rosetta stone for the humanities—"

"We?" I had to interrupt. "Who?"

"A question." He seemed amused at my bewilderment. "I don't know who or where or even when. I'm still searching for the answers. The signals do come out of the Schwarzchild bubble, carried on the Hawking radiation. They may originate in the central singularity. They may come through it. They may come around it."

He sighed and let his thin body sag as if from long exhaustion.

"There's no way to know. I've found no common point of reference. The quantum nature of the singularity upends all our commonsense ideas of space and time." He saw me start to rise. "Sandy, please! Give me a few more minutes."

"Can't we talk on the ship?"

"We're talking now." Impatiently, he beckoned me back

to the chair and limped across the room to uncover the easel. "You've got to see this."

His painting held me for a moment. No scene from the asteroid or anywhere on Earth, it was a seascape. Waves foamed in the foreground. Blue water stretched to a far horizon beyond, with no land in sight. Above them the frame was almost filled with something that took my breath.

I had to stare. It was an island, flying high above the sea. A forest of green plumes like giant bamboo grew along the shore. Inland, red-roofed buildings surrounded a spiral dome the color of gold. It floated on an enormous platform streamlined like the hull of an ocean liner. Tiny mirror-bright globes swarmed around it.

"A glimpse of their world, as I've seen it from there." He pointed to a chalked circle on the floor in front of the easel. "I know nearly nothing of its history, but it was one that NBH swallowed. Its people had no way to save anything material, but a few of them were able to preserve their minds."

He reached to touch the chessboard.

"The individual who reached me has told me all he can. I call him Mr. Other. We've worked out a language for math and physics, but found no words for such complexities as gender—"

I was on my feet.

"One more minute!" He raised his hand to hold me. "Mr. Other has given me a warning you must hear. NBH may be quiescent now, but it's the ultimate bomb."

"Father, please!"

His voice sharpened, the way it did when he had to scold me long ago.

"Here's my news for Earth. As a black hole grows, it contracts. Pressure and temperature in the singularity rise toward infinity. In NBH, they are still contained in the magnetic web woven by increasing spin. The capture of another stray sun could rupture that web at the poles of rotation. Superluminous plumes and bursts of beamed radiation could explode, strong enough to burn the nearer planets and even sear the Earth—"

He stopped at last, frowning at my face.

"I see you don't believe."

"I can't." At the door, I had to turn back. "You've put me in an impossible spot. The pilot will be taking off, with me or without me. I can't leave you here alone."

"You'd better go." He gulped and wiped at his hollow eyes. "I must stay to learn what I can, and hope to get that warning back to Earth." He limped around the easel to give me a quick embrace. "I always loved you, Sandy. It's great that I know enough to solve that problem for you."

He gestured me away from the easel. When I looked back, he was standing on that white-chalked circle. He waved a quick farewell. I caught a glimpse of some object in his hand. I heard a click, and he was gone.

I searched and failed to find him anywhere. I ran back to the ship and got there gasping for breath, with nine minutes to spare. We took off at once. The first long skip brought us in sight of the sun. The second let us pick out Jupiter and Saturn. The third revealed the tiny point of Earth. The last brought it close enough to let us see the whole blue globe, the bright lace of clouds, the familiar continents.

"It looks too green." McKane made a sour face. "I see no cities. I think we've been gone too long."

My own eagerness to see the fruit of change was edged with pain as I recalled all I'd known and loved that the centuries must have erased. He called Earth from low orbit. Watching as he listened, I saw him frown and shake his head, frown and listen again. At last he passed the headphones to me.

"We're expected," he said. "A Director Ivor Cheung wants to talk to you."

I heard a snatch of strange music and then a woman's voice.

"Sir, will you hold for just a moment?"

In only a moment I heard a hearty boom.

"Sandor Fenway! I speak for the Arkwood-Fenway

Foundation." Accents had changed, and I begged him to slow his speech. "Your father told us to expect you."

"My father? How? When?"

"After his return from NBH, two hundred years ago."

I felt dazed. "With no ship?"

"With Arkwood science, he required no ship." I heard a genial chuckle at my confusion. "We're here to welcome you home. A briefing has been prepared. It will cover Dr. Fenway's return and its historic aftermath. A pilot craft is now on the way to guide you in."

The pilot craft was a little silver globe that spoke in a crisp robotic voice. It guided us down, but not to the shabby old brick-and-mortar building my father had leased for it on the outskirts of Atlantica. We landed on a flying island like the one my father had shown me on his easel. It floated over the Gulf Stream, a hundred miles off Sandy Hook. A final skip brought us low above it.

McKane held us there, staring. Its sleek white hull was a full mile long. Green parkways edged its decks. It had no funnels, but a gold-hued spiral dome towered out of its superstructure. Tiny silver globes whirled like birds around it. Our pilot craft brought us through them, down to an open platform.

McKane opened the lock. Rousing music greeted us, tantalizingly half familiar. A little group of men and women stood waiting. All wore neat white jackets with red-black patches on the breasts. Smiling, a tall, dark man advanced to greet us.

"Mr. Sandor Fenway? Captain McKane? " He paused to see which was which. "I am Director Cheung." He turned to gesture at those behind him. "These are fellow foundation officials, all members of the Black Light Society."

McKane muttered a question.

"You'll be learning," he said. "The society is devoted to the study and teaching of what Dr. Fenway knew of Arkwood science and culture. Their mastery of space and time may surprise you. They were even conquering gravity, but too late to save themselves."

He turned to me.

"We'll be briefing you on the historic consequences of his return. Before we go in, however, we have a gift left for you."

He stepped aside. A slender young woman came forward, holding a white plastic box. She lifted it toward me, checked herself, and stepped back, flushing pink.

"Mr. Sandor—" She stopped to take a breath, and I had time to note how well the white jacket became her. "Your father left this message with his gift." She read it from a strip of yellow plastic.

" 'Dear Sandy,

" 'I understood your doubts. Don't brood about them. You'll learn to like Mr. Other. You'll find him a great science teacher and a master at the game.' "

She held the box for me to open. The lid snapped back at my touch, and I saw the jade-and-jet chessmen I had last seen on my father's desk at Black Hole Station.

"Shall we take care of them for you?" she asked. "The update is ready for you now."

Director Cheung took us through a little park where he showed me a statue of my mother, and on to the Lily Arkwood Hall. He spoke to us there, from a stage where the whole wall behind him became an enormous window that could look out on another city, a ship in space, another planet, even Black Hole Station.

Through the first centuries since we left, the skipships had carried colonists out to terraform new planets while Earth itself was in decline. With resources depleted and opportunities rare, it had been almost abandoned. Back from NBH, my father had been its savior.

"The Arkwood legacy." Cheung turned to gesture at a strange-shaped spacecraft dropping out of an orange-red sky. "Arkwood science has reshaped human history. The science of truly instant flight has bypassed the relativity limit and unified the scattered and isolated planets into our great galactic civilization."

He paused to let us watch the spacecraft landing in a city of golden spiral towers.

"The richest gift, however, has been the Arkwood philosophy. Our own evolution had left us driven by herd instincts, forever fighting for survival. We strove to be leaders, but most of us had to follow the winners. Chiefs and priests and prophets. Patriarchs, pharaohs, presidents. Captains of industry and heads of the house. When men were not enough; we invented autocratic gods."

He bowed toward me.

"We honor your father, Mr. Fenway, most of all because he declined to become a god. Instead he helped us grow up. We had aspired to conquer nature and rule the universe. With NBH, he showed us the folly of such infantile illusions.

"The omnipotent destroyer! Itself a dark god, it has taught us our true place in the universal process. The cosmos has neither master nor slaves. It is simply a river of energy where we are droplets of life, or better the climbers of an infinite stair that can take us up forever."

He touched the black circle on his jacket.

"That's the Arkwood way, the gospel of the Black Light Society. We are not a religion, though our message may reflect ancient faiths. We follow no doctrine and enforce no commandments. All we preach is understanding as your father gave it to us, truth instead of illusion, altruism instead of aggression, love instead of hate, peace instead of terror."

The Arkwood way has made sense to me. Though this altered Earth often seems as alien to me as our old one must have been to my father four centuries ago, I've found contentment here. Loving friends have asked me to join the Black Light Society. At the foundation academy, I have begun to learn Arkwood science and Arkwood culture.

I want to discover more. The foundation has restored Black Hole Station. When my studies here on Earth are finished, I plan to go back there and try to reach my father's Mr. Other. NBH has no sun in its ravenous grasp, and that old dread of high places has left me. Looking down from the skyship's rail at the Atlantic whitecaps a mile below, I can hardly recall my terror of falling toward that baleful red star at the bottom of its dark pit.

Station Spaces

by Gregory Benford

Gregory Benford is a working scientist who has written some twenty-three critically-acclaimed novels. He has received two Nebula Awards, first in 1981 for Timescape, *a novel which sold over a million copies and won the John W. Campbell Memorial Award, the Australian Ditmar Award, and the British Science Fiction Award. In 1992, Dr. Benford received the United Nations Medal in Literature. He is also a professor of physics at the University of California, Irvine since 1971. He specializes in astrophysics and plasma physics theory and was presented with the Lord Prize in 1995 for achievements in the sciences. He is a Woodrow Wilson Fellow and Phi Beta Kappa. He has been an adviser to the National Aeronautics and Space Administration, the United States Department of Energy, and the White House Council on Space Policy, and has served as a visiting fellow at Cambridge University. His first book-length work of nonfiction,* Deep Time *(1999), examines his work in long duration messages from a broad humanistic and scientific perspective.*

YOU KNOW many things, but what he knows is both less and more than what I tell to us.

Or especially, what we all tell to all those others—those simple humans, who are like him in their limits.

I cannot be what you are, you the larger.

Not that we are not somehow also the same—wedded to our memories of the centuries we have grown together.

For we are like you and him and I, a life-form that evolution could not produce on the rich loam of Earth. The blunt edge of selection could birth forth and then burst forth, yes. But to conjure a Station thing—a great, sprawling metallo-bio-cyber-thing such as we and you—takes grander musics, such as I know.

Only by shrinking down to the narrow chasms of the single view can you know the intricate slick fineness, the reek and tingle and chime of this silky symphony of self.

But bigness blunders, thumb-fingered.

Smallness can enchant. So let us to go to an oddment of him, and me, and you:

He saw:

A long thin hard room, fluorescent white, without shadows.

Metal on ceramo-glass on fake wood on woven nylon rug.

A granite desk. A man whose name he could not recall.

A neat uniform, so familiar he looked beyond it by reflex.

He felt: light gravity (Mars? the Moon?); rough cloth at a cuff of his work shirt; a chill dry air-conditioned breeze along his neck. A red flash of anger.

Benjan smiled slightly. He had just seen what he must do.

"Gray was free when we began work, centuries ago," Benjan said, his black eyes fixed steadily on the man across the desk. Katonji, that was the man's name. His commander, once, a very long time ago.

"It had been planned that way, yes," his superior said haltingly, begrudging the words.

"That was the only reason I took the assignment," Benjan said.

"I know. Unfortunately—"

"I have spent many decades on it."

"Fleet Control certainly appreciates—"

"World-scaping isn't just a job, damn it! It's an art, a discipline, a craft that saps a man's energies."

"And you have done quite well. Personally, I—"

'When you asked me to do this I wanted to know what Fleet Control planned for Gray."

"You can recall an ancient conversation?"

A verbal maneuver, no more. Katonji was an amplified human and already well over two centuries old, but the Earthside social convention was to pretend that the past faded away, leaving a young psyche. "A 'grand experiment in human society,' I remember your words."

"True, that was the original plan—"

"But now you tell me a single faction needs it? The whole Moon?"

"The Council has reconsidered."

"Reconsidered, hell." Benjan's bronze face crinkled with disdain. "Somebody pressured them and they gave in. Who was it?"

"I would not put it that way," Katonji said coldly.

"I know you wouldn't. Far easier to hide behind words." He smiled wryly and compressed his thin lips. The viewscreen near him looked out on a cold silver landscape and he studied it, smoldering inside. An artificial viewscape from Gray itself. Earth, a crescent concerto in blue and white, hung in a creamy sky over the insect working of robotractors and men. Gray's air was unusually clear today, the normal haze swept away by a front blowing in from the equator near Mare Chrisum.

The milling minions were hollowing out another cavern for Fleet Control to fill with cubicles and screens and memos. Great Gray above, mere gray below. Earth swam above high fleecy cirrus and for a moment Benjan dreamed of the day when birds, easily adapted to the light gravity and high atmospheric density, would flap lazily across such views.

"Officer Tozenji—"

"I am no longer an officer. I resigned before you were born."

"By your leave, I meant it solely as an honorific. Surely you still have some loyalty to the Fleet."

Benjan laughed. The deep bass notes echoed from the office walls with a curious emptiness. "So it's an appeal to the honor of the crest, is it? I see I spent too long on Gray. Back here you have forgotten what I am like," Benjan said. *But where is 'here'? I could not take Earth's full gravity any more, so this must be an orbiting Fleet cylinder, spinning gravity.*

A frown. "I had hoped that working once more with Fleet officers would change you, even though you remained a civilian on Gray. A man isn't—"

"A man is what he is," Benjan said.

Katonji leaned back in his shiftchair and made a tent of his fingers. "You . . . played the Sabal Game during those years?" he asked slowly.

Benjan's eyes narrowed. "Yes, I did." The Game was ancient, revered, simplicity itself. It taught that the greater gain lay in working with others, rather than in self-seeking. He had always enjoyed it, but only a fool believed that such moral lessons extended to the cut and thrust of Fleet matters.

"It did not . . . bring you to community?"

"I got on well enough with the members of my team," Benjan said evenly.

"I hoped such isolation with a small group would calm your . . . spirit. Fleet is a community of men and women seeking enlightenment in the missions, just as you do. You are an exceptional person, anchored as you are in the Station, using linkages we have not used—"

"Permitted, you mean."

"Those old techniques were deemed . . . too risky."

Benjan felt his many links like a background hum, in concert and warm. What could this man know of such methods time-savored by those who lived them? "And not easy to direct from above."

The man fastidiously raised a finger and persisted: "We still sit at the Game, and, while you are here, would welcome your—"

"Can we leave my spiritual progress aside?"

"Of course, if you desire."

"Fine. Now tell me who is getting my planet."

"Gray is not your planet."

"I speak for the Station and all the intelligences who link

with it. We made Gray. Through many decades, we hammered the crust, released the gases, planted the spores, damped the winds."

"With help."

"Three hundred of us at the start, and eleven heavy spacecraft. A puny beginning that blossomed into millions."

"Helped by the entire staff of Earthside—"

"They were Fleet men. They take orders, I don't. I work by contract."

"A contract spanning centuries?"

"It is still valid, though those who wrote it are dust."

"Let us treat this in a gentlemanly fashion, sir. Any contract can be renegotiated."

"The paper I—we, but I am here to speak for all—signed for Gray said it was to be an open colony. That's the only reason I worked on it," he said sharply.

"I would not advise you to pursue that point," Katonji said. He turned and studied the viewscreen, his broad, southern Chinese nose flaring at the nostrils. But the rest of his face remained an impassive mask. For a long moment there was only the thin whine of air circulation in the room.

"Sir," the other man said abruptly, "I can only tell you what the Council has granted. Men of your talents are rare. We know that, had you undertaken the formation of Gray for a, uh, private interest, you would have demanded more payment."

"Wrong. I wouldn't have done it at all."

"Nonetheless, the Council is willing to pay you a double fee. The Majiken Clan, who have been invested with Primacy Rights to Gray—"

"What!"

"—have seen fit to contribute the amount necessary to reimburse you—"

"So that's who—"

"—and all others of the Station, to whom I have been authorized to release funds immediately."

Benjan stared blankly ahead for a short moment. "I believe I'll do a bit of releasing myself," he murmured, almost to himself.

"What?"

"Oh, nothing. Information?"

"Infor—Oh."

"The Clans have a stranglehold on the Council, but not the 3D. People might be interested to know how it came about that a new planet—a rich one, too—was handed over—"

"Officer Tozenji—"

Best to pause. Think. He shrugged, tried on a thin smile. "I was only jesting. Even idealists are not always stupid.

"Um. I am glad of that."

"Lodge the Majiken draft in my account. I want to wash my hands of this."

The other man said something, but Benjan was not listening. He made the ritual of leaving. They exchanged only perfunctory hand gestures. He turned to go, and wondered at the naked, flat room this man had chosen to work in. It carried no soft tones, no humanity, none of the feel of a room that is used, a place where men do work that interests them, so that they embody it with something of themselves. This office was empty in the most profound sense. It was a room for men who lived by taking orders. He hoped never to see such a place again.

Benjan turned. Stepped—the slow slide of falling, then catching himself, stepped—

You fall over Gray.

Skating down the steep banks of young clouds, searching, driving.

Luna you know as Gray, as all inStation know it, because pearly clouds deck high in its thick air. It had been gray long before, as well—the aged pewter of rock hard-hammered for billions of years by the relentless sun. Now its air was like soft slate, cloaking the greatest of human handiworks.

You raise a hand, gaze at it. So much could come from so small an instrument. You marvel. A small tool, five-fingered slab, working over great stretches of centuries. Seen against the canopy of your craft, it seems an unlikely tool to heft worlds with—

And the thought alone sends you plunging—

Luna was born small, too small.

So the sun had readily stripped it of its early shroud of gas. Luna came from the collision of a Mars-sized world into the primordial Earth. From that colossal crunch—how you wish you could have seen that!—spun a disk, and from that churn Luna condensed redly. The heat of that birth stripped away the Moon's water and gases, leaving it bare to the sun's glower.

So amend that:

You steer a comet from the chilly freezer beyond Pluto, swing it around Jupiter, and smack it into the bleak fields of Mare Chrisium. In bits.

For a century, all hell breaks loose. You wait, patient in your Station. It is a craft of fractions: Luna is smaller, so needs less to build an atmosphere.

There was always some scrap of gas on the Moon—trapped from the solar wind, baked from its dust, perhaps even belched from the early, now long-dead volcanoes. When Apollo descended, bringing the first men, its tiny exhaust plume doubled the mass of the frail atmosphere.

Still, such a wan world could hold gases for tens of thousands of years; physics said so. Its lesser gravity tugs at a mere sixth of Earth's hefty grip. So, to begin, you sling inward a comet bearing a third the mass of all Earth's ample air, a chunk of mountain-sized grimy ice.

Sol's heat had robbed this world, but mother-massive Earth herself had slowly stolen away its spin. It became a submissive partner in a rigid gavotte, forever tide-locked with one face always smiling at its partner.

Here you use the iceteroid to double effect. By hooking the comet adroitly around Jupiter, in a reverse swingby, you loop it into an orbit opposite to the customary, docile way that worlds loop around the sun. Go opposite! Retro! Coming in on Luna, the iceball then has ten times the impact energy.

Mere days before it strikes, you blow it apart with meticulous brutality. Smashed to shards, chunks come gliding in all around Luna's equator, small enough that they cannot muster momentum enough to splatter free of gravity's grip. Huge cannonballs slam into gray rock, but at angles that prevent them from getting away again.

Earth admin was picky about this: no debris was to be flung free, to rain down as celestial buckshot on that favored world.

Within hours, Luna had air—of a crude sort. You mixed and salted and worked your chemical magics upon roiling clouds that sported forked lightning. Gravity's grind provoked fevers, molecular riots.

More: as the pellets pelted down, Luna spun up. Its crust echoed with myriad slams and bangs. The old world creaked as it yielded, spinning faster from the hammering. From its lazy cycle of twenty-eight days it sped up to sixty hours—close enough to Earthlike, as they say, for government work. A day still lazy enough.

Even here, you orchestrated a nuanced performance, coaxed from dynamics. Luna's axial tilt had been a dull zero. Dutifully it had spun at right angles to the orbital plane of the Solar System, robbed it of summers and winters.

But you wanted otherwise. Angled just so, the incoming ice nuggets tilted the poles. From such simple mechanics you conjured seasons. And as the gases cooled, icy caps crowned your work.

You were democratic, at first: allowing both water and carbon dioxide, with smidgens of methane and ammonia. Here you called upon the appetites of bacteria, sprites you sowed as soon as the winds calmed after bombardment. They basked in sunlight, broke up the methane. The greenhouse blanket quickly warmed the old gray rocks, coveting the heat from the infalls, and soon algae covered them.

You watched with pride as the first rain fell. For centuries the dark plains had carried humanity's imposed, watery names: Tranquility, Serenity, Crises, Clouds, Storms. Now these lowlands of aged lava caught the rains and made muds and fattened into ponds, lakes, true seas. You made the ancient names come true.

Through your servant machines, you marched across these suddenly murky lands, bristling with an earned arrogance. They—*yourself!*—plowed and dug, sampled and salted. Through their eyes and tongues and ears you sat in your high Station and heard the sad baby sigh of the first winds awakening.

The Station was becoming more than a bristling canister of metal by then. Its agents grew, as did you.

You smiled down upon the gathering Gray with your quartz eyes and microwave antennae. For you knew what was coming. A mere sidewise glance at rich Earth told you what to expect. Like Earth's tropics now, at Luna's equator heat drove moist gases aloft. Cooler gas flowed from the poles to fill in. The high wet clouds skated poleward, cooled—and rained down riches.

On Earth, such currents are robbed of their water about a third of the way to the poles, and so descend, their dry rasp making a worldwide belt of deserts. Not so on Luna.

You had judged the streams of newborn air rightly. Thicker airs than Earth's took longer to exhaust, and so did not fall until they reached the poles. Thus the new world had no chains of deserts, and one simple circulating air cell ground away in each hemisphere. Moisture worked its magics.

You smiled to see your labors come right. Though anchored in your mammoth Station, you felt the first pinpricks of awareness in the crawlers, flyers, and diggers who probed the freshening Moon.

You tasted their flavors, the brimming possibilities. Northerly winds swept the upper half of the globe, bearing poleward, then swerving toward the west to make the occasional mild tornado. (Not all weather should be boring.)

Clouds patrolled the air, still fretting over their uneasy births. Day and night came in their slow rhythm, stirring the biological lab that worked below. You sometimes took a moment from running all this, just to watch.

Lunascapes. Great Grayworld.

Where day yielded to dark, valleys sank into smoldering blackness. Already a chain of snowy peaks shone where they caught the sun's dimming rays, and lit the plains with slanting colors like live coals. Sharp mountains cleaved the cloud banks, leaving a wake like that of a huge ship. At the fat equator, straining still to adjust to the new spin, tropical thunderheads glowered, lit by orange lightning that seemed to be looking for a way to spark life among the drifting molecules.

All that you did, in a mere decade. You had made "the lesser light that rules the night" now shine five times brighter, casting sharp shadows on Earth. Sun rays glinted by day from the young oceans, dazzling the eyes on Earth. And the mother world itself reflected in those muddy seas, so that when the alignment was right, people on Earth's night side gazed up into their own mirrored selves. Viewed at just the right angle, Earth's image was rimmed with ruddy sunlight, refracting through Earth's air.

You knew it could not last, but were pleased to find the new air stick around. It would bleed away in ten thousand years, but by that time other measures could come into play. You had plans for a monolayer membrane to cap your work, resting atop the whole atmosphere, the largest balloon ever conceived.

Later? No, act in the moment—and so you did.

You wovc it with membrane skill, cast it wide, let it fall—to rest easy on the thick airs below. Great holes in it let ships glide through, but the losses from those would be trivial.

Not that all was perfect. Luna had no soil, only the damaged dust left from four billion years beneath the solar wind's anvil.

After a mere momentary decade (nothing, to you), fresh wonders bloomed.

Making soil from gritty grime was work best left to the

micro-beasts who loved such stuff. To do great works on a global scale took tiny assistants. You fashioned them in your own labs, which poked outward from the Station's many-armed skin.

Gray grew a crust. Earth is in essence a tissue of microbial organisms living off the sun's fires. Gray would do the same, in fast-forward. You cooked up not mere primordial broths, but endless chains of regulatory messages, intricate feedback loops, organic gavottes.

Earth hung above, an example of life ornamented by eleborate decorations, structures of forest and grass and skin and blood—living quarters, like seagrass and zebras and eucalyptus and primates.

Do the same, you told yourself. *Only better.*

These tasks you loved. Their conjuring consumed more decades, stacked end on end. You were sucked into the romance of tiny turf wars, chemical assaults, microbial murders, and invasive incests. But you had to play upon the stellar stage, as well.

You had not thought about the tides. Even you had not found a way around those outcomes of gravity's gradient. Earth raised bulges in Gray's seas a full twenty meters tall. That made for a dim future for coastal property, even once the air became breathable.

Luckily, even such colossal tides were not a great bother to the lakes you shaped in crater beds. These you made as breeding farms for the bioengineered minions who ceaselessly tilled the dirts, massaged the gases, filtered the tinkling streams that cut swift ways through beds of volcanic rock.

Indeed, here and there you even found a use for the tides. There were more watts lurking there, in kinetic energy. You fashioned push-plates to tap some of it, to run your substations. Thrifty gods do not have to suck up to (and from) Earthside.

And so the sphere that, when you began, had been the realm of strip miners amd mass-driver camps, of rugged, suited loners . . . became a place where, someday, humans might walk and breathe free.

That time is about to come. You yearn for it. For you, too, can then manifest yourself, your Station, as a mere mortal . . . and set foot upon a world that you would name Selene.

You were both Station and more, by then. How much more few knew. But some sliver of you clung to the name of Benjan—

Benjan nodded slightly, ears ringing for some reason.

The smooth, sure interviewer gave a short introduction, portentous and grim—typical Earther. "Man . . . or manifestation? This we must all wonder as we greet an embodiment of humanity's greatest—and now ancient—construction project. One you and I can see every evening in the sky—for those who are still surface dwellers."

3-D cameras moved in smooth arcs through the studio darkness beyond. The two men sat in a pool of light. The interviewer spoke toward the directional mike as he gave the background on Benjan's charges against the Council.

Smiles galore. Platitudes aplenty. That done, came the attack.

"But isn't this a rather abstract, distant point to bring at this time?" the man said, turning to Benjan.

Benjan blinked, uncertain, edgy. He was a private man, used to working alone. Now that he was moving against the Council, he had to bear these public appearances, these . . . manifestations . . . of a dwindled self. "To, ah, the people of the next generation, Gray will not be an abstraction—"

"You mean the Moon?"

"Uh, yes, Gray is my name for it. That's the way it looked when I—uh, we all—started work on it centuries ago."

"Yet you were there all along, in fact."

"Well, yes. But when I'm—we're—done." Benjan leaned forward, and his interviewer leaned back, as if not wanting to be too close. "it will be a real place, not just an idea—where you all can live and start a planned ecology. It will be a frontier."

"We understand that romantic tradition, but—"

"No, you don't. Gray isn't just an idea, it's something I've—we've—worked on for everyone, whatever shape or genetype they might favor."

"Yes, yes, and such ideas are touching in their, well, customary way, but—"

"But the only ones who will ever enjoy it, if the Council gets away with this, is the Majiken Clan."

The interviewer pursed his lips. Or was this a he at all? In the current style, the bulging muscles and thick neck might just be fashion statements. "Well, the Majiken are a very large, important segment of the—"

"No more important than the rest of humanity, in my estimation."

"But to cause this much stir over a world which will not even be habitable for at least decades more—"

"We of the Station are there now."

"You've been modified, adapted."

"Well, yes. I couldn't do this interview on Earth. I'm grav-adapted."

"Frankly, that's why many feel that we need to put Earthside people on the ground on Luna as soon as possible. To represent our point of view."

"Look, Gray's not just any world. Not just a gas giant, useful for raw gas and nothing else. Not a Mercury type; there are millions of those littered out among the stars. Gray is going to be fully Earthlike. The astronomers tell us there are only four semiterrestrials outside the home system that humans can ever live on, around other stars, and those are pretty terrible. I—"

"You forget the Outer Colonies," the interviewer broke in smoothly, smiling at the 3-D.

"Yeah—ice balls." He could not hide his contempt. What he wanted to say, but knew it was terribly old-fashioned, was: *Damn it, Gray is happening now, we've got to plan for it. Photosynthesis is going on. I've seen it myself—hell, I caused it myself—carbon dioxide and water converting into organics and oxygen, gases fresh as a breeze. Currents carry the algae down through the cloud layers into the warm areas, where they work just fine. That gives off simple carbon compounds, raw carbon and water. This keeps the water content of the atmosphere constant, but converts carbon dioxide—we've got too much right now—into carbon and oxygen. It's going well, the rate itself is exponentiating—*

Benjan shook his fist, just now realizing that he *was* saying all this out loud, after all. Probably not a smart move, but he couldn't stop himself. "Look, there's enough water in Gray's deep rock to make an ocean a meter deep all the way around the planet. That's enougn to resupply the atmospheric loss, easy, even without breaking up the rocks. Our designer plants are doing their jobs."

"We have heard of these routine miracles—"

"—and there can be belts of jungle—soon! We've got mountains for climbing, rivers that snake, polar caps, programmed animals coming up, beautiful sunsets, soft summer storms—anything the human race wants. That's the vision we had when we started Gray. And I'm damned if I'm going to let the Majiken—"

"But the Majiken can defend Gray," the interviewer said mildly.

Benjan paused. "Oh, you mean—"

"Yes, the ever-hungry Outer Colonies. Surely if Gray proves as extraordinary as you think, the rebellious colonies will attempt to take it." The man gave Benjan a broad, insincere smile. *Dummy*, it said. *Don't know the real-politics of this time, do you?*

He could see the logic. Earth had gotten soft, fed by a tougher empire that now stretched to the chilly preserve beyond Pluto. To keep their manicured lands clean and "original" Earthers had burrowed underground, built deep cities there, and sent most manufacturing off-world. The real economic muscle now lay in the hands of their suppliers of fine rocks and volatiles, shipped on long orbits from the Outers and the Belt. These realities were hard to remember when your attention was focused on the details of making a fresh world. One forgot that appetites ruled, not reason.

Benjan grimaced. "The Majiken fight well, they are the backbone of the Fleet, yes. Still, to give them a *world*—"

"Surely in time there will be others," the man said reasonably.

"Oh? Why should there be? We can't possibly make Venus work, and Mars will take thousands of years more—"

"No, I meant built worlds—stations."

He snorted. "Live inside a can?"

"That's what you do," the man shot back.

"I'm . . . different."

"Ah yes." The interviewer bore in, lips compressed to a white line, and the 3-Ds followed him, snouts peering. Benjan felt hopelessly outmatched. "And just how so?"

"I'm . . . a man chosen to represent . . ."

"The Shaping Station, correct?"

"I'm of the breed who have always lived in and for the Station."

"Now, that's what I'm sure our audience really wants to get into. After all, the Moon won't be ready for a long time. But you—an ancient artifact, practically—are more interesting."

"I don't want to talk about that." Stony, frozen.

"Why not." Not really a question.

"It's personal."

"You're here as a public figure!"

"Only because you require it. Nobody wants to talk to the Station directly."

"We do not converse with such strange machines."

"It's not just a machine."

"Then what is it?"

"An . . . idea," he finished lamely. "An . . . ancient one." How to tell them? Suddenly, he longed to be back doing a solid, worthy job—flying a jet in Gray's skies, pushing along the organic chemistry—

The interviewer looked uneasy. "Well, since you won't go there . . . Our time's almost up and—"

Again, I am falling over Gray.

Misty auburn clouds, so thin they might be only illusion, spread below the ship. They caught red as dusk fell. The thick air refracted six times more than Earth's, so sunsets had a slow-motion grandeur, the full pallet of pinks and crimsons and rouge-reds.

I am in a ramjet—the throttled growl is unmistakable—lancing cleanly into the upper atmosphere. Straps tug and pinch me as the craft banks and sweeps, the smoothly wrenching way I like it, the stubby snout sipping precisely enough for the air's growing oxygen fraction to keep the engine thrusting forward.

I probably should not have come on this flight; it is an uncharacteristic self-indulgence. But I could not sit forever in the Station to plot and plan and calculate and check. I had to see my handiwork, get the feel of it. To use my body in the way it longed for.

I make the ramjet arc toward Gray's night side. The horizon curves away, clean hard blue-white, and—*chung*!—I take a jolt as the first canister blows off the underbelly below my feet. Through a rearview camera I watch it tumble away into ruddy oblivion. The canister carries more organic cultures, a new matrix I selected carefully back on Station, in my expanded mode. I watch the shiny morsel explode below, yellow flash. It showers intricate, tailored algae through the clouds.

Gray is at a crucial stage. Since the centuries-ago slamming by the air-giving comets, the conspiracy of spin, water, and heat (great gifts of astro-engineering) had done their deep work. Volcanoes now simmered, percolating more moisture from deep within, kindling, kindling. Some heat climbed to the high cloud decks and froze into thin crystals.

There, I conjure fresh life—tinkering endlessly.

Life, yes. Carefully engineered cells, to breathe carbon dioxide and live off the traces of other gases this high from the surface. In time. Photosynthesis in the buoyant forms—gas-bag trees, spindly but graceful in the top layer of Gray's dense air—conjure carbon dioxide into oxygen.

I glance up, encased in the tight flight jacket, yet feeling utterly free, naked. *Incoming meteors.* Brown clouds of dust I had summoned to orbit about Gray were cutting off some sunlight.

Added spice, these—ingredients sent from the asteroids to pepper the soil, prick the air, speed chemical matters along. The surface was cooling, the Gray greenhouse winding down. Losing the heat from the atmosphere's birth took centuries. *Patience, prudence.*

Now chemical concerts in the rocks slowed. I felt those, too, as a distant sampler hailed me with its accountant's chattering details. Part of the song. Other chem chores, more subtle, would soon become energetically possible. Fluids could seep and run. In the clotted air below, crystals and cells would make their slow work. All in time . . .

In time, the first puddle had become a lake. How I had rejoiced then!

What joy, to fertilize those still waters with minutely programmed bacteria, stir and season their primordial soup—and wait.

What sweet mother Earth did in a billion years I did to Gray in fifty. Joyfully! Singing the song of the molecules, in concert with them.

My steps were many, the methods subtle. To shape the mountain ranges I needed further infalls from small asteroids, taking a century—ferrying rough-cut stone to polish a jewel-world. Many died, of course, caught in the great grinding gears that bored 'roids, made the rock-flinging tunnels, did the hard brute labors in cold and vacuum.

Memories . . . of a man, and more. Fashioned from the tick of time, ironed out by the swift passage of mere puny years, of decades, of the ringing centuries. Worlds take *time.*

My ramjet leaps into night, smelling of hot iron and —*chung!*—discharging its burden.

I glance down at wisps of yellow-pearl. Sulfuric and carbolic acid streamers, drifting far below. There algae feed and prosper. Murky mists below pale, darken, vanish. *Go!*

Yet I felt a sudden sadness as the jet took me up again. I

had watched every small change in the atmosphere, played shepherd to newborn cloud banks, raised fresh chains of volcanoes with fusion triggers that burrowed like moles—and all this might come to naught, if it became another private preserve for some Earthside power games.

Not that Earthers were all vermin, I allow that. Many of them, through the stretched centuries, sent their own bodies to a final obliterating rest. Their funeral pyre was a bright spark as they hit the still-forming atmosphere's upper edge, adding a tad of carbon and water to the burgeoning chemistry. Still . . .

I could not shake off the depression. Should I have that worry pruned away? It could hamper my work, and I could easily be rid of it for a while, when I returned to the sleeping vaults. Most in the Station spent about one month per year working. Their other days passed in dreamless chilled sleep, waiting for the slow metabolism of Gray to quicken and change.

Not I. I slept seldom, and did not want the stacks of years washed away.

I run my tongue over fuzzy teeth. I am getting stale, worn. Even a ramjet ride did not revive my spirit.

And the Station did not want slackers. Not only memories could be pruned.

Ancient urges arise, needs . . .

A warm shower and rest await me above, in orbit, inside the mother-skin. Time to go.

I touch the controls, cutting in extra ballastic computer capacity and—

—suddenly I am there again, with *her*.

She is around me and beneath me, slick with ruby sweat.

And the power of it soars up through me. I reach out and her breast blossoms in my eager hand, her soft cries unfurl in puffs of green steam. *Aye!*

She is a splash of purple across the cool lunar stones, her breath ringing in me—

as she licks my rasping ear with a tiny jagged fork of puckered laughter,

most joyful and triumpant, yea verity.

The Station knows you need this now.

Yes, and the Station is right. I need to be consumed, digested, spat back out a new and fresh man, so that I may work well again.

—so she coils and swirls like a fine tinkling gas around me, her mouth wraps me like a vortex. I slide my shaft into her gratefully as she sobs great racking orange gaudiness through me, *her*, again, *her*, gift of the strumming vast blue Station that guides us all down centuries of dense, oily time.

You need this, take, eat, this is the body and blood of the Station, eat, savor, take fully.

I had known her once—redly, sweet and loud—and now I know her again,

my senses all piling up and waiting to be eaten from her.

I glide back and forth, moisture chimes between us, *she* is coiled tight, too.

We all are, we creatures of the Station.

It knows this, releases us when we must be gone.

I slam myself into *her* because *she* is both that woman—known so long ago,

delicious in her whirlwind passions, supple in colors of the mind, singing in rubs and heats

I knew across the centuries. So the Station came to know her, too, and duly recorded her—so that I can now bury my coal-black, sweaty troubles in her, *aye!* and thus in the Shaping Station, as was and ever shall be, Grayworld without end, amen.

Resting. Compiling himself again, letting the rivulets of self knit up into remembrance.

Of course the Station had to be more vast and able than anything Humanity had yet known. At the time the Great Shaping began, it was colossal. By then, humanity had gone on to grander projects.

Mars brimmed nicely with vapors and lichen, but would

take millennia more before anyone could walk its surface with only a compressor to take and thicken oxygen from the swirling airs.

Mammoth works now cruised at the outer rim of the Solar System, vast ice castles inhabited by beings only dimly related to the humans of Earth.

He did not know those constructions. But he had been there, in inherited memory, when the Station was born. For part of him and you and me and us had voyaged forth at the very beginning . . .

The numbers were simple, their implications known to schoolchildren.

(Let's remember that the future belongs to the engineers.)

Take an asteroid, say, and slice it sidewise, allowing four meters of headroom for each level—about what a human takes to live in. This dwelling, then, has floor space that expands as the cube of the asteroid size. How big an asteroid could provide the living room equal to the entire surface of the Earth? Simple: about two hundred kilometers.

Nothing, in other words. For Ceres, the largest asteroid in the inner belt, was 380 kilometers across, before humans began to work her.

But room was not the essence of the Station. For after all, he had made the Station, yes? Information was her essence, the truth of that blossomed in him, the past as prologue—

He ambled along a corridor a hundred meters below Gray's slag and muds, gazing down on the frothy air-fountains in the foyer. *Day's work done.*

Even manifestations need a rest, and the interview with the smug Earther had put him off, sapping his resolve. Inhaling the crisp, cold air (a bit high on the oxy, he thought; have to check that) he let himself concentrate wholly on the clear scent of the splashing. The blue water was the very best, fresh from the growing poles, not the recycled stuff he endured on flights. He breathed in the tingling spray and a man grabbed him.

"I present formal secure-lock," the man growled, his third knuckle biting into Benjan's elbow port.

A cold, brittle *thunk*. His systems froze. Before he could move, whole command linkages went dead in her inboards. The Station's hovering presence, always humming in the distance, telescoped away. It felt like a wrenching fall that never ends, head over heels—

He got a grip. *Focus. Regain your links. The loss!* —It was like having fingers chopped away, whole pieces of himself amputated. *Bloody neural stumps*—

He sent quick, darting questions down his lines, and met . . . *dark*. Silent. Dead.

His entire aura of presence was gone. He sucked in the cold air, letting a fresh anger bubble up but keeping it tightly bound.

His attacker was the sort who blended into the background. Perfect for this job. A nobody out of nowhere, complete surprise. Clipping on a hand-restraint, the mousy man stepped back. "They ordered me to do it fast." A mousy voice, too.

Benjan resisted the impulse to deck him. He looked Lunar, thin and pale. One of the Earther families who had come to deal with the Station a century ago? Maybe with more kilos than Benjan, but a fair match. And it would feel good.

But that would just bring more of them, in the end. "Damn it, I have immunity from casual arrest. I—"

"No matter now, they said." The cop shrugged apologetically, but his jaw was set, hands ready, body in fight posture. He was used to this. "I command your compliance," he finished formally.

Arrest was a ritual Earthside, as stylized as a classical drama. Very well, use it to throw off his guard . . . "I submit to the ordained order."

Benjan vaguely recognized him, from some bar near the Apex of the crater's dome. There weren't more than a thousand people on Gray, mostly like him, manifestations of the

Station. But not all. More of the others all the time . . . "And you, sir, you're Majiken."

"Yeah. So?"

"At least you people do your own work."

"There're plenty of us on the inside here. You don't think Gray's gonna be neglected, eh?"

In his elbow he felt injected programs spread, clunk, consolidating their blocks. A seeping ache. Benjan fought it all through his neuro-musculars, but the disease was strong.

Keep your voice level, wait for a chance. Only one of them—my God, they're sure of themselves! Okay, make yourself seem like a doormat.

"I don't suppose I can get a few things from my office?"

" 'Fraid not."

"Mighty decent."

The man shrugged, letting the sarcasm pass. "They want you locked down good before they . . ."

"They what?"

"Make their next move, I'd guess."

"I'm just a step."

"Sure, chop off the hands and feet first."

A smirking thug with a gift for metaphor. So much for the formal graces of the arrest ritual.

Well, these hands and feet can still work. Benjan began walking toward his apartment. "I'll stay in your lockdown, but I'll stay home."

"Hey, nobody said—"

"But what's the harm? I'm deadened now." He kept walking.

"Uh, uh—" The man paused, obviously consulting with his superiors on an in-link.

He should have known this was coming. The Majikens were ferret-eyed, canny, unoriginal, and always dangerous. He had forgotten that. In the rush to get ores sifted, grayscapes planed right to control the constant rains, a system of streams and rivers snaking through the fresh-cut valleys . . . a man could get distracted, yes. Forget how people were. *Careless.*

Not completely, though. Agents like this usually nailed their prey at home, not in a hallway. Benjan kept a stunner in the apartment, right beside the door, convenient.

Distract him. "I want to file a protest."

"Take it to Kalespon." Clipped, efficient, probably had a dozen other slices of bad news to deliver today. To other manifestations of the Station. Busy man.

"No, with your boss—direct."

"Mine?" His rock-steady jaw went slack.

"For—" he sharply turned the corner to his apartment, using the time to reach for some mumbo jumbo,"—felonious interrogation of inboards."

"Hey, I didn't touch your—"

"I felt it. Slimy little gropes—yeccch!" Might as well ham it up a little, have some fun.

The Majiken looked offended. "I never violate protocols. The integrity of your nexus is intact. You can ask for a scope-through when we take you in—"

"I'll get my overnight kit." Only now did he hurry toward the apartment portal and popped it by an inboard command. As he stepped through he felt the cop, three steps behind.

Here goes. One foot over the lip, turn to the right, snatch the stunner out of its grip mount—

—and it wasn't there. They'd laundered the place already. "Damn!"

"Thought it'd be waitin', huh?"

In the first second, when the Majiken was pretty sure of himself, *act*—

Benjan took a step back and kicked. A satisfying soft *thuunk.*

In the low gravity the man rose a meter and his *uungh*! was satisfying. The Majiken were warriors, after all, by heritage. Easier for them to take physical damage than life trauma.

The Majiken came up fast. He nailed Benjan with a hand feint and slam. Benjan fell back in the slow gravity—and at a 45-degree tilt, sprang backward, away, toward the wall—

Which he hit, completing his turn in air, heels coming hard into the wall so that he could absorb the recoil—

—and spring off, head-height—

—into the Majiken's throat, hands knifing as the man rushed forward, his own cupped hands ready for the put-away blow. Benjan caught him with both hand-edges, slamming the throat from both sides. The punch cut off blood to the head and the Majiken crumpled.

Benjan tied him with his own belt. Killed the link on the screen. Bound him further to the furniture. Even on Gray, inertia was inertia. The Majiken would not find it easy to get out from under a couch he was firmly tied to.

The apartment would figure out that something was wrong about its occupant in a hour or two, and call for help. Time enough to run? Benjan was unsure, but part of him liked this, felt a surge of adrenaline joy arc redly through his systems.

Five minutes of work and he got the interlocks off. His connections sprang back to life. Colors and images sang in his aura.

He found his arm panels in the back closet. With all the work, he hadn't used them for years, alas. They strapped to his back comfortably, he took a cleansing breath, and—

He was out the door, away—

The cramped corridors seemed to shrink, dropping down and away from him, weaving and collapsing. Something came toward him—chalk-white hills, yawning craters.

A hurricane breath whipped by him as it swept down from the jutting, fresh-carved mountains. His body strained.

He was running, that much seeped through to him. He breathed brown murk that seared but his lungs sucked it in eagerly. Plunging hard and heavy across the swampy flesh of Gray.

He moved easily, bouncing with each stride in the light gravity, down an infinite straight line between rows of enormous trees. Vegetable trees, these were, soft tubers and floppy leaves in the wan glow of a filtered sun. There should be no men here, only machines to tend the crops.

Then he noticed that he was not a man at all. A robo-hauler, yes—and his legs were, in fact, wheels, his arms the working grapplers. Yet he read all this as his running body. Somehow it was pleasant.

And *she* ran with him.

He saw beside him a miner-bot, speeding down the slope. Yet he knew it was *she,* Martine, and he loved her.

He whirred, clicked—and sent a hail.

You are fair, my sweet.

Back from the lumbering miner came, *This body will not work well at games of lust.*

No reason we can't shed them in time.

To what end? she demanded. Always imperious, that girl.

To slide silky skin again.

You seem to forget that we are fleeing. That cop, someone will find him.

In fact, he had forgotten. *Uh . . . update me?*

Ah! How exasperating! You've been off, romping through your imputs again, right?

Worse than that. He had only a slippery hold on the jiggling, surging lands of mud and murk that funneled past. Best not to alarm her, though. *My sensations seem to have become a bit scrambled, yes. I know there is some reason to run—*

They are right behind us!

Who?

The Majiken Clan! They want to seize you as a primary manifestation!

Damn! I'm fragmenting.

You mean they're reaching into your associative cortex?

Must be, my love. Which is why you're running with me.

What do you mean?

How to tell her the truth but shade it so that she does not guess . . . the Truth? *Suppose I tell you something that is more useful than accurate?*

Why would you do that, m'love?

Why do doctors slant a diagnosis?

Because no good diagnostic gives a solid prediction.

Exactly. Not what he had meant, but it got them by an awkward fact.

Come on, she sent. *Let's scamper down this canyon. The topo maps say it's a shortcut.*

Can't trust 'em, the rains slice up the land so fast. He felt his legs springing like pistons in the mad buoyance of adrenaline.

They surged together down slippery sheets that festered with life—spreading algae, some of the many-leaved slim-trees Benjan himself had helped design. Rank growths festooned the banks of dripping slime, biology run wild and woolly at a fevered pace, irked by infusions of smart bugs. A landscape on fast-forward.

What do you fear so much? she said suddenly

The sharpness of it stalled his mind. He was afraid for her more than himself, but how to tell her? This apparition of her was so firm and heartbreakingly warm, her whole presence welling through to him on his sensorium . . . Time to tell another truth that conceals a deeper verity.

They'll blot out every central feature of me, all those they can find.

If they catch you. Us.

Yup. Keep it to monosyllables, so the tremor of his voice does not give itself away. If they got to her, she would face final, total erasure. Even of a fragment self.

Save your breath for the run, she sent. So he did, gratefully.

If there were no omnisensors lurking along this approach to the launch fields, they might get through. Probably Fleet expected him to stay indoors, hiding, working his way to some help. But there would be no aid there. The Majiken were thorough and would capture all human manifestations, timing the arrests simultaneously to prevent anyone sending a warning. That was why they had sent a lone cop to grab him; they were stretched thin. Reassuring, but not much.

It was only three days past the 3-D interview, yet they

had decided to act and put together a sweep. What would they be doing to the Station itself? He ached at the thought. After all, *she* resided there . . .

And *she* was here. He was talking to a manifestation that was remarkable, because he had opened his inputs in a way that only a crisis can spur.

Benjan grimaced. Decades working over Gray had aged him, taught him things Fleet could not imagine. The Sabal Game still hummed in his mind, still guided his thoughts, but these men of the Fleet had betrayed all that. For them, ritual and the Code were a lulling drug they dispensed to the masses. They thought, quite probably, that they could recall him to full officer status,and he would not guess that they would then silence him, quite legally.

Did they think him so slow? Benjan allowed himself a thin, dry chuckle as he ran.

They entered the last short canyon before the launch fields. Tall blades like scimitar grasses poked up, making him dart among them. She growled and spun her tracks and plowed them under. She did not speak. None of them liked to destroy the life so precariously remaking Gray. Each crushed blade was a step backward.

His quarters were many kilometers behind by now, and soon these green fields would end. If he had judged the map correctly—yes, there it was. A craggy peak ahead, crowned with the somber lights of the launch station. They would be operating a routine shift in there, not taking any special precautions.

Abruptly he burst from the thicket of thick-leaved plants and charged down to the verge of a cliff. Above him lay the vast lava plain of Oberg Plateau, towering above the Fogg Sea. From that muddy, scum-flecked sea below came a warm wind, ruffling his hair, calling to his nodules. *Come.*

He unclipped his panels and attached them at shoulder and wrists. Here was a handy spire, ancient volcanic thrust out above the hundred-meter abyss. He paused, called Geronimo!—the ancient cries were always the best—and jumped.

In a sixth of Earth grav, with an atmosphere nearly Earth-thick, the winds were the easiest conveyance. Wings scarcely longer than a big man's arms could command the skies. He flapped a bit, but holding hawklike and still lifted him steadily. He rose through clouds of condensing murk, so no vagrant satellite spy could find him . . . and let Grayworld push him softly, silently up the rough-cut face of the mesa. Streams laughed at him, sawing their way into the fresh flanks. Moving with the wind, he hung in stillness. Banked. Even got in a moment's meditation.

And rose above the launching field. A mudflat, foggy, littered with ships. A vast dark hole yawned in the bluff nearby, the slanting sunlight etching its rimmed locks. It must be the exit tube for the electromagnetic accelerator, now obsolete, unable to fling any more loads of ore through the cloak of atmosphere.

A huge craft loomed at the base of the bluff. A cargo vessel probably; far too large and certainly too slow. Beyond lay an array of robot communications vessels, without the bubble of a life-support system. He rejected those, too, ran on.

She surged behind him. A satiny self, a delight . . . yet they had to keep electromagnetic silence now.

His breath came faster and he sucked at the thick, cold air. He had to stop for a moment in the shadow of the cruiser to catch his breath. *Feeling your years?* she sent, and he nodded. Part of him was centuries old, to be sure, but only inside his skull.

Above, he thought he could make out the faint green tinge of the atmospheric cap in the membrane that held Gray's air. He had labored to lay that micron-thick layer, once, long ago. Now he would have to find his way out through the holes in it, too, in an unfamiliar ship.

He glanced around, searching. To the side stood a small craft, obviously Jump type. No one worked at its base. In the murky fog that shrouded the mudflat he could see a few men and robo-servers beside nearby ships. They would wonder what he was up to. He decided to risk it. He broke from cover and ran swiftly to the small ship. The hatch opened easily.

Gaining lift with the ship was not simple, and so he called on his time-sense accelerations, to the max. That would cost him mental energy later. Right now, he wanted to be sure there was a later at all.

Roaring flame drove him into the pearly sky.

Finding the exit hole in the membrane proved easier. He flew by pure eyeballed grace, slamming the acceleration until it was nearly a straight-line problem, like shooting a rifle. Fighting a mere sixth of a g had many advantages.

And now, where to go?

A bright arc flashed behind Benjan's eyelids, showing the fans of purpling blood vessels. He heard the dark, whispering sounds of an inner void. A pit opened beneath him and the falling sensation began—he had run over the boundaries this body could attain. His mind had overpowered the shrieking demands of the muscles and nerves, and now he was shutting down, harking to the body's calls . . .

And she?

I am here, m'love. The voice came warm and moist, ancient warmth wrapping him in it as he faded, faded, into a gray of his own making.

She greeted him at the Station.

She held shadowed inlets of rest. A cup brimming with water,

a distant chime of bells, the sweet damp air of early morning.

He remembered it so well, the ritual of meditation in his Fleet training,

the days of quiet devotion through simple duties that strengthened the mind.

Everything had been of a piece then.

Before Gray grew to greatness, before conflict and aching doubt,

before the storm that raged red through his mind, like—

—wind, snarling his hair, a hard winter afternoon as he walked back to his quarters . . .

—then, instantly, the cold prickly sensation of diving through shimmering spheres of water in zero gravity. The huge bubbles trembled and refracted the yellow light into his eyes. He laughed.

—scalding black rock faces rose on Gray. Wedges thrust upward as the tortured skin of the planet writhed and buckled. He watched it by remote camera, seeing only a few hundred yards through the choking clouds of carbon dioxide. He felt the rumble of earthquakes, the ominous murmur of a mountain chain being born.

—a man running, scuttling like an insect across the tortured face of Gray. Above him the great membrane clasped the atmosphere, pressing it down on him, pinning him, a beetle beneath glass. But it is Fleet that wishes to pin him there, to snarl him in the threads of duty. And as the ship arcs upward at the sky he feels a tide of joy, of freedom.

—twisted shrieking trees, leaves like leather and apples that gleam blue. Moisture beading on fresh crimson grapes beneath a white-hot star.

—sharp synapses, ferrite cores, spinning drums of cold electrical memory. Input and output. Copper terminals (male or female?), scanners, channels, electrons pouring through p-n-p junctions. Memory mired in quantum noise.

• *Index. Catalog. Transform.* Fourier components, the infinite wheeling dance of Laplace and Gauss and Hermite.

• *And through it all she is there with him, through centuries to keep him whole and sane and yet he does not know, across such vaults of time and space* . . . who is he?

• Many: us. One: I. Others: you. *Did you think that the marriage of true organisms and fateful machines with machine minds would make a thing that could at last know itself? This is a new order of being but it is not a god.*

• Us: one, We: you, He: I.

• And yet you suspect you are . . . different . . . somehow.

* * *

The Majiken ships were peeling off from their orbits, skating down through the membrane holes, into *my air*!

They gazed down, tense and wary, these shock troops in their huddled lonely carriages. Not up, where I lurk.

For I am ice ball and stony-frag, fruit of the icesteroids. Held in long orbit for just such a (then) far future. (Now) arrived.

Down I fall in my myriads. Through the secret membrane passages I/we/you made decades before, knowing that a bolt-hole is good. And that bolts slam true in both directions.

Down, down—through gray decks I have cooked, artful ambrosias, pewter terraces I have sculpted to hide my selves as they guide the rocks and bergs—*after them*!—

The Majiken ships, ever wary of fire from below, never thinking to glance up. I fall upon them in machine-gun violences, my ices and stones ripping their craft, puncturing. They die in round-mouthed surprise, these warriors.

Tumble down, spinning. Gray can always use the extra mass.

I, Station master of hyperbolic purpose, shred them.

I, orbit-master to Gray.

Conflict has always provoked anxiety within him, a habit he could never correct, and so:—in concert we will rise to full congruence with F(x) and sum over all variables and integrate over the contour encapsulating all singularities. It is right and meet so to do.

He sat comfortably, rocking on his heels in meditation position.

Water dripped in a cistern nearby and he thought his mantra, letting the sound curl up from within him. A thought entered, flickered across his mind as though a bird, and left.

She she she she

The mantra returned in its flowing green rhythmic beauty and he entered the crystal state of thought within thought, consciousness regarding itself without detail or structure.

The air rested upon him, the earth groaned beneath with

the weight of continents, shouting sweet stars wheeled in a chanting cadence above.

He was in place and focused, man and boy and elder at once, officer of Fleet, mind encased in matter, body summed into mind

—and *she* came to him, cool balm of aid, succor, yet beneath her palms his muscles warmed, warmed—

His universe slides into night. Circuits close. Oscillating electrons carry information, senses, fragments of memory.

I swim in the blackness. There are long moments of no sensations, nothing to see or hear or feel. I grope—

Her? No, she is not here either. Cannot be. For she has been dead these centuries and lives only in your Station, where she knows not what has become of herself.

At last I seize upon some frag, will it to expand. A strange watery vision floats into view. A man is peering at him. There is no detail behind the man, only a blank white wall. He wears the blue uniform of Fleet and he cocks an amused eyebrow at:

Benjan.

"Recognize me?" the man says.

"Of course. Hello, Katonji, you bastard."

"Ah, rancor. A nice touch. Unusual in a computer simulation, even one as sophisticated as this."

"What? Comp—"

And Benjan knows who he is.

In a swirling instant he sends out feelers. He finds boundaries, cool gray walls he cannot penetrate, dead patches, great areas of gray emptiness, of no memory. What did he look like when he was young? Where was his first home located? That girl—at age fifteen? Was that *her? Her?* He grasps for her—

And knows. He cannot answer. He does not know. He is only a piece of Benjan.

"You see now? Check it. Try something—to move your arm, for instance. You haven't got arms." Katonji makes a thin smile. "Computer simulations do not have bodies, though they have some of the perceptions that come from bodies."

"P–Perceptions from where?"

"From the fool Benjan, of course."

"*Me.*"

"*He* didn't realize, having burned up all that time on Gray, that we can penetrate all diagnostics. Even the Station's. Technologies, even at the level of sentient molecular plasmas, have logs and files. Their data is not closed to certain lawful parties."

He swept an arm (not a real one, of course) at the man's face. Nothing. No contact. All right, then . . . "And these feelings are—"

"Mere memories. Bits from Benjan's Station self." Katonji smiles wryly.

He stops, horrified. He does not exist. He is only binary bits of information scattered in ferrite memory cores. He has no substance, is without flesh. "But . . . but, where is the real me?" he says at last.

"That's what you're going to tell us."

"I don't know. I was . . . falling. Yes, over Gray—"

"And running, yes—I know. That was a quick escape, an unexpectedly neat solution."

"It worked," Benjan said, still in a daze. "But it wasn't me?"

"In a way it was. I'm sure the real Benjan has devised some clever destination, and some tactics. You—his ferrite inner self—will tell us, *now,* what he will do next."

"He's got something, yes . . ."

"Speak *now*," Katonji said impatiently.

Stall for time. "I need to know more."

"This is a calculated opportunity," Katonji said offhandedly. "We had hoped Benjan would put together a solution from things he had been thinking about recently, and apparently it worked."

"So you have breached the Station?" Horror flooded him, black bile.

"Oh, you aren't a complete simulation of Benjan, just recently stored conscious data and a good bit of subconscious motivation. A truncated personality, it is called."

As Katonji speaks, Benjan sends out tracers and feels them flash through his being. He summons up input and output. There are slabs of useless data, a latticed library of the mind. He can expand in polynomials, integrate along an orbit, factorize, compare coefficients—*so they used my computational self to make up part of this shambling construct.*

More. He can fix his field—there, just so—and fold his hands, repeating his mantra. Sound wells up and folds over him, encasing him in a moment of silence. *So the part of me that still loves the Sabal Game, feels drawn to the one-is-all side of being human—they got that, too.*

Panic. Do something. Slam on the brakes—

He registers Katonji's voice, a low drone that becomes deeper and deeper as time slows. The world outside stills. His thought processes are far faster than an ordinary man's. He can control his perception rate.

Somehow, even though he is a simulation, he can tap the real Benjan's method of meditation, at least to accelerate his time sense. He feels a surge of anticipation. He hums the mantra again and feels the world around him alter. The trickle of input through his circuits slows and stops. He is running cool and smooth. He feels himself cascading down through ruby-hot levels of perception, flashing back through Benjan's memories.

He speeds himself. He lives again the moments over Gray. He dives through the swampy atmosphere and swims above the world he made. Molecular master, he is awash in the sight-sound-smell, an ocean of perception.

Katonji is still saying something. Benjan allows time to alter again and Katonji's drone returns, rising—

Benjan suddenly perceives something behind Katonji's impassive features. "Why didn't you follow Benjan immediately? You could find out where he was going. You could have picked him up before he scrambled your tracker beams."

Katonji smiles slightly. "Quite perceptive, aren't you? Understand, we wish only Benjan's compliance."

"But if he died, he would be even more silent."

"Precisely so. I see you are a good simulation."

"I seem quite real to myself."

"Ha! Don't we all. A computer who jests. Very much like Benjan, you are. I will have to speak to you in detail, later. I would like to know just why he failed us so badly. But for the moment we must know where he is now. He is a legend, and can be allowed neither to escape nor to die."

Benjan feels a tremor of fear.

"So where did he flee? You're the closest model of Benjan."

I summon winds from the equator, cold banks of sullen cloud from the poles, and bid them *crash.* They slam together to make a tornado such as never seen on Earth. Lower gravity, thicker air-a cauldron. It twirls and snarls and spits out lightning knives. The funnel touches down, kisses my crust—

—and there are Majiken beneath, whole packed canisters of them, awaiting my kiss.

Everyone talks about the weather, but only I do anything about it.

They crack open like ripe fruit.

—and you dwindle again, hiding from their pursuing electrons. Falling away into your microstructure.

They do not know how much they have captured. They think in terms of bits and pieces and he/you/we/I are not. So they do not know this—

You knew this had to come
As worlds must turn
And primates must prance
And givers must grab

So they would try to wrap their world around yours.
They are not dumb.
And smell a beautiful beast slouching toward Bethlehem.

Benjan coils in upon himself. He has to delay Katonji. He must lie—

—and at this rogue thought, scarlet circuits fire. Agony. Benjan flinches as truth verification overrides trigger inside himself.

"I warned you." Katonji smiles, lips thin and dry.

Let them kill me.

"You'd like that, I know. No, you will yield up your little secrets."

Speak. Don't just let him read your thoughts. "Why can't you find him?"

"We do not know. Except that your sort of intelligence has gotten quite out of control, that we do know. We will take it apart gradually, to understand it—you, I suppose, included."

"You will . . ."

"Peel you, yes. There will be nothing left. To avoid that, tell us *now.*"

—and the howling storm breaches him, bowls him over, shrieks and tears and devours him. The fire licks flesh from his bones, chars him, flames burst behind his eyelids—

And he stands. He endures. He seals off the pain. It becomes a raging, white-hot point deep in his gut.

Find the truth. "After . . . after . . . escape, I imagine yes, I am certain—he would go to the poles."

"Ah! Perfect. Quite plausible, but—which pole?" Katonji turns and murmurs something to someone beyond Benjan's view. He nods, turns back and says, "We will catch him there. You understand, Fleet cannot allow a manifestation of his sort to remain free after he has flaunted our authority."

"Of course," Benjan says between clenched teeth.

(But he has no teeth, he realizes. Perceptions are but data, bits strung together in binary. But they feel like teeth, and the smoldering flames in his belly make acrid sweat trickle down his brow.)

"If we could have anticipated him, before he got on 3-D . . ." Katonji mutters to himself. "Here, have some more—"

Fire lances. Benjan wants to cry out and go on screaming forever. A frag of him begins his mantra. The word slides over and around itself and rises between him and the wall of pain. The flames lose their sting. He views them at a distance, their cobalt facets cool and remote, as though they have suddenly become deep blue veins of ice, fire going into glacier.

He feels the distant gnawing of them. Perhaps, in the tick of time, they will devour his substance. But the place where he sits, the thing he has become, can recede from them. And as he waits, the real Benjan is moving. And yes, he *does* know where . . .

Tell me true, these bastards say. All right—

"Demonax crater. At the rim of the South Polar glacier."

Katonji checks. The verification indices bear out the truth of it. The man laughs with triumph.

All truths are partial. A portion of what Benjan is/was/will be lurks there.

Take heart, true Benjan.
For *she* is we and we are all together,
we mere Ones who are born to suffer.
Did you think you would come out of this long trip alive?
Remember, we are dealing with the most nasty of all
species the planet has ever produced.

Deftly, deftly—

We converge. The alabaster Earthglow guides us. Demonax crater lies around us as we see the ivory lances of their craft descend.

They come forth to inspect the ruse we have gathered ourselves into. We seem to be an entire ship and buildings, a shiny human construct of lunar grit. We hold still, though that is not our nature.

Until they enter us.

We are tiny and innumerable, but we do count. Microbial tongues lick. Membranes stick.

Some of us vibrate like eardrums to their terrible swift cries.

They will discover eventually. They will find him out.

(Moisture spatters upon the walkway outside. Angry dark clouds boil up from the horizon.)

They will peel him then. Sharp and cold and hard, now it comes, but, but—

(Waves hiss on yellow sand. A green sun wobbles above the seascape. Strange birds twitter and call.)

Of course, in countering their assault upon the Station I shall bring all my hoarded assets into play.

And we all know that I cannot save everyone.

Don't you?

They come at us through my many branches. Their smallness has its uses.

Up the tendrils of ceramic and steel. Through my microwave dishes and phased arrays. Sounding me with gamma rays and traitor cyber-personas.

They have been planning this for decades. But I have known it was coming for centuries.

The Benjan singleton reaches me in time. Nearly.

He struggles with their minions. I help. I am many and he is one. He is quick, I am slow. That he is one of the originals does matter to me. I harbor the same affection for him that one does for a favorite finger.

I hit the first one of the bastards square on. It goes to pieces just as it swings the claw thing at me.

Damn! it's good to be back in a body again. My muscles bunching under tight skin, scents swarming thick and rich,